The stirring story of the life and times of Richard Bolitho is told in Alexander Kent's bestselling novels.

1756	Born Falmouth, son of James Bolitho
1768	Entered the King's service as a Midshipman on *Manxman*
1772	Midshipman, *Gorgon* (*Midshipman Bolitho*)
1774	Promoted Lieutenant, *Destiny*: Rio and the Caribbean (*Stand into Danger*)
1775–7	Lieutenant, *Trojan*, during the American Revolution. Later appointed prizemaster (*In Gallant Company*)
1778	Promoted Commander, *Sparrow*. Battle of the Chesapeake (*Sloop of War*)
1780	Birth of Adam, illegitimate son of Hugh Bolitho and Kerenza Pascoe
1782	Promoted Captain, *Phalarope*; West Indies: Battle of Saints (*To Glory We Steer*)
1784	Captain, *Undine*; India and East Indies (*Command a King's Ship*)
1787	Captain, *Tempest*; Great South Sea; Tahiti; suffered serious fever (*Passage to Mutiny*)
1792	Captain, the *Nore*; Recruiting (*With All Despatch*)
1793	Captain, *Hyperion*; Mediterranean; Bay of Biscay; West Indies. Adam Pascoe, later Bolitho, enters the King's service as a midshipman aboard *Hyperion* (*Form Line of Battle!* And *Enemy in Sight*)
1795	Promoted Flag Captain, *Euryalus*; involved in the Great Mutiny; Mediterranean; Promoted Commodore (*The Flag Captain*)
1798	Battle of the Nile (*Signal – Close Action!*)
1800	Promoted Rear-Admiral; Baltic; (*The Inshore Squadron*)
1801	Biscay. Prisoner of war (*A Tradition of Victory*)
1802	Promoted Vice-Admiral; West Indies (*Success to the Brave*)
1803	Mediterranean (*Colours Aloft!*)
1805	Battle of Trafalgar (*Honour This Day*)
1806–7	Good Hope and the second battle of Copenhagen (*The Only Victor*)
1808	Shipwrecked off Africa (*Beyond the Reef*)
1809–10	Mauritius campaign (*The Darkening Sea*)
1812	Promoted Admiral; Second American War (*For My Country's Freedom*)
1814	Defence of Canada (*Cross of St. George*)
1815	Richard Bolitho killed in action (*Sword of Honour*) Adam Bolitho, Captain, *Unrivalled*. Mediterranean (*Second to None*)
1816	Anti-slavery patrols, Sierra Leone. Battle of Algiers (*Relentless Pursuit*)
1817	Flag Captain, *Athena*; Antigua and Caribbean (*Man of War*)
1818	Captain, *Onward*; Mediterranean (*Heart of Oak*)

Also by Alexander Kent

Midshipman Bolitho
Stand Into Danger
In Gallant Company
Sloop of War
To Glory We Steer
Command a King's Ship
Passage to Mutiny
With All Despatch
Form Line of Battle!
Enemy in Sight
The Flag Captain
Signal – Close Action!
The Inshore Squadron
A Tradition of Victory
Success to the Brave
Colours Aloft!
Honour This Day
The Only Victor
Beyond the Reef
The Darkening Sea
For My Country's Freedom
Cross of St George
Second to None
Relentless Pursuit
Man of War
Band of Brothers
Heart of Oak

Sword of Honour

Alexander Kent

arr

Reissued in the United Kingdom by Arrow Books in 2007

7 9 10 8

Copyright © Bolitho Maritime Productions 1997

Alexander Kent has asserted his right under the Copyright,
Designs and Patents Act, 1988 to be identified as
the author of this work

First published in the United Kingdom in 1997 by Century
First published in paperback in 1998 by Arrow Books

Arrow Books
The Random House Group Limited
20 Vauxhall Bridge Road, London SW1V 2SA

Addresses for companies within The Random House Group Limited
can be found at:
www.randomhouse.co.uk/offices.htm

The Random House Group Limited Reg. No. 954009

A CIP catalogue record for this book
is available from the British Library

ISBN 9780099497769

Penguin Random House is committed to a sustainable future for
our business, our readers and our planet. This book is made from
Forest Stewardship Council® certified paper.

Printed and bound in Great Britain by Clays Ltd, St Ives plc

To Chris Patten, a man of honour,
in admiration

Sail forth – steer for the deep waters only,
Reckless O soul, exploring, I with thee, and thou with me,
For we are bound where mariner has not yet dared to go,
And we will risk the ship, ourselves and all.

– *Whitman*

CONTENTS

1

Decisions

Vice-Admiral Sir Graham Bethune put down his pen and waited for the elderly Admiralty clerk to gather up the letters and despatches he had signed. As the tall double doors closed behind him, Bethune stood up and glanced at the nearest windows. Bright sunshine; he could even feel the warmth across the room, with a sky so clear that it was almost colourless.

He heard a clock chime, and wondered how the meeting was progressing along the passageway. Senior officers, lords of Admiralty, and civilian advisers who had been called here to discuss the state of the dockyards and the needs of the medical services. At the Admiralty, it was another ordinary day.

He moved restlessly to the window and opened it, and the sounds of London rose to greet him. The clatter of carriages and the jingle of harness, the cry of a street pedlar risking the wrath of Admiralty porters to sell his wares to the passing throng.

Bethune caught his own reflection in the window, and smiled. Once he had thought he would never hold such an appointment; now he could hardly imagine anything else. After ships and the sea, it had seemed like something foreign. He touched the front of his waistcoat. Graham Bethune, Vice-Admiral of the Blue, one of the youngest flag officers on the Navy List. Like the uniform, the appointment fitted him perfectly.

He leaned over the sill and watched the procession of people. Many of the carriages were open to the sunshine, revealing women in colourful hats and fine gowns. It was April of the year 1814, but the war was still a brutal fact.

Like most serving officers, Bethune had become accustomed to the exaggerated assurances and the promises of final victory.

Reports arrived daily with news that Wellington's armies were breaking through one French strongpoint after another; the invincible Napoleon was claimed to be on the run, deserted by all but his faithful marshals and his Old Guard.

What did all those people down there really believe, he wondered. After so many years of war with the familiar enemy, was the prospect of peace still only a dream? He moved back into the room and stared at the painting on one wall, a frigate in action, sails pitted with shot, a full broadside spitting fire at the enemy. It was Bethune's last command. He had confronted two big Spanish frigates, unfortunate odds even for a captain as eager as he had been. After a brisk engagement, he had run one Spaniard ashore and captured the other. Flag rank had followed almost immediately.

He looked at the ornate clock with its simpering cherubs and thought of the one man he admired, perhaps envied, more than any other.

Sir Richard Bolitho was back in England, fresh from that other war with the United States; Bethune had seen the letter the First Lord of the Admiralty had sent to him in Cornwall, recalling him to London. Bolitho had been his captain all those years ago in the sloop-of-war *Sparrow*. Another war, but they had been fighting Americans even then, a new nation born of revolution.

No reason for the recall had been offered. Surely Sir Richard Bolitho deserved a rest after all he had done? He thought, too, of the lovely Catherine Somervell, who had come to this very office to see him. He often thought of them, together.

And when the impossible had come to pass, and there was peace again, permanent or not, what would happen to Bolitho, and to all the men he had known on his way up the ladder from midshipman's berth to Admiralty? *What will happen to me?* It was the only life he knew. It was his world.

The streets and seaports were full of crippled and tattered remnants of war, rejected by a life which had all but destroyed them. Bethune was sometimes surprised that he could still be sensitive about such matters. Perhaps he had inherited that trait, too, from *Sparrow*'s youthful captain.

He heard voices in the adjoining room, where his clerk held unwanted visitors at bay. He looked at the clock again. Too early for a glass. Bethune did not drink heavily or overeat; he had seen too many of his contemporaries deteriorate because they did not heed such things. He took exercise when he could, a luxury after a ship's restricted quarters, and he enjoyed the company of women, as much as they enjoyed his. But he was discreet, or tried to be, and he told himself it was for the sake of his wife and his two young children.

His servant was standing in the doorway.

Bethune sighed. 'What is it, Tolan?'

'Captain McCleod is here to see you, sir.'

Bethune looked away. 'Ask him to come in.'

What had made him so nervous? Guilt? Thinking perhaps of Bolitho's mistress, who had faced the scandal and had triumphed?

The tall captain entered the room. He had an impassive, melancholy face; Bethune could not imagine him at sea, fighting a gale or the enemy.

'More despatches?'

The captain shook his head. Even that seemed mournful. 'From Portsmouth, sir. By telegraph, just received.' He glanced at the ceiling as if to see through it to the device which could link the Admiralty building to the south coast more swiftly than any courier, faster than any horse, provided the weather was perfect, as it was today.

Bethune opened it, and then hesitated. It was round, school-boy writing, but afterwards he thought it was as though each word had been written in fire. Or blood.

He strode past his servant and the clerk at his desk, his steps seeming unusually loud in the deserted corridor. Great paintings watched him pass, sea battles: courage and heroism, without the human agony which was so seldom shown.

A lieutenant jumped to his feet. 'I'm sorry, sir, but the meeting is still in progress!'

Bethune did not even see him. He thrust open the door, and watched the mingled expressions of surprise, irritation, perhaps alarm.

The First Lord frowned. 'Is it so urgent, Graham?'

Bethune wanted to lick his lips, to laugh, to weep. He had felt nothing like it before.

'From the admiral commanding at Portsmouth, my lord. A despatch has just been received.'

The admiral said evenly, 'Take your time.'

Bethune tried again. It was a great moment, and he was a part of it, and yet all he could feel was sadness. 'Marshal Soult's army was defeated by the Duke of Wellington at Toulouse. Totally. Napoleon has abdicated, surrendered to the Allies, four days ago.'

The admiral stood, very slowly, and looked around the table. 'Victory, gentlemen.' The word seemed to hang in the air. 'If only brave Nelson could have seen it.'

Then he turned to Bethune. 'I shall see the Prince Regent immediately. Attend to it for me.' He dropped his voice to exclude the others. 'It could mean Paris for you, Graham. I would feel more secure with you there.'

Bethune found himself back in his spacious office again, without remembering the return.

When he looked out of the window once more, nothing had changed, not the people nor the horses and carriages. Even the pedlar was still standing with his tray of wares.

The elderly clerk was hovering by the desk. 'Sir?'

'Pass the word to the Officer-of-the-Guard for the First Lord's carriage and escort.'

'At once, sir.' He hesitated. 'Difficult to accept, sir. To believe . . . .'

Bethune smiled and touched his arm, even as Bolitho might have done.

Difficult to accept? It was impossible.

Lieutenant George Avery reined his hired mount to a halt and leaned back in the saddle to admire the view. The house was beautifully designed; magnificent was the only description, he thought, and probably larger than the one where he had spent the night.

It had been a pleasant ride from central London to this place on the bank of the Thames, and it had given him time to think, to prepare for this meeting with his uncle, Lord Sillitoe of Chiswick. He had sensed the jubilant mood of the people all around him, had seen their smiles and waves when he had passed; apparently it was unusual to sight a naval officer on horseback.

But it was more than that, so much more. The impossible had become a fact, and it seemed as if every man and woman in the city was in the streets to make certain that the news

4

was not just another cruel rumour. Napoleon, the tyrant, the oppressor who had sought to enslave a continent, was beaten, a prisoner of the victorious Allies.

This morning she had watched him while he dressed and readied himself for this meeting. He could still feel the power and the passion of their intimacy. Could this relationship, too, be more than a passing dream?

He glanced at a church clock. He was five minutes early. His uncle would expect it, even though it was said that he made a deliberate point of being late for his own appointments.

And yet, Avery scarcely knew him. His uncle, Sir Paul Sillitoe as he had been then, had suggested that he should apply for the appointment of flag lieutenant to Sir Richard Bolitho. As the date for that first meeting had drawn near, he had almost withdrawn the application, knowing that it would only end in another disappointment. He had been wounded, and had been a prisoner of war. Upon his exchange, he had been required to face a court-martial for the loss of his ship, even though she had been lost through the captain's recklessness, and his own wound had rendered him helpless and unable to prevent his men striking to a superior enemy.

The memory of his first meeting with Bolitho, the hero and the legend, was very vivid; it would never leave him, and their association had restored him, had perhaps even made him something he might otherwise never have been.

But his uncle? A man of enormous power and influence; and now that Sillitoe had also become a personal adviser to the Prince Regent, that power was greatly feared, if not respected.

He patted the horse's flank, and spoke to the stable-hand who had come running to take his rein.

'See to her, will you. I doubt that I shall be here very long.'

Doors opened before he reached them, the sun streaming in to greet him from windows that faced the Thames, and the slow-moving masts of local traders making use of the tide. A fine staircase, elegant pillars, but also a spartan lack of ornaments and paintings, which his uncle would doubtless find flippant, and obtrusive.

A hard-faced servant in gilt-buttoned livery confronted him in the spacious hallway. Avery had heard it said that most of Sillitoe's servants resembled prize-fighters, and now he saw that it was true.

'If you will wait in the library, sir.' He did not drop his eyes, again, like a fighter wary of a treacherous attack.

Avery nodded in acknowledgement. The man did not ask for his name; he would know. Otherwise, he would not be here.

He walked into the library and stared out across the river. *Peace.* He felt the pain in his wounded shoulder, always a reminder, should he need one. He thought of her body arched against his; she had insisted on seeing the deep scar, and had kissed it with such gentleness that he had been both surprised and moved.

He caught sight of himself in a tall mirror; like a stranger, he thought. He still could not get used to the single epaulette on his shoulder.

They had all endured so much together. But when he tried to imagine the future, beyond the day or the week, it was like being lost, in a fog.

The war was over. Hostilities continued along the border of Canada and the United States, but that could not last much longer. *And what of us?* 'We Happy Few', as Bolitho had often called them. Adam Bolitho was still in Halifax as flag captain to Rear-Admiral Keen; Captain James Tyacke would be waiting for a new appointment, with the frigate *Indomitable* paid off to await her own fate.

He stared at his reflection. Still only a lieutenant, with streaks of grey in his dark hair to show what the war had cost him. Thirty-five years old. He grinned, surprised that he was able to consider a future without prospects, once Sir Richard Bolitho came ashore for good. In his heart, it was what Bolitho wanted, and Avery felt very privileged to know the inner, private man. Brave in his decisions, unwavering in their execution, but after the cannon had fallen silent and the enemy's flag had come down through the smoke, Avery had seen the other man, sensitive, grieving for those who had fallen, because he had required it of them.

What then for himself? A command of his own? Perhaps a little schooner like the lost *Jolie*, although that was unlikely. The navy would begin ridding itself of ships and men as soon as the terms for peace were settled amongst the Allies. Countless soldiers and sailors would be paid off, unwanted, left to fend for themselves. It had happened before. It would always be so.

'If you will come this way, sir.'

6

Avery left the library, very conscious of the silence; it made him realise how empty the place was. After a noisy, lively ship, it was to be expected. All sailors were like fish out of water when they came ashore. But compared with Bolitho's house in Cornwall, with its endless comings and goings of people from the farm and the estate, neighbours or well-wishers, this splendid residence echoed like a tomb.

His uncle rose from his desk as he entered, closing a large file which he had apparently been studying, although Avery sensed that he had been sitting facing the door for some while. To compose himself? That seemed unlikely. *To get it over quickly, duty done*, was that it?

They shook hands, and Sillitoe said, 'That will be all, Marlow.' A small man whom Avery had not noticed got up from another desk and scurried away. It must be his uncle's secretary but, typically, Sillitoe did not introduce him.

He said, 'I have some claret. I think you will approve of it.' He faced him again and Avery was very aware of the dark, compelling eyes, the hooded lids, the gaze which took in every detail. He could well imagine people fearing him.

'I am glad you are here. It becomes ever more difficult to find the time.' He frowned slightly as another servant entered with the claret and glasses. 'It is fortunate you were in London, and that you received my note.' The stare was impassive, no hint of triumph or contempt. He added calmly, 'How is Lady Mildmay, by the way?'

'She is well, sir. It seems there are few secrets left in London.'

Sillitoe gave a faint smile. 'Quite so. But then, you have not exactly taken pains to conceal your . . . how shall we describe it? Your liaison with this lady, who, I gather, was the wife of your last captain? Of course I *knew* of it. And I am not certain that I approve, not that I expect you would care.'

Avery sat down. What did it matter? *I owe this man nothing.*

He thought suddenly of Bolitho. *I owe him everything.*

'You will not have heard.' Sillitoe took a glass and regarded it severely. 'Sir Richard is recalled to London. He is needed.'

Avery sipped the claret without tasting it. 'I thought he was to be released from active duty, sir.'

Sillitoe gazed at him over the rim of his glass, a little startled

7

by the force of the words. He liked his nephew, and had felt moved to act on his behalf after he had been released from a French prison, only to face a court-martial. A wretched and unnecessary affair, he had thought. But then, he had little time for the navy and its strictures and traditions. His elder brother had been a captain and had been killed in action; it had been that captain who had inspired the young Avery to enter the navy, and it had been that same man who had sponsored him as a midshipman. But Avery's outburst had taken him by surprise, and he did not like surprises unless they were his own.

Avery said, as though to himself, 'Then he will still need me after all.'

Sillitoe frowned. 'I have a deal of influence. I am also a wealthy man, some might say very wealthy. I have business interests in this country, and in Jamaica and the Indies. I need someone of integrity.' He smiled briefly. 'And, if you like, honour.'

Avery put down his empty glass. 'Are you offering me an appointment, sir?'

Sillitoe paced to the window and back. 'A new life, would be a fairer description.'

Avery watched him, suddenly aware of Sillitoe's discomfort. He was ill at ease, and because it was a state unknown to him, he was unable to contain it.

'Why me, sir?'

Sillitoe turned on him angrily. 'Because you should have something to show for your sacrifices, and your treatment, which I thought unfair.' He shook his head as if to silence some hidden voice. 'And because I intend that you should be my heir.' He faced him again. 'My half-brother is dying of fever and a self-indulgence which would have sickened his father, hard man though he was.'

The door opened a few inches.

'The carriage will be in attendance in fifteen minutes, m'lord!'

Sillitoe said, 'I must see His Royal Highness. Louis of France is passing through London, *en route* to claim his throne.' He grimaced. 'There will be much to do.'

Avery found himself on his feet and at the door, his hat again in his hand.

Sillitoe shaded his eyes to watch the river. 'Enjoy your freedom with the beautiful Susanna.' He reached out and took Avery's wrist in a grip of steel. 'Then come back, and tell me your decision.'

Avery heard the horses stamping impatiently.

Surprising that he should be so calm. Like that last day, when *Indomitable* had fought gun to gun with the enemy and men had died within inches of him. And Bolitho had been with him, depending upon him.

And suppose Sillitoe was wrong about Susanna, and that there might be something deeper than the mere fire of sexual excitement?

He said, 'I thank you, sir, but I fear I do not deserve your offer.' He thrust a coin into the groom's hand. 'My loyalty is to Sir Richard.'

Sillitoe watched him without expression. 'Then you are a fool.'

Avery settled in the saddle and gazed down at him. 'Very likely, sir.' He would have said more, but as he dragged at the reins he saw his uncle perhaps for the first time. The man of power and influence.

A man completely alone.

Bryan Ferguson vaulted down from his two-wheeled trap and made sure that the pony was within reach of water.

'You bide here, Poppy.' He glanced at the feed-bag, but decided against it; the pony was getting plump enough as it was.

Then he turned and looked at the low, white-painted inn, The Old Hyperion. Its sign, with the ship heeling to wind and sea, was barely moving. A warm April evening, but the inn would be empty with all the men working late on the farms. He could see the glint of water through the trees, the Helford river; it was a pleasant place. And being the only inn on the edge of Fallowfield village, it could capture what trade there was.

Earlier in the day he had been in Falmouth, and had been very aware of the changes brought about by the news of Napoleon's surrender. There had been more young men in the streets than usual, a sure sign that the dreaded press gangs had been stood down. It would take some getting used to. He flexed his one arm grimly. These days he hardly noticed that he was lacking an arm; it was equally hard to believe that he himself had been pressed into the fleet, along with John Allday.

Fate played strange tricks. Now Allday was coxswain and friend to Sir Richard Bolitho, and Ferguson was steward to the Bolitho estate. And Bolitho had been the captain of that ship, which had snatched them from the beach to serve the King.

He sighed. It was better to get it over with. They had doubtless seen or heard the trap rattle into the yard.

Unis, Allday's wife, was waiting to greet him.

'Why, Bryan, this is a surprise. You're allus at the market today!'

Ferguson walked through the doorway and glanced at the scrubbed tables, the flowers and the polished brasses. Welcoming and neat, like the woman who had greeted him.

'John's out the back, doing something or other.' She smiled. '*My* John, that is.'

The other John was Unis's brother, a one-legged soldier of the line, without whom she could never have managed with Allday at sea much of the time. Then she asked, 'You want to see him? Nothing wrong up at the house, is there?'

He said, 'A messenger came today, Unis.' It was pointless to try and make light of it. 'From the Admiralty.'

She sat on a bench and stared at her arms, which were dusted with flour. 'I thought . . . with the surrender an' that . . . it was all behind us. Will Sir Richard be needed again?' She touched the flour on her skin. 'My John?'

'It may be so.' He thought of Catherine Somervell's face after the messenger had departed. He had heard her exclaim, 'It's so unfair! *So wrong!*'

Just weeks since his return from the war across the Atlantic. Maybe they wanted to honour him in some way.

He heard Allday scraping his shoes at the parlour door and said, 'John would not be forced to go, Unis. Sir Richard would not do it.'

She was quite calm again, her breathing steady. 'I know that, Bryan. But you don't *think* like John, not about the sea an' Sir Richard.'

Allday strode into the room. 'Kate's asleep again, I see.' He shook his friend's hand. 'Going to be as smart as paint when she grows up, just like her mother!'

Unis said, 'I'll fetch a wet for you, Bryan.' She touched the big man's shoulder, and Ferguson saw the pain in her eyes. 'You too, of course!'

Allday looked steadily at him. 'She's left us alone. So what is it, bad news?'

'Sir Richard's called to London. The Admiralty.' He shrugged. 'Same old story, eh?'

'They didn't waste much time. When do we leave?'

Ferguson was both moved and troubled. Like the last time, and all the times before that.

'He'll not expect you to go to London, you know that, man. You've responsibilities here now, Unis and that bonny little mite sleeping in the parlour. The fighting's over, with the French anyhow, and the Yankees will never come this far!' It was no good. What had he expected?

Allday said, 'My place is with him, you knows that. He needs me more than ever now. That eye of his is no better.'

Ferguson said nothing. Allday trusted him with the secret, knowing he would tell nobody else, not even his wife. Especially not Grace. He loved her with all his heart, but he had to admit that she loved gossip.

Allday looked at his hands, strong hands, with scars to mark the years at sea. 'Is Sir Richard put aback by the news?'

'It's hard to say. I watch him and his lady together – like you, I feel proud to be a part of it, but his thoughts he keeps to himself.'

Unis returned with two sweating tankards. 'When my brother gets back I must tell him to set up some more ale. I think we shall be busy this evening.' She looked at Ferguson. 'You told him, then?'

'Aye.'

Allday stared at the tankard between his hands, as if he wanted to crush it. 'Can you see Sir Richard taking on somebody else? It's hard, but we don't expect things to change, not overnight.'

She touched his shoulder again. 'You'll *never* change. I'd not want you to. I'd know you were pretending, putting up with it, just for me an' Kate. She's taken a real shine to you since you got back.'

She turned away, remembering the surprise and hurt he had shown when the child had gone to her brother John, as if he, her own father, was a stranger. It took time. But now he would be going away again. And she must face it.

She thought of Lady Catherine, that day when she had seen her waiting on the harbour quay at Falmouth, watching the little fleet schooner *Pickle* picking up her moorings, Bolitho coming home. And her own man had been with him, as always. Catherine, so brave, so defiant in the face of all the scandal and the cruel gossip. She would take it badly.

There were voices in the yard, and she said brightly, 'The fish man. I asked him to stop by.' She wiped her hands on her apron. 'I'll deal with him.'

Alone again with Allday, Ferguson said, 'She's a marvel, John.'

'I knows it.' He looked around as if he were searching for something. 'I'll go and put up some ale. It'll not take a minute. You sit there and finish your wet. I needs to think awhile.'

Ferguson sighed. Next thing, Allday would be up at the house on some pretext or other, just to speak with Sir Richard, to tell him he would be ready.

He looked round, startled by a thud and something like a cough. He went quickly into the adjoining room, a cool place where the casks were stowed, ready to be tapped and moved to their trestles. One cask, a four-and-a-half-gallon pin, was lying against the wall. Allday sat with his back to it, his hands to his chest, his breathing loud and uneven, like a man dragged from the sea.

Ferguson knelt and put his arm around him.

'Easy, John! That damned wound again!' He watched his friend struggle for breath and wondered how long it had been like this. When Allday turned his head, he was shocked to see that his face was quite pale, grey beneath the weathered tan.

He said, 'I'll fetch Unis.'

Allday shook his head and gritted his teeth. '*No!* Stay with me!' He nodded heavily, and took a deep breath. 'It's goin'. I'll be all right.'

Ferguson watched the colour returning to his rugged face, the breathing becoming more even.

Allday allowed him to help him to his feet, and then said thickly, 'Not a word, mind. It comes an' goes.' He tried to grin. 'See? Bright as a bullock's bayonet!'

Ferguson shook his head, resigned. He was beaten; he should

have known. Allday and Bolitho, like master and faithful dog, someone had once said, each fearful for the other.

Together, they lifted the cask on to its trestle, and Allday said, 'I needs something stronger than ale, an' that's no error!'

Unis found them sitting by the unlit fire, her husband holding a taper for his friend's clay pipe as if they had not a care in the world. She bit her lip to contain her despair. It was all a show, for her sake. Like the new cask on its trestle. The rest she could guess.

Ferguson said, 'Must be getting back. I have to look at the books.' Allday followed him out to the yard, and watched as he swung himself up on to the seat.

He said, simply, 'Thanks, Bryan.' He stared across the fields to the glint of the river beyond the trees. 'You weren't *there*, see. Sir Richard, a full admiral, the finest ever, leading our boarders across on to that bloody renegade's deck like some wild lieutenant! You should have been there. *To me, Indoms!*' He shook his shaggy head. 'I could never leave him now.'

He raised one hand and grinned. It was one of the saddest things Ferguson had ever seen.

And one of the bravest.

Richard Bolitho sat in the corner of the carriage and stared out at the crowds and the horses, vehicles of every size jostling for position with apparent disregard for one another.

Despite the warm evening, he was wearing his boatcloak to conceal his uniform and rank. In the frenzied aftermath of Napoleon's surrender, any such reminder brought cheers and mobbing from ordinary people who had probably never displayed such emotion for any but Nelson.

A long day; a very long day. First Bethune, and then a meeting with the First Lord and his senior advisers. Napoleon had been sent into exile on the island of Elba; the giant who had raped a continent was to be marooned, forgotten. Even as the First Lord had said it, Bolitho had questioned the wisdom of the decision. It was like trying to cage a lion in an aviary, and it was too close, too close . . . .

The First Lord had spoken at length of the American war, and of Bolitho's participation with the squadron under his command. The Americans were being starved of trade due to the activity of the British squadrons, and the chain of command from Halifax to the Caribbean. Little short of a thousand American merchant ships had been captured, and, with France no longer a drain on the navy's resources, more men-of-war could now be sent to seal the last gaps in the blockade.

The First Lord had finished by saying that no war could be won by stalemate. *An example must be made*, a ready warning for the future.

Bethune had been watching Bolitho, and had tossed in some comment on the American attack on York.

The First Lord was old but he was no fool, and he had recognised in this Bethune's attempt to distract him.

'What do *you* think, Sir Richard? I know you hold advanced ideas on the war at sea, and I heard you myself say in this very building that the line of battle was, or should be, a thing of the past?'

Bolitho turned his head and saw the Thames, and the lucid glow which would promise a fine sunset.

'I'll stand by that, my lord. I also believe that a desire for revenge is no good reason for prolonging a war which neither side can hope to win.'

Even then, he had believed that some kind of attack was being planned. Now, during this slow journey from the Admiralty to Chelsea, with time to go over it again in his mind, he was certain of it. Sir Alexander Cochrane had taken over the station; a man of action in every sense, but hardly a peacemaker.

Alone with Bethune, he had asked about Valentine Keen and about his nephew. Bethune had replied cautiously, 'Rear-Admiral Keen will return to England this year. His flagship will more than likely be paid off.' He had looked up from his desk, and for an instant Bolitho had seen the midshipman again. There were only a few years between them, and beneath the charm and the confidence Bethune was much the same. Above all, he was honest. Loyal. 'I am certain that your nephew will find employment even with the fleet reduced, as it certainly will be.'

'He is probably the best frigate captain we have. To be put on the beach after what he has done and endured would be intolerable.'

It must have been at that moment that Bethune had come to his decision.

He had said, 'We are good friends, Richard, and I regret that our paths have crossed only rarely.' He had shrugged lightly. 'As is the way of our calling. I have never forgotten that I have owed everything to you, from the moment you took command of *Sparrow*. And there have been many like me, who gained everything from that contact with you.'

'And there were many who fell because of it, Graham.'

He had shaken his head, dismissing it. 'We shall see the First Lord again when he returns from his audience with the Prince Regent. Their meetings are usually brief.' He paused, and the smile was gone. 'I have to tell you that the First Lord will offer you Malta, will insist that you are the obvious choice for it. Until the peace is finally agreed amongst the Allies, the Mediterranean must serve as a reminder to friends and foes alike that no further territorial claims on land or at sea will be tolerated.' He had watched Bolitho then in silence. 'I thought you should hear it first from me.'

'That was good of you, Graham.' He had glanced around the spacious room. 'But it can be dangerous here, also, so be warned!'

He rapped the roof of the carriage, and said, 'I shall walk from here.'

The coachman in his Admiralty livery barely glanced down from the box. Perhaps he had become too used to the ways of senior officers to question any whim.

He walked beside the river. Kate's London. She had made it his London now, or this small part of it, at least.

What shall I say? What must I tell her?

The First Lord had had no doubts at all. 'Not since Collingwood held this command has there been stability and leadership. Your reputation, your sense of honour are more valuable now than in the line of battle!' He had neglected to mention that Collingwood, Nelson's second-in-command at Trafalgar, had died in the Mediterranean without ever being relieved of that command, despite his repeated requests to be allowed to come home, and despite the illness which had eventually killed him.

He walked on, disquieted by his thoughts.

It had been bad enough when he and Catherine had left Falmouth. Allday visiting the house, ostensibly to ensure that the swords were in good trim, then coming straight out with it. Not pleading, but insisting on his right to be at Bolitho's side, wherever his flag should lead. And his secretary, Yovell, a man of many faces, and the secretive Ozzard. His little crew. And now there was Avery to consider. Bethune had hinted that he had been offered a great opportunity, a chance of security and prosperity. God knew he would never find either as a lowly lieutenant.

The door was open and she was standing at the top of the steps, her hair piled above her ears, like silk in the candlelight.

She slipped his arm around her waist. 'Come into the garden, Richard. I have some wine there. I heard you were coming.' She seemed to sense his tension. 'I had a visitor.'

He turned. 'Who?'

The strain was very evident in his face.

'George Avery. He had come on a mission, with an invitation to some reception.' She caressed his hand. 'Tomorrow. After that, we can leave for Falmouth.'

He said nothing, and walked into the garden, into its deepening shadows. He heard her pour the wine, then she said quietly, 'So it is to be Malta, Richard?'

Nothing of the anger she had shown in Falmouth. This was the poised, determined woman who had dared everything for his sake, who had even shared the ordeal in an open boat off the coast of Africa.

'I have not decided, Kate . . . .'

She put her fingers lightly on his mouth. 'But you will. I know you so well, better than any other, even yourself. All those men you have led and inspired, they will expect it. For them, and the future they have been fighting for. You told me once, they are never allowed to ask, or to question why they should sacrifice so much.'

They walked together to the low wall and watched the sunset over the river.

She said, 'You are my man, Richard. I will be with you, no matter how unfair or unjust I believe this decision may be. I would die rather than lose you.' She touched his face, the cheekbone beneath the damaged eye. 'And afterwards?'

'*Afterwards*, Kate. That is a very beautiful word. Nothing can or will part us again.'

She took his hand and pressed it to her breast. 'Take me, Richard. Use me as you will, but always love me.'

The wine remained in the garden, untouched.

2

More Than a Duty

Captain James Tyacke sat by the small table in his room and half listened to the muffled murmur of voices from the parlour below his feet. The Cross Keys was a small but comfortable inn on the road which headed north from Plymouth to Tavistock. Few coaches paused here because of the narrowness of the track, and he had sometimes wondered how the inn managed to make a living, unless perhaps it had some connection with the smuggling trade. It suited him very well, however, away from the stares and the swiftly averted glances. The pity, the curiosity, the revulsion.

It was hard, even unnerving, to accept that he had last stayed here all of three years ago. It had been run at the time by a pleasant woman named Meg, who had spoken to him often, and had looked at him directly, without flinching. Three years ago; and when he had left the inn on that last occasion, he had known they would not meet again.

The new landlord was welcoming enough, a little ferret of a man with quick, darting movements, and he had done his best to ensure that Tyacke was not disturbed.

Three years. It was a lifetime. He had been about to take command of *Indomitable*, Sir Richard Bolitho's flagship, before they had made sail for American waters. So many miles, so many faces, some already lost from memory. And now that same *Indomitable* lay at Plymouth, paid off, an empty ship, waiting for a new future, or with no future at all.

He glanced at the big brass-bound sea chest by the bed. They had travelled a long, long way together. His whole world was contained in it.

He thought of the past weeks, spent mostly aboard his ship attending to the thousand and one details of paying off, and worse, the rough farewells and handshakes from men he had come to know, men whose confidence and loyalty he had won by his own example.

And Sir Richard Bolitho; that had been the most difficult parting of all. As admiral and flag captain they had discovered a mutual trust, and an admiration which might never be truly understood by an outsider.

And now Napoleon was beaten; the war with the old enemy was over. Perhaps he should have felt elation, or relief. But as Tyacke had watched the fleet schooner *Pickle* standing out to sea, taking Bolitho and Allday on to Falmouth, all he had been conscious of was a sense of sorrow and loss.

The port admiral was a friend of Bolitho's, and had been both cordial and helpful to his flag captain. He had no doubt thought Tyacke's request to be transferred once more to the anti-slavery patrols off the coast of West Africa, exchanging the comparative comfort of a larger ship, or some well-earned extended leave ashore for cramped quarters and the risks of fever and death, bizarre. Bolitho's written support had added a great deal of weight. But, as the admiral had explained, the transfer might not be possible for another year or more.

He remembered *Indomitable* as he had last seen her. Yards sent down, her usually immaculate decks littered with unwanted cordage and spars, her powerful cannon, which had roared defiance at the American *Retribution*, silent and disarmed. Now she was no longer needed, like the men who had served her so long and so well, men who had been pressed into the navy, for the most part. His mouth softened into a smile. But then, so had Allday been a pressed man. And the wounded, what of them? Cast ashore to try and find their places in a world which had all but forgotten them, to fend for themselves as best they could, to beg on the streets when all most people wanted now was to forget the war.

And Sir Richard Bolitho, the hero and the man. One who could inspire others when all hope seemed lost, and who could not conceal his compassion, or his grief for those who had fallen.

Again he gave the small smile. Bolitho had given him back his own hope, his pride, when he had believed them gone for ever. He touched the side of his face. Scored away by fire, rendered inhuman during the great battle when Nelson had led his ships to the Nile. How the eye had survived was a miracle. *He had been so lucky*, some said. What did they know? All the years since he had been smashed down by a French broadside, when men had been killed and maimed on every side and even the captain of his ship, *Majestic*, had died in that bloody embrace, the disfigurement had haunted him. The stares, the way his young midshipmen had dropped their eyes, glanced away, anything but look at him. *The devil with half a face*, the slave-traders had called him. And now he was asking to go back to that lonely world of solitary patrols, pitting his wits against the traders, until the sighting and chase; the stinking vessels with their holds packed with chained slaves living in their filth, knowing they would be killed at the slightest provocation, their bodies pitched to the sharks. Slavers and sharks were rarely far apart.

No, they would not let Bolitho leave the navy. To many people who served in the fleet, he *was* the navy. Between them, Bolitho and his mistress had defied convention and the censure of society. Tyacke touched his face again. He remembered her climbing up *Indomitable*'s tumblehome at Falmouth, disdaining a boatswain's chair, and arriving on deck with tar on her stockings, raising the loudest cheers from the ship's company because of it. The sailor's woman who had come aboard to wish them well: men about to be carried to the other side of the world, torn from wives and families by the relentless press gangs, or felons freed by the local judges provided they were put aboard a King's ship.

And she had done it because she cared for them. She had even disdained formality that day in Falmouth, and had kissed him on the cheek in greeting. *You are so welcome here*. He could still hear the words. And then she had looked along the crowded deck at the watching crowds of seamen and marines and had said, *They will not let you down*. Nor had they.

Perhaps she had been the only one who had truly under-stood the torment he had suffered when he had agreed to be Bolitho's flag captain. He might be envied, feared, respected, even hated, but a captain, especially one who commanded a flagship, must be beyond self-doubt and uncertainty. Few could have guessed that those were the emotions he had felt when he had first stepped aboard to read himself in at Plymouth.

His own words then came back to him now, as if he had spoken aloud. *I would serve no other.*

He glanced around the room. He would have to leave it soon, if only to let them clean it. And suppose the appointment to the anti-slavery squadron was delayed even beyond the port admiral's estimate of a year? What then? Would it always be like this, hiding in rooms, walking out only at night, avoiding every kind of human contact?

He touched the dress coat which hung over a chair, and bore the twin gold epaulettes of a post-captain; a far, far cry from his previous command, the little brig *Larne*.

His mind explored the years since the Nile, and his slow recovery from his wounds. Fifteen years had passed since hell had burst into *Majestic*'s lower gundeck and turned it into an inferno. He had been in Haslar Hospital at Portsmouth for what little treatment could be offered, and Marion had eventually dared to come and see him. She had been young then, and pretty, and he had hoped and expected to marry her.

It had been an ordeal for her, like all the others who had ventured to Haslar in search of friends or relatives. Officers wounded in a dozen or more sea-fights, their faces so hopeful and so pitiful each time another visitor arrived. The burned, the maimed, the limbless and the blind, the living price of every victory, although few ever saw it.

After that, she had married another, an older man who had given her a pleasant house by Portsdown Hill, not far from that same hospital. There had been two children of the marriage, a boy and a girl.

Eventually her husband had died. Tyacke had received a letter from her while *Indomitable* had been at Halifax, the first news he had had of her for those fifteen years. It had been a letter written with great care, offering no excuses, no compromise, very mature, so different from the young girl he had once loved.

He had written a reply to her, and had locked it in the strongbox before the last battle with *Retribution*; she would only have received it if he had died that day. Afterwards, he had torn it into pieces and had watched them drift away beneath his ship's shot-pitted side. When he had needed her, and had sometimes found himself praying for death, she had turned away from him. He had told himself often enough that it was understandable. But she had not returned. So why had her letter disturbed him so much? The years had been another man's reward, and, like the two unknown children, were a part of something he could never share.

There was a quiet tap at the door, and after a moment it opened a few inches.

Tyacke said, 'It's all right, Jenny, I am just going out for a walk. You can see to the room.'

She gazed at him gravely. 'Not that, zur. There's a letter come for you.'

She held it out and watched him carry it to the window. She was a local girl and had six sisters, and at the inn she often saw the uniforms of army or navy, so that she did not feel so cut off from Plymouth, that bustling seaport which her sisters were always quick to compare with this place.

But she had never met anyone like this man before. He spoke only when it was necessary, although everybody knew all about him. A hero: Sir Richard Bolitho's friend and his right arm, they said. They said a lot more too, probably, when she was not within earshot.

She studied him now, his head lowered while he held the letter to the light of the window; he always turned his terrible injury away from her. He had a strong face, handsome too, and he was courteous, not like some of the gentry who called in for a glass. Her mother had warned her often enough about the dangers, about other girls who got themselves into trouble, especially with the garrison near Tavistock.

She felt herself flushing. All the same . . . .

Tyacke was unaware of the scrutiny. The note was from the port admiral. *To present himself at his earliest convenience*. Even addressed to a post-captain, that meant *immediately*.

'I'll need the carter, Jenny. I have to go to Plymouth.'

She smiled at him. 'Right away, zur!'

Tyacke picked up his coat and brushed the sleeve with his fingers. The walk would have to wait.

He stared around the room, the revelation hitting him like a fist. It was what he wanted. It was the only life he knew.

The carriage slowed, and Bolitho saw groups of idlers and

passers-by shading their eyes against the evening sun to peer in at the occupants. Some even waved their hats, although they could not possibly have recognised him, he thought.

He felt her hand on his sleeve. 'It's their way of showing their feelings.' She raised the hand to the nearest crowd and a man shouted, 'It's Sir Richard an' his lady, lads! Equality Dick!' There were cheers, and she murmured, 'You see? You have many friends there.'

The house on the river was ablaze with lights, the chandeliers burning even more brightly than this late sunshine.

How Sillitoe must hate it, Bolitho thought. Wasteful but necessary. *Necessary* was the word for it. His world.

Catherine said, 'I hear there are receptions all over London tonight to celebrate the victory.' She watched his profile, and wanted to put her arms around him, and let the crowds think what they liked.

He said restlessly, 'I wish it was young Matthew up there on the box, and we were heading down to Falmouth.' He looked at her and smiled. 'I am poor company for one so lovely, Kate.' Strangely, the realisation seemed to give him strength. She was wearing a new gown in her favourite green shot silk, high-waisted, her shoulders bared, the diamond pendant resting between her breasts. Beautiful, poised, and outwardly very calm, and yet the same woman who had given herself to him with such passion, again and again until they were exhausted, in the house on the Walk at Chelsea, around the next great sweeping bend of this river.

She said, 'At least it will not be like that terrible feast at Carlton House. I have never eaten so much in my life!' She watched his mouth lift, the way he smiled when they spoke of such things together.

She peered out at the other carriages turning in Sillitoe's drive, the crowds of footmen and grooms. Sillitoe must have gone to a great deal of expense.

There were women too, but not many wives, she decided. She never forgot that Sillitoe had helped her when there had been no one else. He had made no secret of his feelings for her after that. Like the man, it had been a statement of fact, cool and deliberate, not something open to doubt.

She glanced down at her gown. Daring perhaps, as some

would expect of her. She lifted her chin and felt the pendant shift against her skin: Bolitho's woman, for the whole world to see.

And then they were there; the door was opened, and Bolitho stepped down to assist her from the carriage.

Servants bowed and curtsied, while here and there Sillitoe's own men, hard and watchful, reminded Catherine of that last visit to Whitechapel. Some of Sillitoe's men had accompanied them then; there was always an air of mystery and danger where Sillitoe was concerned.

Bolitho handed his hat to another servant, but she retained the silk shawl, which she wore across her bare shoulders. There were no announcements, no footmen to scrutinise invitations, only waves of noisy conversation, and, from somewhere nearby, music. It was neither joyful nor martial, merely an unobtrusive background for people who quite obviously knew one another, either by sight or reputation.

'You look well, Sir Richard!' Sillitoe appeared from behind a pillar, his hooded eyes everywhere. Then he took Catherine's hand and held it to his lips. 'As always, my lady, I never find words for such beauty.'

She smiled, and saw several of the other women turning to stare. Sillitoe gestured impatiently as a footman appeared with a laden tray.

Then he said, 'Rhodes is here. I thought you should meet him, in view of the immediate future.'

Bolitho turned towards her. 'Admiral the Right Honourable Lord Rhodes is Acting Controller at the Admiralty, but he is also said to be the most likely contender for the role of First Lord.' He watched her, reading her eyes. She mistrusted the mention of senior officers she did not know, in case they meant him harm in some way.

Sillitoe said, 'I have put him in another room. I think it might be wise to see him.'

She said, 'I shall wait on the terrace, Richard.'

But Sillitoe interjected, 'This is my house and you are my guests. I see no reason to separate you.' He touched her hand lightly. 'To divide the legend?'

His small secretary was hovering close by, and Sillitoe said, 'I shall come and disturb you shortly.'

One of Sillitoe's men led the way to the library, and then

into a smaller ante-room adjoining it. There was a chair by the fireplace. Catherine recognised it. As if it had never been moved since she had sat there that day, when she had come for Sillitoe's help. When he had brushed past her, and she had felt him fighting the desire to touch her, to lay his hand on her shoulder. But he had not.

Admiral Lord James Rhodes was a tall, solidly built man who had once been handsome. His face was dominated by a strong, beaked nose, while his eyes were surprisingly small, almost incidental by comparison. He glanced quickly at Catherine, but was careful to reveal nothing. A man used to hiding his feelings, if he had any, she thought.

Bolitho said, 'May I present the Viscountess Somervell, my lord?' He felt her look at him, sensed the anxiety, in case there would be some lurking insult or rebuff. But Rhodes gave a stiff bow and said, 'I've not had the honour before, my lady.' He did not take her hand and she did not offer it.

Catherine walked to a window to watch as yet another carriage clattered across the stones. She could feel the admiral staring at her, but found no pleasure in his uncertainty.

She thought suddenly and with longing of Falmouth. To be parted again was too brutal to consider.

She leaned closer to the window and observed the new arrivals. No admiral or politician this time, only a tall lieutenant, removing his hat as he gave his hand to the woman who stepped down beside him. Even in the fading light, she could see the grey in his dark hair, saw him laugh, and the way the fair woman looked at him. So this was George Avery's lover, to whom he seemed to have lost his heart.

And yet, when he had brought Sillitoe's invitation and had warned her of the prospect of Malta, he had said nothing about staying behind when Richard was ordered to sail.

She heard Rhodes say, 'I'm giving you *Frobisher*, d'you know her?'

And Richard's reply, his mind already grappling with his new task.

'Yes, my lord. Seventy-four – Captain Jefferson, as I recall.'

Rhodes sounded relieved, she thought. 'No more, I fear. Slipped his cable two years back. Buried at sea, poor fellow.'

Bolitho said quietly, 'A French prize. She was named *Glorieux*.'

'Does that trouble you, Sir Richard? If so . . . .'

'A ship is as good as you use her.'

Rhodes grunted. 'New, too, compared with some of your recent vessels. Eight years old.'

She heard him pick up a goblet and drink noisily. Yes, he *was* relieved. She turned from the window and said, 'And when will this be required, my lord?'

He regarded her warily. 'Weeks rather than months, my lady. But you need not concern yourself with such matters. I have always found . . . .'

'Have you, my lord? I am glad to know it. Out there, people are celebrating a victory, the cost of which is still to be calculated, and *I am concerned* for this man and for myself. Is that so strange?'

Bolitho said, 'I have not yet decided.'

Rhodes looked around as though trapped. 'You were chosen because of your reputation, because of the honour you have won for your country.' He regarded Catherine grimly. 'It should be plain to see why this is of paramount importance.'

The door opened softly, and Sillitoe entered without speaking.

She said quietly, 'All I see is two islands and two men. A tyrant who has fought and murdered his way through Europe on one, and an admiral of England, a true hero, on the other. That is no comfort at all!' She touched her eyes with her glove, and when she looked again, Rhodes had departed.

Sillitoe said, 'I do regret this. Rhodes is a good controller, but he has no tact. If you decide against hoisting your flag in the Mediterranean, Richard, it will be his head on the block, not yours. And he knows it.' He glared at his secretary again, and then said, 'Join me presently. There are some people you should meet.' He gave a wry smile. 'Including my nephew's guest.'

The door closed and they were alone; only the strains of music and the muffled murmur of voices reminded them where they were.

She lowered her face. 'I am so sorry, Richard. I spoke like an angry, embittered wife. I had no right.'

He raised her chin and studied her. 'If you were my wife in the eyes of the church, I could not love you more. You had every right. You are my life.'

26

'Then let them see it.' She tossed the shawl from her shoulders and touched the pendant, and looked at him again.

'And tomorrow we shall leave London.'

Lieutenant George Avery stared around at the crowd and began to doubt the wisdom of having accepted his uncle's invitation. Important people all, well known to those who shared this unfamiliar world, politicians, senior officers of both army and navy, and a few diplomats adorned with honours he did not recognise. It was the utter transformation of his uncle's house which was the most astonishing thing. The silent austerity had been replaced by music, noise and laughter, and liveried servants pushing through the throng this way and that to satisfy the guests and refill the goblets.

He glanced down at his companion. 'Perhaps we should have made our excuses, Susanna.'

She smiled, observing him thoughtfully, like one discovering or seeking some new and unknown quality in him.

'I recognise some of the faces here. I have seen them on other occasions. I suspect that this is where all the real decisions are made, like the turn of a card.'

Avery felt vaguely jealous, without understanding why. She was used to such affairs, like the one at her own London house, where she had invited him to stay. To be her lover.

He had seen heads turn to look and compare. The beauty and the lowly lieutenant. The most junior sea officer Avery had seen so far had been a post-captain. They walked through the throng, and he saw her acknowledge one or two people. Most of the women she ignored.

When he mentioned them, she replied softly, 'Like the extra footmen, they are paid for their services!' She had gripped his arm and almost laughed at his embarrassment. 'Lord, *Mister* Avery, you still have much to learn!'

She released his arm now, and said, 'That is Lady Somervell, is it not? It must be.'

Avery saw Catherine and Bolitho by a low balustrade, and said, 'Would you care to meet them?'

But Sillitoe stepped between them, and held out his hand. 'Lady Mildmay, what a pleasure. I had been so looking forward to making your acquaintance. I hope everything is to your satisfaction? A great pity you are to be separated from my nephew so soon, but then, I shall never attempt to understand the navy!'

She looked at Avery. 'Separated? I thought. . . . I understood that you would be remaining in England until some suitable appointment could be found.'

Avery said, 'I am Sir Richard's flag lieutenant, Susanna. It is more than a duty, or an excuse. It is what I must do.'

Sillitoe shrugged. 'Believe me, I offered him an alternative, Lady Mildmay. I do, of course, admire loyalty but. . . .' He broke off as one of his footmen signalled to him. 'We will speak later.'

Avery said, 'I was going to tell you. I have been happier with you than I could have believed possible. I love you, I always have.'

'But you'd leave me, because of duty?'

She turned, startled, as Catherine said, 'I think we should meet.'

She offered her hand.

'I do know what you are thinking. I try to accept it, but I shall never do so without pain.' She glanced around the room, seeing the quick glances, the knowing smiles, recognising them. Sir Wilfred Lafargue, one of London's leading lawyers and a friend of Sillitoe's, who had helped with her unexpected inheritance from her dead husband. And a red-faced city merchant to whom she had been introduced, probably at some similar reception. Men of influence, and authority. Not the kind who fought and died in battle, at sea with Richard's ships, or those who stood shoulder to shoulder in the line. And those like Lord Rhodes, solid, reliable and unimaginative, who planned their battles behind the desks of Admiralty.

She said, 'You must ask yourself, my dear, do I love this man enough? Enough to wait?'

A man she knew to be Sillitoe's uncomplaining secretary peered up at her. 'My lady, I am asked to escort you to the terrace.' He blinked rapidly as a clock began to chime. The music had stopped, she noticed.

Bolitho said, 'I shall find your shawl. It will be cool outside.'

She smiled and touched his face. 'No matter. I want people to see us like this, as we are.'

There were lights on the terrace, but the river beyond the wall was in darkness, like black glass.

Bolitho looked over the water, his ear picking up the heavy stroke of oars. A barge of some kind, moving steadily against the current with little regard for the oarsmen.

Sillitoe turned to greet them. 'Now you will understand why I did not invite the prime minister. The Prince Regent cannot *abide* the fellow!' It seemed to amuse him.

Sillitoe glanced up at a cluster of lanterns, and took Catherine's arm.

'Here, if you please. Trust me.' She could feel the intensity, the tenacity which he did not try to conceal.

She stood quite still in the light, oblivious to the others chosen by Sillitoe to be present at this moment, feeling the cool breeze playing over her bare shoulders. She knew Richard was close by, but for just these fleeting moments, she was alone.

The oars were tossed and the barge came alongside the jetty, men leaping out to make fast the mooring lines, others to lay a scarlet carpet on the pale stones.

The Prince would pass her without a glance; he would not even remember her. He knew many women, and had an appetite to match.

She almost held her breath, and thought suddenly of Sillitoe's enigmatic words. *Trust me.* When she looked again, she saw the Prince striding towards her, exactly as she remembered him from the evening at Carlton House.

He was elegantly dressed in the very latest fashion, but even in the flickering lights it could not disguise completely the physical price he was paying for his excesses. His hair was swept forward in a style followed by many of the younger bloods, and no one could doubt his energy or the quickness of his mind.

She realised that no one was speaking, that the Prince had stopped, facing her, his eyes moving over her face and throat, and to the glittering diamond pendant shaped like an open fan. It was like being stripped naked, like an insistent caress.

He said, 'Lady Somervell! Had I known you were to be here, I would have ridden with all haste on the finest charger in the Royal Mews!' He took her hand and held it. 'Indeed, I have thought of you often. The lady who is always *too busy* to become bored, I think you said when last we met?' He

29

kissed her hand, taking his time. 'You are very beautiful.' He released her hand and looked at the others. 'Ah, Lord Rhodes. I trust you have affairs in order for me?' He did not wait for or expect an answer. 'There you are, Sillitoe, you rascal.' They shook hands. More like conspirators than friends, thought Catherine.

The Prince saw Bolitho and greeted him warmly. 'My admiral of England.' Catherine knew that was for her. What she had said on that same occasion at Carlton House. So long ago. Before *Indomitable*; before she had forced herself to write and tell Richard of Zenoria's terrible death. *Tell Adam. . . .* Like yesterday.

He continued, 'I have studied all your reports on the American war. I agree that the sooner it is settled the better for all concerned.' He turned and looked at Catherine. 'And what of Malta, Sir Richard? It is important for our security. And it is important to *me*. I must know, so what say you?' He reached out and took Catherine's arm. 'Shall you do it?'

Catherine could sense Richard's anguish, something like physical pain, just as she was very aware of the others standing nearby. How would they see it, even if they understood? Arrogance, or a display of temperament, when it was neither.

Sillitoe stepped into the circle of light. 'A moment, I pray you, sir.' He held out a piece of paper. 'This was just delivered to me by Admiralty messenger.'

Rhodes muttered angrily, 'First I knew of it!'

Sillitoe ignored him. 'May I, sir?'

The Prince smiled, when seconds earlier he had been angered by the interruption. 'This is *your* house, damn you.'

Sillitoe looked at Catherine but spoke to Bolitho. 'A despatch from the port admiral at Plymouth, Sir Richard. Captain James Tyacke has withdrawn his request for transfer to the West African squadron and has placed himself at your disposal for his duties as flag captain.'

Catherine slipped away from the Prince's grasp, and went to him.

'They have spoken for you, Richard. The need is theirs, too.'

The Prince Regent pursed his lips in a little smile. 'Thank you, Lady Catherine. Thank you. I know I have been a witness to something, although I know not what. I am not ungrateful.

Something might be arranged to enable you to visit Malta.'
He nodded to himself, as she had seen him do before. 'Yes,
it *shall* be done.' He seemed to relax. 'Now, there was talk of
a special claret, Sillitoe. Lead on!' But his eyes lingered on
Catherine, and her hand on Bolitho's arm. Desire certainly,
but there was also envy.

Later, much later, when they were leaving Sillitoe's house,
there were still several carriages waiting in the drive. The
Prince Regent had disappeared in his barge as quietly as he
had arrived.

Bolitho looked up at the stars, and thought, again with
disquiet, of Catherine and the Prince.

She said, 'I left my shawl behind!'

'I shall fetch it.'

He was surprised at the strength of her grip. '*No*. Let us go
to Chelsea. Be together. Lie together. It is all I want.'

Bolitho turned quickly. 'Who is that?'

It was Avery.

'Still here, George? What is it?' Although he thought he
knew. Like Tyacke. The Happy Few.

'I wondered if I could ride with you to Chelsea, Sir Richard.'

Catherine stepped between them, her shoulders pale in the
reflected lights.

'Did she leave without you, George?' She saw him nod. She
slipped her arms through theirs, linking them; she was almost
as tall as they.

'Then ride with us. And tomorrow, you will come to
Falmouth with us.'

He smiled, the sadness held at bay. 'Willingly, my lady.'

From his study window Sillitoe watched the carriage move
out on to the road. He frowned. There were still too many
overstaying their welcome. He would do something about
that.

He picked up the thin silk shawl, which she had left in the
ante-room by the library. He could smell her. Like jasmine.

Then he kissed it and folded it inside his coat and strode out
to do what he must.

31

3

Adam

Captain Adam Bolitho flattened the chart across his cabin table and glanced at the final calculations of the passage, although he knew them by heart. Around and above him the frigate, His Britannic Majesty's Ship *Valkyrie* of forty-two guns, held steadily on course, her reduced sails barely filling. It was early May but there was still an edge to the wind, as he had discovered during his customary morning walk on deck.

It was a time he usually liked. A ship coming to life, with the first glimpse of a horizon. Decks swabbed and holystoned, the boatswain and the carpenter comparing their lists of work for the new day. Sails to be brought down and repaired, rigging inspected and spliced wherever necessary. Water casks scoured out and prepared for refilling, and the end of stale, monotonous food, for the moment. *Valkyrie* was returning to harbour, to the main naval base at Halifax, Nova Scotia, the last real British foothold on the North American coast.

And what would they feel when they reached there? He stared around the cabin, at the lively wavelets falling astern beneath the frigate's counter, feeling again the resentment and impatience he tried so hard to conceal from his ship's company.

For *Valkyrie* was no ordinary or private ship; she was still officially the flagship of Rear-Admiral Valentine Keen, his uncle's friend. *And yours also*, a voice seemed to insist.

Somehow they had grown apart, even since the total destruction of two American frigates with the loss of only one man, a midshipman. Not so long ago, yet Adam could scarcely recall his face. Keen spent more and more time ashore concerning himself with the transport of troops. *Valkyrie* was returning from yet another such convoy. And for what purpose, he wondered. The news from England was optimistic; the war in Europe would soon be over, so that more ships could be released to fight the Americans. But for how long? The build-up of military strength here had to be for some reason.

He heard the marine sentry outside the screen door tap his musket on the deck and call, 'First Lieutenant, *sir!*'

He straightened his back as Lieutenant William Dyer stepped into the cabin.

It still came as a surprise, as if he expected John Urquhart to be presenting himself. Urquhart had gone to a command of his own, one for which he had been little envied. He had been promoted at Keen's suggestion to command the frigate *Reaper*, a ship torn apart by mutiny, inhuman discipline, and murder.

Adam had known that Urquhart could do it, and had been rewarded by the occasional news of *Reaper*'s performance and various successes. A rebirth. But Adam was missing him now.

'Ready?'

Dyer looked at a point above his captain's left shoulder. 'The master says that we shall be up to the anchorage within the hour, sir. If the wind holds steady from the nor'east, we should be in before six bells.'

A pleasant enough officer, and one who had made good use of his experience in this ship, one of the largest frigates on the station since *Indomitable*'s departure for England. But it went little beyond that.

'I shall come up directly.' He did not see the lieutenant's quick glance around the cabin, but he could imagine it. Dyer probably thought that his captain wanted for nothing. *As I once thought of mine.*

Adam had been more than successful as a frigate captain, and he was sensible enough to appreciate it, and that luck rarely came into it except to provide the opportunity to meet with an enemy, and to know his thoughts like your own. After that, it was skill, determination, and the men who depended on you. He smiled. And good gunnery.

The lieutenant saw the smile, and, encouraged, asked, 'Will we be hoisting the admiral's flag again after this, sir?'

'In truth, I do not know.' He moved restlessly to the stern windows and leaned his hands on the sill. He could feel the thud and shiver of the rudder-head, picture the ship as she would appear to any landsmen watching her careful approach.

A flagship. Only a frigate captain would understand the difference. It meant being tied to the fleet's apron strings and the whims and fancies of a flag officer. Keen was a good commander, but it was not the same. He tried to steer his mind away from his own ship, *Anemone*, which had fallen to the American commodore, Nathan Beer. Only an explosion below deck had foiled her capture and salvage, and spared her an enemy's flag. No, it was not the same.

Dyer withdrew, and Adam suspected he would soon be discussing their future with the other lieutenants. Wardroom gossip was only to be expected, but Dyer had not yet realised how quickly it could misfire.

He touched his side where the iron splinter had smashed him down, when *Anemone* had hauled down her colours and he had been unable to prevent it.

He watched the sea again, the fish leaping in *Valkyrie's* untroubled wake.

And what of Keen? Would he marry Gilia St Clair, and if so, why should he allow the prospect to torment him? Zenoria was dead, but his grief for her had not lessened. He picked up his hat and strode from the cabin. The fact was that Keen needed a wife, even if love did not enter into it.

He ran lightly up the companion ladder, and gazed at the familiar panorama which lay across the bows like a ragged barrier. Ships of every kind. Men-of-war, merchantmen, transports, captured prizes, and small, butterfly-like sails which created the movement in every living harbour.

He nodded to Ritchie, the sailing master, and saw him stand away from the compass box; he had been leaning against it. So his wounds were troubling him again. The surgeon had said that he should be discharged.

Adam frowned. Discharged? It would kill him more quickly than any American splinters.

A glance aloft at the newly trimmed sails, and the long, flapping tongue of the masthead pendant. She would make a proud sight, all sails clewed up except topsail and jib, her company at their stations at braces and halliards, topmen ready to take in the last of her canvas once the anchor was dropped.

A sight which, in the past, had always warmed and excited him. But the exhilaration eluded him now, like something beyond his reach.

'Lee braces there! Hands wear ship!'

Bare feet thudded along the deck, and blocks squealed as more men threw their weight on the snaking lines.

'Tops'l sheets!'

Adam folded his arms, and saw one of the young midshipmen turn to study him.

'Tops'l clew lines! Lively there! Take that man's name, Mr M'Crea!'

'Helm a-lee!'

Adam walked to the side to watch as the big frigate came slowly round and into the wind, the way falling off her, her remaining sails already being dragged and fisted into submission.

'*Let go!*'

Dyer hurried aft, his eyes everywhere as the ship came to rest at her cable.

'Will you require the gig, sir?'

Ritchie, the master, grimaced against the pain and then exclaimed, 'Cheering, sir!'

Adam took a telescope and trained it on two other frigates anchored nearby. Their shrouds and rigging were filled with shouting, waving seamen and marines.

He closed the glass with a snap. 'Yes, Mr Dyer, I shall want the gig as soon as possible.'

Dyer stared at him. 'What does it mean, sir?'

Adam looked at the land. 'It means peace. Not here perhaps, but peace, the hope of a lifetime.' He glanced at the staring midshipman. 'He was not even born when the first guns in this war were fired.'

Some of the seamen were grinning at one another, others were shaking hands as if they had just met in some lane or harbour street.

'I shall visit Rear-Admiral Keen. He will expect it.' He saw the first lieutenant trying to grapple with it. 'Take charge, Mr Dyer. I will speak with the hands later when I return.' He touched his arm, and felt him jump as if he had just been nicked by a musket ball.

'They have done well. There are many who were not so fortunate.'

Later, as he climbed into the gig, he recalled his last words.

Like an epitaph.

Rear-Admiral Valentine Keen looked up from his desk and saw his flag lieutenant, the Honourable Lawford de Courcey, watching him through the door.

'Yes?'

De Courcey glanced only briefly at Keen's visitor, and said, 'It is reported, sir, that *Valkyrie* is approaching the anchorage.'

'Thank you. Let me know as soon as Captain Bolitho arrives.'

He looked around the room, which he used as his headquarters in Halifax. Charts, files, and books of signals. With de Courcey and some borrowed clerks, he had managed to stay abreast of the work as he could not have done if he had been at sea for long periods. It had made him feel that he belonged, and that what he was doing was progressive, enabling every ship and facility to give of its best. Until a few days ago, when the frigate *Wakeful* had arrived from England with news of the victory and of Napoleon's surrender. So far away, on the other side of the Atlantic, and yet the word of victory in Europe had affected him far more than the war which was being fought here against the Americans; perhaps because it had been his war for so long, with many enemies involved, but always the French.

He would have received the news earlier but *Wakeful*'s young captain had lost a couple of spars in a Western Ocean storm in his eagerness to be the first to bring the despatches. *Wakeful* had also carried a passenger.

Keen looked at him now: Captain Henry Deighton, the next acting commodore of the Halifax squadron, and soon to be directly under the command of Sir Alexander Cochrane, who had taken over the whole station.

It had all happened so quickly that Keen could not decide if he was pleased or disturbed by the unseemly haste.

There had been several letters among the despatches, including one from the First Lord, to reassure him, perhaps, that the next phase of his career was about to begin. There had been no letters from his father, a sure sign of his continuing disapproval.

And there was Gilia. He would delay no longer in asking her, and of course her father, if his proposal of marriage would be acceptable.

Deighton said, 'Captain Bolitho – what is he like, sir?'

Keen studied him. He was a senior post-captain, with several years of blockade duty and two fleet actions to his credit. Squarely built, with short, gingery hair and restless eyes. Not an easy man to serve, harder still to know, he thought.

'A good frigate captain. Successful, too.'

'Yes, I know him by reputation, of course, sir. It must have been a great asset to have Sir Richard Bolitho at his shoulder.'

Keen said nothing. Deighton had already made up his mind, or had had it made up for him.

Deighton said, 'Originally one of Sir Richard's midshipmen, I understand.'

Keen said, 'So was I. Vice-Admiral Bethune at the Admiralty was another. A good influence, it would seem.'

Deighton nodded. 'I see. I look forward to meeting him. Lost his ship, taken prisoner of war and then escaped . . . he sounds resourceful, if a trifle reckless.'

'He is my flag captain, at least until I leave here.'

It was quietly said but he saw the shot go home. Deighton had come from England; he would know better than anyone what was intended. It would mean further promotion, to vice-admiral. He still could not believe it.

He thought of Richard at home now in England, with his Catherine. He had seen and shared the legend himself. He opened the drawer very slightly and saw the miniature of the girl looking up at him. It could be his, too. *Ours*.

He half-listened to the tramp of boots outside the building, the raucous shouts of drill sergeants. This part of the place was on loan to him because of the general; it would soon revert to the army once his flag came down.

What would Adam think of the peace? He had agreed to be his flag captain, and the decision had surprised Keen. Adam was his own man, Deighton was right about that, and reckless to some degree, although Keen would never say so to someone outside the Happy Few. He could stay here and serve under the new commodore, or he could apply to be relieved, to take his chances in England while he hunted for a new command. It would not be easy; he knew that from his experience of other treaties, other respites in the long years of war.

He thought of all their faces, Inch, and Neale, and others like Tyacke who had somehow survived. The word was rarely used in the fleet, but each man was a hero. Perhaps that was what his father had implied more than once. That in war you needed heroes if you were to succeed. In peace, they were an embarrassment to those who had risked nothing.

It made him feel vaguely uneasy, as if he were letting Adam down. That was absurd. The choice was made, and by the time the next courier vessel arrived, everything might have changed yet again.

He closed the drawer, realising that de Courcey had returned.

'*Valkyrie*'s gig has been sighted, sir.'

De Courcey withdrew. The perfect aide, always there when he was needed, although Keen very clearly understood why he and Adam could not endure one another.

Deighton got to his feet. A heavy man, but he moved lightly, with an air of urgency and purpose. Commodore would be a big step for him. Sir Alexander Cochrane had gathered so many senior officers under his command that it was unlikely Deighton would rise any higher. And he would know it.

Deighton said, 'I must leave, sir. I have arrangements to complete.'

'We shall meet again this evening, Captain Deighton. I shall introduce you to Halifax society!'

Deighton stared at him, as if searching for a trap of some kind. Then he left the room.

Keen sighed, and thought, unexpectedly, of England, of Hampshire. It would be spring there. And there would be Gilia.

Suddenly, he was glad to be leaving.

Adam Bolitho opened the shutters of the two lanterns in his cabin to give it an air of welcome and seclusion. He rubbed his shin, cursing silently to himself; he had just collided with a chair in the darkness.

He touched the watch, heavy in his pocket, but did not look at it. It was about three o'clock in the morning, with *Valkyrie* riding easily at her anchor, a ship at rest, as much as she could be with some two hundred and fifty souls, seamen and marines, throughout her hull, some probably still awake after hearing of Napoleon's submission, and wondering what it might mean to them.

When he had returned from his visit to Keen's temporary headquarters he had ordered the lower deck to be cleared and the hands to muster aft. All those upturned faces: men he had come to know well, and those others who had managed to stay at arm's length from him, and all other authority. United by discipline, by the ship, and by their loyalty to one another, the strength of any man-of-war.

Later, he had explained to his officers what the immediate future might bring. With the arrival of better weather, it would almost certainly mean increased action against the Americans. That had been expected.

Dyer had been quite outraged when he had told them that there would be an acting commodore, as if the exchange of a rear-admiral's flag for a mere broad pendant was akin to a personal insult.

The day after tomorrow *Valkyrie* would sail in company with another small convoy, but her main duty would be to demonstrate to Commodore Deighton the importance and the efficiency of the squadron's scouts and offshore patrols.

Adam slumped in a chair and rubbed his shin again. He had had too much to drink, although he could scarcely remember it. And that was not like him.

He had changed into his best uniform and returned ashore for the evening reception which Keen had felt was necessary to welcome his successor. It had been a noisy, uninhibited gathering, which had shown no sign of ending even when Adam had made his excuses and walked back to the jetty, where his gig's crew had been dozing at their oars.

David St Clair and his daughter Gilia had been there, as he had known they would be, as well as local merchants and suppliers to the fleet, officers of the garrison, and several other captains. Benjamin Massey, a close friend of Keen's father, had not attended; it was said that he had returned to England. But Massey's mistress, Mrs Lovelace, had been present. She had smiled at Adam, that same direct, challenging look she had given him before. But this time her husband had accompanied her. The invitation in her eyes had been very clear.

Gilia St Clair had made a point of greeting him, and had hinted that Keen was about to propose marriage. She had watched his face while she spoke to him, remembering, perhaps, when she had asked him if he had known Keen's wife, and his unhesitating reply. *I was in love with her.* She might have told Keen while *Valkyrie* had been away, but for some strange reason he was certain that she had not.

Then she had mentioned Keen's promotion, and the possibility of his becoming port admiral at Plymouth, and the despair that was ever waiting for its chance seized him once again.

She had even mentioned the house in Plymouth. *Boscawen House.* It had been all he could do to hide his emotion.

It had been at the port admiral's house that he had met Zenoria, purely by chance. She had dropped a glove while alighting from her carriage. It had been the last time he had seen her, before she had taken her life. She had been in Plymouth to visit Boscawen House, accompanied by a London lawyer.

Had Keen, in fact, bought it as long ago as that? Did it signify nothing more to him than a suitable house for a senior officer and his wife?

Like yesterday . . . Zenoria in the admiral's house, surrounded by other officers and their wives, and yet completely alone. . . . And her glove, which he had been carrying when the American broadsides had done for his *Anemone.* That, too, was another fragment of this undying pain.

Her voice. *'Keep it for me. Think of me sometimes, will you?'*

He would never forget.

He jerked around in the chair. 'Who is that?'

It was John Whitmarsh, his servant. Another reminder. He had been the only survivor from *Anemone*, except for those men who had surrendered when they had seen their captain fall. Just a boy, who had been 'volunteered' by an uncle when his father had been drowned off the Goodwins. He could have been no more than ten or so when he had been sent to sea in *Anemone.*

'Me, zur.' He stepped carefully into the circle of light. 'I thought you would likely be staying ashore, zur.'

Adam ran his fingers through his dark hair. He must not go on like this. He would destroy himself, and those who depended on him.

'I considered it.' He gestured to his cupboard. 'A glass of cognac, if you please, John Whitmarsh.' He watched him bustling about, always so content, so eager. When Adam had offered him the position of servant the boy had treated it with open delight, as if he had been thrown a lifeline. How could he know that he, in turn, had offered the same to his captain?

And now, all the changes. What might happen next? He looked at the boy grimly. He had nobody. Father dead, and no word from his mother, although Adam had written in an attempt to discover her whereabouts, and her interest, if any, in her son. He was thirteen years old. *As I once was.*

He took the goblet and held it to the lamplight.

'Stay a while, John Whitmarsh. I have been meaning to speak with you.'

'Is something wrong, zur?'

'Have you thought about your future, in the navy, or beyond that?'

He frowned. 'I – I'm not sure, zur.'

Adam studied him for several seconds. 'I received no reply from your mother, you see. Someone must decide for you.'

The boy seemed suddenly anxious. 'I'm very happy here, zur. You've taught me so many things, how to read an' write. . . .'

'That was not all my doing, John Whitmarsh. You are a quick learner.' He looked at the goblet again. 'Would you consider being sponsored as midshipman, or transferred as a volunteer to some ship more suitable for advancement? Have you thought of that?'

The boy shook his head. 'I don't understand, zur. A midshipman . . . wear the King's coat like the young gentlemen, like Mister Lovie who was killed?' He shook his head again, determination making him suddenly vulnerable. 'I shall serve *you*, zur, an' one day perhaps I'll become your cox'n like old Mister Allday does for Sir Richard!'

Adam smiled, and was strangely moved. 'Never let Allday hear you describe him as old, my lad!' He became serious again. 'I believe you could be a midshipman, and eventually a King's officer, with some education and the right guidance.

41

And I would be prepared to sponsor you.' He saw that he was achieving nothing. 'I shall pay – even your mother cannot object to that!'

The boy stared at him, his eyes filling his face. It was all there, despair, anxiety and disbelief.

'I want to stay with you, zur. I don't want anybody else.'

Overhead feet moved back and forth, the watch changing. It must be four o'clock. But to this boy it meant nothing; all he saw was the one life he knew being taken from him.

'I shall tell you a story. There once was a young boy who lived with his mother in Penzance. They did not have much money, but they were happy together. Then his mother died, and this boy was left with nothing. Nothing but a piece of paper and the name of his uncle, whose home was in Falmouth.'

'An' be that you, zur?'

'Aye, John Whitmarsh, it was. I walked all the way to Falmouth. Not as far as India, but far enough, and there I was taken in and protected by the lady I grew to know as my Aunt Nancy. I could have stayed with her, and I would have had no fear of want again. But I waited until my uncle's ship returned to Falmouth. He was her *captain*.' He was surprised at his own voice. Pride, love for the man who was one of England's greatest admirals.

The boy nodded gravely. 'An' you became a midshipman, zur.' There was a silence, then he said, 'When I met Sir Richard that day, when he asked about you, an' what I saw when our ship went down, I *felt* it. How he felt, what you meant to him, just like me an' my father.'

'So think about it, for your own sake. And for mine. We take much from this strange life we lead. It is sometimes a comfort to put something back into it.'

The boy picked up the empty goblet but Adam shook his head, and he left it.

Then he said, 'I only ever had one real friend, zur, that was Billy, an' he was lost that day.'

Adam stood up and yawned. 'Well, now you have another, so be off and catch some rest before they pipe the hands.'

He turned to watch as the slight figure melted into the shadows, and was pleased by what he had done.

They were two days out of Halifax on passage for the Bermudas once again, and *Valkyrie*, with her heavily laden charges, had barely logged five hundred miles. Long, monotonous days when some of the hands had to be chased even to their routine duties watch by watch.

In other circumstances it might have been ideal. There was a light north-easterly wind, enough to fill the sails and no more, with clear skies and sun to drive away the memories of winter cold and darkness.

At noon Adam stood by the quarterdeck rail and shaded his eyes to watch the three heavy transports lying downwind, with the outline of *Wildfire*, a smaller twenty-eight-gun frigate, almost invisible in a shimmering heat haze.

He heard the murmuring voices of the midshipmen, who were gathered with their sextants to estimate and compare their calculations from the midday sights, while Ritchie and one of his mates moved amongst them with the tired patience of schoolmasters. Lieutenant Dyer was with the boatswain by the foremast, discussing work to be done on the crosstrees, although Adam guessed that he had chosen the moment merely to keep out of his way.

This endless convoy work, soldiers and guns, stores and ammunition; it might be necessary, but it was not a life he cared for. A slow passage and limp canvas when he was more used to questions of whether to reef or not, with spray bursting over the beakhead to send the unwary flying.

He glanced at the skylight. He had scarcely seen Captain Deighton since he had come aboard. He was down there now, using the large stern cabin. Deighton was probably relishing it, thinking of the moment when it would be his stepping-stone to higher rank.

He glanced at the masthead. At least there was no broad pendant yet. *This is still my ship*.

Ritchie was writing in his log, and looked up as Adam's shadow fell across it.

The sea was empty, a glittering, blinding desert, and yet in his mind's eye he could see the land, exactly as Ritchie's spidery calculations and estimated position described it. New York lay some hundred and fifty miles to the west. Ships, movement, the enemy. But for how much longer?

'How are you feeling, Mr Ritchie?'

He saw the immediate alarm, the anxiety. Like the boy, when he had asked him about his future.

43

'Fair enough, sir.' He sighed. 'Some days is better'n others.'

Adam regarded him gravely. 'Take heed of the bad times, Mr Ritchie. Have a word with the surgeon, perhaps?'

Ritchie's worn face split into a grin. 'Of course, sir.'

George Minchin was a surgeon of the old school, one of the butchers. And yet, even sodden with rum, he had probably saved more lives in his brutal trade than others more mindful of the risks. He had been Bolitho's surgeon in the old *Hyperion* when she had fought her last fight. Drink should have sent him aloft long since, Adam thought, but he was still with them. He could understand Ritchie's reluctance to fall into his hands.

He saw Ritchie turn his head slightly. 'He's one of the walking dead if ever I saw one, sir!'

The man in question was tall, narrow-chested and bony, like a living skeleton. Except that Adam had seen him carry Captain Deighton's chest and other gear up from a boat alongside with neither a tackle nor another hand to aid him; he had muscles of steel. He was Deighton's personal servant and went by the name of Jack Norway. If that was indeed his name.

When spoken to, he would listen attentively, his gaunt head slightly on one side, his gaze never leaving the speaker. Dyer had remarked irritably, 'Never says a word, damn his eyes! More like a bodyguard than a servant, if you ask me!' He had shown no interest in mixing with those around him, and the others seemed content to keep it so.

Adam tugged out his watch and flicked open the guard. Then he turned it slightly to catch the sun's reflection on the engraved mermaid, which had immediately attracted him in the shop in Halifax. Chiming clocks, watches of every kind, and this one. His old watch had gone missing after he had been wounded in *Anemone*, or had been stolen during his imprisonment. *The little mermaid.* Like the one which was said to visit the church in Zennor, where Zenoria now lay. Or did she . . . ?

'We shall exercise the starboard battery after the hands have been fed, Mr Ritchie.' He could smell the heady aroma of rum in the warm air, another part of a ship's daily life. *Mine, too.*

He saw one of the midshipmen cleaning his sextant, then turning away as Deighton appeared on the quarterdeck.

He glanced at the men working on deck, the sailmaker's crew with their needles and palms, stitching and repairing, letting nothing go to waste. Fasken, the gunner, was bending over one of the larboard carronades, watched anxiously by Lieutenant Warren, who until recently had been a midshipman. There were probably about forty years between them.

Deighton remarked, 'Some experienced men, Captain Bolitho, but some very young ones, would you agree?'

Adam said, 'The ship has a good backbone of seasoned men, warrant officers and the like. I have been lucky. Some of the others are quite young, and I'm still short-handed despite volunteers from Halifax, but even the young ones have experience enough of battle.'

He studied Deighton's profile, the short ginger hair, the ever restless eyes.

Almost to himself, Deighton added, 'Keep them busy, drive them hard, that's the answer. But I'm sure you know that, eh?'

'This is not a ship of the line, Captain Deighton. We are often engaged in chasing enemy vessels, with a prize or two at the end of the day. We always need extra hands to crew the prizes, when and where we can find them.'

Deighton nodded slowly. 'And you have been more than successful, I hear.'

Adam gestured over the starboard side. 'There are prizes a-plenty out there for those who will run them to earth.'

Deighton took a telescope from the rack and scanned the horizon immediately ahead of the ship, pausing at each transport, and the hazy frigate beyond.

'She must be *Wildfire*. Captain Price.'

Adam half-smiled. Price, the wild-eyed Welshman. But all he said was, 'A good officer.'

'Yes, yes. We shall see.'

The afternoon watch had taken over its various stations, the men glancing at the other captain as they trooped aft, their eyes curious, perhaps hostile.

Adam wondered why. Because Deighton was a stranger? *But then, so was I.*

Deighton asked abruptly, 'And who is *that*?'

Adam saw the boy, John Whitmarsh, pausing by the boat tier to stare at the sea.

'My servant.'

Deighton smiled, for the first time. 'A damn sight prettier than mine! Where did you find him?'

45

He was surprised that Deighton could rouse such resentment in him.

'He was one of the few to survive when my ship was sunk.' He turned and looked at him directly. 'I am putting him up for advancement.'

'I see. Is he from a good family? His father, has he . . . ?'

Adam replied shortly, 'His father is dead. He has no means of support.'

'Then I don't understand.' He touched Adam's sleeve. 'Or . . . perhaps I do.'

A squad of marines had lined the quarterdeck nettings, and a sergeant was inspecting their muskets. At a signal from forward, some old pieces of boxwood were hurled outboard by the carpenter's mates.

'Marines, *ready*!'

Adam beckoned to the lieutenant of marines. 'Carry on!'

The pieces of woodwork floated past, and as the order rang out each marine fired his musket in turn. There were a few grins and some derisive cheers from idlers on the gundeck as splashes burst around the makeshift targets.

Adam reached out and took the marine officer's pistol, and tested the weight in his palm; it was heavier and clumsier than his own. He climbed up on to some bollards and took aim. The driftwood was further away now, and he heard Deighton remark, 'Not much chance there!'

'I think, Captain Deighton, that you were right the first time. You *don't* understand.'

He felt the pistol buck in his grip and saw one of the wood fragments splinter. Then he handed the pistol to the marine lieutenant, and said, 'Now, I think we all do.'

46

4

The Longest Day

Catherine carefully raised the window catch, and paused to glance over her shoulder at their bed. The curtain around it was partly drawn to shield his face from the first light; he was asleep, one arm flung out toward her pillow, at peace, perhaps his only refuge.

She opened the window and looked down at the garden, the rich colours of her first roses. The sun was warm on her skin even so early in the morning, the air clean, and bearing only a hint of salt from the sea.

If she had leaned out, she would have seen the blue-grey water of Falmouth Bay beyond the headland. But she did not lean out. Today, of all days, the sea was an enemy.

Her gown had fallen open and she felt the breath of that sea on her skin. There was no one to see her. The estate workers were in the fields, and she could hear the faint sound of hammers chipping on slate. She had once believed she would never get used to this place, or call it home, and now it was a part of herself.

She touched her breast as he had done, could still feel the depth of his embrace and his desire. As if he had only just withdrawn from her.

How quickly time had passed since their return from London. Riding, walking, and being alone with each other.

Now the house was so quiet, as if it was holding its breath. George Avery had visited them several times, and with Richard had gone through the canvas pouches which arrived regularly from their lordships. She had listened to them, trying to share it, to make it last. Like Richard's new flagship, *Frobisher*. They

47

discussed the ship like the professional sailors they were, as if she were human, a living creature.

Avery had stayed at the inn at Fallowfield, perhaps to allow them as much time as possible alone together, and also to ponder over his rejection by Susanna Mildmay. She knew it had saddened Richard; he had blamed himself, because Avery had put loyalty before his own personal happiness. If she was really the woman for him. . . . She watched a pair of wagtails darting amongst the flowers. *Is that not what society said about me?*

She pressed her hand to her side, feeling the ache, the heaviness, the pain which today would bring.

They had dined alone last night, although neither of them remembered the meal which had been so carefully prepared.

She had told him she wanted to ride with him all the way to Portsmouth, where *Frobisher* lay waiting to receive him. Like the other times, like the last time when she had climbed up *Indomitable*'s side. It was not to be. Richard had said that he wanted to take his leave of her in this house. *Where I always think of you.*

How could she do it? How could she let him go like this, so soon? She knew he hated the idea of her making the long journey, some one hundred and fifty miles, back from Portsmouth. Even with the roads in good condition and the coming of better weather, there was always the risk of footpads, or deserters from the army or navy who robbed or even killed if resisted. He would not be alone. He would be among friends when he saw his flag hoisted above his new flagship. Avery, Allday, Yovell, and of course Ozzard, who had given no hint of what he thought about leaving yet again. And perhaps the strongest of all, James Tyacke, who had cast aside his idea of returning to Africa. Or perhaps he had decided that there would be no escape and no solace even there.

Yes, Richard would have friends, but he needed memories also. Like last night. It had not been a last, desperate passion, an act which if missed would haunt them as something lost. It had been a *need*; she had felt it when they had come to this room, when he had turned her towards the finely carved cheval glass, and had undressed her while she had watched his hands, knowing they explored her, and yet sensing that it was happening to someone else. A stranger.

He had taken her to the bed and had said, 'Do nothing.'

He had kissed her from her throat to her thigh, from her breast to her knees and then, very slowly, back again. She could not believe that she had been able to contain her desire for him, and when she tried to pull him down to her, he had gripped her wrists and held them while he had looked down at her, wanting her, but needing it to last. Lovers, as if for the first time.

And then he had smiled at her. Even though the light had been from a single candle only, she thought it was the most beautiful thing she had ever seen.

He had entered her without hesitation, and she had cried out his name while she had arched her body to receive him.

She felt a tear fall on her breast, and wiped her skin angrily with the lace of her gown.

Not now. Not now, of all times.

She walked to the bed and pulled the curtain aside. His face was relaxed, even youthful. More like Adam than most of the other faces in those ever-watchful portraits. His hair still black across the crumpled pillow, except for the one rebellious lock above his right eye. It was almost completely white, and she knew he hated it. It concealed the savage scar which ran deeply into his hairline . . . so close to death even then.

She sat on the bed and realised he was awake, watching her. She did not resist as he released the gown from her shoulders, nor flinch when he touched what he had kissed and teased so often. She understood. It was another memory. When he was able to be alone sometimes, to be free from the demands of duty, when he might perhaps be reading the leather-bound sonnets she had given him, he would remember, and would be with her, as she was with him.

She said, 'It is a lovely day, Richard.'

He caressed her hair, which hung loosely over her bare shoulders.

He smiled, searching her face. 'You lie. It is an *awful* day!'

'I know.'

He raised himself on one elbow and looked at the clock, but said nothing.

There was no need. She thought of their walks by the sea, following a receding tide, their footmarks spread in the sand

49

like molten silver. Holding this day at bay. They had visited his sister, and had found her strangely calm, able and willing to talk about her late husband, Lewis, 'the King of Cornwall'.

She had been very definite about one thing. 'I'll not let the estate go. The people always depended on Lewis. He'd expect it of me.' She had glanced around the huge, empty house, and had said, 'He's still here, you know.'

She realised that she had taken his hand. 'I'm sorry, Richard . . . it becomes more difficult to accept.'

They heard the discreet clatter of dishes, the soft murmur of voices beyond the door.

'Not for so long this time, Kate.'

She smiled, and wondered how it was possible. 'I shall come to Malta and torment you. Remember what Prinny said about that?'

Grace Ferguson, the housekeeper, nodded to the maid. 'Give a knock.' She smiled. 'Sounds all right.'

She thought of the barely touched meal of the previous night, the unopened champagne, which always seemed to take their fancy for some reason. But you could never be sure, especially with her ladyship. She had never forgotten when her husband had told her about that terrible day when the girl Zenoria had jumped to her death from Trystan's Leap. He had described how Lady Catherine had lifted the slight, broken body and held her like a child while she had opened her clothing to find the one mark which would identify her. Where a whip had laid open her back; the *mark of Satan*, she had called it. . . .

The maid came out and smiled. 'Good as gold, ma'am. Nothin' worries they much.'

'You mind your manners, girl!' She turned away. *That's all you know*.

Then she walked to a window and stared down at the yard. Young Matthew, as he was still called and probably always would be, was giving the carriage a wipe with his cloth. Heads would turn when they saw the Bolitho crest on the door; people would wave, but, like the maid, they would never understand.

Another Bolitho was leaving the land. She remembered her own bitterness when Bryan had returned home after the Battle of the Saintes, with one arm gone. As she had nursed him over the months and watched him slowly restored to life, she had

50

been almost grateful. He had lost an arm, but he was still her man, and he would never have to leave her again.

Later, when she went downstairs, she saw that Sir Richard's cocked hat lay beside his sword. Ready.

She peered up at the nearest portrait, Rear-Admiral Denziel Bolitho. He had been the only other officer in the family to attain flag rank. He had been with Wolfe at Quebec, probably near to where Sir Richard and John Allday had last been, she thought. But it was not the face or the rank she noticed; it was the sword. The artist had even caught the light on it, exactly as it was falling now. The same old sword.

For some reason, she shivered.

John Allday watched the boy lead the pony and trap around the stable yard, and tried to come to terms with his feelings. All his life he had seemed to be waiting for ships, or coming back to this place from one vessel or another. In the past he had been able to face it squarely, hope for fair winds, and what Mister Herrick had always referred to as *Lady Luck*.

This time it had been hard. Unis putting on a brave face, little Kate wanting to play games with him, unaware of the pain that such partings brought. The next time he saw her she would be bigger, almost a person, and he would have missed the part in between. He grimaced. Again.

So it was another ship, but that did not trouble him. He was the admiral's coxswain, as he had always believed he would be, as he had promised Bolitho when he had been the youthful captain Allday remembered so well.

He had seen the looks on other people's faces until they had grown used to it. Admiral, England's finest, and his coxswain. But so much more. They were friends. It had even taken the flag lieutenant a while to fathom it out. And now he, too, was one of Sir Richard's little crew; he even read Unis's letters to Allday, and replied to them in a way that nobody else could do.

He saw Young Matthew, very smart in his livery, examining the baggage, ensuring it was properly stowed. From the stables Allday could hear the horses stamping their hooves, eager to go. He sighed. *Like me*. Wanting to get started now that the choice was made.

Bryan Ferguson came from the house and nodded to

Matthew. 'You can harness up now.' He joined his friend by the wall. 'Got everything you need, John?'

Allday glanced at the stout black sea-chest which was lashed beside one of the admiral's. He had made it himself; it even had secret drawers in it. He wished he had had time to show them to little Kate.

'Enough, Bryan. Leastways, we should get some good weather at this time o' year.'

Ferguson frowned, sensing the sadness and, at the same time, the overriding determination of this big man.

He said, 'You know that sea well, of course.'

Allday nodded. 'Where *Hyperion* was lost to us.'

Ferguson bit his lip. 'I shall visit Unis as often as I can. She knows we're always here and ready if she needs anything.' He ran his eye over his friend again. The landsman's idea of the true sailor, he thought, in his smart blue jacket with the buttons bearing the Bolitho crest and his nankeen breeches and silver-buckled shoes. God alone knew the people owed everything to men like him. It still did not seem possible that the fear of war and invasion were past.

He saw Allday turn as Catherine Somervell came from the house and stood for a moment in the bright sunshine. Her long, dark hair hung straight down her spine, and she wore a gown the colour of fresh cream. She shaded her eyes while she turned to speak with one of the stable-boys, her ready smile revealing nothing of her emotions.

Allday watched her and waited for her to notice him. She made a beautiful picture, he thought, and he guessed she had taken great care of her appearance. The sun glinted on the pendant Bolitho had given her, the diamond fan hung low on her breast, like pride, like defiance, like the sailor's woman she was.

When he had last visited the house he had seen them together, in her own garden by the wall. They had been holding one another, and had not seen him. Allday had left without a word. It had been too private, a moment which he could not share.

Afterwards, he had recalled the words he had used to describe Captain Adam Bolitho and the girl who had thrown herself from the cliffs. *They looked so right together*. He could have been speaking of Sir Richard and his lady.

He realised that she was looking at him and felt strangely guilty.

She came to him and took his big hands in hers.

'Take good care, John.' For the merest instant, he had seen her mouth quiver. 'And look after my man for me, will you?' She was in control again.

Then she turned and saw the horses being backed into position, Young Matthew speaking to them, careful not to catch her eye. In his quiet way, he too would know how she felt; he had driven them before when they were to be parted, just as he had driven her to the harbour when Bolitho had returned home after leaving *Indomitable* at Plymouth.

She stepped among the roses and chose one, then held it to her face. A perfect red rose, one of the earliest. There would be many more before long, when he was far away from here.

She saw him on the steps now, the house at his back, as he might remember it. He looked rested, his face showing no sign of strain or uncertainty. Her man, youthful again. No wonder people thought he and Adam were brothers, although Richard himself would dispute any such foolish notion.

He came down the steps, carrying his hat, the old sword hanging against his hip, where she had been, where her head had lain. He saw the rose, and took it from her.

'So much a part of you, Kate.' He hesitated, as if suddenly aware of the silent figures nearby. 'It is better this way.'

She touched his shirt, and felt her locket underneath.

'I shall remove it when we lie together again, dearest of men.'

Gently, he placed the rose in her gown, above her breasts.

He said, 'It is time.' He glanced around, but Allday had already climbed into the carriage, leaving them alone but sharing it, as always.

She saw him press his fingers to his eye as he faced into the sunlight, but he shook his head as he sensed her concern. 'It is nothing.' Then he held her hands tightly. 'Compared with this, nothing else signifies.'

She caressed his face and smiled at him. 'I am so proud of you, Richard. And these people too, they all love you and will miss you.' Then she said, 'Kiss me, Richard. *Here*. We are alone in every other sense.'

Then she stepped back and gave him another smile. 'Now, Richard.'

It took an age, an eternity, until at last the carriage moved through the gates. Somebody gave a cheer, and Catherine heard someone else sobbing quietly. Grace Ferguson, who had been a part of it all from the beginning.

She clutched the rose against her skin and waved with her free hand. She could scarcely see now, and yet she was determined that he would remember her like this and feel no despair and no guilt for his departure. When she looked again, the road was empty. She stared blindly at the stables and saw her big mare Tamara tossing her head over the door. She felt her resolve weakening; she would ride after him, hold him again once more.

She heard Grace Ferguson exclaim, 'My lady! My lady, you've cut yourself!'

Catherine glanced down at her breast where she had been pressing the rose; she had felt nothing. She touched the skin with her fingers and looked at the blood.

'No, Grace, it is my heart which bleeds.' Then and only then did she give in, to bury her face against the other woman's shoulder.

Ferguson waited and watched in silence. When the others had all drifted away the two women remained standing together in the sunlight. Only their shadow moved, when quite suddenly Catherine touched his wife's arm without speaking and walked slowly away towards the house, the bloodied rose still held against her breast like a talisman.

James Tyacke opened a window slightly and stared down at the busy street. Portsmouth, called by some *the heart of the British Navy*, and a place which had been so familiar to him as a young lieutenant, seemed completely different. He knew, in truth, that he was the one who had changed.

He had chosen this small boarding house on Portsmouth Point partly because he had stayed here before, and because he knew it would afford him some peace over the next few days, before he went to the dockyard to take command of *Frobisher*. He could still scarcely believe he had abandoned his decision to return to the slave coast with so little hesitation.

He watched the jostling crowds of sailors and marines, the

trusted men who were unlikely to desert, and had been allowed ashore. In peace or war, it was every captain's main concern that he might be left too short of hands to work his ship out of harbour.

He had seen for himself the mass of shipping at Spithead, the misty hump of the Isle of Wight beyond. Familiar, and yet so alien. He sighed. When would he accept it? He had no past, and his future was only today and tomorrow. It had to be enough.

The owner of the boarding house had obviously been surprised to number a post-captain among his guests, and had done everything he could to make Tyacke welcome. He was a small goblin of a man, completely bald, who wore an outdated and shabby wig, usually somewhat awry and, Tyacke thought, not properly athwartships. There was an unspoken etiquette in naval circles as to where sea officers should lodge. Senior officers stayed at the George in the High Street, where a room had already been reserved for Sir Richard Bolitho when he arrived from Cornwall. Lieutenants and the like used the Fountain further down the street, and the 'young roosters', the midshipmen of the fleet, frequented the Blue Posts, famous for its rabbit pie, if rabbit it was.

Here, too, on the Point, separated only from the respectable properties by the same rules which governed the teeming world of a ship of the line, were lodging houses, some so squalid that it was a wonder they had not been burned down; tailors, pawnbrokers and moneylenders; and narrow lanes where the ladies of the town paraded their wares, and were rarely lacking in customers. It was so often the last place a sailor would see or snatch a moment to enjoy himself, before weighing anchor and sailing perhaps to the other side of the world, often never to return.

He thought of Lieutenant George Avery; he would be arriving soon in Portsmouth if he was not already here. Another who had chosen uncertainty instead of a life ashore. For some reason, Tyacke was pleased that Avery had made the decision to join them.

And there was the ship. He had studied her details, which the Admiralty had made available to him in their weighty folder of orders and sailing instructions. A strange ship, without familiar faces, so he would start from the beginning once more. *Indomitable* had taught him that he could do it, and much more besides.

All the way to Portsmouth, he had gone through the folder. He had travelled alone. It was still difficult to accept that he was wealthy, by his own standards, as the result of slave bounty still trickling through the Admiralty channels, and prize money which he had gained under Bolitho. He touched his burned face. *His own coach*. And, had he wanted it, he could have taken a room at the George.

He closed the window and sat down. *The ship*. If he could get through the next two days, he knew he could take the next all-important step. From a commander of a schooner and a lowly brig to *Indomitable*, and now *Frobisher*, a ship of the line. And all because of one man. *I would serve no other*.

He thought of Bolitho's Catherine, and wondered how she would deal with this new appointment so soon after Bolitho's return from Halifax. He was certain that Bolitho would not bring her to Portsmouth. Crowds, cheers and mindless well-wishers. What would they know of the cost of separation?

Tyacke looked at his open chest. Another journey. This time, how might it end?

He touched his leg, where a splinter had torn into it. It had been *Indomitable*'s last battle; she would never fight again, according to the dockyard people at Plymouth.

It was like recalling someone else. He had taken a boarding-pike and driven it into the deck and had supported himself, despite the pain and the blood, until the guns had fallen silent. *Were we really like that?*

And Bolitho leading the boarding party over to the enemy's deck, that old sword dangling from his wrist, with Allday at his side.

The sounds from the street intruded again. It would be worse at night; he should have considered it. No private places to walk, to travel with his thoughts alone for company. That he did remember about the Point. Somebody had once proclaimed that it was *crowded with a class of low and abandoned beings who seem to have declared open war against every habit of decency*. Obviously not a sailor, he thought.

Then he would spend his last few days here in this room. Perhaps he might read *The Gazette*, and any newssheet that might tell him how the war with the Americans was progressing.

He looked round as the door opened an inch.

'I am sorry to intrude, Captain Tyacke, I know you insisted on privacy. We have to be careful, of course, with so many sea officers waiting for ships.'

Tyacke nodded. *Praying for them, more likely.*

The shabby wig was awry again, but his eyes were busily going around the room. Probably wondering why a post-captain, soon to assume command of a flagship, should choose such a humble place to stay.

Tyacke said patiently, 'I am all attention, Mr Tidy.'

'There is a *lady* come hence to see you, sir. Say the word, and I will make the necessary excuses. I would not like people to think . . . .'

'What is her name?'

He already knew. Had he merely been trying to avoid a decision, like tearing the letter to fragments?

'Mrs Spiers, sir.' Encouraged, he added, 'A very pleasant lady, I would say.'

'I'll come down.'

'Please use my parlour.' He paused. 'Or this room, if you prefer.'

Tyacke stood up. 'No.' How many women had been ushered into these rooms? And how often?

As he followed the small goblin figure down the creaking stairs, Tyacke was aware of something almost unknown to him. *Fear.* But of what?

She was facing the door when he entered the parlour, hands folded, the ribbons of a wide-brimmed straw hat dangling from her fingers. She must have changed over the years, had been married, borne two children, been widowed. But she was the same. Brown hair curled above her ears; the level, open gaze he had believed gone for ever, lost in that other darkness.

She spoke first. 'Don't turn away, James . . . I did that once to you. I have thought of it so many times. I wrote to you.'

'I wrote to *you*.' His mouth could not form her name. 'But you would have seen it only if I had fallen. I said . . . I said. . . .' He imagined the little man in his wig listening outside the door. But there was nothing outside, nothing beyond this room or this place. He saw her move towards

57

him, and said, '*Don't*, Marion. Not now. Not like this. I've tried so hard . . . .'

She was very close, looking up at him; the same curved lashes. She reached up deliberately and touched his scarred face, without revulsion, without obvious emotion. Like her letter. Understanding, not asking forgiveness.

He heard himself ask, his voice that of a stranger, 'How did you know? Who told you?'

She glanced at his epaulettes. 'I read about Sir Richard Bolitho, and I knew you would be here as his captain again. The rest was easy, but you know what Portsmouth is like. A village, if you let it become one.'

'I take command the day after tomorrow. After that, who can say. . . .' He looked away and asked abruptly, 'Are you well, Marion? Provided for?'

She nodded, her eyes never leaving him. 'My husband was a good man. It was very sudden.'

He glanced around the small, untidy parlour, with its smells of tobacco and wet soot.

'And the children . . . two, you said.'

'Caroline is quite grown now.' Then she did lower her eyes. 'James is twelve. He hopes to enter the navy one day.'

Tyacke said quietly, 'They are not my children.'

She smiled. It made her look vulnerable, and suddenly defeated.

'They could be, James. If you wanted. If you wanted enough.'

He heard the landlord say loudly, 'No, Bob, I've got somebody in there.'

Tyacke turned into the light and said gently, '*Look at me*, Marion. Not at the captain, but at me, the survivor. Could you lie with me, search for a future, when we had no past?'

He had put his fingers to his face, where she had touched him. He could still feel the touch, and wanted to curse himself for his stupidity, for the hope which would betray him, if he allowed it.

He had not seen her move, but she was at the door, one hand on the catch.

'I had to come, James. I was very young . . . at that time.'

58

Young, and transparent like gossamer. But I loved you then. I never forgot.'

She played with her hat, and shrugged. 'I'm glad I came. I had hoped we might be friends again.'

'Nothing more?'

She watched him, perhaps trying to rediscover. 'Write to me, James. I know you will be busy with your affairs, but please try to write, if you want to.'

He was reminded sharply, vividly, of Catherine and Bolitho, as if he had just seen them. What they had overcome, what it had cost them, and how they had triumphed. As he had seen that day in Falmouth, when she climbed up the ship's side to the delight of his men . . . .

. . . Of the yellow gown he had carried in his chest over the years, which Catherine had worn to cover her nakedness when *Larne* had found the open boat, when all hope of their survival had been abandoned. *Except by me* . . . .

He replied, 'I'm not much of a hand with writing, Marion.'

She smiled, for the first time.

'If you want to.'

She had put a small card in his hand. 'If you have time, James. It is not so far.'

He stared at the card, his mind, usually so cool and accurate, now like a ship taken all aback.

Where was the anger, the condemnation which had been his companions for so many years? Perhaps, like the pity, it had been something shared.

'I shall leave now.' When he did not move, she came to him again, and said, 'You are still that man, James.' She felt him hold her, carefully, as if she might break, and wanted to cry when she saw how he turned the terrible scars away as she kissed his cheek. It was a small beginning.

When Tyacke looked again, she was gone, and the landlord was in the doorway beaming at him. As if it had all been only in his mind.

'All done, sir?'

Tyacke did not answer, but climbed the stairs to his room. He propped the card on a table, and opened a bottle of cognac.

Tomorrow Avery might come, so that they could begin their preparations. Everything else would fall into place. . . .

But he knew it would not, as he should have realised when he had torn his letter into pieces.

He lay down and stared at the ceiling.

The longest day. *For all of us.*

5

The Prize

Bolitho placed his sealed letter to Catherine on the table and pictured her reading it, perhaps by her roses, or more probably in the privacy of their rooms. It had been bad enough, leaving her in Falmouth, and this letter was little comfort. Not yet; even sending it was like breaking a precious link.

He pulled out his watch and flicked open the guard: almost two o'clock in the afternoon. No turning back.

He sighed and replaced the watch in his pocket, his eyes moving around the room, its dark timbers almost black with age and the smoke from a thousand fires. He had only stayed at the famous George Inn once before, then as a young captain. It was a timeless place, which had seen more admirals and captains come and go than he could imagine.

The room looked bare now that his chests had been taken out to be sent to his new flagship, empty, ready to forget him and welcome another.

It was not difficult to see Nelson here, perhaps in this very room, on his last days ashore in England. He had left his beloved Emma at their house in Merton. What was she doing now? And what of those who had promised Nelson that she would be taken care of?

He turned away, angry with himself for making the comparison. There was none. Only the bitter rift of separation was the same.

He heard voices on the stairs; one was Avery, the other Allday. It was time.

Down the stairs, the scene was exactly as he had expected. The landlord, anxious to please, careful not to show it. There

61

were plenty of uniforms in evidence, sea officers obviously enjoying themselves, each careful to catch his eye as he passed. Some might have served with him, most had never seen him in the flesh before. But they all knew him.

It was said that when Nelson left the George for the last time the streets had been packed with people trying to catch a glimpse of him, and show their admiration for their hero. Perhaps it had even been love.

He himself had never met 'Our Nel', although even Adam had exchanged a word or two with him when he had been carrying despatches.

He saw Avery watching him from the doorway, his eyes tawny in the reflected sunlight. Beyond him, Allday stood with his back to the inn, as if he had already rejected the land.

The street was busy, but quite ordinary. No cheering crowds or curious sightseers this time; but then, there was no war raging across the Channel.

'We'll walk to the Sally Port.' He saw Allday turn and touch his hat to him, the admiral's coxswain.

Avery observed him thoughtfully, trying to guess the mood of the man to whom he was loyal before all else.

Bolitho said, 'No bands, no parades, George.' He smiled. 'Like God, the navy is only fully appreciated when danger is at the gates!'

Avery tried to sense bitterness or regret, but there was none. He had seen the letter Bolitho had given to the landlord, and knew the truth would be in it, for her alone. For Catherine.

He said, 'The ship is short-handed, sir. I think Captain Tyacke is eager to put to sea, to learn the strengths and weaknesses amongst the people.' Even Tyacke was different, he thought. Once a hard man to know, he had become as close to a friend as was possible within their ordered lives. And he had seemed withdrawn, as if a part of him were still lingering elsewhere.

He wondered what Bolitho truly thought about the choice of flagship; he himself had only had a few days aboard *Frobisher*, and he had found little time to meet the other officers, or get the feel of the ship. In a rare moment of confidence, Tyacke had told him that *Frobisher*, if properly manned and drilled, would be a fast sailer, and had a hull so well designed that even in heavy seas she might remain a relatively dry ship.

That would prove a godsend for her seamen when required to make or reef rebellious canvas, finding what warmth and comfort they could between decks afterwards.

Avery had expected there might be some resentment at Tyacke's appointment, but he had discovered that *Frobisher*'s previous captain had been suddenly discharged as medically unfit, and sent ashore with the Admiralty's blessing. Avery had served Bolitho long enough to know that the real reason for the captain's hasty departure was probably something very different, and he had gained the impression that the ship's lieutenants, at least, were glad to see him go. Tyacke had revealed nothing of his own thoughts. He had his own methods of gaining a company's loyalty, and would tolerate nothing less than the standards he had set in *Indomitable*.

Bolitho tugged his hat down more firmly as they rounded a corner and the wind off the sea swept to greet them.

Avery had explained that Tyacke had changed the anchorage after leaving the dockyard, and the ship now lay off St Helens on the east coast of the Isle of Wight. A long, stiff pull for any barge crew, he thought, and Allday would be watching their behaviour and that of the barge with a critical eye. Like other old Jacks, he had always maintained that a ship could be judged by the appearance and handling of her boats.

He considered his own change of role. Tyacke would have attended to everything, food and stores, fresh water, and any fruit juice he could lay hands on, keeping his subordinates at arm's length until he had learned the reliability, or otherwise, of lieutenants and warrant officers, purser, gunner and boatswain. Bolitho gave a brief smile. And, of course, the midshipmen, the 'young gentlemen', for some reason he had not yet discovered always the bane of Tyacke's life.

He saw Allday on the jetty, apparently relaxed and untroubled, but Bolitho knew him so well. He would already have learned everything he could about the *Frobisher* of seventy-four guns, once the French two-decker *Glorieux*. Completed too late for Trafalgar, she had had only a brief career under the Tricolour before she was attacked and captured by two of the blockading squadron while on passage from Belle Isle to Brest. That had been four years ago. Allday would be thinking of that, too: the same year he had married Unis at Fallowfield.

Prize ships, put to work against their old masters, were

commonplace in the navy. There had been times when even ships rated as unfit through rot or disrepair had been pressed into service, like his own *Hyperion*, a ship of which they still yarned and sang in the taverns and alehouses. *How Hyperion cleared the way* . . . . Would their lordships make the same mistake of running the fleet down to the bare bones, simply because the immediate danger had been withdrawn?

He glanced at Avery, who was speaking with a waterman, noticing the stiffness with which he held and moved his shoulder when he was not conscious of it. Like Allday and his wounded chest, where a Spanish blade had hacked him down.

They were loyal; it was more than mere loyalty. But they were both sacrificing so much, perhaps a last chance, for his sake.

'Ah, here she be!' Allday scowled. 'A fresh coat of paint will be the first thing!'

Bolitho shaded his eyes to watch the barge, which had suddenly appeared around the stern of an anchored frigate. It had probably been obtained direct from the dockyard where *Frobisher* had just completed an overhaul; there would have been no time to paint it dark green, as was the custom for flag officers' barges. Again, he felt the same sense of doubt. The last captain, Charles Oliphant, might have remained as his flag captain unless he had explicitly requested James Tyacke.

He recalled Admiral Lord Rhodes's obvious eagerness for him to take *Frobisher* as flagship.

He looked at Avery again; perhaps he had noticed the flaw. Captain Oliphant was related in some capacity to Rhodes, although he could not recall where he had heard it mentioned. He frowned. But he would remember.

The barge turned in a wide arc and tossed oars, the bowman hooking on to the jetty while a seaman vaulted onto the worn stonework. Smart enough, with a lieutenant in charge, no doubt wondering what this first encounter would be like.

Avery said quietly, 'That's Pennington, second lieutenant, sir.'

Allday conceded, 'Not too bad.'

The lieutenant stepped ashore and doffed his hat.

'I am ready to take you directly to your flagship, Sir

Richard.' The eyes, Bolitho noticed, were careful not to meet his own.

'It is a long pull to St Helens, Mr Pennington.' He saw the surprise at the use of his name. 'I think they might rest easy for ten minutes.'

The lieutenant stared at the oarsmen, their raised blades dripping like wet bones.

'That will not be necessary, Sir Richard.'

Bolitho said gently, 'Have you so short a memory, sir, that you cannot remember what it was like when you first pulled an oar?'

Pennington dropped his eyes. 'I see, Sir Richard. Very well.' He turned away, and nodded to the boat's coxswain. 'Rest easy, O'Connor!'

Allday saw the ripple of surprise run through the boat. *Put that in your pipe and smoke it*, he thought.

Eventually, they were cast off and pulling strongly into the Solent. There were ships of every size and rate, and Bolitho saw sunlight flash on several telescopes as they watched him pass. It would soon be all around Spithead, he thought; the navy was a family, whether you liked it or not.

'What is the state of the ship, Mr Pennington?' Again, he was aware of an immediate caution, as if the lieutenant suspected a trap.

'All provisioned and watered, Sir Richard.'

'Short-handed?'

'Thirty trained men short, Sir Richard. Full complement of marines.'

Thirty short, out of a full company of six hundred souls, was not crippling, but the last captain should have used his time in the dockyard to recruit or poach men from other sources.

He peered over at a small brig which was scudding abeam, and preparing to set her courses. A fine-looking little ship, he thought, and he wondered if Tyacke had seen her, and was remembering his own command, *Larne*, which he had given up for *Indomitable. For me*.

Allday leaned forward as they passed another anchored man-of-war, and Bolitho saw the quick glance from the stroke oarsman, seeing it for himself: the admiral's coxswain who sat close to his master like a companion.

65

Allday said, 'There she is, Sir Richard. I'd know them Frenchie lines anywhere.'

Bolitho shaded his eyes again, aware of the blurring of his vision. The reminder. The taunt.

What Allday had said was true. The longer line of the upper hull, the planking extended beneath the beakhead to offer added strength and protection, were distinctively French. British shipbuilders had continued to end their upper gundeck with a flat bulkhead, which rendered the forepart of the ship weaker than the sides. Tyacke would have made full note of that; his own terrible injury at the Nile was the result of French fire devastating the gundeck where he was serving at the time.

Slightly broader in the beam than her English counterparts, *Frobisher* would provide a better platform for her artillery in poor sailing conditions.

He shook himself mentally. *The war was over.* It was to be Malta, not Halifax this time. He thought suddenly of Adam, and of Valentine Keen. Nothing more must happen to them, with the war in North America so nearly finished. Neither side could win, even as neither side could demonstrate a willingness to submit.

He put his hand to his eyes again as the barge swept beneath the ship's long and tapering jib boom, and did not see Avery's immediate concern. And here was the figurehead, shining in fresh paint and gilt: Sir Martin Frobisher, explorer, navigator, and one of Drake's fighting captains. He had been portrayed with jutting beard, staring blue eyes, and a black Elizabethan breastplate.

He wondered what had become of the original figurehead, so obviously unsuitable when the ship had changed names. It was not unknown for a prize to retain its old name, but the navy already had a *Glorious* on the list, and confusion might have occurred in the endless ebb and flow of signals and fleet orders.

The lieutenant called, '*Bows!*'

And there it was. The curved tumblehome, the new black and buff paint, the entry-port and the waiting rank of scarlet.

His flagship. It was a proud moment.

He touched the locket beneath his shirt, and prepared to stand as the barge surged alongside.

I am here, Kate.

He turned, momentarily off guard, convinced that he had heard her voice; he could not have been mistaken.

Don't leave me.

The Royal Marine sentry outside the screen door of the great cabin was as stiff and motionless as a man could be with the ship swaying gently at her anchor. After the bright sunlight, the shouted commands, the fifes and drums, the din of a flagship's welcome to her new lord and master, it seemed peaceful here, protected.

The ceremony had been brief, with his flag breaking at the mainmast truck, timed to the exact beat of a drum, and standing out in the Solent breeze like painted metal.

There had followed a quick presentation to the assembled ranks of lieutenants and senior warrant officers: a nod here, a nervous smile there, each man glancing surreptitiously at him before he, in turn, came under scrutiny.

Like the marine sentry, given time, he would get to know them, some better than others. It was always the hardest part to accept: the division, the barrier which rank had thrust upon him. *He was not the captain.* He could never again be as close as a captain to the people he commanded.

He nodded to the sentry, and although the man's eyes did not flicker beneath his glazed leather hat, the contact had been made.

The stern cabin was broad, spacious, and strangely welcoming. Even the strong smells of paint and fresh tar which pervaded the whole ship could not interfere with the familiarity of these things. The wine cooler with the Bolitho crest carved upon it, which Catherine had had made to replace the one lost with *Hyperion*, the high-backed chair in which he sometimes slept, his desk, his books, some old, some she had given him because of the clarity of their print. He saw Ozzard hovering by what was apparently his pantry door, and he had already seen his secretary, Yovell, observing from his own vantage point during the ceremony, when the admiral's flag had been broken out. They had worked very hard to prepare this place for him, and he had been moved by it.

Tyacke followed him into the cabin. 'All fair, Sir Richard?'

He nodded. 'You have done well, James, in so short a time.'

Tyacke glanced around. 'There's more room here than there would have been. Four eighteen-pounders were removed.'

Bolitho watched him carefully, but saw no sign of strain or discouragement. A new command, an unknown company, a way of doing things which might offend or irritate him, but Tyacke's face gave nothing away.

'Take a glass, James.' He guessed that Avery, like Allday, had purposely stayed away for this first meeting since they had shaken hands at Plymouth, where *Indomitable* had been paid off.

'I'd relish that, sir.' He made to take out his watch, and then hesitated. 'But only one glass. I've still a few ends to splice before I'm ready.'

Bolitho watched Ozzard pouring the wine, apparently indifferent to the sounds of a ship at anchor, muffled voices, the clatter of blocks and tackles as more provisions or equipment were hoisted aboard. The Caribbean, Mauritius, Halifax, and now Malta. His thoughts were unknown, the barrier here the greatest of all.

Tyacke sat, but Bolitho knew his ear was pitched to that other world.

He said, 'I've been through the books and the signals. They seem to be in order.'

Bolitho waited, knowing what was coming next.

'The punishment book lists nothing unusual.' He looked at Bolitho. 'Not like some we've seen together, sir.' He was referring to the frigate *Reaper*, but, almost superstitiously, avoided mentioning her name. 'Discipline is fair enough, but they need more gun and sail drills before I'm handing out any bouquets!'

'And what of your officers?'

Tyacke raised his glass, and paused as a boatswain's call twittered in the distance.

Then he said, 'The senior lieutenant, Kellett, seems very competent.' He looked at him directly, no longer averting the burned face, as he had in the past. 'I may be speaking out of turn, sir, but I think the first lieutenant has been carrying this ship, not just during the overhaul, but before that. I can *feel* it. Sense it.'

Bolitho sipped the wine. Perhaps it had come from the shop in St James's Street, where he had gone with her.

He would force the issue no further. It would be an intrusion, and Tyacke would tell him when he had made up his mind. When he was certain.

Tyacke said, 'The midshipmen now, they're another story. Most of them are newly joined and come from naval families. Some are young, *too* young for my taste.'

Any ship on an important commission, or Admiralty or government business, would have encouraged parents, who saw it as an opportunity only too rare in peacetime, and with the fleet being cut down. William Bligh of the ill-fated *Bounty* had had no difficulty in acquiring very young midshipmen for his command.

Tyacke said suddenly, 'But given time and a good run through Biscay, we might see the makings of something.' For a moment his blue eyes were very clear and distant, like Herrick, Bolitho thought, or perhaps more like the man Tyacke had once been. 'But I still find myself looking around expecting to see old faces, the ones who can make or break any ship.'

Who did he mean? *Indomitable, Larne*, or further back still, perhaps even before the Nile?

Bolitho said, 'I do it myself. All the time.'

He did not see the sudden, searching expression in Tyacke's eyes.

He said, 'You are satisfied, James? Being here, when perhaps you could have found a different sea to challenge?'

Tyacke seemed surprised, or relieved, that he had not asked something else. He touched his face, although Bolitho sensed that he did not even notice it.

'There is no escape, sir. There never was.' Then, firmly, 'It suits me well, sir.'

He put down the glass and got to his feet, his eyes resting briefly on the gleaming presentation sword, which Allday had already placed on its rack; *part of the show*, he once called it. Unlike the old family blade at his hip. The legend. The charisma, as his flag lieutenant Oliver Browne had described it. Another lost face. He smiled reminiscently. *Browne with an 'e'.*

Tyacke hesitated. 'I was wondering, sir . . . .'

Bolitho said, 'Ask me, James. You may always do that.'

Tyacke seemed, again, to hesitate. 'When we weigh tomorrow, will you miss England?'

Bolitho looked at him steadily. *Will I miss her*, he meant. But he did not know how to ask, without overstepping the mark.

'More than I would have believed possible, James.' He watched him leave, taking his hat from Ozzard without even seeing him. Bolitho heard Allday in the adjoining cabin, and was suddenly grateful.

It was like stumbling on to a secret, something so private that any wrong word could destroy it, and the man who carried it. The gown Tyacke had always carried in his sea chest, the one he had given Catherine to cover herself when *Larne* had plucked them from the ocean and the nearness of death. The woman . . . .

After all this time.

He stood up and walked to the stern windows, and then sat on the curved bench seat above the glistening water.

It was just as well that *Frobisher*'s great anchor would show itself tomorrow.

But the voice persisted. *Don't leave me.*

Bolitho heard Allday putting his shaving gear away and speaking quietly to Ozzard in the sleeping-cabin, and walked slowly to the sloping stern windows.

Since the hands had been called, *Frobisher* had been alive with muffled sounds and occasional shouted commands. A ship preparing to sail was so familiar a sight in these waters that most people would take no notice, but in his heart he knew that this departure was different. There would be many ashore today to watch them leave. Wives, lovers, children, wondering when they would meet again. The sailor's lot. They would be pondering on the man whose flag flew from *Frobisher*'s main; would he care enough for the many he commanded? Not an ordinary day for them. *Or for me.* The shave and the clean shirt were all part of it. He glanced at Ozzard's tray. He could still taste the fine coffee Catherine had bought for him; he had even eaten breakfast, slices of fat pork, fried pale brown with biscuit crumbs. He knew Ozzard disapproved of this meal, considering it fit only for a lowly lieutenant or midshipman, when the admiral he served could demand what he liked. *Neither of us will change now . . . .*

He leaned on the sill and stared at the bright water, criss-crossed by ranks of low, white crests. The wind had backed

70

overnight, perhaps to the north-east. He had had little sleep, and not because of the ship's unfamiliarity; he had overcome that sensation a long time ago. He had lain awake in his cot, half-listening to the ship's sounds, *her voices*, as his father would have described them. Creaks and mutterings, as if from the keel itself, the occasional hiss of wind and spray against the side, the responding thrum of stays and shrouds.

And once, when he had fallen asleep, he had found himself in a dream which had exploded into a nightmare. Catherine being carried away from him, her clothes torn from her, hands reaching out to touch her.

After that he had unshuttered a lantern, and had read through the last batch of instructions from the First Lord; they were lengthy, diplomatic, but meaningless. Like most senior commands, responsibility would eventually rest on the shoulders of the officer in charge.

It would be another reminder, if one were needed, of Napoleon's overwhelming power and his successes, Spain and Portugal, Italy, and onward into Egypt. Marshal Murat's crushing victory over the Egyptians at Aboukir had been the removal of the last obstacle. The gateway to India had lain open, and all Napoleon's grandiose schemes appeared to have been forged into one unstoppable force, until Nelson had taken his ships into Aboukir Bay and had destroyed the French fleet.

He glanced at some small boats passing astern, making heavy weather of it in the stiff breeze and choppy sea.

The Battle of the Nile, they called it now. Something Tyacke would never forget, or be allowed to forget. He smiled at the sharpness of memory. *Hyperion* had been there, too. Today the peace was still to be settled amongst the victors. But there would always be the predators, just outside the firelight, seeking an easy prey: the aftermath of every battle.

Allday entered the cabin, and said, 'Lively up top, Sir Richard. This will mark out the boys from the men!'

Bolitho turned to face him. He had not heard Allday leave to go on deck. A big, shambling figure, yet he could move like a fox when he wanted to. Ozzard was there too, his sharp eyes moving to the breakfast tray, the empty plate and coffee cup. And then, critically, to the coat, which he had already laid out for this occasion.

Allday saw it and smiled privately, thinking how the people

71

on deck would see the admiral. Not in the beautiful gold lace and gleaming buttons, but in the old, familiar sea-going coat which had even survived a battle or two. *Like us*, he thought grimly.

Ozzard patted the coat into place, almost scowling at the tarnished epaulettes.

Allday took the old sword down from its rack and turned it over in his hands. Yes, that was how they should see him. Not as the admiral, but as the man.

The ship's company would find it hard to get used to. Like the old *Indom*, when Sir Richard had made a point of speaking to the men on watch, the marines at their endless drills. He had heard him say to an officer once, 'Remember their names. In many cases, it is all that they own.'

The man.

Bolitho tugged out his watch. Tyacke would be here very soon. The shouting and the thudding bare feet were silent now. The capstan was manned, the lieutenants at their stations, on the quarterdeck, at each mast, and right forward when the anchor came home.

He thought of Avery, who had been much quieter than usual. Going over it, perhaps. Reliving what he had found, and what he had thrown away.

He saw Ozzard glide to the screen doors; his keen hearing had detected Tyacke's footsteps despite all the other noises.

Tyacke entered, his hat tucked beneath one arm. There were fine droplets of spray on his coat, and Bolitho guessed he had been up and about since before the cooks had been called.

'Ready to get under way, Sir Richard. Wind's holding fresh an' steady, nor'easterly. Once clear of St Helens, I've laid a course to weather the foreland. When we've got sea room I'll come about and steer sou'west.' He smiled briefly. 'It'll be a bit lively until then, but I shall be able to see what they can do.'

No hesitation or uncertainty, despite a different ship, people he scarcely knew, and every glass in the fleet watching him, waiting for a mistake.

'I'll come up.' The formality must wait a little longer. 'Thank you, James. I know what it cost you.'

Tyacke looked at him, perhaps remembering that other beginning. 'The cost is shared this time, sir.' As he turned to leave, he added, 'Twelve hundred miles from Spithead to Gibraltar, our first landfall.' He grinned. 'They'll have learned something of our standards by that time!'

Bolitho touched the sword at his side, and turned to Allday. 'What are *your* thoughts, old friend?'

Allday glanced up at the skylight as the boatswain's calls shrilled impatiently. Spithead Nightingales, the Jacks called them. They ruled your life.

He replied slowly, 'I'm a mite older, Sir Richard, but I *feels* the same.' He glanced at the nearest empty gunport. 'It's going to be strange, never facing an enemy broadside again.'

They went on deck, beneath the poop, and past the big double wheel where the helmsmen were already in position. Four of them: Tyacke was taking no chances.

Despite the wind, it was warmer on deck than he had expected; he felt the new pitch sticking to his shoes as he crossed to the quarterdeck rail. From here to the beakhead there were men everywhere, with more already swarming aloft to the topsail yards. Aft by the mizzen mast, the marines were waiting in squads to man the braces and halliards. The old hands claimed it was because the mizzen's sail plan was the simplest, and could mostly be handled from the deck, so that even a 'bullock' could manage it!

Bolitho saw the quick glances, the word passing along the upper deck. Avery was standing by the opposite rail, hat tugged down over the greying hair which was part of the price of his service. Tyacke was speaking with the sailing master, Tregidgo, a straight-backed man with an unsmiling, taciturn countenance. He was a Cornishman, and he had served in *Frobisher* for the four years since her capture, and under her two captains, Jefferson, whom Rhodes had casually dismissed – *slipped his cable two years back, buried at sea, poor fellow* – and Oliphant, who had left in such haste.

Tyacke faced him and touched his hat. 'Ready, Sir Richard.'

Bolitho glanced up at his flag, streaming against an almost cloudless sky.

'Carry on, Captain Tyacke.'

Calls trilled and parties of men dashed below, where they were needed on the other capstan to add their weight to the straining cable. Bolitho shaded his eyes to watch a few passing boats. There were women in one of them, whores going to greet another new arrival at Spithead. It was, unofficially, common practice to allow prostitutes on board, if only to prevent men from desertion and the aftermath of punishment.

'Anchor's hove short, sir!' That was Kellett, the first lieutenant. He was right up forward by the cathead where he could watch the lie of the cable as the heaving, straining men at the capstan bars hauled their ship to her anchor by muscle alone.

Kellett came from an admiral's family. Bolitho had seen him only once since he had come aboard, a young, serious-faced officer with deceptively mild eyes.

'Stand by on the capstan!'

'Loose the heads'ls!'

Some confusion ensued, but there were trained hands well placed to assist or knock the offender into position.

'Hands aloft, loose tops'ls!'

The men were already poised to swarm out along the tapering yards. It was no place for anyone with a bad head for heights. He smiled at himself.

Clank – clank – clank. The pawls on the capstan were slowing; he imagined the great anchor moving below the ship's shadow, a last grip upon the land.

A fifer and a fiddler broke into a tune, and across the backs of crouching seamen and those at the braces with their eyes lifted to the yards, Bolitho saw Allday watching him, as if nothing stood between them.

So that was what he had been doing.

Bolitho lifted one hand, and he saw a midshipman turn to stare at him. But he saw only Allday, with the shantyman's reedy voice rising even above the squeal of blocks to remind him. To bring it all back once more.

There was a girl in Portsmouth Town. . . . Heave, my bullies, heave!

He touched his eye. *Portsmouth Lass.* Only Allday and perhaps one other would have thought of it.

'Anchor's aweigh, sir!'

Frobisher was already swinging round, leaning above her own reflection as the anchor was hoisted up and catted home.

He beckoned to Avery. 'Walk with me, George.'

While men bustled past them and cordage slithered along the deck like snakes, they walked together, as they had before when the guns had flamed and thundered all around them.

'Is there anything I can do, Sir Richard?'

Bolitho shook his head.

How could he explain, to Avery, of all people, that he could not bear to watch the land slide away, and to be alone with his thoughts. And his sense of loss.

Instead, he looked up at his flag, high and clean above the deck.

The last command. He acknowledged it as if he had spoken aloud. Then so be it.

6

Know Your Enemy

Lieutenant George Avery felt the warmth of the noon sun across his shoulders, and walked to the quarterdeck nettings to obtain a better view of the Rock. There were vessels of every description anchored, to take on stores or to await new orders, and around and amongst them boats under sail or oars bustled in endless activity. The towering mass of Gibraltar dwarfed them all, watchful, eternal, a guardian of the gateway to the Mediterranean.

Frobisher's slow approach, the crash and echo of gun salutes, and the brisk exchange of signals were part of the tradition, and once anchored, the ship's company were soon hurrying to other duties, lowering boats and spreading awnings. As during the passage out from England, they were left little time to ponder on their first landfall.

Ten days since the Isle of Wight had vanished astern, not a fast passage by any means, but deliberately planned to exercise the whole company, sails, guns, lowering and recovering boats, until Captain Tyacke was satisfied. If satisfied he was. Hate him, curse him, it made no difference, because every one from seasoned seaman to ship's boy knew that Tyacke never spared himself, nor shied away from anything he demanded of others.

On occasion, he had ordered lieutenants and senior warrant officers to stand down, to be replaced by subordinates, or anyone Tyacke thought should discover the true responsibility of his rank or station. They had skirted Brest and the French coast and entered the Bay of Biscay, unpredictable as ever

76

despite the shades of spring, passing close even to Lorient, where *Frobisher* had been launched.

Then the coast of Portugal, like dark blue smoke in the morning light; into bright sunshine, where, although driven hard, Avery had sensed a change in the company, had seen men pause to grin at one another. To respond.

In the wardroom he had seen it and heard it, too. But as the flag lieutenant he was never part of any company, and that suited him. Until they knew him better, other officers might imagine that he was the admiral's ear, Tyacke's too, ready to pass on their more outspoken opinions. These were divided on Tyacke's ruthless insistence upon drills. Some protested that it was pointless, as there was little likelihood now of action. Others took the view that, as flagship, it was a matter of pride.

Avery had noticed that Kellett, the deceptively mild-mannered first lieutenant, was rarely drawn into these heated discussions. Only once, he had turned suddenly on a junior lieutenant and had said, 'I fully realise that you likely speak more out of drink than conviction, Mr Wodehouse, but do so again in my presence and I'll take you aft myself!' It had been quietly said, but the wretched Wodehouse had cringed as if he had just received a torrent of obscenities.

Avery realised that one of the midshipmen was waiting to catch his eye.

'Yes, Mr Wilmot?'

'Signal from *Halcyon,* sir. *Have despatches on board.*' He pointed helpfully over the nettings. 'Yonder, sir. *Halcyon,* twenty-eight, Captain Christie.'

'Very well.' Avery smiled. 'That was quickly done. I shall inform the captain.' He saw the youth glance across at the lithe frigate. She was small, by modern standards, but still the dream of most young officers. Maybe even this midshipman, with one foot on the bottom rung.

Tyacke strode across the deck, his head turned to give some instructions to a master's mate.

He saw Avery, and said, '*Halcyon,* eh? Left Portsmouth three days after us. She'll be joining Sir Richard's command at Malta.' He glanced at the midshipman. 'Make to *Halcyon. Deliver despatches on board.*'

Avery watched the midshipman scurry away to his signals

party, where the flags were all ready to bend on to the halliards.

'Mr Midshipman Wilmot is a brighter one than some. Didn't wait to be told.'

But Avery had seen the midshipman drop his eyes from Tyacke's face. How could he ever come to terms with it?

Tyacke turned as the flags shot up to the yard and broke to the offshore breeze. 'We might hear some news.' He smiled wryly. 'Or it may be a recall!'

Avery said, 'Do you know Malta well, sir?'

Tyacke said, 'Look at those damned boats!' His arm shot out and he called, 'Mr Pennington? You are the officer-of-the-watch, I assume?'

The lieutenant swallowed hard. 'I *saw* the boats, sir.'

'Well, tell them to stand away. I'll not have the flagship trading with scum like that! I don't care what they're trying to sell!' He turned away. 'Drop a round shot through the first one that tries to come alongside!'

Avery sighed. Tyacke would not be drawn about the past. *We make a fine pair.*

A seaman who was intently polishing the spokes of the big double wheel glanced across at him and said, 'The admiral's comin' up, sir.'

Pleased, Avery acknowledged it. It was another beginning.

Bolitho walked over to join him. 'I have just heard about *Halcyon.*' He shaded his eyes and stared across the busy anchorage. 'Which is she?'

Avery pointed her out. He thought Bolitho looked rested and untroubled, although he knew he had been working with Yovell almost every day since they had left Spithead. Instructions, details of ships and their captains, a thousand things which Avery could only guess at.

He had seen him pacing the deck at night under the stars, or standing with his open shirt rippling in the wind when the hands were turned up to take in a reef, or to change tack on the run south. Thinking of his Catherine, perhaps. Holding on, while the leagues rolled away from *Frobisher*'s great rudder.

Perhaps he did not need sleep like other men. Or was it denied him?

'Strange to be here.' Bolitho touched his eye and massaged

it slowly. 'I was out here after the revolution, when the royalists hoped to raise a counter-action at Toulon. It was doomed from the conception, George. So much waste.'

He stared across at the opposite side: the coast of Spain, almost swallowed in heat-haze. Another memory. Algeciras. He could remember someone pointing to it and saying, 'Look. Yonder lies the enemy.' But the face eluded him.

Avery wanted to speak, but after Tyacke's abruptness he was afraid to break the moment, which like all the others had become a part of his life. A part of him.

He asked, 'You will know what to expect, sir?'

Bolitho did not seem to hear. 'All that time ago, George. But later when I was here as flag captain in *Euryalus*, I can see it so clearly. The old *Navarra* being attacked by Barbary pirates. People smile when you mention them now, but they're as dangerous as they ever were. They'll not be tamed simply because we say so.'

'*Navarra*, sir? What was she?'

Bolitho looked at him. 'Just an old ship. She had no place in any line of battle. No prize court would have parted with a handful of gold for her.' He smiled, as if he was reaching out. 'Catherine was on board that ship with her husband. Where we met. Where we found and lost one another.' He paused. 'Until Antigua.'

Avery tried to imagine it, Catherine as she must have been; like *Golden Plover*, which Tyacke had described in one of these rare moments of intimacy.

Bolitho looked round as a seaman called, 'Boat's cast off from *Halcyon*, sir!' Then he said, 'I've seen so many victories and failures in this sea, but nothing could outshine that meeting.'

Tyacke appeared, and said sharply, 'If you're mistaken, Mr Pennington . . . .'

The second lieutenant stood firm. 'No, sir, the boat carries *Halcyon*'s captain!'

Tyacke glared at him. 'Then man the side, if you please.' He saw Bolitho and touched his hat. 'From England, sir. Got here ahead of us.' Then he relaxed slightly. 'Hardly surprising!'

Avery watched them. *From England*. Maybe new orders for Bolitho. And letters? It was too soon. He thought of Allday; he might want one written for him before they weighed.

79

The marines fell into two ranks at the entry port, and Tyacke waited to greet the visitor. Routine.

The calls trilled, the salutes were exchanged, hats raised to the quarterdeck, the flag.

Captain Christie said, 'Despatches, sir, and some personal mail.' He was a tall, serious-faced officer, probably in his late twenties, his gleaming epaulettes marking him out as a post-captain. War or no war, he had been posted, and he had his own ship.

Bolitho said, 'Come aft and take a glass.'

Avery followed them, knowing that the young captain had been unprepared for this invitation from the admiral.

They all sat down in the spacious cabin, and Ozzard appeared silently with his tray.

Christie said, 'It is an honour to be serving under your flag, Sir Richard. In these uncertain times one cannot be sure what . . . .'

He turned as Tyacke said quietly, 'Do I know you, sir?'

Christie took a goblet and almost spilled the wine. But his eyes were level enough.

'I know *you*, sir.'

Bolitho knew it was difficult for some reason, as difficult as it was important.

Christie said, '*Majestic*, sir.'

Just the name. The ship where it had happened. A ghost from the past.

Tyacke did not speak but studied Christie, trying to put the pieces together. As he had so many times, until it had almost driven him insane.

Christie said to Bolitho, 'I was a midshipman in *Majestic*, Sir Richard. My first ship, and I had barely been aboard her for more than a couple of months.' He looked around, as if searching for something. 'When Lord Nelson led us to Aboukir Bay.' He hesitated. 'To the Nile.'

Tyacke said slowly, 'I remember you.'

Christie continued, 'We were amongst the French fleet in no time at all, and were locked with the big eighty-gun liner, *Tonnant*. Broadside after broadside.' His voice was contained and unemotional, which made his description all the more vivid and terrible. 'Dead and dying lay everywhere. I was too junior to have a proper station and I was kept running messages from the quarterdeck to the guns.' He stared at the misted goblet. 'Our captain was killed, people I knew were being torn to pieces, calling for help when there was none to be given. I – I almost broke that day. I was carrying a message to the lower gundeck, and I was terrified that the ship would be blown apart before I could find somewhere to hide. All the training meant nothing. I wanted to hide. To escape.' Again, he hesitated. 'And then . . . .'

Outside, Avery could hear another boat being ordered to stand away, someone laughing. But only this was real.

Christie said, 'The lieutenant in charge of the forrard division of guns called to me, Sir Richard. He put his hand on my shoulder and shook me back and forth until I was calm again.'

Avery saw Tyacke nod, his blue eyes distant, unseeing.

'He said to me, "Walk, boy. *Walk*. To these poor devils you are a King's officer, but today you are the captain's voice, so use it clearly and show them what you can do."'

Avery thought of the midshipman called Wilmot. How Christie must have been.

Christie said, 'You sent me aft. Then the French broadside found us again. But for you I would have died with all the others. I told my father about it, and he tried to write to you. I wrote to you myself, but heard nothing.' He looked directly at Bolitho. 'It is wrong of me to speak of things so personal, but they have always meant so much to me, ever since that day. It made me a man, and I hope a better one.'

He stood up and said, 'I shall return to my ship now, Sir Richard. It has been an honour.' He raised his hand as Tyacke made to follow. 'No, sir, I shall see myself over the side.' Then he smiled. Relief, gratitude, surprise, it was all there. 'In the fleet they always spoke of The Happy Few. Now I understand.'

Behind the pantry hatch Allday put down his rum, his 'wet', and considered what he had heard.

In the navy you had to expect it. Faces from the past, like old wounds, were not easily forgotten. *Always the pain*. But they were safe now. And yet, why was he so uneasy? He wanted to ask Lieutenant Avery to write a letter to Unis for him. But not about this. It was something he could not talk about through another man's pen.

Ozzard came back, frowning.

Allday tried to shrug it off. 'Did I ever tell you about the time when me an' Sir Richard was fighting them Barbary pirates, Tom?'

'Yes.' He relented slightly, and Allday thought he had felt it, too. 'But spin it again, if you like.'

'The sea's face is fair enough today.'

The two women stood side by side by the old stile at the beginning of the cliff path and looked out across Falmouth Bay. The surface of the sea was unbroken, but heaving gently in the sunlight, as if it were breathing.

Catherine glanced at her companion, Richard's youngest sister, Nancy. She was looking better than expected. In life, her husband Lewis had been too large to ignore; in death, perhaps his strength was still her support.

Catherine ran her palm over the stile, the step and beams polished by countless hands and feet. How many had paused there to rest and reflect, as she had often done? She looked along the winding cliff path, hardly used nowadays. She rarely walked there, and certainly never alone, not since Zenoria's fall from Trystan's Leap.

Nancy said gently, 'Never fear, you'll have a letter soon from him.'

'I know. He never forgets. It is like hearing his voice.' She brushed some hair from her eyes. 'Tell me, Nancy. How are your affairs progressing?'

Nancy smiled at the change of subject. This tall, beautiful woman had become dear to her, had helped her through the grief of Lewis's final days and immediately after his death. A woman known and admired, envied and hated, who, with her brother, had defied every convention to proclaim their love. The hero and his lady. Lewis, too, had always admired her, and had made no secret of it. He had always had an eye for women. She stopped her thoughts, like closing a door.

'The lawyers from London are still at the house. Lewis's affairs were in good order, despite what I may say were his occasional extravagances. They will arrange for someone to manage the estate, at least until the children become involved.' She shook her head. '*Children*. Hardly that any more!'

They turned away from the stile. Catherine could remember

him holding her beside it, the need of one for the other, after a reunion, or before another separation.

She said, 'Two weeks since he left. It will be three soon. I try to see his ship in my mind, where she is, what they may be doing.' She shrugged. 'The Mediterranean . . . where we first met. Did you know that, Nancy?'

She shook her head. 'Only that you lost one another soon afterwards. That he did tell me.' She smiled, as though remembering. 'To think what he has become, in the navy, and to this country, and he remains uncertain of himself in many ways.' She added with sudden emphasis, 'I'll be thankful when he comes home.' She touched Catherine's arm. 'And stays here.'

They turned towards the gentle slope which led down to the old grey house and its attendant cottages, so that the headland seemed to screen them from the murmur of the sea, its constant presence.

It would seem different to Nancy, daughter of a sailor, from a family of sailors, sister of Falmouth's most famous son and England's naval hero. Born and raised here with these people of the sea around her, the courageous fishermen who ventured out in all weathers to supply the tables of manor house and cottage alike. The coasters and the famous Falmouth packet ships, who sailed with the tide in peace or war. Nancy had grown up with them and their tradition.

She felt Nancy hesitate as she saw the carriage waiting in the stable yard. Perhaps their meeting and walk together had made her forget, if only for a moment. But now she would be driven back to that huge house with its folly, another of Lewis's little indulgences.

How empty it must seem now. *I count the days and weeks. But Nancy will never have even a letter to sustain her.*

Nancy said, 'You have a visitor.'

Catherine stared past the carriage, aware of her painful heartbeat. There was no other vehicle, no horse to denote some courier, or messenger from Plymouth. But she could see somebody inside the estate office, in dark clothing, his back towards her, and she heard Ferguson's sudden laugh. Perhaps he had sensed her return and was trying to reassure her. What would she do without him and without Grace? The link with Bolitho's earlier life, which she could never share.

Nancy said, 'I'll wait a moment. Just to be sure.'

Her protective caution made Catherine grip her arm.

'I am always safe, dear Nancy!'

Then, as she walked into the yard, the man with Ferguson turned and faced her. Uncertain, anxious, but, as ever, determined.

She quickened her pace. 'Rear-Admiral Herrick! I had no idea you were in Cornwall, or in England, for that matter. I am pleased to see you.' She half turned, ashamed that she had offered her right hand when Herrick's pinned-up sleeve should have reminded her. She said, 'This is Lady Roxby, Richard's sister.'

Herrick bowed stiffly. 'We met but briefly, ma'am. Some years ago.'

Nancy smiled at him. 'We *met* seldom, but through my brother you have always been a part of us.'

She allowed her coachman to help her into the carriage. 'Please call and see me again, Catherine. Soon.' She glanced briefly at Herrick. Like an unspoken question.

Catherine took Herrick into the house. Someone she should know so well, and yet he was still a stranger.

'Please be seated, and I shall fetch you something cool. Some wine, perhaps?'

He sat down carefully and looked around the room. 'Some ginger beer if you have it, my lady. Or cider.'

She regarded him steadily. 'No titles today. I am Catherine – let it be so.'

Grace Ferguson peered in at them. 'Why, 'tis Rear-Admiral Herrick! I scarce recognised you without your fine uniform!'

Catherine turned. She herself had not truly noticed. Perhaps it had been the surprise, or relief that he was not some courier bearing the news she dreaded.

Herrick said awkwardly, 'I am still of that rank, in name, in any case.' He waited for the housekeeper to leave them, and added, 'I am sent to Cornwall by their lordships.'

She watched him, his struggle to share something with her. He was not attempting to be secretive or superior, like other men she had known; he was simply unused to confiding his thoughts to any one. Perhaps only with his beloved wife Dulcie had he ever been able to do so.

His blue eyes were as clear as ever, but his hair was

completely grey, and there were sharp lines at the corners of his mouth which deepened, she thought with pain, when he sat, or, as now, when he leaned forward to accept the proffered glass. Richard had told her some of it, how Herrick had been captured and had had his hand savagely smashed, to destroy forever his ability to 'lift a sword for the King'. When he had been rescued, they had discovered that the wound had already succumbed to gangrene. The ship's surgeon had taken off his arm.

Most of all she remembered Bolitho's pride, his love for this stubborn, unyielding, courageous man. She sat opposite him and watched him drink the ginger beer.

She said, 'Richard is at sea.'

He nodded. 'I know, my . . . Catherine. I heard something of it. I guessed the rest.'

She waited. If she spoke now, Herrick would lose his sudden confidence. Or perhaps it was trust.

'I will never get another sea appointment. I did think I would be put out to grass, especially after the *Reaper* affair.' He looked around again. 'I have always remembered this place, and this room. I walked up from the town just now, as I did all those years ago. I was here when Richard's father was still alive, when he gave him the old sword. Over yonder, by the library door. And again, when we came back from the Indies . . . Richard's father was dead by then.'

She turned involuntarily as if she would see them, saw only Captain James Bolitho's unsmiling portrait. He, too, had lost an arm.

'I have been in Plymouth. I am appointed to the revenue service here.' He smiled briefly, and she saw him as he must once have been. 'So dress uniform is hardly appropriate for such a *popular* and respected commission.'

She thought of Nancy again; she had often mentioned the folklore of local smugglers, the 'gentlemen', as Tom the coastguard had called them. Richard had always spoken harshly of them, and of their brutal trade.

'Will it suit you, Thomas?'

She saw him flinch at the use of his name, as she had known he would.

'I needed to do something. The sea is my life. Unlike Richard, I have nothing else now.' He leaned forward and added, 'There is a lot to be done. New boats – there are four cutters building at Plymouth, and I must find men who can be trusted to perform what is sometimes a dangerous duty. The country is desperate for revenue, and free trade in the dark of night cannot be allowed to flourish unchecked.'

It was there, as Richard had described it to her. The grasp, the enthusiasm; once Herrick established a grip on something, he would never let go.

'Where are you staying, Thomas? There is plenty of room here, if you wish . . . .'

He put down his glass. 'No, I am settled at the inn. It is easier for the coach. Besides . . . .'

She nodded, careful not to smile. '*Besides*, Thomas. What a span that word must carry.'

Herrick studied her gravely. 'I shall be back and forth. If you need me, I will be easy to find.' He stood slowly, and she sensed the pain of the amputation, like so many she had seen in the streets.

'Will you not stay a while, Thomas?'

He glanced through to the library, as if to reassure himself. 'Another time, I would be honoured. Proud.' He turned away, as if unable to speak otherwise. 'When I lost Dulcie I was blind to everything, to that which I owed Richard, and above all else to you, for staying with her when she was beyond aid.' Then he faced her again, his eyes very clear. 'Blind. But not any more. You risked everything for Dulcie, and so for me. I shall not lose my way in self-pity again.'

He took her hand and kissed it with great care, and without pretence.

He took his hat from one of the servant girls and said, almost abruptly, 'You met Lord Rhodes, I believe?'

She had her hand to her breast without knowing it. She nodded. Herrick turned his hat over in his own, strong hand. Like Ferguson, he had become used to it, if ever any man could.

'A close friend of Hamett-Parker.' His mouth hardened. 'The president at my court martial.'

She followed him out into the sunlight, and he added, 'I do not trust that man. Not one inch.' Then he took her hand in his again, and smiled. 'But Richard once taught me well enough. *Know your enemy*, he said. But never reveal that knowledge!'

She watched him stride out along the track, stooped, troubled by his injury more than he would allow anyone to guess, and, out of uniform, almost shabby.

She raised her hand as he turned to look back. But at that moment, he was a giant.

James Tyacke paused outside the chart room to allow his eyes to adjust to the darkness, and then made his way beneath the poop to the quarterdeck. The ship was still strange to him, and any vessel under cover of darkness was always a threat to the unwary.

He looked up at the sky beyond the topsails, at the millions of faint stars from horizon to horizon, and the merest sliver of a moon which showed itself only occasionally on the restless water.

He saw the dark shapes of the watch on deck, the third lieutenant, Tollemache, who was officer-of-the-watch, conferring quietly with another shadow, a master's mate.

He moved to the compass box and glanced at the card: south-east-by-east, the ship moving easily but slowly under reduced canvas. According to the chart, they were some fifty miles to the south-west of the Sicilian coast. To any landsman this would seem like an ocean, an endless, open waste, but Tyacke could feel the difference, and smell it. The nearness of land, with the shores of Africa somewhere across the opposite beam. The Mediterranean was like no other sea, and always the land seemed ready to surprise or ensnare you.

Tomorrow they would sight Malta: the end of the passage. It was still too early to judge if his exercise and drills had left their mark on the ship's company. The officers remained wary of him, like Tollemache, who was standing the middle watch only a few feet away. Uneasy, perhaps, at his captain's presence, which he might interpret as a lack of trust in his ability.

Three weeks since they had weighed anchor at Spithead. Faces, names, pride and resentment. Typical enough in any company with a new captain, and an admiral's flag at the masthead.

His thoughts had repeatedly returned to *Halcyon*'s captain, Christie, the way this sea and the past kept returning. When he had taken command of *Indomitable* there had been another such recurrence, in the person of a one-legged ship's cook. The very day he had read himself in, the man, like a spectre, had brought it all back. *Majestic*, and Christie coming out with it, despite Bolitho's presence. And the cook, who as a young seaman in Tyacke's division had been smashed down by the same broadside which had left Tyacke for dead.

Would it never leave him? Sometimes, like tonight, it haunted him, so that he was unable to sleep.

He moved to the quarterdeck rail and saw the helmsman's eyes in the dim compass light as he turned to observe him.

Christie, at least, had gained something from it. *It made me a man.* Simple, genuine sincerity. *So why not me?*

He glanced around again as two seamen paused to take the slack out of some halliards before making them fast again.

Did this ship have any memories? Perhaps she was not old enough. It was difficult to imagine French voices and orders being uttered where his own men now stood.

A midshipman was writing on his slate, pencil squeaking, recording something for the log; Tyacke could see his white patches clearly in the darkness. Like Christie must have been . . . .

He walked impatiently to the empty nettings, angry with himself, with what he must regard as a weakness. It was none of those things which defied him to sleep, which put an edge to his voice when he had known he was asking, expecting, too much from people who had been allowed to *run down*, as Allday would have put it.

He had sworn to himself that it was over and done with. His anguish, his shame and his resentment had been like a defence. He had even told himself that, once out of England, it would fall back into place, into the mist of time and memory.

But it had not gone away, and his practical mind could not accept it.

He turned from the nettings and said, 'I've made a note in the log, Mr Tollemache. When the morning watch is aft, you can set the forecourse. We may sight local shipping at first light, and I shall want enough agility to avoid it.'

He felt the lieutenant staring after him as he made his way to the poop. Outside his cabin he looked aft to where the sentry stood in a pool of light, as if he had never moved. There was a faint glow beneath the screen door. Could Bolitho not sleep, either?

With his cabin door closed behind him, he unshuttered the lanterns and looked at the cot beyond the screen, and then at the cupboard where he kept his brandy, one of the bottles which Catherine Somervell had sent aboard for him, as she had before in *Indomitable*. Who else would have thought of it? Would have cared?

Eventually he sat down, his head in his hands, his ears only half-aware of the shipboard sounds, the unending chorus in any living vessel.

Then he straightened his back and pulled some writing paper from a drawer. Surprisingly he felt quite calm, unnervingly so. Like the moment of decision, before going into battle, or at the first sight of the enemy's masts and sails spanning the horizon. An awareness, simply because there was no choice, perhaps never had been.

How long he sat there, the pen gripped in his hand, he could not remember.

And then, as if driven by another force, he began to write.

Dear Marion . . . .

When Lieutenant Kellett strode aft to muster the morning watch, Tyacke was still writing.

Then, at dawn, he went on deck and examined the log. He was the captain again.

Eight bells had just chimed from the forecastle belfry when Richard Bolitho came on deck, and crossed to the weather side while *Frobisher* settled down on the final leg of her approach. His mouth was still tingling to the coffee Ozzard had prepared while Allday had been shaving him. Something which had become a routine, as much a part of the ship's own procedure.

He shaded his eyes and stared along the length of the upper deck. Malta seemed so small, so insignificant on any chart, and yet from here it reached out on either bow as if snared in the tarred shrouds and standing rigging, a sprawling mass of sandstone. They were still too far away to distinguish houses and fortifications, or the batteries which guarded the anchorage, and made Malta the most formidable obstacle to any hostile fleet or squadron which might attempt to slip through the strait between Sicily and the coast of North Africa.

This was an island fought over, occupied and reoccupied, it was said as far back as 800 BC, when the Phoenicians had arrived. Sicilians, Arabs, all had left their mark upon architecture, religion and trade.

He felt a trickle of sweat run down his spine; his fresh shirt would be like a rag within the hour, and he envied the bare-backed seamen, skins already sunburned, as they dashed up and down the ratlines in response to the shouted orders from the quarterdeck.

Some of the unemployed men stared at passing craft, brightly coloured fishing boats with bat-like sails. Most of them had an eye painted on the bow, the eye of Osiris, believed to enable the boat to see where it was going and so avoid danger. A few of the occupants waved as the black and buff seventy-four passed, but not many. Men-of-war, large and small, had become commonplace to these people throughout a war they had never truly understood.

Bolitho moved slightly into the shade of the mizzen topsail, and winced as a reflected shaft of sunlight pricked his injured eye. He saw Tyacke speaking to Tregidgo, the sailing master. They were probably satisfied with their calculations, and their arrival at the estimated time. The master was competent, Tyacke had told him, an old hand, four years in *Frobisher* and ten as a master before that. Tyacke had also said that he was not an easy man to know.

Bolitho had spoken to him only once, a fellow Cornishman, but with entirely different beginnings. Tregidgo had been the first of his family to go to sea; the others were all tin miners, Cousin Jacks, as they were called in Cornwall. He had not waited to be taken by a press gang, but had walked into Redruth and volunteered. It must have been a hard climb to his present rank, Bolitho thought.

He saw Allday moving around the boat tier, his face set in a frown of concentration. The barge had been painted green at his instruction, but it was impossible to know if Allday was pleased with it.

Lieutenant Avery joined him. 'My first visit here, sir.'

Bolitho said, 'I doubt if you'll find much time to explore.'

They looked up as more men clambered out along the topsail yards, like monkeys against the pale sky.

Bolitho had seen the date in the ship's log: the sixth of June, 1814. Adam's birthday. He thought of the war he had left behind in those disputed American waters, the risks and dangers to Adam; afraid that his despair and bitterness at Zenoria's death might make him reckless, and too eager for a fight with the enemy which had destroyed the only other thing he had loved, the frigate *Anemone*. He knew what it was like, how grief could blunt even the most experienced captain's judgement; he had suffered it himself, at a time when he believed he had nothing to live for. A death wish, someone had called it.

If only Adam were here. Another in his position would use his influence as admiral to arrange such a transfer, but it would be seen as favouritism, and Adam would decline for that very reason.

Tyacke said, 'Take in your courses, Mr Kellett, and have the marines mustered aft.'

He never seemed to raise his voice, but they were coming to know their captain, and aspire to his standards, even if they could not understand why he drove himself so hard.

Allday had come aft, but was careful to keep his distance. Thinking, perhaps, of the child who would be even more grown up when he eventually reached home again.

Bolitho bit his lip. June. His own daughter, Elizabeth, would be twelve years old this month.

I do not know her.

More shouted commands, and the way going off the ship as she moved steadily towards the land and the gleaming expanse of anchorage. The gunner was on deck speaking with Gage, the fourth lieutenant, making sure that each gun would fire exactly on time when the salutes began. A few men looked towards the quarterdeck where the admiral and his aide stood side by side, apparently beyond the reach of doubt, or any ordinary concerns.

Bolitho smiled to himself, and Avery saw the smile and found comfort in it, without knowing why.

There was a Spanish frigate anchored nearby, some of her company mustered on deck to dip her ensign in respect as the ship with the admiral's flag moved abeam.

Bolitho tried to accept it. They were enemies no longer.

He thought of Catherine's words, when they had first met. It was as though she had just spoken them aloud.

Men are made for war, and you are no exception.

But it was not a reminder. It was a warning.

No Choice at All

Adam Bolitho stood by the entrance of *Valkyrie*'s great cabin and watched in silence as Rear-Admiral Valentine Keen strode to the stern windows, his hair almost brushing the deckhead beams. It was impossible to know what he was thinking, but Adam sensed that he no longer regarded this as his flagship.

Valkyrie had anchored at Halifax in the early morning, and with scarcely a word Captain Henry Deighton had gone ashore to report to Keen. It had not been an easy passage, either to the Bermudas or on the return. Deighton had questioned Adam relentlessly about almost everything, from the various patrol areas to recognition signals; Adam had expected that, after their bad beginning. Deighton had hardly spoken to any of the officers, and had confined himself to this, Keen's cabin, for his meals and to write endless reports, for whose benefit was still unclear.

Keen looked well, he thought, his fair hair almost white against his tanned features. He showed no sign of strain, and Adam suddenly realised what had changed. Here, in *Valkyrie*, he had become a stranger.

Keen said, 'Much has happened in your absence, Adam. I hear from Captain Deighton that you were most thorough, by the way.'

'It was somewhat different from blockade duty, I imagine, sir.'

Keen glanced at him curiously. 'You disliked him?'

'I have served better men, sir. In *my* opinion.'

Keen nodded. 'Honesty is what I would expect from you.

As my flag captain, and as my friend.' He moved to the windows again and watched several boats pulling past the stern. 'Hard to remember all the snow and ice.' He seemed to come to a decision, visibly, like some physical effort.

'I have to tell you now that Deighton's promotion to commodore has been confirmed. I gave him his commission this morning when he came ashore.' He swung round, his eyes in shadow. 'I shall be leaving soon for England. As my flag captain, you are of course entitled to come with me.' He hesitated. 'Although with matters as they are in England I cannot make you the promise of a new command. It may take time.'

Adam tensed, his mind prepared, like waiting for the first shot in a battle. Or in a duel.

Keen said, 'Great matters are afoot. You will know soon enough, but I can assure you that *Valkyrie* will be in the thick of it. A small but experienced inshore squadron will be needed to defend some of those soldiers you have escorted of late. I should think the Bermudas might well sink under their combined weight!'

Adam said quietly, 'And Commodore Deighton, sir?'

'He will be in command of the squadron. Four frigates, including yours.'

Adam felt his jaw tighten. *Mine*. Keen had already decided. It was no choice at all. With Urquhart promoted and gone to command the redeemed *Reaper*, who of similar experience did *Valkyrie* have in her company? Dyer, the first lieutenant, was competent and reliable, when he was told exactly what to do. Two other lieutenants had been midshipmen only months ago. The sailing master was a fine seaman and navigator, but sometimes he could barely draw breath because of his wounds, although he would fall dead rather than admit it. And there was a drunken surgeon, George Minchin, who had been serving with Sir Richard Bolitho when *Hyperion* had gone down.

Keen knew him better than he realised. No captain would quit his command when his ship was on the eve of something dangerous, where skill and experience would count more than anything.

Keen said, 'Another captain could be found for *Valkyrie*. But Commodore Deighton is new amongst us. The burden of his responsibility will be great enough.'

No choice at all. 'You mentioned the army, sir?'

Keen plucked at something on his coat. 'An attack on American soil. It is all I can say.'

Adam said flatly, 'I shall stay, sir.'

He sensed that Keen had been prepared for any decision, but he could not conceal his relief.

'Your presence, your name alone, will make all the difference. And, of course, I shall be following your exploits as closely as I can.'

England. The admiral's house at Plymouth, where he had walked with Zenoria, so careful to remain in sight of the other guests. The last time he had seen her.

Keen said suddenly, 'My proposal of marriage was accepted, Adam. I wish you could have been here when it was announced.'

Adam licked his lips. 'Congratulations, sir. I would say as much to Miss St Clair, as well.'

Keen opened a drawer and closed it again. 'She is on passage to England with her father at this moment. Yes, I wish you had been here.'

Adam wondered if she had told him what he had said about Zenoria, that his absence had been planned.

He looked at Keen's open features. She had told him nothing.

The first lieutenant had appeared in the screen doorway.

'The boat is returning, sir.' He spoke to his captain, but his eyes were on the rear-admiral.

'Thank you, Mr Dyer.'

Keen glanced around the cabin, remembering perhaps the long days at sea, the boredom of routine, and the sudden fury of danger and battle. 'There is nothing of mine here.'

As the lieutenant's footsteps faded away, Keen said, 'Have the ship fully provisioned, Adam.' He hesitated. 'Be patient with him. He is an experienced officer, but he is not like us.' He tried to smile, but it evaded him. 'Not like *you.*'

They went out into the sunshine, and Keen turned once more to look at the watching seamen and marines.

He said simply, 'I shall miss you.'

Adam removed his hat, and the Royal Marine guard slapped their muskets and bayonets into a salute.

Who did he mean? Me? The ship? The assembled hands

would mean little to him; some he would already have forgotten.

Perhaps he was bidding farewell to this life, and exchanging it for higher authority, promotion too, where Adam would be the intruder.

Dyer dismissed the side party and joined him to watch Keen's boat pulling away.

'May I ask something, sir?'

Adam turned to him, surprised, even slightly shocked by the first lieutenant's nervousness.

Have I been so unapproachable? Did I forget the first responsibility of command? The most coveted gift, his uncle had called it.

He reached out and touched Dyer's arm. 'I am remaining with *Valkyrie*. Is that what you were about to ask?'

Dyer could not hide his relief, and a genuine pleasure. His was not a face which could conceal anything.

'I shall pass the word, sir!'

Adam looked towards the land, but Keen's boat had disappeared. Then he gazed up at the gently swaying masthead, where Deighton's broad pendant would soon appear. *Not like you.*

He turned sharply as a chorus of cheers broke from the forecastle, although every one was careful not to catch his eye.

Despite everything, he was glad of his decision. As if the ship had spoken for herself.

'All present, sir.' Adam waited for the other captains to be seated, and glanced around the cabin, searching for some sign or hint of its new occupant, a portrait of someone, some memento from a past ship or port of call. There was nothing. The cabin looked exactly as it had when Keen had stood here, moments before leaving it for the last time. That had been three days ago, and in the meantime, while the other vessels of the new inshore squadron had anchored nearby, Commodore Henry Deighton had spent much of his time either ashore or here in his cabin, going through the ship's books and navigational logs, and had made no attempt to meet his captains in advance of this first gathering.

96

Adam knew them all, Morgan Price, the wild-eyed Welshman who commanded the frigate *Wildfire*, and Isaac Lloyd, captain of *Chivalrous*, the second largest frigate in the group, who had held two commands in the West Indies and was burned as dark as any islander.

He saw Urquhart meet his eyes. His ship, *Reaper*, had been a challenge, but Keen had agreed that he was the obvious choice. There were others who had watched *Reaper*'s return to the fleet with both doubt and mistrust. A ship which had been cursed by mutiny could be seen as a threat, a dire warning to any captain who abused his authority in the name of discipline.

And there was Jacob Borradaile, commander of the fourteen-gun brig *Alfriston*. His ship had been there when *Reaper*'s mutiny had broken out, and her despairing company had turned on their captain and flogged him to death. Borradaile was probably the most unlikely figure present today, like some gaunt caricature, with sprouting, badly cut hair and deep, hollow eyes. He was no one's idea of the commander of a King's ship, but those who knew him swore by his skills and impressive knowledge of those he was fighting. James Tyacke had once described him as 'a good hand. Came up the hard way'. From Tyacke there could be no higher praise.

Commodore Deighton sat behind his table, shoulders very stiff, fingers interlocked, his restless eyes moving quickly from face to face. Adam introduced them one by one, and in response there was a quick smile, almost a grimace.

To Urquhart he said, 'And what of *Reaper*? Learned their lesson, have they?'

Urquhart replied calmly, 'I think others have, because of her, sir.'

Commodore Deighton frowned, and turned to Isaac Lloyd. 'Your ship has performed very well, I believe. I shall be looking to you.' His gaze settled on the hollow-eyed Borradaile. '*Alfriston*. I shall need you to maintain contact with the main squadron. It will be a demanding assignment.'

Borradaile watched him without expression. 'We'll be ready, sir.'

Adam saw Morgan Price glancing round. Perhaps he was expecting a glass of wine, a small thing, but usual enough at such a gathering as this. There was no wine; not even Deighton's strange-looking servant, Jack Norway, was present. A rumour, probably originating in the wardroom, had suggested that Norway had been rescued from the gallows, which might explain why he held his head at such an acute angle, and seemed barely able to speak.

Deighton was opening a long envelope and drawing out some papers. Adam could see the seals of Admiralty, and others too, which seemed to lend added importance to this meeting.

Deighton said, 'What I tell you is in the strictest confidence.' He frowned as Borradaile dragged his heels across the deck. 'A combined naval and military operation is planned, to take place while the weather is favourable, and to gain the maximum advantage. Admiral Cochrane will be in overall command, but the operation will be divided into separate sections.' He reached up and touched his ginger hair as if he were thinking of something else. Then he said deliberately, 'An attack on Washington, gentlemen.'

He had their full attention now, and Adam could see the amusement in his eyes. Pleased with his timing, with its effect.

These were experienced officers, and Adam knew that each man was regarding the challenge in a different light. Borradaile was used to prowling in American coastal waters, picking up intelligence where he could, and then making off if any enemy patrol vessel came upon him. Morgan Price was more concerned with the presence and size of American frigates; he had crossed swords with several of them already, and, like Lloyd of *Chivalrous*, he was never averse to prize money when it came his way.

Adam realised that Deighton's eyes, now quite steady, were on him.

'Captain Bolitho, what is your opinion of this honourable undertaking? You are experienced as anyone, I should have thought.'

Adam stared out at the blue-grey water beyond the stern windows. *How do I feel? Truly feel, setting aside my dislike of this man?*

He answered, 'The timing will have to be perfect, sir. Every care must be taken to avoid the leakage of information to the enemy. They would not be slow to rally against such an attack.'

'Of course, Captain.' Deighton played with the corners of his papers. 'You have no reason to love the Americans. You have had too close a contact for that.'

'I lost my ship to them, sir, and I was a prisoner of war.'

Deighton's eyes gleamed. 'Ah, but you *escaped*. I recall reading the full account.'

This was the man he could understand. 'The account of my court martial, sir?'

Price grinned wildly, and Lloyd took an interest in his cuff. Deighton nodded, unmoved.

'How did you find your captors – *the enemy*?'

'They fight for what they believe. They are like us in many ways.' He thought of his uncle. 'It is like fighting people of your own blood.'

'I shall have to take your word for that, Captain.' He smiled, but there was no warmth in it. Then he continued, 'And what are our chances of success, would you say?'

Adam saw Urquhart watching him, hating this casual interrogation in the presence of the others.

He answered, 'It can be done, sir. Others have said as much. But without ships and the necessary military strength, it has not been possible.' He paused. 'Now we have both. It would be a gesture, rather than a victory. Some might describe it as revenge for the American attack on York.'

Deighton raised a hand. 'And what do *you* say?'

Adam heard someone laugh, one of his men. One of those he had almost left behind, abandoned.

'I say *I do not care*, sir. Tomorrow we may be at peace.' He glanced around at the others, sensing that he had their understanding. 'But while we are still at war we must strike them as hard as we can. So that it will be remembered, and, with it, the many who have died for it. Too many.'

Deighton laid his hands flat on the table. 'Then we are agreed.'

His servant entered the cabin as if to a signal, with a tray of glasses.

The commodore stood up, and the others followed suit.

'I give you a sentiment, gentlemen. To the squadron.' His eyes rested on Adam again. 'And to *victory*!'

One glass each, and the servant had departed as silently as he had entered.

Deighton smiled. 'Your orders will arrive tomorrow. In the afternoon we shall weigh and take station as I direct.' The smile was fading. 'That is all, gentlemen.'

Adam was on the quarterdeck to see each captain into his gig. The last to leave was Borradaile, as he had known it would be.

Adam said quietly, 'Well, my friend? What are your feelings?'

Borradaile looked at him and made some attempt to adjust his ill-fitting uniform before going down to his waiting boat.

'I was thinking just now, sir, while I watched and listened.' His deep, hollow eyes were hidden in shadow, ageless, a man of the sea. 'So like your uncle, I was thinking. So very like that fine, caring sailor.' He almost smiled. 'But all eyes open for storms. I was thinking that too, sir.'

He shambled to the entry port, outwardly oblivious to the calls and ceremonial of his departure.

Adam found himself more moved by the simplicity and honesty of Borradaile's remarks than he had thought possible. Perhaps after Deighton's hints and suggestive asides, it had been what he most needed. He stared across the anchorage. Four frigates and a brig. At least they would be doing something again, instead of playing watchdog to helpless transports.

He saw the marines falling out and hurrying below to their messes, their barracks, as they insisted on calling them. Washington, then. But he could find no excitement in the prospect. Was that, too, gone for ever?

Whatever the outcome, the blame would lie with the man in command. The margin would be a narrow one: success or utter disaster. Then he thought of his uncle. *That fine, caring sailor.* It had made him seem closer. He smiled. And *that* was what he had needed.

Adam Bolitho stood loosely by the quarterdeck rail and stared along the full extent of his command, beyond the taut rigging and the jib sails to the empty sea ahead. It was angled now, and quite steady, as if *Valkyrie* were riding a sloping bank of dark blue, eye-searing water.

Below the larboard gangway the ritual of punishment was drawing to a close; it was something which Adam had learned to accept without flinching. Three weeks had passed since the newly formed squadron had left Halifax, and to the masthead lookouts the other frigates would still be in sight, ready to run down and investigate any suspicious vessel, or to respond to the commodore's signals.

Three weeks of drills and yet more drills, the messdecks humid in the unwavering heat, and tempers fraying. It was not unusual in any ship of *Valkyrie*'s size.

He glanced down as the boatswain's mate paused and ran his fingers through the lash, to separate each of its nine tails, then the drum rolled again and the lash came down with a crack across the naked back.

Bidmead, the master-at-arms, chanted, *'Thirty-six, sir!'*

There was something like a sigh from the ship's company, who had been piped aft to witness punishment. The victim's back was a mass of torn and bleeding flesh. But as his wrists were cut free from the upended grating he stepped clear and stood unaided, only his heaving chest revealing the pain he had suffered.

It had been a severe punishment, but Spurway was one of the ship's hard men, a troublemaker who had been flogged many times, and had boasted, and proved, that he could take it without a whimper.

Adam hated the ritual for many reasons. In a ship like this one, there were always accidents, falls, cuts and bruises as men, some inexperienced, were driven to work aloft in pitch darkness when the pipe came to shorten or make sail. For trained hands like Spurway to be excused work because of a flogging was nothing but waste. Nor would it deter others like him. But discipline was vital, and Spurway had struck a petty officer who had sworn at him for malingering.

At his back, he could sense the line of marines across the poop, a captain's final authority if all else failed.

He saw Minchin, the surgeon, peering up at him, his face as red as raw meat.

'Take him below. And don't be too soft with him.'

Minchin squinted into the sun, and grinned. 'He would have been better off in the army, sir. They'd have hanged him!' He strolled away, a man isolated from all the others.

Dyer touched his hat. 'Permission to fall out the hands, sir?'

'Yes.' Adam stared past the lieutenant's shoulder at the small courier schooner which had met with them soon after dawn to pass across a satchel of despatches for the commodore.

He watched the schooner's sails turning slowly end on in the haze, like pink shells. *Free*, he thought, her commanding officer able to move at will as he sought out his next rendezvous.

He looked at the gangway. The grating was gone, and two seamen were swilling away the remaining blood.

He said, 'Have a word with Mr Midshipman Fynmore. He hopes to sit for lieutenant soon. He should have prevented the trouble with Spurway.'

Dyer said, 'He's very young, sir.'

Adam faced him. 'He was there. He was in charge. *Tell him!*'

He turned as his servant John Whitmarsh hurried from the poop.

'What is it?' Although, in truth, he was glad of the interruption. He had been over sharp with the first lieutenant. But he, too, should have known.

Whitmarsh said, 'The commodore sends his compliments, zur. Would you join him aft.'

Adam smiled. 'Directly.' Perhaps the schooner had brought final orders for the proposed attack. So much time seemed to have passed since Deighton had announced it in his cabin that it had lost all sense of urgency.

He walked into the poop's cool shadow and saw two seamen glance at him, and as quickly look away. No one in the ship liked the man who had been punished, but a flogging was a flogging, and they would never take sides against one of their own.

He paused before entering the great cabin.

Rather like us, he thought.

Deighton was at his table, leaning on his hands while he studied an opened chart and a file of carefully written instructions.

'Ah, good – here you are.' He had raised his head, but remained in silhouette against the glistening panorama of

102

the sea. 'Punishment carried out, eh? Just what the brutes deserve. No one respects a gentle hand, no matter how well intended.' He gestured to a chair and added, 'I thought you were against flogging, on principle.'

Adam sat down. 'I am, sir. But until some other means of punishment is suggested by their lordships or the King's regulations, I shall flog any man who tries to undermine the discipline in this or any other ship.'

'I am glad to know it, sir.' Deighton tapped the chart. 'It is all here in the admiral's despatches. The attack will take place in two weeks' time. I would like you to read the instructions as soon as possible. I have every faith in the strategy proposed, of course, but you might wish to challenge something.'

'Yes, sir.' Strange to hear someone other than his uncle or Keen referred to as 'the admiral'. It was like wearing a blindfold, not knowing the mind behind it, except by reputation. Bolitho had always known the importance, and also the folly, of such an undertaking unless it was certain of success.

'It will be a twin-pronged attack, by way of the River Potomac, and supported by another along the River Patuxent.' He opened and closed his fist, like a crab. 'Major-General Robert Ross will be in command of the land operations.' He glanced at him quickly. 'Do you know him?'

Adam said, 'He has the name of a man of action, sir.' A major-general. So it was that important.

Deighton nodded. 'Good, good. Our squadron will be placed and in position on the first day, and our main task will be to prevent any interference from the enemy while our soldiers are landed.' He waited while Adam stood and walked to the table. The charts were current, and fully corrected, something that could never be taken for granted, particularly with the Americans' insistence upon altering the names of so many towns and landmarks. He could feel Deighton watching him, perhaps searching for doubts.

He said, 'It will depend on the weather. Transferring the troops from transports to boats will take time; it always does.' He paused, expecting Deighton to interrupt. He traced the coastline with his finger. 'There are too many ships. It will take too long to prepare.'

'Are you saying it cannot be done?'

103

Adam bent closer to the chart; in his mind he could already see it. Soldiers tumbling into boats, many of whom had never taken part in an amphibious landing. It only needed a few small, determined vessels to work amongst them, and even with overwhelming support from the navy, any invasion would end before it began.

He straightened his back and looked at the sea. The wind was powerful but steady, with the ship still on the same tack, but he knew from experience and from what the old hands had said that it could change within the hour. Too many ships had driven aground off Chesapeake Bay to take the approaches lightly.

'It *will* be done, sir, if so ordered. I should like to discuss it with Mr Ritchie.'

Deighton stared at him. 'Ritchie? Who is he?'

'The sailing master, sir. He has great experience of these waters, and I value his judgement.'

'Oh, very well, I suppose that. . . .' He turned away. 'It is not an issue open for discussion.'

Adam waited. What did it matter? Another battle, probably planned in a comfortable room somewhere, by minds already dulled by years of war, overreached by new methods, driven by fresh ambitions which were rarely taken into account.

But it does matter. It always had, and it always must. When the drums rattled and beat to quarters and men ran to their stations, some would look aft, to see their captain, to attempt to discover in his face some hope, some hint of their chances. They never questioned what they were ordered to do. *Of course it matters.*

He said quietly, 'When we next rendezvous with *Alfriston*, I think we should speak with Commander Borradaile.'

Deighton squared his shoulders. 'If you think it useful. Coastal experience, that sort of thing?'

'We must seize and hold an advantage, sir, no matter how small.' He could see an argument forming on Deighton's face. 'As I said before, sir, the enemy are too much like us. They will fight with all they have. As we would, if the French were to sail up the Thames and attack London.'

Deighton studied him, seeking something more. But he said only, 'Signal the squadron to close on *Valkyrie*. I will pass each captain his final instructions. After that. . . .' He did not

104

continue. Instead, he changed tack. 'I know that Rear-Admiral Keen had great faith in you. Doubtless, he had his reasons. I shall expect the same confidence and competence from you myself. Is that understood?'

'It is understood, sir.'

'Perhaps you would care to take a glass with me, Captain?'

Adam sat again. This new Deighton, the caution, the wariness, was not easy to accept.

'Thank you, sir.'

But Deighton would never allow a breach in the wall of formality, unlike Keen. *The day that Deighton calls me by my first name, I shall shake his hand.*

The strange servant entered noiselessly and prepared some goblets.

Deighton said abruptly, 'Of course, Captain, you're not married, are you?'

'No, sir.' Always a reminder, a barb.

'Not all a bed of roses, y'know.' Deighton took a glass and held it to the reflected glare. He turned to the table again, and opened a drawer. 'With all these details to examine and decide upon, it slipped my mind. There was a letter in the despatch bag for you.' He forced a smile. 'From a lady, I'll swear to it.'

Adam took it and glanced at the seal and the written instructions. It must have been passed from ship to ship before it came to the courier schooner.

Adam saw her without effort, the dark eyes and high cheekbones, and the confidence which she gave to others. *To me.*

He said, 'Catherine, Lady Somervell, sir.' He watched him, for some surprise or innuendo, that he should know her so well, well enough to receive a letter from her.

'A lady of magic, they tell me.' He raised one ginger eyebrow. 'Perhaps she will bring us luck in this great venture.'

Adam left the cabin, the taste of the wine clinging to his tongue. He did not know one vintage from another, but he did not think Keen or his elegant flag lieutenant would rate it very highly.

John Whitmarsh was in his cabin, and made to leave when he entered. He was polishing his captain's sword, the short, curved fighting blade which Adam had selected with such care after his other had been lost in *Anemone*.

'No, stay. You'll not disturb me.' He sat down beneath the skylight and slit open the letter.

My dear Adam. . . . It was dated in May, three months, a lifetime ago. How much worse it would be for her.

He could even imagine her writing it, perhaps in the library, which looked over the garden she had made her own. So many memories, countless pictures, the last being the one he carried like a penance, Catherine on the beach with Zenoria's broken body in her arms.

By the bulkhead the boy John Whitmarsh watched his captain's face, while his cloth moved up and down the keen-edged blade without a pause.

So remember, dear Adam, that you are not alone. Last week I visited Zennor again, no better place to rest. I tell you this, Adam, she is at peace now. I could feel it. The last thing she would have wanted would have been for you to lose yourself in grief. You have your life to live, and so much to offer and to discover. Do not throw it away for any cause or reason. You will find your love again. As I have.

The boy's hand stilled on the hanger as Adam unlocked his cabinet, and took out the small velvet-covered book.

Very gently, he opened it, and looked at the pressed remains of the wild rose he had picked for Zenoria. A book which Keen had casually given him, without understanding what it had meant. He held it to his cheek for several seconds, remembering, and yet very aware of the woman who had written to him, that she cared enough for him to reach out to him and give him this comfort.

The boy asked carefully, 'Is it bad, zur?'

Adam looked at him. 'No, not bad, young John.' He folded the letter, and heard her voice again. *She is at peace now.*

Catherine understood, better than anyone, that neither the love nor the peace could ever have been his; that, without her, there would only have been grief, tearing him apart.

He said quietly, 'With someone's help, I have reached an understanding.'

Catherine had returned to Zennor for his sake, to the church where he had stood with her and with Bolitho, when Keen had taken Zenoria for his wife. Perhaps she had discovered

106

that the little mermaid had gone back to the sea. And found peace. *For both of us*.

The boy watched him leave the cabin. He did not understand any of it, but that did not matter. He had been a part of it.

8

One Hand for the King

Commodore Henry Deighton prowled restlessly about his great cabin, reaching out to touch pieces of furniture and equipment, obviously without seeing them.

Adam waited beneath the cabin skylight, glad that somebody had closed it. Deighton was almost beside himself, unable to control his disbelief even in front of Adam and the hovering Lieutenant Dyer, an unwilling spectator. Anyone working on deck would otherwise have heard him.

Deighton swung round, one hand jabbing the air to emphasise each word. 'And are you telling me, Captain, that just because of some *scrap* of information which *Alfriston*'s captain. . . .' He snapped his fingers and Dyer offered helpfully, 'Borradaile, sir!'

Deighton ignored him. 'You are telling me that I should contact Rear-Admiral Cochrane's ships, and the transports, and suggest that he delay the attack! Hell's teeth, man, do you know what you're asking me to do?'

Adam felt his impatience changing to anger, but knew that any outburst now would be like a match in a powder magazine. He said, '*Alfriston* stopped a Portuguese trader, sir. One known to Commander Borradaile. In exchange for information, the trader . . . .'

Deighton shouted, '*Smuggler*, you mean!'

'Smuggler, sir. One who has proved very useful in the past.'

He waited while Deighton peered at his chart again. 'There is an American commodore named Barney. He has a flotilla of small vessels in the bay. It seems he is sheltering at the mouth of the Patuxent, perhaps because of information about us, or perhaps merely as a precaution.' His voice hardened. 'Where our ships and four thousand troops are to be conveyed and landed, *the day after tomorrow.*'

Deighton snapped, 'The admiral must be well aware of that!'

Adam glanced at Dyer and wished he was somewhere else. When *Valkyrie* was next committed to action Dyer would remember today, and the men he served.

'And there is this battery.' He did not move or indicate on the chart what Borradaile had told him. Deighton had already challenged that, too. 'Old or new, we don't know, but the Americans have been working on it these past weeks. It is not an easy approach at any time, but with a battery sited and ready, perhaps with heated shot . . . .'

Deighton sat down heavily as if the deck had given out beneath him.

'I *know* about heated shot, Captain, and I also know that a slow-moving force of vessels entering a confined passage is no match for a shore battery.'

Adam said to Dyer, 'Wait for me in my cabin.'

The lieutenant left without a word. Only then did Deighton realise he had gone.

'You are leaving me no sea room, Captain. The responsibility is mine.'

Adam thought of Dyer in his cabin. Had he guessed that he had been sent there to prevent him from describing how the new commodore had seemed snared by his own vital but damning authority?

'The whole fleet will be expecting results.' Deighton was on the move again, his hands clasped beneath his coat-tails, his head bowed under the weight of his decisions.

Adam watched him, and found no comfort in the contempt he felt. He recalled Keen's words. *Not like us. Not like you.*

Individual faces stood out in memory. His coxswain, Starr, who had been hanged by the Americans for setting charges to destroy *Anemone* when otherwise she might have been saved, to serve under the Stars and Stripes. John Allday's son, who had fallen in the battle with the USS *Unity*. And the young midshipman, Lovie, their only casualty when they had destroyed the American prize and her would-be rescuer. Wiped away, like chalk from a slate.

Washington was the impossible, the unobtainable trophy. In war, what did motives matter any more? Glory or revenge, it made little difference to the men who fought and died.

He said suddenly, 'I have a suggestion, sir.' It was like hearing someone else, a stranger: calm, impersonal.

He saw Deighton turn to stare at him, as though he were offering him a lifeline. 'Destroy the battery before the attack begins.' He watched the surprise change to disbelief, then to something like disappointment.

'No time. And besides, what chance have we?'

'Boat action, sir.' It was like a rising madness, and although he knew he should guard against it, he felt himself being carried by it.

Deighton nodded, very slowly. 'And you would lead this venture, I presume? Another laurel for the family garland? For your uncle?'

Adam said, 'That is unworthy, *sir.*'

Surprisingly, Deighton laughed. 'Well, let us assume if it were at all possible, and lead it you would – by God, where would you begin?'

He considered it, unnerved that it should seem so straightforward, something already written in orders. *You are commanded to proceed.* Like the great paintings of famous sea fights; there was never any pain or blood.

'I would transfer to *Alfriston* immediately.' He saw the caution in Deighton's eyes. 'Which would leave you with the full company of frigates.' He saw Deighton nod, although he thought he had not known that he had done so. 'I would require forty marines, and a hand-picked party of seamen.'

Deighton swallowed. '*Thirty* marines.'

Adam felt his fingers tingling. Part of the madness.

He asked quietly, 'You agree, sir?'

Deighton stared around the cabin, as if he had suddenly become a stranger there.

'I shall put your suggestion in writing.'

Their eyes met. 'And I shall sign it, sir.' That way, there could be no recriminations. 'Willingly.' He picked up his hat. 'I will attend to the transfer, and signal *Alfriston* to lie downwind in readiness.'

110

He left the cabin, breathing deeply. The sun had shifted, but the normal day-to-day work was going on as before. As if nothing had happened. As if he had not committed himself, and others, to disaster. Suppose he was wrong? Should he have remained silent, and so forced Deighton to make a decision?

A scarlet-coated marine stepped out smartly.

Adam looked at him: a round, sunburned face, familiar, but at a distance, observing some rule of his own making.

He said, 'Corporal Forster?'

The corporal glanced around, suddenly unsure of himself. Some other marines were watching from the starboard gangway.

'Beggin' yer pardon, sir. It's not for me to say, but I was wonderin' . . . .'

Adam said, 'Tell me.'

'Well, sir, before you asks my officer, I'd like to put me name down for the raid.'

Adam looked away. It was only a vague idea, and yet they all knew about it.

And I almost left them.

The corporal added nervously, 'I'm a fine shot, sir.'

Adam touched his sleeve and did not see the other marines nudge one another.

'That you are, Forster. Give your name to the first lieutenant.' He tried to summon a smile, some kind of reassurance. 'I'll see you a sergeant yet!'

He strode on, his mind busy with details, then paused to glance round as signal flags dashed up to the yard.

There was no time to write a letter to Catherine. Perhaps Deighton had deliberately kept hers from him.

He felt the breeze across his face and saw the sailing master watching him, as if reading his thoughts.

And if I fall, there will be no letter. Only peace.

Alfriston's chart room was small, even by a brig's standards; she had begun her life in the merchant service, and space was at a premium aboard her.

It had been a red, angry sunset, the horizon fading eventually to a hard line. But the wind was steady, and Borradaile had insisted that the weather would not 'go sour', as he had put it. Adam could feel the man close by him now, his patched

111

elbows on the chart, a large magnifying glass gripped in one bony hand.

The brig seemed to be moving beneath him, an illusion, but she felt heavier in the water with her extra seamen and thirty of *Valkyrie*'s marines packed between decks. Even at the last minute, before he had been pulled across to *Alfriston*, he had expected the commodore to change his mind, to rely on the written details of the admiral's plan, and to do nothing beyond his orders.

In the fading light he had seen faces watching him from *Valkyrie*; a few had even called out to wish him well. It had moved him more than he had expected. The first lieutenant had been almost severe.

'If you think it's too much of a risk, sir, *fall back*. We shall get you out of there, somehow.'

And Minchin, observing silently from the poop. Perhaps calculating how many would end up on his table, or in the 'wings and limbs' tub on the orlop deck.

The worst part had been the very moment of departure, glancing around his cabin so as not to leave anything vital behind. John Whitmarsh had watched him kick off his shoes and tug on the hessian boots he often wore when called to action.

'I want to come too, zur! It's my place!' He had even been wearing the dirk Adam had given him for a birthday present. It seemed likely that it was the only gift he had ever received.

Adam had heard the bark of orders, the feet on the deck and the creak of tackles, the more measured tramp of marines preparing to climb into the boats. He was well aware that it might be the last time he would stand in that cabin, in that ship, or anywhere, and yet the boy's despair had made all the rest seem insignificant.

'Not this time, John Whitmarsh. When you wear the King's coat and have someone like *old Mister Allday* at your side, you'll see the sense of it.' It had been no use.

'When we lost *Anemone*, zur, we helped each other!'

Adam had laid a hand on his shoulder. 'That we did, and we still can.'

At the door he had looked back. 'Remember all our friends who were not so lucky. Stay with the ship.'

He sighed, and felt Borradaile turn to watch him.

112

He said, 'Tell me your thoughts, my friend.'

Borradaile frowned. 'I shall land you an' your party here, sir.' He poked the chart. 'My guess is that the admiral will make an early start, to get his ships into position and to land his soldiers up here.' His bony finger jabbed the chart again, by the river called Patuxent. 'A place named Benedict, the most suitable ground for the military.' He spoke of them almost with contempt, as was often the way with sailors.

Adam said, 'The flotilla of small vessels sheltering there, they will have to be boarded and taken first.'

Borradaile grunted; it might have meant anything, and Adam could sense his impatience. Good or bad, time was against them. He could even smell the man, tar, tobacco, salt and rum.

His was a small, tight command, where there would be no secrets, their strength the dependence of one upon the other, and an utter trust in one another. He smiled in the lamplight. *Like my first command. The fourteen-gun* Firefly. *At the age of twenty-three.* How proud his uncle had been of him. He often wondered what the old veterans like Borradaile thought of the boy-captains with all their dash and arrogance. *Like me.*

Borradaile said, 'The army will have a fight on their hands, an' that's no mistake.' He chuckled. 'But then, no sense, no feeling!'

Adam stood away from the table and winced as he struck his head against a beam.

'I'll tell the others.' Their eyes met. 'If we fail, it will not be laid at your door.'

Borradaile led the way to the main messdeck where the landing party had been stowed away like so much additional cargo. In the half-light the white facings and crossbelts of the marines stood out sharply, each man gripping his weapons and various items of equipment. Their officer was Lieutenant Barlow, a competent but unimaginative man who never questioned an order and expected his men to behave in the same way. Deighton had refused to allow the captain of marines to join the landing party, and that officer would be fuming about it, no matter what their chances were.

He saw *Valkyrie*'s third lieutenant, Howard Monteith, sitting apart from the rest. He had risen from a junior lieutenant to third by way of death or promotion, and he was young, but he had the eye for detail of a much more senior officer: Adam had seen him checking his men and their weapons, have a few words with each one and getting the right responses.

There was Jago too, a gunner's mate who had been with Urquhart when they had blown up the American prize and her would-be rescuer, and a tough, reliable seaman.

Adam waited until they had all coughed and shuffled into expectant silence.

He said, 'We are a small part of much greater affairs, but one which could make the difference between success and defeat. Be mindful of that.' They would be wondering why their captain was taking charge and not some other officer. The experienced men would see it as a sign of the mission's importance; the sceptics would say that it must be without risk if the captain was sharing it with them.

He thought of Deighton, who apparently believed that such men as these had no right even to ask why they were being sent. And of his uncle, who thought it was all they did have.

He said, 'There is an enemy battery up yonder.' He saw a couple of men stare at the ship's side as if it were as near as that. 'It is not big, but, like a poacher and his piece, it is well-sited to wreak havoc amongst our people.'

He looked up, caught off-guard as canvas cracked out like gunfire; for an instant he thought the wind had defied Borradaile's predictions and was rising. Perhaps it was safer to be like Barlow, the marine lieutenant. Borradaile was making more sail. The word moved in his mind again. *Committed*.

'You will be fed now, and there will be a good measure of rum.'

He saw the grins, and thought again of his uncle, the pain in his eyes when he had said, 'Is that all they ask for what they do?'

He nodded to Monteith, and ended simply, 'Keep together, and fight bravely if you must. We shall have the sea at our backs.'

He found Borradaile waiting for him by the compass box.

'West by north, sir. Holding steady on the starboard tack.' He sounded satisfied.

Adam thought of the men he had just left, drinking their rum. *If I began now I would never be able to stop.*

114

He turned as he realised Borradaile had asked him something.

'My apologies, I am leagues away at present!'

Borradaile shrugged. 'I was thinking, sir, about going ashore.' He waited, perhaps expecting a rebuff. 'After what happened to you, being a prisoner an' the like, how d'you feel about it?'

Adam looked at his gaunt shadow. 'Not fear, my friend. Perhaps it gives me an edge.' He thought suddenly of the boy Whitmarsh, and added, 'It is my place.'

After the close confines of *Alfriston*'s hull, the air across the black, heaving water felt fresh, even cold.

Adam stood in the sternsheets of the barge, his hand on the coxswain's shoulder to steady himself as he strained his eyes to see the boat ahead. Five boats in all, oars rising and falling like dark wings, with only an occasional pale splash to mark a blade cutting against the inshore current.

The next boat astern was packed with marines, and he could see the white belts and pouches without difficulty. Like the noise, looms creaking in the rowlocks, the stem thrusting toward the deeper darkness of the land. Surely someone must see or hear them?

He knew from experience that his apprehension was unfounded. The sounds of the sea and the moan of a steady breeze would muffle almost everything. Each oarsman was handpicked, some from *Valkyrie*, and others put forward by Borradaile. In the leading boat he had stationed one of his own master's mates, a veteran like himself, who was very aware of the responsibility he had been given.

No matter what happened they must keep together. If the boats lost sight of one another, the raid would become a shambles before it had begun.

He saw another faint splash, and knew that the first boat was using a lead and line simply to ensure that they were not wandering amongst the rocks he had noted on the chart. Some were as big as islets.

He felt the coxswain lean forward to gesture to the stroke oarsman. No words; they were too experienced to need more than a hint. What were they thinking? Like most sailors, probably anxious when *Alfriston*'s ghostly shape had faded into the darkness. Now, each man would be wanting to get it over and done with, to return to familiar surroundings, and their friends.

The lookout in the bows called in a hoarse whisper, 'Jolly boat's comin' about, sir!'

The coxswain snapped, '*Oars!*' Another seaman shuttered a lantern just once toward the following craft, and Adam saw the untidy disturbance of spray as the blades backed water to avoid running them down.

The jolly boat circled round until it dipped and lifted in the shallows, and Lieutenant Monteith called out as loudly as he dared, 'Ship at anchor, sir! Off the point! Brig or brigantine!'

Always the unexpected to raise the stakes, but Monteith sounded calm enough.

He could feel the coxswain's shoulder under his fingers, hard and tense. *Waiting*. They were all waiting.

Adam replied, 'Take over the others, Mr Monteith.' He glanced at the pale faces of the oarsmen, watching and listening. How many times had he seen Keen brought to the ship in this barge, or pulled ashore to meet his lady? He thrust it from his mind. *His new wife*.

The jolly boat was too small, and by the time support could be organised even the sleepiest watch might have been roused. The unknown vessel had to be taken without delay. Any sort of alarm might bring troops, even a man-of-war hurrying to head them off.

He thought of Deighton. *Another laurel for the family garland, for your uncle?* He felt a grin breaking the fierce tension in his jaw. *He could damned well think what he liked!*

He said, 'Boarding party, be ready! Cox'n, as soon as we sight the brig, or whatever she is, make for the chains where we can hook on!'

He stared around for the jolly boat, but it had already drifted clear and merged with the darkness. Monteith was left to his own devices, perhaps the first time he had carried out such a mission. *If I fall, he will be on his own.* He drew his hanger and said, 'No shooting. You know what to do!'

'Give way all!'

The barge sighed into a low trough and gathered way again.

116

Perhaps the bearing was wrong? He glanced up, but even the stars were elusive. Some of the oarsmen were beginning to breathe more heavily: it had been a long pull with an overloaded boat; they were tired. All they had left was hope, and trust.

Something moved across the faint scattering of stars, like birds on passage. He gripped his hanger until the pain steadied him, and the birds hardened into shape, into the masts and yards of the anchored vessel. She loomed out of the night, so close that it seemed impossible that no one had yet sighted them.

'Easy, lads!' It was pointless to think of the other possibility: that the bulwarks were already lined with marksmen and swivels, that their carefully guarded secret was just another myth.

The coxswain hissed, 'Oars!'

Adam groped along the boat, holding a man's arm here, another's ready hand there, until he was in the bows with the waiting boarders. Jago was one of them, and Adam guessed he had detailed the spare hands when he realised what was happening.

He watched the rigging rising above him. '*Now!*'

A grapnel flew over the bulwark and snared into place, and the gunner's mate, Jago, was up and over the vessel's side before anyone else could move. Adam found himself on a littered, unfamiliar deck, men hurrying past him, brushing him aside in their eagerness to get aboard.

There was a single cry, and Adam saw Jago drag a limp corpse down from the forecastle where the luckless seaman had been supposedly guarding the anchor cable.

Jago bent down and wiped his blade on the dead man's shirt and said between his teeth, 'Never sleep on watch! Bad for discipline!'

Incredibly, Adam heard somebody stifle a laugh.

He said, 'Rouse the others.' He walked to the vessel's deserted wheel and glanced at the masts and furled sails. Brigantine. Small, and very useful in these waters.

A few thumps and startled shouts, and then it was over. There were ten of them; the others, including the vessel's master, were ashore.

Jago said, 'They'll give no trouble, sir.'

Adam smiled. There was no point in telling Jago that the swivel guns on the brigantine's poop and foredeck were fully loaded and primed. But for the sleeping watchman, things would have been very different, and that would have left Monteith to make the biggest decision yet in his young life.

'Tie them up. Tell them what to expect if they try to raise an alarm.'

Another seaman, one of Borradaile's, as Adam did not recognise him, said, 'She's the *Redwing*, out of Baltimore, sir. Carries stores for the army.' He jerked his thumb towards the land. 'To the battery. Their last visit, they tells me.'

Adam did not ask how he obtained the information, but it was priceless. So the battery was there. And it was completed.

There was no time to spare. He beckoned to Jago. 'Could you work this vessel into open water? The truth, man – no heroics.'

Jago faced him defiantly. ''Course I can, sir! I was servin' in one such out of Dover when I first got pressed!'

Adam matched his mood and gripped his arm, hard. 'She's yours, then. When you hear the charges blow, weigh anchor and try to rejoin the supporting squadron. I shall see you get a fair share of the prize money.'

Jago was still staring after him as the barge crew climbed down to their boat. Then he spat over the side and grinned. 'If you lives after today, *Cap'n*!'

The barge felt lighter as they pulled steadily toward the darker wedge of the land, and Adam saw the gleam of Monteith's white shirt as he stood in the jolly boat to wave as they surged abeam.

A lantern shutter lifted and light blinked across the water, and in what seemed like seconds men were leaping into the shallows on either bow to control and guide the boat in the last moments before the impact of driving ashore.

The marines were wading towards the beach, their bayoneted muskets held high, their heads turning like puppets as they fanned out to protect the other boats.

Adam felt the water surge around his boots and drag at each step forward. He could almost hear Borradaile's question. *How do I feel, then, stepping once again onto a land that almost destroyed me, when even now there might be a marksman taking aim, holding his breath . . . .*

But fear? There was none. A light-headedness which was

no stranger to him, a reckless courage that matched Jago's defiance.

He waved his hanger, and saw faces turn towards him. 'Lively, lads! One hand for the King and keep one for yourselves!'

But the King was insane . . . so where was the sense of it? He knew that if he laughed now, he would be done for.

Then he thought of Bolitho, of his face when he had told him about Zenoria, and all those watching portraits which had condemned him. There had never been any choice for them, either.

Lieutenant Monteith rolled on to his side, an arm upraised as if to withstand a sudden blow, then gasped with relief as Adam dropped down beside him.

Adam pulled his small telescope from his coat. 'All quiet?'

'Yes, sir. Our people are in position and the marines have three pickets to guard each possible approach.'

He heard the anxiety in Monteith's voice. It was not unjustified. There was still enough darkness to cover them, but in less than an hour. . . . He closed his mind to it. The admiral's report had claimed that the nearest artillery post was some five miles away, but without surprise they could not hope to destroy the battery in time.

Monteith said, 'I thought I could smell fire, sir. Like burning.'

Adam glanced at him. 'It must be the new oven for heating shot.'

There was no point in deceiving the young lieutenant. If they succeeded in destroying those guns, Borradaile would be ready and waiting to pick them up. If they failed, *Alfriston* would be the battery's first victim.

Monteith said between his teeth, 'Where the *hell* is that man?'

That man was a foretopman named Brady, as nimble and sure-footed as any cat when working high above the deck in every kind of weather. But before he had agreed to join the navy rather than face deportation or worse, he had been a poacher. A man very much at home in territory like this.

Adam said, 'He'll not run, Howard.' He smiled. 'We'd know by now if he had.'

He felt Monteith staring at him in the darkness, surprised that he could appear so confident, or unnerved by the casual use of his first name.

A marine said in a fierce whisper, 'Here comes the little bugger now!' He must have seen Adam's epaulettes, and added, 'Brady's back, sir!'

The man in question dropped beside them. 'Five guns, sir, an' the magazine is on the side slope.' He was making slicing motions with his hands. 'Two sentries, and the rest of 'em are in a hut.'

Adam looked towards the bay, but it was still hidden in darkness. In his mind's eye he could see the battery, hacked from the hillside with the remainder of the slope rising behind it. No fear of attack from inland; the only enemy would come by sea. Five guns. A landsman would not think it much, but with heated shot they could cause a damage and destruction no landsman could begin to imagine.

'Pass the word, Brady. We will move now.' He let his words sink in. '*As planned!*' He gripped the little man's shoulder. There seemed no flesh at all, only muscle and bone. No wonder he could kick and fist freezing canvas in a screaming gale with the best of them. 'That was well done.'

He heard the marines moving carefully on the hard, sun-dried ground. They were all well concealed, but in the faintest daylight their scarlet coats would stand out like beacons.

Adam stood up. He was suddenly very thirsty, but calm enough. He searched his feelings, as if he were examining a subordinate. He had no inclination to yawn; he knew from past experience that it was a first sign of fear.

Dark shapes hurried away to the right, men used to cutting out ships in the night, so experienced that they could take out a strange vessel as if it were their own. Like Jago and the brigantine.

He heard Lieutenant Barlow draw his sword, and snap, 'Marines, *advance!*'

Adam said, 'If I fall, Howard, get them back to the boats.'

He was running now, his hanger held across his body, his heart pounding painfully, and suddenly the crudely-made wall was stretching out in front of him. Had his eyes adjusted to the darkness, or was it lighter? Nothing made sense. Only the wall. *The wall . . . .*

The crash of musket fire was deafening, the echo of the shot rebounding like a ricochet.

But the shot had come from behind; he had felt it fan past his head. One of the marines must have caught his foot on something, probably some of the building material scattered about on the slope. He raised his hanger and shouted, '*At 'em, lads!*' There was no such thing as luck now, good or bad. '*Go for the guns!*'

A marine was first on to the wall, but plummeted to the ground as someone fired up at him at what must be pointblank range. Another shot came from the other side of the clearing, but more seamen were already running across, cutlasses and boarding axes hacking at the sentry before he could reload or plead for his life.

A marine was on his knees, staring at blood on his tunic. The knowledge steadied Adam more than anything. He, too, could see the blood, and when he tore his eyes from the figures around the hut he realised that he could also see water, very still, and the colour of pewter. The bay.

He saw a marine level his bayonet and stand astride a fallen figure by one of the guns.

Adam flicked the bayonet with his hanger and said, 'Enough! Join your squad!'

But the marine could only stare from him to his victim.

'But he done for my mate Jack, sir!' The bayonet wavered, as the marine gauged the distance.

Adam repeated, '*Enough!*' He could not remember the man's name. 'You can't bring him back!'

Sergeant Whittle roared, 'Over 'ere, that man!'

The marine obeyed, hesitating only to look once more at his dead friend. Discipline was restored.

The man on the ground had been wounded, but he seemed to be attempting to grin, in spite of the pain.

'That was thoughtful of you, Captain!'

Adam looked at him. An officer, very likely the only one here. *Yet.* He called, 'Take this one, Sergeant!' To the injured officer, he said, 'You and your people are prisoners. Do not resist. I think my men are beyond the mood of reason.' Another bayonet darted between them as the American slid a hand into his coat. But the effort was too much, and the hand fell back again.

121

Adam knelt and reached into the coat, and drew out nothing more dangerous than a small portrait in a silver frame. He thought of Keen and the girl, Gilia.

Monteith was shouting, 'Break this door open! You, Colter, fetch the fuses.' And Lieutenant Barlow's voice restoring order and purpose, guarding their flank.

He replaced the portrait in the wounded man's coat, and said, 'A very pretty girl. Your wife?'

So much to be done. Fuses to be laid, wounded to be moved, the five guns to be spiked. But it all seemed unreal, beyond himself.

He called, 'Attend this officer, Corporal.' He realised it was Forster, the marine who had volunteered. 'Well done.'

The American gasped, 'Not yet. Maybe never. . . .' He grimaced as pain probed through him again.

Adam stood. 'Flesh wound. You'll be well enough.' The corporal leaned down with his bandages, no doubt wondering why he bothered.

The American held up his hand as Adam turned to leave him.

'Your name, sir. I would like to tell her . . . .'

Adam sheathed his hanger; there was blood on the blade, but he remembered nothing about it.

'Bolitho.'

Monteith was back again. 'I'm moving the wounded now, sir.' He glanced at Forster with his bandage. 'Theirs and ours. We lost five killed, seven wounded.'

Adam shook his arm. 'Get them to the boats.' He raised his voice. 'This officer will give his word that they will not interfere.'

Monteith listened, and wondered. He had expected to be killed, even though he had not dared to contemplate it; he had expected to fail this youthful, remote captain. But now he was shaking his arm, smiling at him. *Will I ever be so confident?*

It took an hour, and still no one raised an alarm. It seemed as if the rest of the world had ceased to exist.

Adam said, 'Go with the others, Howard. *Alfriston* will be there to collect the boats directly.' He pulled out the watch and opened the guard with its finely engraved mermaid. He

122

imagined he could feel warmth on his cheek although he knew that the morning was still grey.

Monteith hesitated. 'Are you *certain*, sir?'

Adam walked to the parapet. The guns had been spiked, and when the magazine exploded there would be nothing left. When he glanced around, Monteith had gone. Only the dead lay where they had fallen.

At this moment more of the enemy might be marching or riding with all despatch to this place. He walked to the open trapdoor, which led down to a crude powder magazine.

He looked around at the sprawled corpses. A small price to pay for what they had done; that would be in the eventual report.

Aloud he said, 'But not small to you.'

He felt the skin on his neck tingle, an instinct he never took for granted; his pistol was in his hand and cocked before he realised it.

But it was Jago, the tough gunner's mate.

'I *ordered* you to stay with the prize!' There was an edge to his voice which warned him how close it had been.

Jago said evenly, 'The others said you was standing fast until the fuses was lit, sir.' There was no humility, and no resentment either.

'And you took it upon yourself to come looking?'

Jago almost grinned. 'No more'n what you did when you come looking for Mr Urquhart and me after we blowed up the Yankee frigate!' He peered around, and examined the dead without concern or conscience. 'Worth it, sir?'

Adam raised his arm; it felt like lead. 'Tomorrow, our soldiers will land. After that, it's only fifty miles to Washington.'

He took a slow match and held it out to Jago.

'Here. Perform the honours.' He gazed once more at the dead. 'For us all.' And, half to himself, 'And for *you*, Uncle.'

But Jago heard, and, hardened though he was, he was impressed; and for him that was something.

Then he lit the fuses.

9

Too Late for Regrets

Adam Bolitho watched the last of the boats being hoisted inboard, and then lowered on to their tier where the boatswain's party was ready to make them secure. Even the barge had survived, and had been towed with the others by Borradaile's *Alfriston*.

Lieutenant Dyer had scarcely been able to hide his excitement and pleasure. Perhaps, like the commodore, he had expected the mission to fail, and that they would all be killed or taken by the enemy.

He gripped the quarterdeck rail and suddenly realised how drained and tired he was.

Soon it would be dark. But the last sunlight was still clinging to the horizon, and touching the horns of the figurehead's helmet as if unwilling to depart.

He thought of the moment when the battery's magazine had exploded, great rocks and pieces of stonework crashing through the trees, some splashing down dangerously close to the boats as they pulled towards *Alfriston*, and was reminded of Deighton's satisfaction with the mission, tempered only by an angry disbelief that Adam should have gone personally with the landing party.

Adam had said, 'When you order men ashore to carry out a task which might normally be executed by the military, you cannot simply abandon them to it. On deck, ship against ship, that's a different matter. But in unknown and hostile territory . . . .'

Deighton had interrupted, 'And I suppose *you* could not bring yourself to abandon the chance of further glory for yourself?'

Eventually he had contained his sarcasm. 'I shall send a full report to the admiral, and then to their lordships. A battery destroyed, the way opened for the attacking squadron, and a useful prize to boot . . . the brigantine should fetch a good price. I hope you explained to that Borradaile fellow about the arrangements for sharing prize money?'

'I believe he is well aware of them, sir.'

Of the casualties, he had told Deighton that one of the wounded was unlikely to survive an amputation. A brave man, he had not complained once during the painful transfers from boat to brig, and then to *Valkyrie*. But when he knew he was being carried down to the surgeon, he had pleaded and sobbed like a child.

Deighton had said, 'Can't be helped.' He might have been talking about a breakage in the galley.

Adam watched the brig *Alfriston* leaning to the freshening breeze as she changed tack and headed away to the south-west. Despatches for the admiral. He tried to control his bitterness. To ensure that Deighton's own part in the attack did not pass unnoticed. . . . He himself had thought *Alfriston* should remain in company, at least until they had made contact with their own frigates again.

Deighton had scoffed at his suggestion. 'Where's your zest for battle now, Captain? My orders are to cover the squadron's flanks. *That I shall do.*'

Adam turned as one of the surgeon's loblolly boys appeared on deck, and then walked to the lee side and pitched a bloody bundle outboard. A man's leg. He thought of the dead left behind at the battery, blasted to pieces when the charges had exploded. Surely better than what he had just seen.

He ran his fingers through his hair, feeling the salt and the sand, remembering the wounded American officer with the miniature of his girl. . . . Without thinking, he touched the scar in his side where the *Unity*'s surgeon had probed for splinters. Perhaps the American would tell her one day.

He heard voices below the poop and saw the gunner's mate, Jago, with some of his messmates. He was carrying a shirt which he had just washed out after his experience ashore, and, even in the fading light, Adam could see the livid scars of the cat across his muscular back. Unjustly flogged by *Valkyrie*'s previous captain, he would carry the scars to his grave like any felon. It had been John Urquhart, then *Valkyrie*'s first lieutenant, who had protested to the captain, and had spoken up for Jago, to no avail; it was obvious that Urquhart had been damned to oblivion because of his intervention. Until Keen had given him *Reaper* to command, another ship which had been torn apart by the cruelty of a sadistic captain.

He came to a decision, and beckoned to the gunner's mate. Jago ran lightly up the quarterdeck ladder and waited. 'Sir?'

Adam saw his eyes flit over his captain's torn breeches and crumpled shirt; he himself had not found the time to change into cleaner clothes.

He said, 'I shall not forget what you did. And I wanted to ask you something.' He could almost feel Jago's guard come up, but continued, 'I lost my old cox'n.'

Jago nodded. 'We know, sir. They 'anged 'im.'

'Would you consider taking his place?'

Jago stared at him. '*Your* cox'n, sir?' He glanced up as one of the topmen yelled something to some hands working aloft.

'I'll be gettin' discharged after this, sir. I've done my share, though some might say different.' He shook his head. 'I'm a gunner's mate. That'll do for me, sir.' He looked at him in the same thoughtful manner. 'But you done kindly by me for askin'.'

Adam dismissed him and watched him rejoin his friends, and drag the damp shirt over his head, hiding the savage scars. No wonder he held Urquhart in such respect. He smiled. *If not his captain.*

Dyer murmured, 'The commodore, sir.'

Deighton strode across to the weather side and stared at the men working on the tiered boats.

'The sea and the wind are moderate, Captain. I think we shall lie-to tonight, and rejoin the squadron tomorrow.' And, sharply, to the sailing master, 'What time would *you* estimate, Mr Ritchie, all things being even?'

Ritchie regarded him with a certain wariness. 'During the dog watches we should make contact with *Wildfire*, sir.'

'Then make it so, Mr Ritchie.' He grinned. 'We have done what we set out to do, eh?'

Adam saw some of the others looking over with the same caution. This relaxed, almost jovial mood was something new to them.

He said, 'I do not think we should lie-to, sir.' He kept his voice low, but he saw Ritchie nod in agreement.

Deighton said, 'You *disagree*, Captain, is that it?'

'It is my duty to advise you, sir.'

'It is not your duty, sir, to criticize me in the presence of the ship's company!' The joviality was gone.

'The enemy will call for reinforcements, sir. It would be their first reaction.'

'And this is mine, Captain. We shall lie-to until the morning watch is mustered. Make a note of it in the log.' He gave the fierce grin again. 'Now!'

He walked away, and a few moments later a faint glow appeared at the cabin skylight.

Adam turned, and saw Lieutenant Monteith waiting for him. 'Yes?'

'The wounded man, Simpson. He died, sir.'

There was blood on his sleeve, and Adam guessed that he had stayed with the wretched Simpson until the end. He could see it as clearly as if he had been there: Monteith, and the seaman he could not recall but for his courageous silence, and the surgeon, his face as red as the blood he spilled. And he thought of Deighton's indifference. His arrogance.

Jago was right. *Leave it when you can. Walk away from it while you still have limbs, wipe it from your mind.*

Perhaps he was too tired to think. No such thing as luck, good or bad. *Was that really me?* There was always a possibility that Deighton was right; he had been an experienced and senior captain before this appointment.

He touched Monteith's arm and said, 'Dine with me tonight, Howard.' He saw the lieutenant's surprise. 'We shall drink to damnation and drown our sorrows. . . . I fear we shall be busy men tomorrow.'

Monteith said, 'I would have liked nothing better, sir. But I have the middle watch.'

He should have known. 'Then rest while you can.' He made his way down to his cabin, as the marine sentry was relieved outside the commodore's quarters.

John Whitmarsh was waiting for him, and the table had been carefully laid.

Adam shook his head. 'I find that I cannot eat. Some cognac, please.'

127

Then he sat down and dragged open his drawer. It was as well that Monteith had declined the invitation, he thought.

The cognac burned his throat, but it seemed to steady him.

He picked up a pen and began to write. *Dear Catherine* . . . .

When Whitmarsh entered the cabin again he removed the pen from Adam's out-thrust hand, and looked at the empty sheet of notepaper. *Dear Catherine.* The captain had even done that for him, taught him to read. Like so many things. Almost shyly, he reached out and touched the bright epaulette on the shoulder; Adam, deeply asleep, did not wake.

The captain was back. It was all that mattered. Tomorrow could wait.

When the hands were piped on deck with the morning watch, their captain was already in his customary place on the weather side of the quarterdeck.

Adam watched the familiar preparations, hammocks being stowed in the nettings, petty officers checking their lists and waiting to report to their lieutenants. He had had only a few hours' sleep, but a great deal of coffee and a change into clean clothing had made all the difference. He touched his chin. And a shave. He thought of Bolitho, and the restorative power of the customary shave from his faithful Allday. Impossible to think of them being separated. But it would come . . . .

Old Mister Allday. Young Whitmarsh had better not let him hear himself so described, he thought. Whitmarsh was very quiet these days, almost withdrawn, as he went about his duties. Another separation; but it would be for the best. His aunt would be more than willing to take care of the boy while he attended a local school. You could learn a lot in a man-of-war, but if Whitmarsh was to be sponsored as a midshipman he would need preparing for the other 'young gentlemen' he would eventually meet. *As I did.* It had been his Aunt Nancy then, another stranger who had become one of his own family, who had taught him to feel at ease in a world he had never known. But that was what was troubling Whitmarsh. Leaving the ship. *Leaving me.*

He turned as Ritchie called, 'West by north, sir. Starboard tack. Wind's backed a piece overnight.' He did not need to be able to see the masthead pendant. He knew. He could feel it.

Dyer was here, too. 'Ready, sir!'

'Very well. Hands aloft, set tops'ls and forecourse.' He saw one eyebrow rise very slightly. 'We shall save the t'gallants, Mr Dyer, until we can see where we are going!' It brought a few grins from the helmsmen and the master's mate of the watch. All old hands, they knew what the captain meant. There was no sense in showing all your top canvas at first light, until you knew who else was about. He laid his hands on the quarterdeck rail, still ice-cold from the night. It would be a different story in a few hours' time.

He loved to hear a ship coming alive again; he had hardly ever given the order to lie-to, unlike some captains. Like Deighton. . . . A ship should be moving. He recalled an old sailor's advice to him once. *An equal strain on all parts, hull and spars, and she'll not let you down.*

Valkyrie leaned over to the thrust of wind, spray glinting above the beakhead as the darkness loosened its grip.

He thought about Deighton. Perhaps they were both at fault. It was not the first time he had served with a man he could scarcely tolerate. It was all too common. The cramped confines of a crowded hull made few allowances for personal dislikes.

They would receive new orders, either to continue their patrols and the stop-and-search tactics which had been so successful, or they might be returning to Halifax. All of the inshore squadron would need to be restocked with fresh water and, if possible, fruit. He turned it over in his mind. *And if I should be offered another command?* Because of Deighton, or because he needed a new beginning?

'West by north, sir. Steady as she goes!'

Dyer crossed the deck. 'Dismiss the watch below, sir?'

Adam saw a tendril of smoke from the galley funnel, earlier than usual, but sailors could eat at any time.

'Very well.' He looked for the sun. 'D'you have some good eyes aloft?'

Dyer nodded, relieved. 'I picked them myself, sir.' He hesitated, sensing the barrier which still separated them. 'Are we likely to meet with an enemy, sir?'

Adam smiled. 'Well, we know where most of our *friends* are, Mr Dyer!' Even the nearest ones would be further away by now because of the commodore's insistence on lying-to.

And it was getting lighter. He could see the pale outlines of the brigantine's sails against the heaving water, and thought

129

of Borradaile's uncanny knack of obtaining information from any vessel he sighted . . . .

He heard a splash, and knew it was Deighton's strange servant flinging some water over the side. Perhaps he had been shaving his master.

He took a few paces across the deck, and back again. It was no use; he would have to make allowances, be ready to bend more easily, even if he never understood Deighton's sudden fits of anger and his inability to conceal it.

The figures around him were assuming identity and purpose: men flaking down lines, another splicing a damaged halliard. Two midshipmen, their white patches very clear now, were making notes on their slates, a master's mate watching with a critical eye.

Perhaps they might meet with another courier vessel. But there would be no letters, unless Catherine had written again. He wondered where his uncle was, at sea, or performing some tedious duty ashore. How they would be missing one another. How they belonged. . . . And Keen, soon to be married. He thought of her letter, her visit to Zennor, the mermaid's church. Only she would have cared enough to write of it to him.

The sort of woman who could fascinate and thrill any real man. She was never truly absent from his thoughts; once he had even dreamed about her, when she had come to him not as a friend but as a lover. He had been ashamed and disgusted with himself because of it; it had seemed a betrayal of them both. But, in the wildness of the dream, she had not rejected him.

He heard somebody mutter, 'Another early bird.'

It was Deighton, wearing a boat cloak, with his hat tugged down over his eyes. He grunted as the officers touched their hats to him.

He saw Adam and remarked, 'That coffee – like damned bilge water.'

Adam said, 'I'll have some of mine brought to you, sir. It comes from London.'

'From a lady, no doubt.' But there was no bite to his tone. 'I'd take it as a favour.' He glanced around. 'You're not under all plain sail yet.' Again, it was not a complaint. Perhaps he was making an effort.

Adam said, 'A precaution. You know, sir, first sunlight on their skyscrapers.'

Deighton said suddenly, 'Rear-Admiral Keen, you've known him for a long while?'

'Yes, sir. We've served together from time to time.'

'Lost his wife, I understand.'

Adam waited, tensed, for the next question.

But instead Deighton said, 'Getting married again, I hear. Shapely little piece, to all accounts.'

'When he's promoted, she will be an asset to him.' It was as far as he would go.

Deighton said abruptly, '*Promoted*, of course! Vice-Admiral. No stopping him now. But for the damnable blockade duty, I would have been in that fortunate position. As it is, after this . . . .'

Adam said, 'It's a question on everyone's mind.' He thought suddenly of Jago. *I've done my share*. Perhaps he was the lucky one after all.

Deighton turned to face him. 'You're young. Good reputation, successful, many would say. It will be different for you.'

It was the closest they had been, probably would ever be, and Adam was oddly moved by it.

Deighton said, 'When we rejoin the squadron I might discover more about this campaign . . . .'

'Deck there!' The masthead lookout's voice seemed unnaturally loud. 'Sail to the nor'east!'

Adam was already pulling off his coat, and tossed it to one of the midshipmen.

'I'll take a glass and go up myself. I might know better then.'

Deighton restrained him. 'An enemy?'

He knew how it would appear to the lookout. Whatever it was, it was coming out of the sun. They would not sight *Valkyrie* in the lingering darkness just yet. It was little enough.

He replied, 'Unlikely to be one of ours, sir.'

Deighton peered over the side. 'They'll not snatch our prize, damn them!'

Adam hurried to the shrouds, faces turning on every side to watch him. How could he destroy the frail confidence which Deighton was trying to build between them?

He gripped the ratlines and began to climb.

How could he explain to Deighton? *It's not the prize. It's us they're coming for!*

*   *   *

Adam's heels hit the deck as he completed his descent from the crosstrees by way of a backstay. It was hardly dignified for a captain, but it saved time, and he was a little surprised that he could still do it; the palms of his hands felt raw from the slide, and his clean shirt was stained with tar.

'I'd like to have a look at the chart, sir.'

Deighton's face was filled with questions, but he was experienced enough not to voice them in front of the listening watchkeepers.

It was dark in the small chart room, but he held the image as sharply in his mind as he had seen it minutes ago. The lookout had pointed unwaveringly. 'Frigate, sir. Starboard quarter!'

In the first, uncertain light he had seen the other ship for himself, a perfect pyramid of pale canvas, running before the wind with each sail hard and full. Through the telescope he had been able to see part of her hull. The lookout had good eyes indeed, but what he had not seen was a second ship, a sliver, perhaps of equal size, hull up on the shining horizon.

Deighton asked impatiently, 'What was it?'

Adam did not look up from the chart. 'One, maybe two frigates, sir. Yankees, carrying all the sail they can muster.' He tapped the chart with the dividers. 'Probably out of New York, or even Philadelphia. They hadn't sighted us just now, but it won't be long.'

Deighton stared at the chart. 'What do you think?'

'Two choices, sir. Run, and hope to meet up with the squadron or the admiral's ships.' He wished he could see Deighton's face more clearly in the shadows. Only his hand was visible, drumming on the edge of the chart table.

Deighton said, 'And the other choice?'

Adam dropped the dividers on the chart. 'Stand and fight. There'll be no surprises this time.'

Men were moving about the decks again; the initial excitement was past. But not for long; there were no secrets in any ship.

'Two frigates? We'd be outgunned.'

'The sailing master said that it would take until the dog watches to meet up with our ships. Twelve hours at best, sir.'

The hand moved again, agitated, as if separate from its owner. 'That Ritchie doesn't know everything, dammit!'

'He's the best sailor in the ship, sir.'

He waited, feeling no pity for the man who had insisted on letting *Alfriston* go without informing the other frigates of his intentions. To extend their patrol area and so lose signalling contact was nothing but folly. All he felt now was a sick despair.

He said, 'We have an empty ocean. By setting every sail, we might avoid a stern chase and any serious damage to masts and rigging. We would lose the prize, but we did what we came to do.'

Deighton glared at him '*You* did, that's what signifies to you!' He moved to the door, where the glare of sunlight seemed to catch him unawares.

He said thickly, 'I've never run from an enemy. Nor shall I now. What would they say of me?' He laughed, a bitter sound. 'Some would find pleasure in it, I daresay!'

Adam looked past him, at the familiar figures near the big double-wheel, the two midshipmen with their slates. Men, and boys like these, to be sacrificed because of one officer's vanity.

He heard himself ask, 'Then you'll fight, sir?' Like somebody else. A stranger's voice.

Deighton gripped his arm and as quickly released it, as if he had just realised what he was doing.

'You will fight this ship, Captain Bolitho. That is an order! *I* am going aft. I shall not be long.' He looked up at the deckhead as a muffled thud made the air shiver.

One shot. To attract the most distant vessel. *Valkyrie* had been sighted, perhaps even recognised; she was well known enough in these waters.

Deighton had gone. To do what, he wondered. To pray?

He walked out and on to the quarterdeck again, taking his coat from the midshipman who held it with barely a glance. He stared up at the masthead pendant curling and hardening in the wind; real, everyday things. All the rest had been a dream, an illusion.

He beckoned to the first lieutenant, and said, 'Two Yankees to the nor'east.' He knew others were turning to listen. 'We will continue on the same tack for the present, but you may loose the t'gallants, if only to show them we are all awake this day. Then send the remainder of the hands to breakfast.' He

133

looked at Ritchie. 'Put it in the log. The commodore wishes it to be known. We shall fight.'

He found that Monteith was beside him. 'What is it, Howard? It is too late for regrets.'

Monteith shook his head. 'May I ask, sir? But for the order, would you have run for it?'

Do they know me so little? 'No, by Christ, I would not! Not for any man!'

Monteith nodded, and touched his hat. 'I never doubted it, sir.'

Adam saw Whitmarsh's small figure below the poop, carrying his short fighting sword, and what appeared to be his best hat; the other must have been lost somewhere between here and Chesapeake Bay. He shaded his eyes to look up at the freshly-set topgallant sails. Again, he saw the enemy ships as he had watched them through the powerful telescope. Three hours, four at the most, and then this deck would be in torment.

He raised his arm so that Whitmarsh could clip on his scabbard, then took the hat and examined it. *Make me strong today . . . .*

Valkyrie's previous captain had been a tyrant and a coward. How would he be judged?

He laid his hand on the boy's shoulder, and saw the gunner's mate, Jago, pause to watch them.

'It will be warm work today, John Whitmarsh. Take station below when we engage.'

The boy gazed up at him. 'I'll be close by, zur. If you needs me.'

It was little enough, but Adam clapped the hat with its gleaming gold lace on his unruly hair and exclaimed, 'Then so be it!' He looked over at the helmsmen and felt the grin spread across his dry mouth.

'Let us make this a day to remember!'

Adam closed his watch with a snap and said to the first lieutenant, 'That was well done, Mr Dyer. A minute off your record for clearing for action!'

After the strident rattle of drums and the seemingly uncontrolled stampede of running men, the silence seemed unreal; even the ticking of his watch was audible.

Now all was still, the crews around their guns, most of them stripped to the waist, outwardly relaxed now while they waited for the next order. *Valkyrie* was cleared for action, screens torn down, chests and cabin furniture stowed below. But the boats still lay on their tier, and no nets had been spread overhead to protect the hands from falling wreckage.

He walked aft, where the marines waited on either side, muskets resting against the packed hammock nettings, their only protection if it came to close action.

He found Deighton, alone but for his servant, right aft by the taffrail. Both the enemy ships were clearly visible now, and with a soldier's wind directly under their coat-tails were almost bows-on. The smaller of the two ships was overhauling her larger consort, with even her studding sails set to achieve her maximum speed. Twenty-eight guns. Certainly no more.

He said, 'This is what I intend, sir.' He was surprised that he could sound so formal, as if it were just another daily drill. 'The leading ship intends to close the range as quickly as possible.'

Deighton did not take his eyes off the other frigates.

'Huh, you can blow *him* out of the water!'

Adam recalled his own early days in a frigate, the ruses and tricks he had seen some captains attempt, not always successfully.

'Like a hound after a stag, sir. He intends to try and slow us down, cripple us if possible, so they can close in for a kill.' He glanced forward again; it seemed so bare without the nets spread above the gundeck.

The lieutenants would explain, and the older hands might see the sense of it. They must seem to be running away from a superior force of ships; if they dropped the boats astern and were seen to spread the nets, their intent to fight would be obvious.

He added, 'They will hold the wind-gage, but I shall use it to our advantage.'

There was a sharp bang, and seconds later he saw a ball skip across the blue water like a dolphin. The pursuing captain had used his bow-chaser to test the range; it was always a difficult shot, but it only required one good hit.

He went forward and waited for Dyer to meet him. 'I shall luff presently.' He saw Ritchie listening, taking it all in. 'Then we shall sail as close to the wind as we can. It should give us some advantage and extra elevation.' He watched his words going home. 'Double-shotted, chain-shot, too, if we have any. No full broadside.' He paused, holding Dyer's eyes. '*Gun by gun.* Do it yourself. I want that terrier dismasted before we are!'

He snatched a glass from the rack and climbed into the shrouds to search for the second vessel. He found her and settled her in the spray-dappled lens. One of their large frigates. Like Beer's *Unity* . . . .

He strode aft again, feeling the eyes upon him, knowing their thoughts.

'Sergeant Whittle. Choose your marksmen, then clear the poop. Your scarlet coats make a good aiming point!' Some of them even laughed, as if it was a huge joke.

Whittle, an impressive figure with iron-grey hair beneath his leather hat, bawled an order, and his men moved to their usual stations.

Deighton said, 'I don't see the wisdom of that, Captain. Those ships are out for a kill, you said as much yourself!'

Perhaps he felt safer with the armed marines around him. Adam almost smiled. What was *safe* today?

He flinched, although he had been expecting it, as a long orange tongue shot from the other frigate's bow, and the bang followed like an echo.

It was well aimed, but the range was still too great. Maybe a nine-pounder; he imagined he could see the brief blur as the ball reached its maximum elevation. He saw the splash, and felt the hull jerk violently as the shot found its mark below the waterline. He glanced sharply at the wheel; Ritchie had three helmsmen on it now, but she showed no sign of running free or being out of command. With the steering gone, there would be no hope at all.

He raised his hand. 'Alter course three points! Steer nor'west!'

Men were already hauling on the braces as the helm went over. The effect was immediate, the wind tilting *Valkyrie* like a toy as she came round further and further, as close to the wind as she would hold.

A whistle shrilled. 'Open the ports! *Run out!*'

Squealing like pigs, the guns were hauled up to their ports, extra men running from the opposite side to add their weight

136

to the tackles. At this angle, it was like dragging each gun up a steep slope.

Sails cracked and thundered overhead. Ritchie called, 'Course nor'west, sir!'

Dyer was already at the starboard gangway, oblivious to the demented sails and the men slipping and falling on the spray-drenched deck. He had drawn his sword, and was standing motionless, staring at the enemy frigate as she loomed into view, as if she and not *Valkyrie* had made the violent change of tack.

'*Fire!*' Dyer ran from the side as the gun roared out and hurled itself inboard on its tackles, the crew already working with their sponges and worm to clear the barrel of any smouldering remnants which might ignite the next charge as it was rammed home. Adam had seen it happen, men driven beyond reason by the fury of battle who had neglected to sponge out a gun, and had been blown to bloody fragments when it had exploded.

There was a chorus of wild cheering which Adam could not have prevented even if he had wished to. It must have been one of the last guns to fire; they would never know.

Almost with disbelief, he saw the other frigate's foremast begin to move, in a silence which made it all the more terrible.

Slowly at first, and then like a giant tree, the entire foremast with spars, torn canvas and trailing rigging reeled forward and over the side.

He shouted, 'Stand by on the quarterdeck!' When he looked again, the mast was dragging in the sea alongside the enemy ship, snaring her, dragging her round like a great sea-anchor. From a thing of beauty and purpose to a drifting shambles; but that would not last.

The confusion amongst the flapping sails was even more violent when *Valkyrie* swung round still further, almost aback as she laboured through the eye of the wind.

Adam dragged himself to the compass. 'South-east by east, Mr Ritchie.' He saw Dyer staring at him and shouted, 'Larboard battery! *Broadside!*'

'*Fire!*' The range was about half a mile, but with a full, double-shotted broadside, they could easily have been along-side.

137

As the wind drove the swirling smoke away like fog, Adam raised his telescope and studied the enemy's shattered stern; the fallen mast had dragged her around to expose her full length. Only her mainmast remained standing; topmasts, spars and booms covered her decks; torn canvas and coils of severed cordage completed the picture of devastation.

Deliberately, he made himself turn, testing his emotions as he saw the second frigate, leaning over on a converging tack, her guns already run out like black teeth.

He walked to the quarterdeck rail and saw the men stand back from their guns, one gun captain lifting a fresh ball in readiness for the next shot, and the one after that. Until it was over.

He said, 'They must not board us! We're done for if they overrun the ship!'

He drew the fine, curved hanger and held it over his head. 'On the uproll, lads! Make each shot tell!'

Somebody cheered, and a petty officer silenced him with a threat.

The gun captains stood behind their breeches now, each with his trigger-line pulled taut, their crews crouched and ready with handspikes to change the elevation or training.

'*Fire!*'

The deck reeled beneath his feet, and Adam realised that the enemy had fired at the same moment. There was smoke everywhere, and he heard men screaming as splinters as large as goose quills tore amongst them. He wiped his face with his wrist and saw the enemy's sails, pockmarked with holes, but each yard properly braced, still holding her on the same tack.

The smoke was gone and he saw the upended guns now, the patterns of bright blood where men had fallen, or been crushed beneath the heated barrels.

Deighton was suddenly beside him, and seemed to be shouting, although his voice was muffled, faint.

'Disengage, Captain! That is an order, *do you hear*?'

Adam stared past him at the oncoming ship; she seemed to fill the sea, and there were men in her shrouds, waiting to board, ready to mark down the most valuable targets. As if in a dream, he noticed that Deighton had removed his bright epaulettes. Marines were clambering up the ratlines, some with two muskets slung over their shoulders. Sergeant

138

Whittle's best marksmen. . . . He tried to think, to clear his mind.

'I will not strike our colours, sir! You gave me an order to fight.' He knew Dyer was waiting for the order. 'Fight I will!'

Deighton winced as more iron crashed into the lower hull. 'I'll see you in hell for this!'

Adam pushed past him. 'We shall meet there, *sir*!'

He reached up to his shoulder, thinking somebody had tried to take his attention. His epaulette was gone, the cloth shredded into rag where a musket ball had torn it away.

'*Fire!*'

Men were coughing and retching as the smoke billowed inboard through the open gun ports; the enemy's sails seemed to be towering right alongside, and yet the guns still fired, and were reloaded. The dead lay where they had fallen; there were not enough spare hands either to throw them outboard, or to carry the whimpering wounded below.

Adam saw the other ship's tapering jib boom and then her bowsprit passing over the larboard bow like a giant's lance. There were shots everywhere, a rain of iron hammering the deck, ripping into the torn hammocks where several marines had already fallen.

So they would not collide. The American was carrying too much canvas.

Wildly he swung round, and shouted, '*Carronade!*' Then, 'Let her fall off, Mr Ritchie!'

A master's mate ran to throw his weight on to the wheel. Ritchie was propped against the compass box, his eyes fixed and staring as if still watching his ship's performance, even in death.

Adam waved his sword, and someone on the splintered forecastle jerked the lanyard. The carronade, the smasher as it was known, recoiled on its slide, and where seamen had been massing, ready for a chance to board, there was only a blackened heap of remains, men and fragments of men, and one officer standing, apparently untouched, his sword dangling by his side, perhaps too shocked to move.

Dyer had rallied the gun crews and had brought more men from the disengaged side. *Valkyrie* shivered to another broadside, their own or the enemy's Adam did not know.

Somebody was yelling at him. 'The commodore's bin hit, sir! They've took 'im below!'

The other frigate, her hull pockmarked with holes and with great, livid scars in her timbers, was being carried past by the press of canvas. Shots still ripped across the broadening arrowhead of water between them, but the shooting was less controlled. He saw two men fall from the shrouds as the Royal Marines in the fighting tops kept up their fire. In his heart, he knew that the engagement was over, but his reason could not accept it. One enemy crippled, and unlikely to reach safety once the other ships in the squadron came upon her. And the other – he could see her name now, in bright gold lettering across her counter, *Defender* – was unwilling to continue.

He rubbed his ear; there was cheering too, which seemed very faint, although he knew it was here, in his own ship. The guns' roar had rendered him almost deaf. He saw men peering at him and grinning, teeth white in their smoke-blackened faces.

Dyer was here, shaking his arm. 'The lookout has sighted *Reaper*, sir! The enemy must have seen her, that's why they're standing away!' He looked stunned, unable to accept that he was alive when so many had fallen.

Reaper, of all ships. So right that it should be John Urquhart, coming to the aid of his old ship, where he had been treated so badly.

'Shorten sail, Mr Dyer.' He wanted to smile, to give them something they could cling to when the final bloody bill was reckoned. 'Report damage and casualties.' He tried again. 'You did well. *Very well*.' He turned away, and did not see Dyer's expression. Pride; gratitude; affection.

He said, 'I must see the commodore. Take charge here.' He saw the man called Jago, a bare cutlass wedged through his belt.

'A victory, sir.' It seemed to have drained him. 'Or as good as.'

Adam shaded his eyes to watch the enemy frigate. *Defender*. They might still meet again. Her flag was flying as proudly as before. Defiant . . . .

He seemed to recall what Jago had said, and stared around. 'My servant! Whitmarsh! Where is he?'

140

Jago said, 'He's below, sir. I took 'im meself, you bein' busy at the time.'

Adam faced him. 'Tell me.' It was almost as if he had known. But how could he?

Jago answered, 'Splinter. Didn't feel nothin'.'

'And you took him below?' He looked away, at the sea. So clean, he thought. So clean. . . . 'That was bravely done. I'll not forget.'

The orlop deck was crowded with wounded men, some fearful of what might happen, others lying quietly, beyond pain.

Minchin, his familiar apron covered with blood, peered at him as a man was dragged from his table and carried into the shadows.

He said thickly, 'The commodore's dead, sir.' He gestured to a covered shape by one massive timber and Adam saw the strange servant on his knees beside the corpse, rocking back and forth, moaning like a sick animal.

Minchin wiped some blood from his knife with a rag, and cut himself a slice of apple with it. 'Quite mad, that one!'

He chewed steadily as Adam turned down a blanket and looked at the dead boy's face. There was not a mark on him; he might have been asleep. Minchin knew that the iron splinter had hit him in the spine, and must have killed him outright. He had seen many terrible things in his butcher's work, men torn apart in the name of duty, who had believed even in extremity that a miracle could save them. At least the captain's servant had been spared that. But there was nothing he could say; there never was. And there were others waiting. He could barely taste the apple because of the rum, which helped him at times like these, but down here in this hellish, lightless place, it reminded him of somewhere. Someone . . . .

He gave a great sigh. Where was the point? And the captain had done what he could. *For all of us.*

It would not help him, or anyone else, to know that Commodore Deighton had been killed by a single musket ball, but not one fired by an American weapon. It had entered the body from high up, at a steep angle. He peered at a wounded marine who was drinking some rum. It could rest.

He gestured with his knife. '*Next!*'

Adam looked at the boy's face. How he must have relived *Anemone*'s death each time the drums had beaten to quarters.

We help each other. He covered his face again with the blanket. It was all that John Whitmarsh had ever wanted.

He climbed once more up to the smoky sunlight, and almost broke when he saw his lieutenants and warrant officers waiting to make their reports, and to ask for his instructions.

One figure blocked his way. It was Jago.

'*Yes?*' He could scarcely speak.

'I was thinkin', sir. That offer of yours, cox'n, weren't it?'

Adam faced him, but barely saw him. 'You'll take it?'

Like the other time he had seized a lifeline.

Jago nodded, and held out his hand. 'I'd want to shake on it, sir.'

They shook hands in silence, men pausing in their work and perhaps forgetting their fear, merely to watch. To share it.

That evening, as predicted by Ritchie, they met with the remainder of the squadron and headed for the Bermudas, for orders. In *Valkyrie*'s wake, the stitched canvas bundles drifted down and down into eternal darkness. One of them was the commodore.

And one was a boy who wore a fine dirk strapped to his side, for the last farewell.

10

A Ship of War

His Britannic Majesty's Ship *Frobisher* lay at her anchor, unmoving above the perfect twin of her reflection in the blazing sunlight. The ensign at her stern and the admiral's flag at the mainmast truck were equally motionless, and between decks, in spite of the awnings and windsails, the air was like an open kiln.

The crash of Malta's noonday gun echoed across the water like an intrusion, but only a few gulls rose from their torpor, squawking in protest before settling down again.

In the great cabin Sir Richard Bolitho, coatless, his ruffled shirt open almost to the waist, shaded his eyes to stare at the land, the craggy battlements where, occasionally, he could see a red coat moving slowly on patrol. He pitied the soldiers in their thick uniforms as they paced up and down in the heat.

Frobisher was a well-built ship, and the sounds which reached Bolitho's quarters were muffled and remote, as if they, too, were stifled by the heat. But in many ways he envied the life and movement from which he was separated, *protected*, as his secretary Yovell had once described it. Even here, right aft, he could catch the heady smell of rum, and imagine the ship's community of some six hundred seamen and Royal Marines preparing for their midday meal.

He sighed and sat at his table again, to the litter of signals and local correspondence awaiting collection. Since their arrival here in Grand Harbour, the ship had scarcely moved. Such inactivity was bad for any fighting ship, and for one with a company far from home, with no immediate prospect of discharge or action, the strain on discipline and routine was becoming evident.

He had received two letters from Catherine; they had arrived together in a courier brig from Plymouth. It was the shortest time they had ever been parted, and yet the uncertainty of the future and the strange, lingering sense of loss he felt seemed to make it worse.

She wrote of things she knew would please him, of the house and the estate. Of the garden, *her* garden, and the roses which gave her so much pleasure.

She touched on her feelings for him, but was careful not to trouble him with her own pain of separation.

There had been one ugly note; she had mentioned it in case he should hear it from someone else. There had been a riot in Bodmin, the county town, although he found it hard to imagine in that sort of community; a local regiment had been disbanded, and the men had mounted a protest to demand work after their service to their country.

If it had happened in Falmouth, Bolitho wondered what Lewis Roxby would have done. He might well have put some of the men to work on his own large estate, and encouraged other landowners to do the same. In Bodmin, a magistrate had read the Riot Act, and called out the dragoons from Truro.

She had told him that she was going to London to see the lawyers again. She would think of him. *Dearest of men . . . always.*

He heard Ozzard's sharp voice from the pantry, and then Allday's. They were bickering about something, as usual. Without them and their concern over his welfare, he sometimes thought that the inactivity would drive him mad.

There were receptions, for him and his officers, and for visiting ships, old enemies who were now classed as allies. That would take a long, long time to accept.

He had seen little otherwise of the island itself, and although he had been offered facilities ashore with as many servants as he might need, he had remained in his flagship. As if it were a last link with the only life he knew and understood.

Malta was full of history, and as one senior officer had described it, 'the stronghold of Christianity'. When the French had been forced to withdraw because of the naval blockade, the Maltese had requested British protection, and a restoration of their rights and privileges. The island, small though it was, had once again become a stronghold. Now, with Napoleon's surrender and his incarceration on Elba, it was assumed by some that Malta would be allowed to resume its own self-government, not so different from that of the old Knights of Malta.

That same senior officer had laughed outright when Bolitho had suggested it. He had exclaimed, 'Have you ever known the flag hauled down after a victory, Sir Richard? If a place is worth dying for, it's worth holding on to, in my opinion!'

He heard the marine sentry's heels click together, and then Ozzard hurrying to the outer screen door.

It was Captain Tyacke, his scarred face very deeply tanned above the whiteness of his shirt. He was so used to the heat and the sun of Africa that he scarcely noticed it.

'Officer-of-the-Guard has just brought a message, Sir Richard.' He glanced around the cabin, made still more spacious by the removal of the eighteen-pounder guns which would otherwise have occupied even an admiral's quarters. They had been replaced by short wooden replicas, quakers as they were termed, so that, outwardly at least, the ship would appear fully armed.

Bolitho slit open the envelope. It bore a military seal on the outer flap. Another visitor . . . .

He said, 'We shall have a major-general coming aboard during the dogs, James. His name is Valancy, although it does not give a reason for this honour.'

'I shall deal with it, sir.'

Bolitho looked at him, aware of the change in him; he had seen it develop during their passage into the Mediterranean, and these dragging weeks in harbour. Perhaps he had found the challenge of the new command stimulating; he had performed miracles with some of the inexperienced hands and the junior officers. But that was only a part of it.

We are so alike in many ways. He will share it with me, when he is ready.

Tyacke said, 'Perhaps we shall be told something, sir.'

'Soon, I trust.' He stood up and walked to the quarter gallery and watched a small boat being pulled across the harbour. A boy and an old man; they did not even glance up as *Frobisher*'s big shadow passed over them.

He said quietly, 'If it does not happen, James, I shall write a suitable report to their lordships.'

Tyacke watched him, the set of his shoulders, his hair still as black as the day they had first met. And later, when Bolitho had asked him to be his flag captain. Not ordered or demanded, as most flag officers would have done, as, indeed, they were entitled to do. He had asked. And had said, *because I need you*. No wonder they spoke of the legend, the charisma, but it was both and neither of them. It was the man himself.

Tyacke said, 'If we can get to sea . . . .'

Bolitho turned towards him. 'I know. Drive her if we must, fight if we have to, but *get to sea*!'

He saw Tyacke glance down at the wine cooler, made for him after the other had been lost in *Hyperion*. Even here, Catherine was very close. He saw the disfigured side of Tyacke's face in the reflected glare from the skylight. Like melted wax, the flesh burned from the bone, the eye, miraculously unblinded, as clear and blue as the other. Even that seemed different. . . . From the moment the ship had left Spithead Tyacke had gone about his duties, explaining his standards to his lieutenants and senior warrant officers without flinching beneath the scrutiny of strangers. Landsmen and some of the younger midshipmen still could not meet his gaze without dropping their eyes; Tyacke had endured this every hour and every day since he had been smashed down at the Nile. Was it possible that he had accepted it? Or was there some other, deeper reason?

He had spoken of his feelings concerning Malta to Tyacke. The reply had been blunt, uncompromising, like the man.

'We'd be fools to let it go, sir. It may be only seventeen miles by nine, a landsman might say the same as the Isle of Wight. But it stands *here*, and who commands it holds the key to the Mediterranean. Every trading nation knows that well enough!'

Bolitho said, 'Perhaps this commission will be shorter than we thought possible.' He touched his eye as the sunlight found its mark. The cruel reminder. *Which I cannot accept.* 'Will you still go back to Africa?'

Tyacke smiled faintly. 'I would have to think on it.' He seemed to consider it. 'Yes, I would have to give it a deal of thought.' He looked at the deckhead as a call twittered, and feet padded across the tinder-dry planking. 'I must see the first lieutenant, if you will excuse me, sir.'

Bolitho watched his hand hesitate on the door, and said, 'If there is anything you wish to talk about, James, I am here.'

Tyacke paused with his hat halfway to his head. Then he smiled fully, and seemed suddenly young again.

'If you were not, sir, then neither would I be.'

Allday entered as the door closed, and glanced at the two swords on their rack.

'Might be another courier vessel soon, Sir Richard.'

So he was fretting, too. Needing to be here, but thinking of his newfound life with Unis and his daughter.

Bolitho gestured toward the cupboard. 'Have a wet, old friend. We are both all aback, it seems.'

Allday stooped beside the cupboard, and said over his shoulder, 'Get this little lot over, an' maybe we can make sail for home.'

Bolitho rubbed his eye. He must have missed something.

Allday held up a glass of rum and grinned.

'To us, Sir Richard!'

'What have you heard?'

Allday looked at the high-backed chair in green leather, which she had given Bolitho. Like the wine cooler, and the locket he always wore when they were apart from one another. *A sailor's woman.* There was no higher compliment.

He said, 'I was talkin' to the men in the guardboat just now, Sir Richard. There's a yarn goin' around about an attack on some local merchantmen. Pirates, they says.'

He felt something like a chill against his damp spine. How they had first met, all those years ago. Barbary corsairs.

He said, 'The officer-of-the-guard left no such message.'

Allday put down the empty glass, careful not to leave any wet mark, which would cause more trouble with Ozzard.

'With respect, Sir Richard, the Royals are all well an' good, in their place.' He tapped his forehead. 'But their officers don't know it all.'

Bolitho smiled. 'Off with you. And don't fret over Unis. She is in good hands.'

Allday went out, unreassured, and found Ozzard in his pantry. He sniffed suspiciously, and said, 'Been at the grog again!'

Allday ignored it. 'Sir Richard's troubled. He worries about Cap'n Tyacke, an' about me, an' about everybody but himself!'

Ozzard regarded him scornfully. 'Captain Tyacke? Don't you *know*, for God's sake?'

Allday sighed inwardly. He could kill the stooping servant with one blow, and he sometimes wondered why they had remained friends. Of a sort.

Ozzard snapped, 'It's a woman, you blockhead! It's always a bloody woman when trouble's at the door!'

Allday left the pantry, touching the little man's shoulder as he passed. If he stayed, he knew he would make matters worse.

It was like sharing a terrible secret. It was not Captain Tyacke's pain Ozzard was describing. It was his own.

Major-General Sir Ralph Valancy stepped into the stern cabin and glanced around while Ozzard took his hat. Bolitho noticed that he showed no sign of discomfort and that his uniform was perfectly pressed, his boots like black glass, although if he had been dressed in rags one would have known him to be a professional soldier. He must keep his orderly very busy, to appear so untroubled by Malta's heat and the dust.

Valancy took a chair. 'I could never have been a sailor, Sir Richard. Too confined, even for an admiral!'

Bolitho waited while Ozzard fetched wine, and wondered why this man reminded him of someone. Then it came to him. Halifax, where he had met the young captain from the King's Regiment, who had been at the siege of York, and had given a miniature of herself back to the girl, Gilia St Clair, who would soon marry Valentine Keen.

That young captain would be very like this major-general, if he lived long enough.

Valancy sipped the wine and made a sound of approval.

Bolitho said, 'It's a mite warm, but cooling anything is not easy with the ship at anchor.'

Valancy's face broke into a grin. 'Any wine tastes good to me, sir! I've ridden, marched and damned well crawled over every kind of territory, and like my men, I've had most dislikes steamed out of me!' He became serious. 'You've heard about the missing transport vessel, the *Galicia*?'

Bolitho recalled Allday's scorn for the military in general, and the marines in particular.

'I have not had an official signal as yet.'

Valancy shrugged. 'I only heard myself this morning. The *Galicia* was under charter to the army, on passage for Malta. A fisherman reported seeing her attacked by a heavily-armed vessel. He made off before he became another victim.'

'Algerine pirates?'

Valancy nodded. 'Sailing too close to the Saracen coast, as they call it. The Dey of Algiers will have had a hand in it. The whole North African coast would be part of the Turkish empire if he and the Bey of Tunis could find enough ships.'

Bolitho thought of his time as a flag captain, when he had been involved with that same coast and the notorious port of Djafou to the west of Algiers. Slavery, cruelty and torture; he had seen even his most experienced seamen sickened by what they had found. Piracy was common in these waters, and when the fleet had been fully employed against the French and maintaining a blockade, some of those same pirates had even flouted all authority to prey as far north as the Channel and the Western Approaches.

If the Mediterranean was to become stable again, this menace to trade would have to be removed. If peace and mutual trust were not restored, Britain's new allies would soon look for other means of enforcement.

Bolitho said, 'I have six frigates, and a few smaller vessels.' He glanced at the nearest quaker. 'And my flagship. Not a great force, but I have worked with far less in the past.'

'Indeed, I know, Sir Richard. You won't remember me, but I was aide to the general at Good Hope when you came to our aid.' He gave a faint smile, remembering. 'I was with the Sixty-First then. It was a fine regiment.'

It was the smile, exactly like the captain who had fought at York. The professional soldier.

'I remember.' He recalled that other general. They would not give the Cape of Good Hope back to the Dutch, either.

The soldier said, 'Yes, we'd not long heard about Trafalgar. And Nelson's death. Such a shock, although inevitable, I suppose. I often wonder what happened to his mistress after his death. Shunned by everyone, I suppose.'

Then he looked directly at Bolitho. 'That was a stupid remark. I apologise, Sir Richard.'

149

Bolitho said, 'It is something I think on myself, Sir Ralph.' He stood up abruptly, thinking now of Catherine, how they had first met, the deadly chebecks closing in under sail and oars, ready to fire into any larger vessel's vulnerable stern. When Catherine's Spanish husband had died. *And we lost one another . . . .*

He said, 'I shall send the only frigate I have in harbour. *Frobisher* will remain here, as she must, until more men-of-war arrive.' He could already hear Tyacke's disagreement, and his doubt.

Valancy nodded slowly, surprised, perhaps, at this sudden decision, but careful not to show it.

'The frigate's captain.' He hesitated, as he might before leading a charge. 'Will he know the instability of these people? They have countless sailors and fishermen, thrown into their rotten jails, and for no other reason than that they are Christians! Barbarians!' He became very earnest. 'And the Dey of Algiers has some six hundred guns, according to our latest intelligence . . . .'

'May I ask you something? If this matter were to be entrusted to the army, who would you send?'

Surprisingly, Valancy laughed. 'A mission like this, which might fan the flames of another war? I'd go myself! Right or wrong, it would be my responsibility.'

Bolitho smiled, and tapped his glass with a paper-knife. 'Another glass, Sir Ralph?'

When Ozzard appeared to pour the wine, Bolitho said to him, 'Ask Allday to find Captain Tyacke, and have him lay aft.' He noticed that Ozzard did not lift his eyes, nor did he show any surprise.

As he left the cabin, Bolitho said quietly to Valancy, 'I thought you would say as much.' He sipped the wine, and added, 'I shall go in *Halcyon*.' He recalled her captain's face when he had described his fear and helplessness aboard *Majestic* at the Nile, when Tyacke had given him back his courage and his pride.

Frobisher, or a larger group of ships would invite disaster . . . .

Allday entered by the other door and paused, as if uncertain. That, in itself, was unusual.

Bolitho said, 'Well?'

'Cap'n Tyacke is with the purser, Sir Richard.' He refused to look at the major-general. 'I left a message, but I thought . . . .'

Bolitho sat again. 'It is why we are here. Why I was sent.' He smiled. 'My compliments to the captain, and *ask* him to come aft.'

Allday departed, and Valancy said, 'Remarkable fellow. Although I don't see that it is possible for anyone to know what you intend.'

Bolitho touched his eye. 'Remarkable, yes. Your general said as much at Good Hope. He also said that he could use a few thousand more like him.'

The soldier got to his feet. 'I shall detain you no longer, Sir Richard.'

Bolitho shook his hand. Tonight Valancy would probably regale his staff with tales of the strange ways of the navy, and how an admiral had taken the time to reassure a common seaman.

And yet, somehow, he knew he would not.

Tyacke entered the cabin as soon as the major-general had been seen safely into his boat.

Bolitho said, 'Have *Halcyon*'s captain repair on board, James. There is something I wish to discuss with you.' He saw the immediate signs of argument. 'It is a matter of some urgency.'

'You're leaving *Frobisher*? Your flagship?'

'Presently. While I am away, I would be pleased if the guns were replaced in my quarters.'

Tyacke left the cabin without asking another question; there was no need.

The sunshine and the brightly painted boats meant nothing to him. His was still a ship of war.

Lieutenant George Avery put down his pen and passed the finished letter across his small table. 'There. I hope it does justice to your thoughts.' He watched as Allday, who had been squatting on a chest in the hutch-like cabin, made his mark carefully and deliberately at the bottom of the page. Avery had asked him once what the distinctive symbol meant, and Allday had told him that it was like the stone Cornish cross that stood outside the church in Fallowfield where he and Unis had been married.

Allday cocked his head to listen to a bosun's call, very clear and shrill in the evening stillness. 'Won't be long now,' he said.

Avery glanced around the cabin. A hutch indeed, but private when he needed to withdraw from the ship's general life and routine.

'How do you feel about it?'

Allday looked at him thoughtfully. Once he would have shown instant caution, if not mistrust.

'I've been with Sir Richard long enough to take things as they comes, but this time, I ain't so sure. Them devils ain't to be trusted an' never were. We should wait until the rest of the squadron is joined here.'

Avery thought of *Halcyon*'s young captain. A good officer, as Tyacke had confirmed, but one twenty-eight-gun frigate against well-sited batteries and, no doubt, ships ready to repel any unwanted visitors, was hardly a bargaining point.

He said, 'At least your letter will be on its way.'

Allday stood up; he had heard somebody outside the door. Avery had not written or received any letters himself, but to mention it might be pushing things too far. It was a pity, he thought. Avery was better than most of his kind. He smiled. But he was still an officer.

'I'll be ready when they calls us, sir.'

Avery got to his feet as Kellett, the first lieutenant, stepped to one side while Allday departed.

'Come in!'

They both laughed as Kellett eased his way around the screen door; the cabin was a twin of his own.

'I won't detain you.' He sat on the same chest and glanced uncuriously at the pen and paper. Avery thought he probably knew about the letters he wrote for the admiral's coxswain, but he would never remark upon it.

He knew Kellett no better than when he had joined the ship at Plymouth. Tall, about twenty-five, and obviously respected by the more seasoned hands and warrant officers; Tyacke had implied that he had carried the ship for most of the time during *Frobisher*'s lengthy overhaul. He was loyal, too; he had never complained to Tyacke about how he had been left with most of the duties, as some would, if only to ingratiate themselves with the new lord and master.

152

Kellett said, 'I would that I were coming with you. Or that *Frobisher* were carrying the flag into Algerine waters.'

Avery waited. Kellett was not here to waste his time before they transferred to *Halcyon*. He wanted to talk.

Avery said, 'You've been in this ship for three years.'

Kellett looked at him, his mild eyes very steady. 'I was appointed as second lieutenant, but my immediate superior was transferred.' He shrugged. 'I thought, ah, my future is brighter already!' But there was no humour in his voice.

Avery prompted, 'The previous first lieutenant was promoted?'

'*Transferred*. To some miserable, rat-infested bomb-vessel. I did not like him much, but he deserved better for all that.'

Avery considered it. The first lieutenant was the Honourable Granville Kellett, and the son of an admiral. His future, war or no war, should be assured. Unless . . . .

'What was the captain like? I understand that he was removed because of illness, although the surgeon claims he had no part in it.'

Kellett's smile was genuine. 'I'm surprised you got anything out of that one. He wouldn't tell you he was taking off your leg, until afterwards!' He nodded his thanks as Avery poured two glasses of cognac. 'Captain Oliphant was rarely aboard during our time in the dockyard. He was ill, but he was receiving treatment ashore.' He paused. 'But not in Haslar Hospital, as you might expect.' He swallowed some of the cognac. 'I discovered that for myself.'

'Was it sudden?'

'I thought so at first. Now, looking back, I can see that he suffered some kind of discomfort . . . pain. It affected his moods, his temper. We received the news about *Frobisher*'s appointment as Sir Richard's flagship, and I thought he was delighted about it. He would have been the flag captain, and, as Lord Rhodes' cousin, his prospects seemed excellent.' He dropped his voice. 'But I can tell you now, I thank God that Captain Tyacke is in command. I have never seen such a change in a ship, the *life* he's put into her!'

Avery smiled. 'I was in awe of him when we first met. I am closer to him now. But he still frightens me more than I'd care to admit!'

Kellett put down his empty glass. 'That was welcome, sir.'

Avery got carefully to his feet. Strange to think of French officers sitting here as they had done, discussing the prospects of battle, promotion, or perhaps love.

Kellett seemed to come to a decision. 'Captain Oliphant was very fond of women. He would get into debt because of them, if it suited. My predecessor was "transferred" because he refused to help him. I suspect I was retained merely because of my illustrious father.' He forced a smile. 'I would deny every word in court, of course!'

Avery said gravely, 'Of course.'

They both laughed, and Kellett shook his hand. 'Be careful on this mission. I would not wish to lose a friend, one so newly gained.' Then he was gone.

Avery thought about it. Rhodes had been the one who had arranged for *Frobisher* to become Sir Richard's flagship. It would have been the making of Oliphant, no matter what the future held. He heard a boat being warped alongside. It was time.

But, related or not, Rhodes would never have suggested Oliphant for flag captain if there had been even the faintest hint of scandal, especially as he valued his own prospective appointment to First Lord.

Captain Oliphant was very fond of women. Kellett's words seemed to linger in the humid air.

It was not their concern. James Tyacke's decision to join them had changed everything, and from what Kellett had said, not only for Sir Richard's little crew.

He thought he could hear Tyacke's voice through the after screen, even before he reached the great cabin. The Royal Marine sentry remained expressionless, his eyes fixed on some point at the opposite end of the ship as he rapped his musket on the deck and shouted, 'Flag lieutenant, *sir!*'

Bolitho looked up from his table and smiled at him.

'I know, George. It is almost time.' If he were glad of the interruption, he gave no sign of it.

He turned to Tyacke and said, 'You have my written orders, James. You are captain-in-charge until our return, unless despatches to the contrary direct you. The ship is in good hands. None better.' He held out his own hand, and Avery knew that although Allday, too, was present, for Bolitho, the cabin was empty but for himself and his captain.

He said, 'Trust me. This is something that must be done. If I wait for a full show of force, it might be too late. You know that.'

Tyacke sounded very calm again, but he was not resigned. 'I worked too long with slavers. I know these scum, no matter what they call themselves. It matters to *me* that we finish our work here.' He hesitated. 'And go home.'

Ozzard had insisted on joining them aboard *Halcyon*, and when he had finished supervising the lowering of the admiral's bag into the boat, he snapped, 'He can't manage his own, can he?'

Allday was still thinking about Tyacke, his mention of home, something previously unknown.

He ventured cautiously, 'About Cap'n Tyacke, an' what you said, Tom. I thought . . . .'

Ozzard peered up at him, in the first shadows of evening. '*Thought?* Leave thinking to horses, they've got bigger heads!'

Allday watched him bustle away, and was troubled by it. Tyacke's talk of home remained uppermost in his mind. *For all of us.*

As sunset touched the ancient battlements like blood, Bolitho and his companions were pulled across to the frigate *Halcyon*. There was a promising breeze, and the capstan was already manned, the sails loosened in readiness to leave.

Within the hour, it was as if she had never been.

11

A Sailor's Woman

The staircase somewhere to the rear of the main Admiralty building was narrow and, Catherine guessed, rarely used. The banister was dusty; she could feel it under her glove, and when she reached the final curve of the stairs she looked down and saw cobwebs on the hem of her gown.

The few windows were sealed despite the heavy air, and the hint of a thunderstorm which hovered over London and the river.

She had once heard Richard mention going to the Admiralty *by way of the back stairs*. This must have been what he meant.

The elderly Admiralty clerk paused to look back at her. 'I am very sorry, m'lady. Sir Graham Bethune was unavoidably detained, and asked that you meet him here.'

Here was a small ante-room, with three chairs and little else. A place of assignations, perhaps.

'Thank you. I will wait.'

She could hear the clerk's heavy breathing, almost painful. He was not used to the back stairs, obviously.

Alone again, Catherine crossed to a window, but saw only the slope of another roof. It could be anywhere. She suppressed a shiver. It was like the view from a prison.

Perhaps she should not have come. But once in London she had kept herself busy, seeing the lawyers again, and sending a note by hand to Bethune. She sighed. And tonight, another reception, as Sillitoe's guest. She would be careful. But she needed his advice, and he would know it.

Then a few more days before returning to Cornwall, to the grey house. Waiting.

She thought about the reception that evening; how different it might have been. It was yet another party in honour of the Duke of Wellington's return to England. She had heard of one held at Burlington House to which nearly two thousand guests had been invited, many wearing grotesque costumes, and with behaviour to match. The wine had been consumed in such quantity that it was doubtful many of the guests would have remembered if the Iron Duke had been there or not.

She was tired, and hoped it did not show. Now, as on other such occasions, she always felt as if she were performing, for both of them, no matter what interpretation others might choose to put upon it.

The main door opened and closed in one swift movement, so that she had only a brief glimpse of dark blue carpet and gilt chairs beyond.

Bethune seized her hands and held them to his lips.

'A thousand apologies, Lady Somervell. I only arrived back from Paris two days ago, and when your note came I could not free myself!' He did not release her hands, and studied her with a warmth and affection which she knew was genuine.

She smiled. 'How was Paris?'

He glanced toward a chair and then flicked it with his handkerchief.

'Crowded. Full of uniforms.' He looked at her again. 'Foreign.'

She sat down and turned her ankle to look for the cobweb, but it was gone. She saw his eyes follow the movement, and could understand why he was so attractive to women.

'Did Lady Bethune accompany you?'

He looked away. 'She did. She is here, at the Admiralty, now.'

It explained the back stairs, the secrecy, if there was such a thing any more.

He sat on the chair opposite her, his knees bent and apart, more like the awkward midshipman he had been than a flag officer. It made him seem more human; a friend.

He said, 'I have had little success so far, Lady Somervell.'

She raised her hand. 'Catherine.'

He smiled. 'Catherine. Sir Richard's squadron is not yet assembled at Malta, but when it is, we may expect more news.'

'And if he is allowed to come home, where then? Where next? Are they so ungrateful that they forget what they already owe him? I had hoped to join him, if only briefly, at Malta.' She looked at him until he dropped his eyes. 'It was my promise to him.'

'I remember. The situation in Malta is complicated. More so because there is trouble with the Algerines.' He tried to lighten it. 'Yet again. It is a sensitive time, not least for Sir Richard.'

'If I joined him, at my own expense and not that of the Treasury, unlike so many, it might offend the proprieties . . . marriage and religion . . . is that it?'

'Perhaps. But I have not abandoned the idea. However, there is one excellent piece of news. The frigate *Valkyrie* is to be withdrawn from the Halifax squadron. Adam will find orders waiting for him to return to England. To Plymouth.'

She shook her head, and did not see his eyes move to her hair and neck. 'I do not understand.'

'At times like these, there will be more captains than ships. It is the way of things when the guns are quiet. For how long, who can say? But there is a new frigate building and almost completed at Plymouth. I spoke with the First Lord and have written to the port admiral.'

She still could not grasp that Keen was there, a vice-admiral now. She had been invited to the wedding, which was arranged for October. She heard herself say, almost in a whisper, 'A new command, a fresh beginning.' Sharing it, seeing his face when he received his orders.

She said, 'Thank you for that, Graham. I should have known.'

He shrugged, unsure of himself, she thought. 'Neither Adam nor Richard will tolerate favouritism. So I thought *I* should do something.'

'It will do much to help both of them.' She looked down as he put his hand on hers. 'I am grateful, Graham.'

He pressed her hand very gently. 'If only, Catherine.'

She withdrew it, and faced him. 'As it is, remember? Not as it might have been. There has been damage enough already.' She gave him a folded note. 'My Chelsea address, in case you have forgotten it. If you receive any news, anything at all. . . .' She did not go on.

She tugged off one glove, and held out her hand. 'This is less dusty.'

He kissed it, lingering over it, while she watched his bowed head in silence. What might he think or say if he knew what she felt at this moment? Did he not realise that she lived on dreams and memories, homecomings and the painful farewells always so close in pursuit?

A clock chimed somewhere in the building, in that other, safe and respectable society where men in power could break the rules but still manage to shield their mistresses and keep them separate from their pious wives. But the anger would not come.

Bethune had pulled out another handkerchief. 'Please. Use this. I – I am so sorry I have upset you, Catherine.'

She shook her head and felt a tear splash against her skin. 'It is not you. Don't you understand? I miss him so much . . . each day without him, I die a little more.' She turned away and groped for the door. She had a vague impression of a figure in uniform bowing stiffly outside the room, and Bethune's curt, almost angry, 'Wait for me inside! I'll not be long!'

She did not remember reaching the bottom of the narrow staircase with him, and yet she felt the urgency, the need for Bethune to go back, where some unemployed captain was waiting to plead for a ship. As Richard had once done.

And where his wife would be waiting to hear about *that woman*.

Bethune was holding the carriage door. 'Tonight then, dear Catherine. Fear not, you have many friends.'

She looked past him at the bustling carriages and carters, the sightseers, and the red coats of soldiers off duty.

'Here, perhaps.' She glanced up at the Admiralty's arched entrance and imposing, pillared façade. 'Elsewhere, I think not.'

She climbed into the carriage and leaned back against the sun-warmed leather. She did not look round, but somehow she knew that Bethune was still gazing after her.

Hampton House, on the Thames Embankment, had been chosen as the venue for this latest of many receptions to honour the Duke of Wellington, and, indirectly, his victorious army. Although it was the London residence of Lord Castlereagh, the foreign secretary, it seemed likely that he saw less of it than anyone. Of all the statesmen and government leaders involved in negotiations with the allied powers, he had probably been the most active. The Treaties of Chaumont, followed two months later by the First Peace of Paris, which Castlereagh had settled with Metternich almost unaided, seemed no less a victory than Wellington's.

Catherine rested her hand on a footman's sleeve as she stepped down from the carriage. The air was still and heavy, with dark, brooding clouds broken only occasionally by a glimpse of early stars. There was still thunder in the air, like something physical. Perhaps, as she had thought at the Admiralty, she should not have come. She sighed, and walked slowly along a dark strip of carpet. If there was a downpour, the carpet would take the brunt of it.

The house was spacious, but seemed anonymous, unmemorable, like so many others on similar occasions. Every window glittering, every chandelier alight, strains of music, and a tide of voices audible even from here.

And now the garden, with more candles and coloured lanterns, people standing about in groups, taking advantage of any light breeze from the river. Faces turned to watch her, probably wondering who she would be with. She lifted her chin. At least Sillitoe did not care. People feared him. Needed him.

If Richard were here, he would see it differently, as no less a part of duty than firing a salute. He would make her smile at the absurdity, and the importance of appearance. Like a code, or a secret signal . . . .

'Lady Somervell?'

It was a well-dressed young man, neither servant nor guest.

He bowed. 'Sir Graham Bethune has asked me to escort you to his party, my lady.' He looked at her, and must have seen the unspoken question in her eyes. 'Lord Sillitoe is delayed.'

They returned to the house. People parted to allow them to pass, young women with daring gowns and bold glances, older women in gowns which neither flattered nor suited them. Uniforms of every kind, but not many sea officers; men who tried to catch her eye, then turned to their companions as if they had succeeded.

Toiling amongst them was an army of footmen, sweating in

160

their heavy coats and wigs, and yet able to pass a glass of wine or retrieve an empty one before it was broken or trampled into the carpet.

Bethune came striding to meet her. 'Welcome, Lady Somervell!'

They both smiled, remembering the informality of that dingy ante-room.

She curtsied. 'Sir Graham, how pleasant.'

She slipped her hand through his arm and saw the eyes following them. Surprised, perhaps disappointed that there was no new scandal.

Without turning his head, Bethune murmured, 'Lord Sillitoe is with the Prince Regent. He sent word that he will not be long.'

She glanced at him. 'He trusts you, Graham.'

'I am not certain that trust means the same thing to him.'

She turned, seeing Susanna Mildmay on the arm of a major of the Royal Irish Dragoons. If Avery's lover had seen her, she did not reveal it.

Perhaps Avery had been saved from something. But he would never believe it.

Bethune said, 'The orders for Adam have been sent.' Her fingers tightened on his arm. 'We shall always need dedicated captains. It would have been a waste, otherwise.'

And the other Adam no one knew. The little mermaid . . . . *No one knows.*

There was a loud bang on the floor, and a footman announced yet another prominent participant in that campaign which had ended so dramatically at Toulouse, when Napoleon had abdicated.

She said, 'You are being watched. People will talk.'

Bethune shrugged. 'They will always do that, when there is beauty like yours to envy.'

She did not have to look at him; his sincerity was obvious.

'Did you find that captain a ship?'

She spoke to calm herself, more than anything else. She had seen the group by an open window, Bethune's wife, poised and unsmiling, staring at her.

Bethune said, 'I could do nothing for him, even if I had wanted to.' He glanced at her. 'Do not concern yourself with them, Catherine. They are friends of mine.'

161

Catherine offered her hand. 'Lady Bethune, this is an unexpected pleasure.'

Bethune's wife said, 'That is a lovely gown. It shows your skin to perfection.' She gazed at the diamond pendant between her breasts. 'Yes, to perfection.' She turned away. 'More wine, I think.'

The others seemed affable enough, older officers and their wives, men employed at the Admiralty, or those who had been there when Bethune had first made his mark.

Catherine flicked open her fan to cool her face. Very dull, she thought. If only Sillitoe would arrive. He, at least, was never dull.

Bethune's wife had returned. Close to, and in spite of the expensive gown and jewellery, she was almost plain, and Catherine found herself wondering, not for the first time, how they had met, what had drawn them to one another.

'Something amuses you, Lady Somervell?'

She said, 'One hears all the time that there is a shortage of senior officers, in the navy at least. And yet, when I look around me, all I see are generals, and not a few admirals! Is that not strange?'

'Do you have any children? By your marriage, I mean to say?'

Catherine controlled her anger. *Oh yes, I know exactly what you mean.* 'No. Perhaps it is a blessing.'

Bethune's wife nodded, her lips tight. 'It could seem so. But my husband and I believe that children are the foundation of any marriage. In the navy, it is sometimes all one can cling to.'

Catherine faced her. 'And love, madam, what part does that play?'

Surprisingly, the tight lips folded into a smile. 'I should have thought you could answer that question better than I.' She raised her hand. 'Why, my dear General Lindsay, how well you are looking! You are quite recovered, I hope?'

Catherine sensed, rather than saw, the footman approach with the tray of glasses. She took one, and said, 'Wait,' and drank the contents; it was hock, and almost cool, or so it seemed. She replaced the glass on the tray and took another.

'That was most welcome. Thank you very much.'

162

If the footman had been another Allday, he might almost have winked.

Instead, he murmured, 'It sometimes 'elps, m'lady!'

Bethune was hurrying toward her.

'Catherine, what has happened?' He looked over at his wife, who was speaking to a portly officer with as much animation as if he were her greatest friend.

She answered softly, 'I should have gone when I heard about Sillitoe.'

What was the matter with her? She had dealt with far worse, endured far worse, and triumphed. But not without pain. So why could she not hide it now, treat this with the contempt it deserved? An innocent remark, then? Never . . . .

'I shall speak with her.' He looked down at her hand on his wrist, perhaps remembering how she had removed her glove for him.

'Say nothing. You have too much to lose.' She gazed at him steadily. 'I can understand why Richard cares so much for you. Please, never change!'

There was more banging on the floor, and it was with some reluctance that the din of voices died down.

But it was not a footman this time.

Catherine thought she felt Bethune tense as Admiral Lord Rhodes climbed heavily to the top of a flight of marble stairs.

'Shortly we shall dine, ladies and gentlemen!' Someone gave a loud handclap, and several of the younger women shrieked with laughter.

Rhodes did not respond. 'Just a few words, if I may.'

One of Bethune's friends murmured, 'Oh, for God's sake.'

Rhodes stared around the room, his face shining in the flickering candlelight.

'I may be biased, some claim it is a fault, but I sometimes believe that upon these occasions, and this one in particular, we tend to offer all the laurels to our military friends.' He paused while Susanna Mildmay's major gave a cheer. 'And overlook the achievements of our own service, without which no soldier would put his foot on foreign soil, nor hope to keep it there!'

This time the cheering was genuine.

Catherine glanced at Bethune again. He was unsmiling, his face grim, like a stranger's.

Rhodes was saying '. . . and, as our naval heroes cannot all be here tonight, let us remember one of our most outstanding and gallant sailors, who serves us still!'

Catherine felt her heart leap as Rhodes added, 'Sir Richard Bolitho, Admiral of the Red.' He reached out, beckoning. 'So who better? A hero's lady!'

Bethune exclaimed, 'God damn the man!'

Catherine watched as Belinda Bolitho was guided up onto the stairs. Rhodes started to clap and then others followed, some barely aware of what was happening.

Then the applause died, but the noise of conversation did not resume.

'Catherine, I had no idea!' Bethune took her hand in his. 'Believe me!'

She looked over at Bethune's wife. So poised. Smiling now, unlike those around her.

She said, 'I shall leave. Make my excuses.' It was like a nightmare, when none of the words you needed were ever there, when all you wanted to do was run.

Bethune stared around, his face cold, beyond anger. 'Sillitoe will be here soon, I am certain of it!'

She touched his arm, and looked directly into the eyes of his wife.

'Some people have short memories. I do not.' She curtsied to the others, wanting to scream at them, to spit in their faces. 'They speak of honour, when they know it not.' She turned round, her gown hissing against a pillar.

Bethune said, 'I shall accompany you to your carriage.'

His wife called, 'Graham! We are to go into the great hall!'

Bethune regarded her with contempt. 'You used my name! I had all but forgotten!'

He guided Catherine to the stairway, his hand firmly on her arm.

'I shall take you to your house.'

She felt the damp heat of the night on her face and bared shoulders, and saw, shining blackly, the Thames.

'No.' She forced a smile. 'It seems I am still vulnerable.' She did not give her hand. 'But I have a strength which others can never begin to understand.'

People moved round her and she was aided into the carriage,

while another footman ensured that her gown was clear of the door.

Like this morning . . . how could it be the same day? Bethune stood watching her, his fists bunched against his sides, then, as the horses nudged forward, he turned abruptly and strode back into the house, with something like hatred in his face.

The carriage rattled across the cobbles and Catherine stared out of the window at the passing river. So many views, so many aspects. The house she had just left; Sillitoe's on that great sweep of the river; and her own at Chelsea.

Far across the other side of this same river she saw the first lightning. Like the opening shots of a sea fight, reflected as they were in the dark water.

She gripped her fan until the pain steadied her.

She said aloud, 'God keep you safe, dearest of men.'

Perhaps he would hear her.

Catherine closed the door and went directly to her room. She heard the carriage clattering away, the driver doubtless glad to be going into shelter before the storm began in earnest.

She lighted another stand of candles near the bed; the housekeeper would ordinarily have done it, but it was her night for visiting in Shoreditch with her married sister.

She listened to another pattern of thunder, closer now but not much. Perhaps it might pass over after all. She walked to the window and watched a livid flash of lightning. How quiet the house was; Mrs Tate would be returning at six in the morning to prepare breakfast. As usual.

She pushed one curtain aside as it hung loose across the window, and with her other hand tugged the combs from her hair and tried to calm herself. But all she could see were the stares, the bewilderment, and the hostility. It had always been there, but she had managed to accept, if not ignore it. Richard must never know. He would not rest until he had dealt with the culprits, high or low.

The window shivered as another roll of thunder broke the stillness, and in the lightning she saw the first drops on the glass. Perhaps the sound of rain would make her sleep.

The air quivered again, and she reached out to raise the loose curtain. She saw the river. There would be no boats moving out there tonight.

She glanced at her reflection in the dappled glass, and felt her heart throb with sudden pain. Her thoughts were gone, scattered in a second. It was real. *It was now.*

She turned very slowly, her back to the downpour and flashes of light. The man stood by the half-open door, his face in shadow, only his eyes alive in the flickering candlelight.

He must have entered the house earlier. Had been intent on robbery, perhaps knowing that she and the housekeeper were not expected to return.

She said, 'Damn you, what are you doing here?' From the corner of her eye, she could see the commode where she kept a small carriage pistol. There was a chance. If only . . . .

The man moved suddenly into the circle of candlelight.

'Do not even think of it. I unloaded it, in any case.' He gave a slight bow. 'A precaution, you understand?'

She watched him, one fist clenched, the nails biting into her skin.

He had a level, resonant voice . . . a man of some breeding and education. As he moved closer, she saw that his shirt and breeches were well tailored. He was without shoes. She lifted her chin slightly.

'What have you stolen?'

He pushed the loosened hair from his forehead, and sounded more angry than she might have expected.

'I'm no thief, damn your eyes! It's you I came to see, *my lady!*'

She took two steps away from the window. 'I can call for help . . . .'

He moved so swiftly and lightly that she barely saw it. He was not tall, but he was very strong, as if he were gaining more strength from this violent determination.

He swung her round and pinioned her arms, his voice insistent across her shoulder. 'If you scream, it will be your last!'

'Tell me who you are – what you want . . . .'

He was muttering to himself, and she could smell gin on his breath. She tried not to show alarm, anything which might provoke him further.

'I saw you looking for the curtain cord just now.' He laughed softly, and she felt the noose dragged around her wrists. She struggled to free herself, but he pulled it tighter. Expertly. She had seen Richard's men doing it.

'There now.' He swung her round to face him. 'I have heard it said that you are something of a spitfire, but I shall have to forgo that pleasure.'

She held his gaze, seeing his eyes move over her. It was not possible, but there was something familiar about him.

She said quietly, 'Have we met?'

He laughed.

'Hardly that, my lady. You were too occupied with your *admirer* Bethune.'

She watched him, trying to give nothing away. The captain who had been asking Bethune for a favour, or for a ship.

He was staring at the diamond pendant as if suddenly mesmerised by it: he took it between his finger and thumb and lifted it slightly into the candlelight.

She said, 'Please . . . don't take it. I'll give you money . . . .'

She did not see him move or raise his arm. The blow seemed to snap her head back with such force that she thought her jaw was broken. She was conscious only of falling, down and down, and yet she was not moving.

He gripped her shoulders and shook her, his face inches away from hers.

'Don't you speak like that to me, *you whore!*' He slapped her with his free hand, again and again, and then dragged her upright and flung her on to the bed.

Her head was reeling; there was no pain, only a numbness, a sense of complete helplessness. She felt the bed beneath her, and tasted blood where he had cut her lip. She tried again, a physical striving to hold on to her wits, her understanding. *I must not lose consciousness.*

She felt the mattress yield as he sat heavily near her. She could hear the painful breathing again, and when she opened her eyes she saw him crouched on the edge of the bed, his hands thrust into his groin, moving his head from side to side, speaking to himself.

He turned, and looked at her. 'I lost my ship because of a whore. Then I saw another chance taken away, because of an act of favour.' He gripped her shoulder, the fingers bruising her skin. 'For another Bolitho! Because of another bloody whore!'

167

She cringed, waiting for another blow.

She whispered, 'It's not true. They know nothing about it.'

He was not listening. 'I was to be his flag captain. I suppose you knew that too?'

She shook her head.

What was the matter with him? Was he ill or insane? Nothing made sense.

He lurched up, and she heard him moving about the room, as if driven by something beyond his control.

Then he came back and raised her head and shoulders and wedged a cushion beneath them.

She wanted to shake her head to clear her mind, but some warning sense made her remain quite still. Perhaps he would leave. It was unlikely, but someone might call, even at this hour. She glanced at the window, the rain sheeting down it. She had been standing there, holding the curtain, and he had been here. Watching, waiting.

His shadow fell over her, and she felt him holding the pendant again.

He said, 'They take everything. They lie and deceive. They ruin you.'

'Please leave now, before it's too late.'

He began to drag the gown from her shoulders, unhurriedly and deftly.

She tried to pull away and felt the cord around her wrists tearing at the skin. In a sudden silence, she heard a clasp fall to the floor, and the more insistent tearing of silk.

She said, *'Don't! Please don't!'*

But he rolled her on her side so that she could not see him, his fingers in her hair, twisting it, making her gasp aloud with pain. She felt him kneeling, pressing against her while he tore at her clothing. He was violently aroused; she felt the warm night air across her legs, his hands on her garters, her stockings, and then hard against her skin.

She knew she must hold on, even as she knew what was happening, and that it was hopeless.

She had never been afraid of any man, except her father, but this was different.

She could feel it like a sickness in her stomach, rising up as if to choke her. Not fear; it was sheer terror. It was rape.

168

His hands were everywhere, exploring her, then dragging her round to rid her of the last of her clothing.

She screamed, and felt her head jar back again to the force of the blow.

He was holding her, his fingers insistent, probing, final.

There was a great clap of thunder, a single crack which seemed inside the very room.

She attempted to open her eyes, to move her aching body, but nothing happened. Tiny pictures flashed through her brain, like fragments in a nightmare. The shadow rising over her, the pain, and the sense of choking. Perhaps he had killed her after raping her.

A voice said, 'I have her. Cut the cord, man!'

Another hand holding hers, rough but steady, the blade barely touching her skin as the cord was pulled away.

She groped, and tried to cover her nakedness, but there was a sheet over her body, and no hands explored her thighs, her hair. A damp cloth dabbed at her mouth and cheek; somewhere, miles away, booted feet thudded on the stairs.

She opened her eyes, and realised that his arm was round her naked shoulders, holding her, while he cleaned her torn mouth. Sillitoe did not allow himself to relax even when the life returned to her eyes, and she reached up to touch the cloth.

Over his shoulder, he said, 'Deal with it. You know what to do.'

She struggled, but he held her. A man used to women, she thought, who knew how to restrain them . . . .

He said quietly, 'I know a good doctor nearby.'

She put her hands under the sheet, shaking her head. 'He did not . . . I fought him, but I couldn't . . . .'

They must have used the same stealthy manner of entry. Taking advantage of the thunder, they had come straight to this room. Otherwise. . . . She retched, and he held her until the spasm passed.

She wanted to ask so much, to discover how he had known what had happened, but all she could say was, '*Why?*'

Sillitoe took a silver flask from his pocket and unscrewed it with his teeth.

'This will burn, but it will do you good. Don't touch any of the other bottles and glasses in here, in case he used them.'

169

She choked. It was cognac, but the shock of the raw spirit on her cut mouth had the desired effect.

He said, 'His name is Charles Oliphant, former captain of what is now Sir Richard's flagship, *Frobisher*.' The hooded eyes were expressionless. 'Are you certain there was no congress?'

'Yes. . . . But for you . . . .'

He said harshly, 'He is diseased, the last stages of syphilis. He is dying from it, God damn his rotten soul!'

She thought of the spasms of apparent pain, the wildness and desperation. He had wanted revenge, but against what? She had heard of men who had been so badly infected that they had gone insane before dying. Too late to spare those they had themselves defiled.

She did not realise she had spoken aloud. 'I would have killed myself if he had done that to me.'

Sillitoe held her, recalling those last tense seconds. The lightning holding her naked body like silver, her pinioned arms, the crouching figure forcing her legs apart, oblivious to everything else. A moment later? He pursed his lips. *I would have killed him.*

She was lying against him, in shock, exhaustion, disbelief. Like a very young girl, the self she had described to him when he had gone with her to Whitechapel, after her father had died.

As his men had kicked Oliphant to the floor he had held on to that picture. Her helplessness. And he had wanted her then.

'What will become of him?'

Sillitoe considered it, without anger, and without emotion. It was not his way.

'Lord Rhodes and his clique have gained too much power by rattling other people's skeletons in public. It will be interesting to see what happens when he has a live skeleton of his own in the closet.'

She could feel his breathing; the strength of the arm around her shoulders. She was safe, even with this man whom no one trusted.

Sillitoe heard his carriage returning. Did no one in this street ever question such nocturnal comings and goings?

He looked at her hair spilling across his arm.

The one woman he could never have. The only woman he would never give up.

12

Face to Face

Richard Bolitho awoke from the dream, and for a few lingering moments was confused by the sounds and movements around him. He lay on his back in the cot and stared up into the darkness and waited for the old familiarity to return. He had once believed that he could never forget the feel of a frigate.

Instinct and experience told him that *Halcyon* was changing tack yet again; the thud of bare feet on the damp planking, the crack of unruly canvas and the squeal of blocks spoke for themselves.

He propped himself on one elbow and swallowed hard. *Halcyon*'s officers had invited him to their wardroom for a last meal before landfall. That had been strange, too. After a big cut-down two-decker like *Indomitable*, and the other ships which had flown his flag in recent years, it had all seemed so small, so intimate: Captain Robert Christie, a guest in his own ship to conform with the time-honoured custom, Avery and himself. *Halcyon*'s three lieutenants, sailing master, surgeon and captain of marines had completed the gathering. And the wardroom itself had been packed tight. One midshipman had also been invited, the youngest in the ship; he had proposed the loyal toast, but otherwise remained awed and silent throughout the meal and lively conversation.

It was hard not to make comparisons. This mixture of youthful exuberance and excitement; the way it had once been for him, when he had taken command of his first frigate, *Phalarope*. He winced and rubbed his eyes. All of thirty years ago. How was that possible? The headache would go when he went on deck. Too much wine . . . the rare chance to relax and speak with just a handful of officers who were typical of all those under his command. . . . He peered over the side of the cot and saw that the door into the main cabin was unfastened, swinging this way and that while the hands on deck brought *Halcyon* back under control and laid on a new tack.

There was an early greyness from the stern windows; in no time, it would be bright and hot once again.

Captain Christie knew his ship well. They had logged six hundred miles in less than four days, in spite of contrary winds one minute and the chance of lying becalmed the next. But that was the Mediterranean, no better place for a frigate captain to work his ship and her company until they became one.

He thought of Tyacke, recalling their last words together before he had transferred to *Halcyon*. Tyacke had been opposed to the idea of his visit to Algiers from the first mention of it.

Christie, on the other hand, had confined his comments to the matters of navigation and a final landfall. He, better than most, would be aware of the possible danger to his ship if their reception was hostile, and if injury or death befell his admiral his chances of further advancement would be ruined. A thinking man, and an intelligent one.

Avery had suggested that he might go ashore and make the first contact with the Dey or his advisers. Like Tyacke, he was not convinced that his admiral was fully apprised of the risks.

Bolitho sat upright. More sleep was out of the question. He felt the ship lean over, and imagined the sea boiling around her stem while her sails filled again to the wind.

He was not here to incite another war. But the Dey had to be made to understand that that was where it would end, if the outrages committed by Barbary corsairs and Algerine pirates were allowed and encouraged to continue. In spite of all the treaties and promises, slavery remained a fact. Six years after prohibition, the trade still flourished; according to his Admiralty instructions, between fifty and sixty thousand slaves were being transported each year. And here in the Mediterranean, the Dey of Algiers condoned the seizure of luckless sailors and fishermen, mostly Sicilians and Neapolitans, simply because they were Christians. It could not be tolerated.

He smiled as he heard someone moving about in the other cabin. Allday had known or guessed he was awake.

172

He would be fetching hot water from the galley, for the morning shave which had become so much a part of their rituals and relationship.

He climbed down from the hanging cot and remembered this time to duck his head; even here down aft, *Halcyon* was smaller than *Phalarope* had been. He glanced up at the skylight. It *was* lighter. He touched the locket around his neck and tried to imagine what she was doing. If she woke missing him as he missed her. Or did she . . . .

Allday's shoes creaked on the painted deck covering.

'Fine morning, Sir Richard.' He watched his pale shape in the gloom, waiting to test his mood, like an old Jack smelling the sea changes.

'We shall anchor during the forenoon.' He saw Allday unshutter a lantern for the shave. How many times, he wondered. How many dawns like this?

Allday saw the lantern throw its light across the cabin. The watch on deck would see it. *The admiral's up and about!* Trying to fathom out a reason, when he could stay in his comfortable cot while they were lashing up and stowing their hammocks to provide some room on the crowded messdecks. The watch below had their hammocks slung so close together they were usually touching. You could hear what a man was thinking.

He grinned. They only knew the admiral. They would never know the man.

Bolitho lay back in the chair. 'What are your thoughts today, old friend?'

Allday worked busily on the blade. 'I think it's a risk. Maybe I don't believe it's worth it. Let somebody else take the weight, or get a bloody nose for a change.'

'Is that what you really think?'

No wonder the imposing major-general had not understood. How could he?

'It's what most of the Jacks will be thinking, an' that's no error!'

Bolitho heard the familiar, uneven step directly overhead. Avery was up and dressed already. There would be another argument from him. But so much better than making them seal it up and say nothing. Like the fragment of news Avery had gleaned about *Frobisher*'s previous captain, Oliphant. A

173

man who gambled heavily and usually lost most of it; a womaniser who hardly came up to the high moral standards of his influential cousin, Rhodes. Perhaps the future First Lord had hoped and intended that Oliphant's future might be assured as flag captain? It was like a puzzle where the clues refused to fit, but sooner or later he would hear about it. Some might already be making comparisons with Hugh, his own dead brother, a gambler who had cost their father so dearly in debts and in grief.

He thought, inevitably, of Adam; but he could find small trace of Hugh in him, apart from his quickness with a sword or pistol. And what some called his recklessness. *What they said of me.*

The deck tilted, and the lantern swung giddily until the rudder took command again.

Allday stood with the razor upraised. He had seen the shaft of light pass over Bolitho's injured eye and his attempt to shield it. Like the time when Bryan Ferguson had caught him trying to lift a cask full of ale, and the agony of his old wound had knocked him witless.

Always the pain . . . .

'Done, Sir Richard.' He watched him get to his feet, his body adjusting to the deck and the lively movement. How it had always been, and they were still together. Instead of comfort, it brought him a momentary sadness.

Bolitho faced him, vaguely silhouetted now against the grey light.

'I *know*, old friend. I want that, too.'

Allday watched him return to the sleeping compartment, and then shook his head.

He could not ask Lieutenant Avery to write about that, either. He would save it and tell Unis himself. When it was all over.

'South-east by east, sir! Steady as she goes!'

Bolitho remained on the larboard side of the quarterdeck, watching the land spread away on either bow, almost colourless in a shimmering haze. The wind had dropped and had backed slightly to the north-west, and it had taken them longer to reach their destination than Christie and his sailing master had predicted.

Bolitho tried to ignore the heat across his shoulders, the stabbing reflections from the sea. A grim, inhospitable place, he thought, with deep water close inshore, so that any strange vessel would have to anchor within easy range of the guns of which Major-General Valancy had spoken.

He took a glass from the midshipman of the watch and levelled it with great care on the nearest land. Rough and broken; he could imagine the dust between his teeth, the heat rising from the ground itself.

The ship had probably been under observation since daylight: a man-of-war, unexpected, and more to the point, unaccompanied. It was a risk, but curiosity might overcome the use of direct action.

He touched the locket beneath his damp shirt. If not . . . .

He looked at the men working on deck, some pausing to peer at the land, then at the officers on the quarterdeck as if to gauge their chances. He recalled Allday's words. *What most of the Jacks will be thinking.* He was rarely wrong.

He returned the telescope to the midshipman and caught him staring at him. It would be something worthy of a letter home.

Christie joined him by the rail, his hat tugged down over his eyes to protect them from the blinding glare.

'When we reach the outer anchorage, Sir Richard, what then?'

Bolitho replied, 'We shall fire a salute to the citadel, if we can see it. Then you may anchor.'

Christie nodded doubtfully. 'The wind troubles me, sir. If it veers we shall be on a lee shore.' Unexpectedly, he chuckled. 'It might make a speedy departure difficult!'

Bolitho smiled at him, and did not see a master's mate nudge his companion by the wheel.

'The next move will be theirs.'

Christie touched his hat and moved away. 'Have the gunner lay aft.'

Another madness, some would think. To fire a salute to a lot of murdering heathen.

Avery said, 'Your flag, sir.' He glanced meaningly at the mainmast truck. 'Is it wise?'

'They must see us for what we are, George. If they fire on my flag without provocation, they will know the consequences.

175

I am relying,' he smiled again and touched his arm, '*depending on their curiosity!*'

He thought of Djafou, the harshness of the land, the cruelty of their enemy. Napoleon was beaten; if the allies did not stand together now, there would be another conflict. It could begin here.

The maintopsail filled and boomed and the hull tilted over very slightly. Men scampered to braces and halliards, cupping the wind while it held.

Avery said, 'Perhaps the major-general was misinformed about the guns, sir. Over six hundred, did he say?'

Bolitho turned to the midshipman. 'Give my flag lieutenant your glass.' To Avery he said, 'You will see it was no exaggeration.' He watched Avery's profile as he trained the big signals telescope; the haze had cleared a little, and he would be able to recognise the telltale stone walls of old fortifications, and newer ones along the high ground.

It would take an army to prepare such defences. *An army of slaves.*

Avery said, 'A lot of shipping, sir. One of them must be the vessel they seized, *Galicia.*'

Bolitho turned away. Avery missed nothing, but rarely seemed to write anything down. It was a great pity about the fair Susanna, like his uncle's offer of security and a prosperous future. He had given up both. *For me. For us.*

Ozzard appeared on the gangway and, after a quick, incurious glance at the land, threw something over the side. He was giving up nothing. This was all he had.

Bolitho saw *Halcyon*'s gunner speaking to his selected gun captains. One of them glanced aft, and his expression was as clear as if a voice had shouted it.

A proper salute? For them bastards!

But whoever was watching their slow approach would be waiting for it, the one gesture of peaceful intent when *Halcyon*'s guns would be empty. When she would be at the mercy of those hidden batteries.

'Hand me the glass.' He was surprised by a sudden edge in his voice. 'Mr Simpson, is it not?' He saw the midshipman's alarm give way to astonishment that he should know his name. 'I shall require your shoulder also!'

It was the worst part. Tricks born out of experience.

Deceit. . . . If he was wrong, this youth could be dead within the hour, and yet he was grinning at one of his companions, the midshipman who had called the loyal toast in the wardroom.

He eased the draw of the glass very slowly and saw the outline of the citadel harden into something solid, like a mist clearing away. As marked and described on the chart, and the information on the chart was about all they knew of this place.

And there it was. A tiny patch of scarlet floating above it as if detached. The flag. He measured the distance with his eye. Half an hour, perhaps less if this breeze continued to favour them.

Christie was there again. 'The salute, Sir Richard?'

Bolitho kept his eye on the land. 'Seventeen guns, if you please.'

Christie said nothing. He did not need to. Seventeen guns: an admiral's salute. He would probably be wishing it was a full broadside instead.

Avery watched him, and thought of Catherine; she must have seen him like this when they had been together in the open boat after shipwreck. Jenour had been his flag lieutenant then, and afterwards, Bolitho had given him a command of his own, when all Jenour had really wanted was to remain with his admiral.

Am I so like poor Jenour? I watch his moods, I share his excitement, and often his pain in the aftermath of victory. And now, we are sailing towards an unknown force, a power of evil. He half-smiled. How his father, the clergyman, would have described it.

And yet I feel no fear, nor would I be anywhere else.

He saw Allday standing by the companion way, his arms folded while he looked along the deck, recognising each move, understanding every sheet and halliard, the *bones* of a ship as he had once described them. Briefly their eyes met, and Allday gave a slight nod. Like that very first time, when Avery had known that he was accepted by others of Bolitho's 'little crew'.

He saw Bolitho return the big telescope and say something to the midshipman. He wondered what it had been. Words which had suddenly made the lively midshipman become so serious. So proud.

177

Bolitho turned and looked at him, his hand touching the hilt of the old sword.

'Soon now, George.'

Someone yelped with alarm as a single shot crashed out from the land, the sound lingering long afterwards. Every glass was raised, but nobody moved, as if the whole ship were under a spell.

Then there was a yell. 'They'm dippin' their flag, sir!'

Bolitho gripped the old sword and stared at the land. His eye was painful, and he could not see the distant citadel. But in his mind it was very clear, like an image in a telescope.

Dipping their flag, not to him, but to His Majesty King George the Third. Perhaps they did not know that His Majesty was shut away, insane. Maybe it no longer counted for anything. He wanted to dab his eye, but knew Avery would see and become anxious.

He said, 'Begin the salute, if you please.'

Halcyon's gunner took charge himself, striding to each crew in turn. As the first shot banged out and the gun recoiled inboard on its tackles, he was already moving on to the next, repeating the couplet slowly and deliberately to time each shot.

If I wasn't a gunner I wouldn't be here. 'Number two gun, *fire!*'

Between shots, Bolitho said, 'Now is the time for eyes and ears, George.' To Christie he called, 'There is a guard boat yonder, Captain! Anchor when it suits you.'

Then he looked at the men who were running to their stations for shortening sail, and murmured, 'Well done.'

Allday heard and understood that, too. He was speaking to the ship.

Captain Christie lowered his telescope and said, 'They're sending a boat, sir.'

Bolitho walked across the quarterdeck, feeling the impact of the heat as *Halcyon* swung listlessly to her anchor. Close inshore now, he could see the old fortifications. You could lose an army trying to work around the town from inland, and a fleet would fare little better against the many guns facing the bay.

Allday was watching the approaching boat with obvious

suspicion. It was double-banked, with two men to every oar, more like a galley than a longboat.

'Man the side!'

Avery murmured, 'It is not difficult to imagine what the marines are thinking about, sir.'

Christie said, 'There's an officer of some kind, sir.' He took another quick glance with his telescope and exclaimed, 'A white man, by God!'

Bolitho watched the oncoming galley, graceful, yet somehow sinister.

He said, 'If things go wrong, Captain Christie, you will cut your cable and put to sea. Fight your way out if you must, *but do it*!' He saw the immediate opposition in Christie's face. 'That is an order. You must get word to Malta.'

He moved nearer to the side and saw the oars backing smartly, holding the galley and then turning it towards the frigate's side. No barge crew could do it better.

The boatswain's mates moistened their calls on their tongues and glanced expectantly at the entry port.

'*Pipe!*'

The squeal of calls died away just as suddenly, and Bolitho stepped forward to meet their visitor.

A white man certainly, perhaps with a mixture of other blood. His uniform was remarkably plain, its only decoration being a pair of tarnished epaulettes.

He doffed his cocked hat and gave a slight bow to the assembled officers.

'Your visit is without invitation, but nevertheless I am commanded to offer you welcome.'

He spoke flawless English, with an inflection Bolitho had heard before.

He said, 'I am . . . .'

The man bowed again, and smiled faintly. 'I know of you, sir. *Bo-lye-tho*, His Majesty's admiral of fame and reputation.'

'And whom have I the honour of addressing, sir?'

'I am Captain Martinez, adviser,' again the small smile, 'and friend to Mehmet Pasha, the Governor and Commander-in-Chief in Algiers.'

'Would you care to come to my quarters, Captain Martinez?'

Martinez held up his hat to shade his eyes from the sun.

179

His hair was sleek, and as dark as Bolitho's own, his skin tanned to the colour of leather; there were deep crows' feet around the eyes. He could have been any age from forty to sixty.

He glanced at the guns, their crews standing by with sponges and worms to clean out the barrels after the salute.

'That will not be possible. I have orders to escort you to the citadel myself.' He made an elegant gesture. 'You will find the craft quite comfortable.' His dark eyes flitted around the upper deck. 'An improvement, I would think?'

Captain Christie said sharply, 'I must *protest*, Sir Richard. Once you were in the citadel, we would be powerless to assist you!'

Bolitho shook his head. 'I am ready, Captain Martinez. My aide will accompany me.'

Martinez frowned as Allday joined Avery by the entry port. 'And who is this?'

Bolitho said simply, 'He is always with me. I trust that will suffice?'

'Yes.'

Bolitho touched his hat to the side party: Christie and his lieutenants, so many faces staring at him, anxious and without understanding. Men he did not even know.

Martinez ushered them to the stern of the galley. It was ornate, with gilded carvings, and long shades to provide privacy for the passengers.

Bolitho heard him giving orders to the boat's crew: a different voice again, fluent and without hesitation.

Avery whispered, 'Martinez is no Turk, sir. Spanish, more likely.' He frowned. 'But there's something else . . . .'

Bolitho nodded. 'It is my belief that he learned his English in America, a long time ago.'

Avery looked relieved. 'I agree, sir.'

Allday loosened the cutlass at his side. 'I'd not trust one of 'em!'

Bolitho raised one of the blinds and was surprised to see *Halcyon* lying half a cable away, so fast were the oars rising and dipping.

He recalled Christie's concern, and hoped he would remember to keep his men working as normally as possible. A thousand pairs of eyes were probably watching the ship at

180

this very moment. The first sign of preparation for action would destroy everything. He touched the locket again.

It was suddenly cool and almost dark, and he realised that the galley had entered something like a cave, a seaward entrance to the citadel here, where there were no tides. It made the place almost impregnable.

They were alongside a stone-flagged jetty, and he saw more uniforms, soldiers this time, observing them in silence, fingering their weapons as if unsure.

Most of the muskets were French, but there were a few British ones among them. Demand probably outpaced supply, hence the seizure of the chartered *Galicia*, which had been carrying powder and shot, and perhaps an unlawful cargo of weapons. It was common enough; army quartermasters were like pursers, not averse to some private profit if it was offered without risk to themselves.

He considered Martinez, his role here, and where he had originated. A survivor of the American Revolution, perhaps? Or a mercenary who had changed sides once too often.

He was striding ahead of them now, full of energy and purpose. Bolitho found he could almost smile. A man you would not turn your back on.

He heard Allday breathing heavily on the steps; Martinez probably reminded him of the day when a Spanish sword had cut him down. He was paying for it now.

'Easy, old friend. We can rest a while . . . .'

Allday turned towards him, his brow furrowed with pain.

'I'll keep with you, Cap. . . .' He shook himself, angry because he had almost called him *Cap'n*, as in those other, reckless days.

Doors opened to receive them and Bolitho saw rich rugs hanging from the walls. There was incense too, and the smell of sandalwood.

Martinez paused and held up his hands. 'We must proceed alone, Admiral Bolitho.' He glanced disdainfully at Allday. 'He can rest here.' He moved his dark eyes to Avery. 'There will be refreshment. Companionship, if you wish.' He smiled again. 'It is permitted.'

Bolitho snapped, 'Women? But I thought the Dey was opposed to such behaviour.'

The glance was almost pitying. '*Captives*, Admiral Bolitho.'

Bolitho's eyes moved quickly to an open, unguarded window. Avery did not even blink. He understood.

Instead he said, 'We shall be here, Sir Richard.'

Bolitho said, 'I never doubted it.'

More doors closed behind him and he saw Mehmet Pasha seated at the opposite end of the room. Another surprise; he had expected him to be rotund and soft, someone used to the spoils and rewards of his rank.

But the man he saw was neat and slight, with bright, intelligent eyes and a cruel mouth. The face of a warrior, or a tyrant.

Martinez said, 'Mehmet Pasha speaks no English.' It seemed to amuse him. 'So you will have to trust me.'

Bolitho gave a stiff bow, and said, 'I am here to represent His Britannic Majesty, Excellency. On behalf of our two nations, and the peace we presently enjoy.'

He half-listened to Martinez's guttural translation and was reassured by it. Mehmet Pasha was not listening. He had understood every word he had said.

Bolitho continued, 'The vessel *Galicia* and her cargo were seized by one of your ships. I ask that you release *Galicia*'s master, so that I may arrange a solution.' He looked at the other man calmly. 'And the release of her company.'

Martinez touched his arm and beckoned him to a window. 'Some of them are there, Admiral. They resisted, they were punished.' He watched him curiously. 'Perhaps you would have done the same?'

The corpses lay where they had been thrown, like so much rubbish. As a warning to others, or with total indifference. The pools of dried blood were still apparent by the rotting remains. They had suffered terribly before they had died.

Martinez returned to his position facing his master.

Bolitho had seen more than the decaying corpses; he had caught sight of some of the guns pointing out across the bay. Perhaps Martinez had intended him to see them. Like a threat.

Mehmet Pasha was speaking, his tone unhurried, and without any sort of emotion. Martinez explained, 'The vessel was carrying an unlawful cargo. It was using waters governed only by the Dey, that also was *unlawful*. You are received here as a guest.' His eyes moved between them. 'But you

182

have no authority, no power in these waters. He has spoken.'

'I shall send his words to His Majesty, Captain Martinez. Of his response, I am not privileged to speak.'

Martinez looked less confident, and said quickly, 'Mehmet Pasha commands here, Admiral Bolitho!'

Bolitho watched the other man. Outwardly calm, even contemptuous, but something, an instinct perhaps, gave another impression. He was waiting to hear Bolitho's answer, and not through his 'interpreter'.

'Please tell him,' he pointed suddenly to the window, the blinding edge of the horizon, 'that I command *out there*!'

In the sudden silence he could hear the echo of his own words, a sentence of death if Mehmet Pasha recognised his bluff.

The other man rose slowly from his chair, his face thoughtful. At any moment he would call for the guards. He would have proved nothing.

Martinez said huskily, 'There will be some refreshment, Admiral, for you and your . . . friends.' He bowed as the slight figure walked unhurriedly to another door. Then he murmured, 'You may take the *Galicia* when you depart from here, but her cargo remains.' He glanced at the closed doors. 'You are a very fortunate man, permit me to say!'

Bolitho saw Avery being ushered into the room, the astonishment and relief in his tawny eyes.

'For a moment, Sir Richard . . . .'

Bolitho forced a smile. 'For a *moment*, George. But it was not to be.'

Martinez persisted, 'Your little ship would stand no chance, but you knew that?'

Bolitho shrugged. 'There would be other ships, as many as might be needed, as well you know. The rightful release of *Galicia* is not an understanding, but it may be the beginning of one.'

Martinez said, 'One of my officers will attend your return to the ship, Admiral Bolitho.'

Bolitho understood. He needed to know what his master's reactions truly were, and Bolitho could accept that he had a kind of courage to serve here, for whatever reason. He thought of the rotting remains by the wall. Martinez would need no warning to remind himself of the constant danger he was in.

Avery fell into step beside him, eager to leave, and perhaps unable to accept that they would be allowed to do so.

'I did as you bid me.' He revealed the end of a small telescope inside his coat. 'A good view of the main anchorage from up there.' He glanced round at Bolitho and said, 'There are two frigates at anchor. Fifth-rates, I'd say, no flags but well guarded. Did you *know*, sir?'

'I'm not certain, George.' He shaded his eyes to watch the same galley gliding towards the jetty. Mehmet Pasha wanted them away from here quickly, hence the release of *Galicia*. But two frigates? From where, and to what purpose?

He thought of the erect figure in the ornate chair. The bluff had not been one-sided after all.

Avery saw the galley come to rest, and a bearded officer in a flowing robe stepped ashore to receive them. He could scarcely conceal his relief.

'And we could have stayed a while longer for "refreshment"!'

Allday glared, and just as suddenly grinned at him.

'A ship's biscuit full o' weevils would do me after this damnable place, an' that's no error!'

Bolitho climbed down into the galley and waited for the bright sunshine to greet them again. With luck, they might be clear of Algiers by dusk. Christie would need no encouragement after this.

He touched the locket, and knew Avery was watching him. Later, he might admit it to himself. It had been a very close thing. How close, only Martinez had known at the time.

'*Boat ahoy?*' Sunlight flashed on fixed bayonets along *Halcyon*'s gangway.

Allday cupped his hands. '*Flag!*'

Bolitho stared at the land, and then up at the frigate's side and rigging.

He was back. He smiled at a memory. Lady Luck had been with him.

13

So Private and So Strong

Captain James Tyacke sat in Bolitho's high-backed chair and watched as his admiral strode from the adjoining cabin, Ozzard trotting behind him trying to adjust the clean shirt, without success.

Tyacke felt vaguely uneasy, uncomfortable seated while Bolitho stood. He paced the cabin, describing what he had discovered at Algiers, pausing from time to time to make sure that his round-shouldered secretary was keeping pace, and that he was not thinking and speaking too quickly for the pen.

It was more than that; Tyacke had felt it within an hour of *Halcyon*'s return to the Grand Harbour. An almost boyish eagerness to put his thoughts into motion, to be doing something again. But Tyacke knew him well enough now to see beyond it. There was a brittleness, a need, perhaps, to convince himself as well as those in the far-off Admiralty.

Bolitho's return had been something else Tyacke would remember: order and discipline momentarily forgotten as *Frobisher*'s hands had swarmed into the shrouds and rigging to cheer *Halcyon*'s boat, as it pulled alongside and hooked on to the chains with a flourish.

Tyacke had seen the effect for himself on Bolitho's features when he had climbed aboard, the wild cheering, from men he scarcely knew, echoed by those from *Halcyon* and the other ships which had joined the squadron during the admiral's absence.

Tyacke shifted in the chair. He had shared it, and his anxiety and relief had been forgotten in that very personal moment.

'The Dey knows he has a strong position, James. All those

guns – it would take a fleet, and even then the cost might outweigh the gains.' He paused, and waited for Ozzard to tug his neckcloth into place. 'And had I requested permission to anchor beforehand it would have been refused, or ignored like those of my predecessors.'

Tyacke nodded. It was pointless to remind him of the risk, and the possible consequences. Bolitho might have spoken the words himself. *That was then. This is now.*

Instead he said, 'The two frigates are another matter. If they are to fly the Dey's colours we might take precautions, but if they are corsairs,' he frowned, '*pirates*, it would put a great strain upon our ships.' He glanced at an open gunport. 'We now have seven frigates, including *Halcyon*, under your flag. There are brigs and schooners too, but no match for fifth-rates.' He looked over at the flag lieutenant, who was leaning comfortably across the stern bench. 'If you are sure of it?'

Avery said, 'I am certain, sir.'

Tyacke touched his disfigured face. 'It is said that Spain intended to dispose of some of her men-of-war. It is possible. But this Captain Martinez . . . I know nothing of him, as a slaver or in any other role.'

Bolitho walked to the sloping stern windows. The sun was high overhead, the buildings along the shore sandy yellow in a dusty glare. The weather would change soon, and it would take weeks more for a decision to be made. He felt the old restlessness churning within him. *Everything took so long . . . .*

He turned his back on the others to study a passing dhow, but his mind was still upon the letter which had arrived with the courier brig. *Time.* Catherine would be thinking of it also. The ever-present barrier. But it was not even that; it was the tone of her letter, different in some way. Or was it his own fatigue after the fast passage from Algiers? He knew it was not.

Tyacke said, 'The frigates are there for a reason. At anchor they are useless, no threat to anybody.' He was thinking aloud. Did he suspect something? *That I am being torn apart?*

Suppose Catherine had given up the fight. She was beautiful; she was rich in her own right. She did not need to endure the separations and the anxieties being thrust upon her. Someone else, then? He thought of her last words in that letter.

186

Whatever you do, wherever you are, remember that I love you and only you, nothing could change that.

He would read it again, slowly, when he was alone. But first . . . .

He said, 'Something from your anti-slavery days, James? Make *them* come out to us?'

Tyacke smiled, but not with his eyes. '*Frobisher*, sir.' He glanced around the cabin, less spacious with the eighteen-pounders returned to their ports. 'They will know she is your flagship. After your visit they might be expecting more to join us. They will not want to risk losing the two frigates.' He shrugged. 'And if their presence is proved innocent, we have lost nothing.'

Bolitho walked away from the windows and the glare, pausing to rest one hand on Tyacke's shoulder. 'Another bluff!'

Tyacke glanced at the hand on his shoulder, strong and tanned, an extension to this man's brain and experience. He was not easily moved, and was careful not to show it now.

'It might succeed.' He looked at Avery. 'At least it will get this ship's company working again!'

They laughed, the tension gone.

Bolitho thought of the big room overlooking the battery, and the scattered remnants of the corpses. *I command out there!* He said, 'There are a few of the *Galicia*'s original company, who were allowed to leave with our prize crew. Captain Christie had them separated. Perhaps they could be questioned, now that their safety is assured.' He recalled Christie's own description, the terror, the disbelief and hysteria amongst the few sailors who had been spared the brutality and eventual death meted out to *Galicia*'s master, and others who had 'resisted'.

Avery glanced at the others, sensing the bond, the quiet understanding. He had seen Bolitho take the letter from the despatch bag, and the expression in the grey eyes as he had read through it. It must be like a hand reaching out, a security which few could understand. He thought of Susanna. Still no letter, but then, he had not hoped for one. He gave a rueful smile. Even that was a lie.

Bolitho said, 'I shall send orders to the squadron, so that each captain is left in no doubt of the kind of enemy we are facing.'

Tyacke watched him. *So that you will carry the blame if we are proved wrong.*

He was glad about Christie. *Majestic* had done precious little for anyone else.

The sentry bawled, 'First lieutenant, *sir!*'

Bolitho looked at his secretary. 'You are frowning.'

Yovell smiled gently, behind his small, gold-rimmed spectacles.

'I was asking myself, Sir Richard, why do the marines always shout so loudly?'

Lieutenant Kellett stood in the doorway, his hat beneath his arm. 'Officer-of-the-guard, sir.' He spoke to Tyacke, but his deceptively mild eyes were on Bolitho.

Tyacke took an envelope from him, and then said, 'Major-General Valancy requests the pleasure of your company at his headquarters for dinner.' He looked up from the page in time to see the disappointment and frustration which, in those few seconds, Bolitho had been unable to hide.

Bolitho said only, 'Make the necessary arrangements, James. It may be important.'

Yovell gathered up his papers. It was time to go.

He said, 'I will have these copied at once, Sir Richard. I have a clerk and one of the young gentlemen to assist me.'

Avery said, 'I shall accompany you, Sir Richard.' He saw the unspoken protest, and added, 'The *army*, Sir Richard. They will expect it.'

He left, and Tyacke said, 'You could refuse, sir.'

Bolitho smiled, rather bitterly, he thought. 'People think we are inspired by duty. In truth, we are its slaves!'

Later, with the barge alongside, the crew in their best chequered shirts and tarred hats and Allday poised massively in the sternsheets, the marines and boatswain's mates were ready and waiting. *Frobisher*'s captain and senior lieutenant saw the admiral over the side.

Allday waited for Bolitho to settle himself beside Avery, and then gave the order to cast off.

He saw it in the eyes of the bargemen as they laid back on their looms. Their admiral, who wanted for nothing.

Allday scowled at the bow oarsman as he stowed his boathook.

How could they ever know? At moments like these, *nothing* was all he had.

The day after Bolitho's return to Malta, *Frobisher* weighed anchor and put to sea. At first light two of the frigates, *Huntress* and *Condor*, had also departed with orders to take station outside Algiers, where their presence would be seen and understood.

Bolitho had been on deck to watch them leave, his heart and mind responding to the sight of the two sleek frigates spreading their sails, and leaning obediently to an early breeze. He had wanted more than anything to have an opportunity to know all of his captains, but he was again reminded that time was the enemy. The ships in his new squadron were mostly known to him by name or reputation, even the small brig *Black Swan*, which was to be the flagship's only companion.

After *Frobisher* had cleared the harbour Bolitho went to his quarters, surprised that he felt no trace of fatigue from the previous evening, despite the heavy meal and entertainment by the army. Avery had fallen asleep at the table, but he had not been alone; their hosts seemed to expect it, and made no comment.

He had returned to the ship to find Captain Christie waiting for him in Tyacke's cabin.

A small thing, a fragment of information, but it was all they had. Of the handful of men who had been released with the *Galicia*, one had been the boatswain, a Greek who, because of his captors, had feared for his life more than the others. He had described to Christie how they had been attacked and boarded, as if *Galicia*'s presence had been known to the Algerines. Every man had been robbed and the vessel looted, and two of the seamen had been killed for no apparent reason. The master's son had been aboard; the attackers had known that, too. Unable to obtain information from the wretched master, they had beaten his son, and then nailed him to a crudely fashioned cross, where he had died. There had been other pirate vessels nearby, which had altered course to the east once the attack had been completed. The boatswain had been certain he had heard someone mention Bona. On the chart it was shown as a small port, little more than a segment of a bay, some hundred and fifty miles from Algiers. *Halcyon* had sailed past it only days ago, and Christie was probably cursing his misfortune that he had not known it was being used as a base by Algerine pirates.

Tregidgo, the sailing master, had confined himself to saying that Bona was known to be used by fishermen for shelter, and sometimes for trade. It would be a likely choice for ships waiting to pounce on some unwary merchantman.

A show of force, then. Afterwards, they would meet up with the two frigates outside Algiers. It would be interesting to know what Captain Martinez would have to tell his master about that.

He sat down and thought once more of Catherine's letter. He had read it very carefully when he had returned from his visit to the garrison. With the lantern unshuttered, and the ship silent but for the secret noises in any living hull, he had sensed again the reserve, the unspoken, as if she wanted to protect him from something, like the riots of which she had written earlier.

The roses are at their best just now. I would that they might last for ever.

The summer would soon be over in Cornwall. In his mind, he could see her on the old path, *their* path. Watching the empty horizon. Waiting. Hoping . . . .

Ozzard hurried to the door and opened it, although Bolitho had heard nothing.

It was Tyacke, outwardly relaxed, glad to be at sea again, even if it proved a worthless exercise.

His blue eyes moved quickly to the untouched coffee, and back again to his admiral.

'*Black Swan* is taking up her station ahead of us, sir.'

Bolitho nodded. The brig might remind Tyacke of his old command, but her commander was not of his world. A forceful, determined young officer, he might go far, if fate was kind to him. When the fleet was reduced in strength and numbers, he would be only one of many trying to prosper in the career of his choosing.

Tyacke had commented bluntly, 'A big mouth to match his head, that one!'

Bolitho said, 'When you hear of slavery even here, does it bring the past back to you, James?'

Tyacke squinted against the sudden glare as *Frobisher* altered course very slightly.

'It was different then.' He did not explain. 'But where there's gold you'll find slavers. In the end they'll not be so quick to run – they'll stand and fight. Turks, Arabs, they are always the hardest to control.' He saw Ozzard by the pantry. 'Would you fetch a chart for me? The master knows which one.'

Ozzard almost frowned, but hurried away after glancing at Bolitho.

When the door closed, Tyacke said, 'I am sorry about the trick, sir. I wanted to talk. A ship can be a small market-place where privacy is concerned.'

Bolitho waited. This was the moment.

Tyacke said, 'Years ago, there was a girl in my life. That was before. . . .' He hesitated. 'The Nile. Then I lost her. I never thought I'd ever see her again. Or want to, for that matter.' He looked at his hands and added simply, 'So I lost her.'

Bolitho wanted to tell him that he understood, but if Tyacke lost the will to speak now, it would not return.

'She wrote to me, and I wrote to her, but never posted it.'

Bolitho said nothing. It was the letter he had put in the strongbox before *Indomitable*'s battle, with another of his own addressed to Catherine. *But we both survived that day.*

Tyacke turned to look at the door, expecting Ozzard or someone else to be there.

'Then, in Portsmouth, just before we commissioned, she came to see me.' He spread his hands, as if he still could not understand or believe it. 'I knew we would meet one day.' He looked now at Bolitho, very directly. 'As you must have known, sir.'

Bolitho said, 'I hoped.'

'I had another letter when the courier came. I should have penned a reply, but with you away, and the future uncertain, I thought I would wait.'

'You still care for her, and for what happened. Do you care enough, James?'

'That's it, sir. I don't know. I have no right. . . . I've lived so much apart from ordinary, decent people for so long that I'm not sure any more.'

He thought of the gown Tyacke had carried in his chest, for

191

the girl who had rejected him. The same gown he had given to Catherine.

'Did you ever tell her about the gown, James? The way you told Catherine?'

Tyacke shook his head. 'There are two children to consider, sir.'

Bolitho saw the door edge open. 'Ah, Ozzard. Some cool wine, if you can lay hands on it!'

Ozzard said, 'The master didn't know about a chart, sir.' It sounded like an accusation. Then he hurried away: always alone.

Bolitho said gently, 'When you write, James, tell her. About the gown. Tell her.'

Tyacke touched his scarred face. 'I never see this. I'm always looking out, watching others.'

Ozzard reappeared, without any change of expression. 'This is cool, Sir Richard.'

Bolitho said, 'Let me.' He held the bottle; in the unmoving air it felt almost cold. Ozzard must have stowed it in the bilges somewhere. It was clear Rhenish wine, from that shop in St James's, in her London. Perhaps she had even held this bottle, before it was packed and sent to Portsmouth.

Tyacke watched, his uncertainty, his inability to speak like this before, momentarily forgotten. Unimportant.

He could never have what this man had and shared with his lovely Catherine, who had kissed him on board *Indomitable* that day in Falmouth, to the delight of the assembled ship's company.

He could see it in Bolitho's grey eyes, the way he shaded the damaged eye to study some detail of the label. So private, and yet so strong that he felt like an intruder.

But aloud he said, 'I shall try, sir. When I write.' He stared at the deckhead, and sensed Ozzard placing a glass within reach. 'Then I shall exercise the gun crews, and blow away these Maltese cobwebs!'

Bolitho raised his glass. 'Let Mr Kellett do it, James. He admires you greatly, you know.'

Unexpectedly, Tyacke laughed, the tension draining away. Bolitho regarded him for several seconds; his wine remained untouched.

'I think we shall fight.' He brushed the rebellious lock of

hair from his forehead, and Tyacke saw the livid scar. 'In fact, I am certain of it.' He smiled, the man he must have been when he had first met Catherine.

'I am glad you told me . . . shared it with me, James. Now we are truly of one company.'

Vice-Admiral Sir Graham Bethune got to his feet, startled by the interruption as the doors of his room were thrown open and Sillitoe, followed nervously by a protesting clerk, strode towards him.

Bethune exclaimed, 'My lord, I had no idea. . . .' He tried again, angry with himself that he was so easily disturbed by this man, powerful or not. 'You were not expected!'

Sillitoe stared around and into the adjoining room, and waited for the clerk to withdraw.

He said, 'I am here to see Rhodes. I trust that will present no obstacles?'

Bethune gestured to a chair. 'I shall see what I can do, my lord. At any other time . . . .'

Sillitoe sat down, outwardly calm, unmoved. '*At any other time* I would prefer not to visit this place. However, I shall use the opportunity to mention a matter to you first.'

Bethune watched him across his desk, dressed all in grey, elegant, assured, with droplets of rain on his coat. He must have walked here from some nearby building. For exercise, or to prepare himself for a meeting with Admiral Lord Rhodes, although Bethune had heard no mention of it; his clerk would have told him.

Lean and sleek; a man who rode, walked and fenced to keep his mind and body sharp. Bethune had heard he used a very respectable house not so far from the Admiralty. Was he like that with women, also, habit rather than need?

Sillitoe said, 'I have just had news of the attack on Washington last month, the burning and destruction of government buildings and stores, and the sinking of American ships there.'

Bethune felt suddenly wary, uneasy. The Admiralty had only received the information this morning, on the telegraph from Portsmouth. The first person to be informed had been the Prince Regent; Sillitoe must have been with him at the time.

'I was relieved to know that the attack had been successful.

193

Surprised, too.' He ignored Bethune's resentment, and continued, 'I understand that Captain Adam Bolitho is to be given a new command.'

Bethune swallowed. Sillitoe's change of tack was like the man, swift and unpredictable. 'He should have received his orders, and be returning to England as we speak, my lord. *Valkyrie* was severely damaged. She will be withdrawn from service.'

Sillitoe studied him coolly, his hooded eyes revealing nothing. 'The squadron commodore was killed? Unfortunate, although it would seem, in my experience, that officers chosen of necessity for this or that command are not always the right ones for the task.' He raised his hand. 'There is another matter. One which I would prefer to remain between us only.' He watched Bethune's growing discomfort, but felt no triumph; if anything, he sensed anger and contempt.

He said, 'Lady Somervell. You were there at the reception for the Duke of Wellington. You attended Lady Somervell when I was detained by His Royal Highness.' He leaned forward as if to emphasise his words. 'As I requested of you!'

'She left before your arrival, my lord.'

Sillitoe leaned back, his head resting on the chair.

'Sir Graham, do not take me for a fool. I know all of that. She left because she was angered by remarks made by Lord Rhodes, his arrogance in introducing Lady Bolitho as an honoured guest. It was an insult.'

'The last thing I wanted was for her to be humiliated!'

Sillitoe regarded him coldly. 'She was not. She was angry. Had I been there, I would have spoken out rather forcefully.'

Bethune looked away. 'I know. I was in no position to prevent it.'

Sillitoe smiled. 'Had you known about it beforehand, I would not be sitting here now.' His eyes flashed. 'And neither, sir, would you!'

Bethune said, 'I wrote to Lady Somervell, to explain. But she had gone down to Falmouth. I shall endeavour to . . . .'

Sillitoe said quietly, 'I thought perhaps you had mislaid her London address?' He watched, waiting for some sign, some hint. But there was none. Bethune might deceive his wife, but he doubted even that. He held out his hand and opened it slowly.

'This piece of paper has her address written upon it.' He saw Bethune's eyes widen; there was a certain anxiety as well. He felt his anger returning. 'It was found on a man I now know to be Charles Oliphant, at one time a captain in command of the seventy-four *Frobisher*.'

Bethune stared at it. 'She gave it to me. In case I had any news of Sir Richard. I must have mislaid it when . . . .'

'When Oliphant came crawling to you to beg for a command before the truth became known.'

'I do not understand.' Bethune leaned forward. 'Please tell me, if anything has happened to disturb Lady Somervell, I must know!'

Sillitoe waited, counting the seconds. 'Oliphant was waiting for her in Chelsea. The house was empty; she was alone.' He paused. 'Mainly because she was allowed to proceed there without an escort.' He saw the shots slam home. 'She was attacked, but I had received word about Oliphant. People tell me things. I got to the house in time to prevent . . . .'

'To . . . prevent what, for God's sake?'

Sillitoe said harshly, 'Oliphant, the officer chosen to be Sir Richard's flag captain, is not only a gambler and a thief, he is one so rotten with disease that he wanted only revenge, in the last and only way he knew.'

'Tell me, sir – is she safe?'

Sillitoe felt his muscles slackening. Had Bethune given a single hint of involvement, he would not have trusted himself.

'She is safe. With no thanks to those who might have protected her.'

Bethune persisted, 'And Oliphant?'

'He is in care.' His mouth hardened. 'And under guard. It seems likely he will either die or be driven to the bounds of madness before much longer. If not, he will face a court martial, where the severest penalty will be demanded.' He dabbed his mouth with his handkerchief. 'And deserved!'

Bethune thought of the night when it had happened. Weeks ago; he should have suspected something. But his wife had been against his becoming further involved. *I should have known . . . .*

Sillitoe added, 'I have a few small suggestions to make to Lord Rhodes. I am confident that they will be easy to act upon.'

Bethune looked at the clock. 'I fear Lord Rhodes has a prior engagement, my lord. As I explained . . . .'

Sillitoe said, 'Announce me.'

Bethune repeated wretchedly, 'A prior engagement . . . .'

Sillitoe gave a faint smile. 'I know. With the new inspector-general.' He laid the envelope on his desk. 'Here are my credentials, Sir Graham.'

Bethune stared from him to the buff-coloured envelope with its royal seal.

'I shall attend to it immediately!'

Sillitoe walked to a window and stared down at the wet streets, the bowed heads and shoulders of people hurrying for shelter. He should feel something beyond the contempt and impatience they afforded him. But all he could think about was the woman, naked and bound in that small, quiet house in Chelsea. Holding her, protecting her. Wanting her.

The doors opened again; Rhodes had come himself.

'I must *congratulate* you – I had no idea!' He darted a quick glance at Bethune, and another officer who had followed him. He smiled. 'I think our meeting should be recorded, Sillitoe. Everything out in the open, eh?'

Sillitoe did not return the smile. 'As you wish. There are several items. To begin with, the desertion from duty by your cousin, Captain Oliphant, and the failure to provide medical evidence when you agreed to discharge him. Court-martial offences, you will not dispute. Gambling debts, frequenting premises used by prostitutes and becoming diseased to such an extent that he is all but out of his mind. And an attempted rape.' He balanced lightly on one foot. 'Need I continue, Lord Rhodes?'

Rhodes stared around, barely able to speak. 'I shall not need you, gentlemen.' When the door closed again he exclaimed thickly, 'I did not *know* about the extent of his illness, I swear it! I wanted only the best chance for him to improve his circumstances.'

'Yes. Under Sir Richard Bolitho, the man you tried to humiliate through another.'

'What must I do?'

Sillitoe glanced at the painting of a sea fight, Bethune's old ship. Men fighting and dying. He suppressed his mounting fury. *For arrogant fools like this.*

'Continue as before, my lord, what else might you expect? Your cousin will not disturb you. You have my word on it.' He reached down and took his hat from a chair. 'I am the new inspector-general, not judge and jury.'

Rhodes made a final attempt. 'When I am offered the post of First Lord . . . .'

Sillitoe waited for the doors to open for him.

'Be assured, Rhodes.' He gave a cold smile. 'You will not.'

He walked out of the building, and was suddenly glad of the wet pavings and the cool, damp air on his face. He could walk for a while, and think. He recalled Bethune's wife on the night of the reception when he had arrived late, to find Catherine gone; it was the closest he had ever seen her to elation. A conniving woman, who would use her husband when he believed it was the other way about.

He nodded to himself, and was unaware of the scrutiny of passers-by. That was it. It would be better for Bethune, for all concerned perhaps, if he was sent to a new appointment. Somewhere a long, long way from England.

Grace Ferguson watched as a housemaid placed a vase of freshly cut roses by the window and gave them her approval.

'Saw you cutting them yourself, m'lady. Did my heart good.'

Catherine smiled. 'I hate it when they are finished.' She glanced at the window, to the grey-blue line of the horizon beyond the headland. 'I shall try to make them last, in case . . . .'

Grace busied herself tidying some books which did not require it. She had mentioned her thoughts to her husband several times, but Bryan had insisted that her ladyship was well enough, missing Sir Richard, but otherwise the same.

Grace was not so sure, but Bryan was like that. All men were. Lady Catherine was a lovely woman. But she was a human being, for all that. Of course she missed her lover, as she herself had fretted over Bryan all those years ago when he had been snatched up by the hated press gang, along with John Allday. *And now look at us . . . .*

She thought of Catherine's eventual return from London, the strain and tension in her face. One night Grace had arranged a bath for her, and had seen the bruises on her arm, the healed cut on her neck. She had said nothing, not even to Bryan.

Catherine said, 'Lady Roxby will be coming this afternoon, Grace.'

Lady Roxby she might be to the outside world, but as Richard's sister she could never be anything but Nancy to Catherine. With only the servants for company, she still lived in the big house, with a steward taking care of the estate. Lewis Roxby's presence was still very tangible whenever Catherine had visited, and she thought that Nancy, in her way, was less lonely than herself.

Grace Ferguson faced her, having made up her mind. 'You'm not eating right, m'lady. You'll fade away if you don't eat! When Lady Roxby comes I shall bring some of those little cakes you like, I made them myself.'

'I don't mean to worry you, Grace – we've all had enough of that in the past few years. All I want is to have him here, with me, with us. He's done so much – can't they see that?' She seemed suddenly troubled by the watching portraits. 'I want to be strong, to be patient, like all the others must have been.'

Grace said, 'You'll be strong, m'lady. I knows it.'

Later, when the Roxby carriage rolled on to the cobbles, Catherine saw that there were two visitors. Nancy was accompanied by a young woman with fair hair. She was neatly but plainly dressed, a servant, or perhaps a companion. She heard Grace Ferguson greeting them and then went to the door, hoping her anxiety and lack of sleep would not be as apparent to Nancy as it obviously was to her housekeeper.

Nancy embraced her, and said, 'This is Melwyn. Her mother is a dressmaker and seamstress over in St Austell. I've known her family for years, since I was a child.'

Catherine looked at the girl, for that was all that she was. Serious, almost grave features, but when she smiled she had an elfin prettiness which would soon draw some young man's attention.

'Melwyn has been staying at the house with me for the past few days. She works hard, and is pleasant company. A fine seamstress too, like her mother.' She smiled, and Catherine saw Richard's warmth in it. 'As you have lost your Sophie, I thought you might consider taking her into your service.'

Catherine said, 'Melwyn. What a pretty name.'

Nancy said, 'It means "honey-fair" in the old Cornish tongue.'

Catherine asked quietly, 'Do you want to leave home, Melwyn?'

The girl seemed to consider it. 'I – I think so, m'lady. I need the work.' She looked at one of the portraits, her eyes distant. 'My father went for a soldier, to the West Indies. He died there. I do still think about him.' She turned again. 'Do 'ee know the West Indies, m'lady?'

Nancy said with unusual severity, 'Don't ask so many questions, my girl.'

But Catherine said gently, 'Yes, I know them. Where I found my love again, after losing him.' She felt the girl's shoulder tremble slightly beneath her hand. *As I once was.*

'They do say that you travelled all over the world, m'lady.'

Catherine patted her shoulder and smiled at her. 'That story grows in the telling!'

Nancy watched, quietly satisfied. Melwyn was not like most of the local girls who served the big houses and estates. She was a dainty worker; her fingers could skim over a piece of silk or linen as if enchanted, and she was sometimes withdrawn, and a bit of a dreamer. Like her remarks about her dead father: a sergeant in the Eighty-Seventh Foot, true enough. But a foul-mouthed braggart until the army had recruited him, probably while he was drunk. Perhaps it was safer to be a dreamer.

Catherine said, 'If you want it, Melwyn, I would be happy to employ you.'

The girl smiled, beautifully. 'Oh my dear life! Wait till they hear about *this*.'

Catherine looked away. Her voice was reminiscent of Zenoria, although she was completely different in every other way.

The door opened slightly; Grace, she thought, to tempt her with her little cakes.

But it was Bryan. She kept her hand on the girl's shoulder, feeling the sudden chill in her body in spite of the room's heavy warmth.

'What is it?'

'A letter, m'lady. I told the post boy to wait, in case. . . .'

He looked round, relieved as his wife entered and took the letter from his hand.

Nancy spoke, saying that she would remain, but Catherine did not hear her. She picked up a knife and slit the envelope; her hand was quite steady, and yet she felt as if her whole body was shaking. The girl made to move away but Catherine said, 'No. Stay with me.' She dashed her hand across her face, angry with the sudden tears. The writing was blurred, unfamiliar. She persisted, turning it to the light, hardly daring to draw breath.

Then she said, 'Bryan, have you heard of a ship named the *Saladin*?'

Bryan watched her, seeing the strength and determination, and something more.

'Aye, m'lady. She's a big Indiaman, fine-looking vessel. Put into Falmouth once – John Allday an' me went down to see her.'

'The *Saladin* sails from Plymouth next week.' They were all waiting, listening, but she was speaking to him. To Richard. 'She sails for Naples, but will stop at Malta. . . . Will you come with me, Melwyn?'

Nancy exclaimed, 'Malta? How is it possible?' She was near tears, and also proud that she was still a part of it, of them.

'It has been arranged. By a friend.' She stared around the room, seeing it come to life again. The loneliness, which she had been forced to share with the memory of that night when she had known raw terror, would now be gone.

A friend. She could almost sense Sillitoe's amusement.

14

The Edge of Darkness

Lieutenant George Avery spread the chart across the cabin table and watched as his admiral examined some notes, before leaning over it in the fading light.

In the afternoon the wind had backed again, and had risen unexpectedly. Tyacke had discussed it with Bolitho and they had decided to reef *Frobisher*'s bulging topsails. Men had fought their way out along the treacherous yards, the wind hot across their bodies as if it were from the desert itself.

Now, looking at the well-used chart with its bearings and the hourly calculations of their progress from Malta, Avery saw that the nearest land was about eighty miles away. The little brig *Black Swan* had taken up her station for the night, and Avery had last seen her through a telescope, tossing about under minimum canvas like a gull in distress. A lively command at the best of times, and Avery had wondered what her youthful captain thought of his present position, under the very eyes of the flagship.

He knew that Bolitho was troubled by the lack of contact and knowledge of his various captains. He had heard him speaking to Tyacke about Norton Sackville of the *Black Swan*. Only recently promoted from lieutenant and highly recommended by his previous flag officer, he was in his early twenties, and eager for a chance to distinguish himself. Tyacke had replied to a question, 'Sackville is clever enough, to all accounts.' He had tapped his forehead. 'But a little lacking in wisdom.'

The ship felt quieter now under reefed topsails, but she yawed occasionally to broken water; so different from the days of calm seas and limp canvas.

Bolitho was aware of Avery's scrutiny, and thought he was probably questioning why it was necessary to divide the squadron on the strength of an idea, a rumour.

Perhaps I am driving myself for the wrong reasons?

He felt the deck shiver, the heavy rudder taking the brunt of sea and wind.

Two days and ten hours to reach this position: the port of Bona was lying to the south of them. To tack any nearer overnight would be inviting disaster; a lee shore would offer no hope if they misjudged the final approach.

He had been thinking, too, of *Black Swan*, and had tried to put himself in her captain's place. Sackville's lookouts would be the vital link, would make the first landfall, and Sackville himself might have to decide on a course of action.

He half-listened to the sounds around and above him, the creak of straining rigging and the rebellious crack of loose canvas. Voices too; the thud of hard, bare feet overhead. Allday was on deck, Ozzard was in his pantry. The ship carried them all.

He glanced across the table and winced as the lantern's light swung across his eyes. Surely it was no worse? Or was it another attempt to delude himself?

He remarked, 'I have asked the surgeon to come aft, George.'

So calmly said. Like a man chatting to his second before a duel.

Avery secured the chart, and did not look up. 'He seems a steady enough fellow, Sir Richard. Not like some we've seen.'

They were both thinking of Minchin and his bloody apron.

Avery ventured, 'Does it trouble you much, sir?'

Months ago he would have turned on anyone, no matter how close, who might have suggested a weakness. He would have regretted it instantly, but even that eluded him now.

Almost distantly, he said, 'You have not been what Allday would term a North Sea sailor, George. It has been like that. A mist on the sea's face when the light is too strong, but gone soon afterwards. At other times, I can see things so clearly I find myself searching for reasons, solutions.' He shrugged. 'But I cannot *accept* it. Not now, not yet.'

He heard the bell chime out, the responding pound of feet

202

as the watch on deck was relieved. He had observed it, and done it so many times that he could see it, as if he were up there with them. Only the ship was different.

Avery was troubled by his mood. Resisting, but already resigned . . . .

He said suddenly, 'After this is over, sir – '

Bolitho looked at him and smiled suddenly, the doubts and the strain falling away.

'Then what shall we do, George? What shall we become?' He paused, as if he had heard something.

'You have been a good and loyal friend to us, George. Neither of us will forget.'

He did not need to explain *us*, and Avery was moved by his intensity.

The sentry tapped his musket and called, 'Surgeon, *sir*!'

He said, 'I shall be in my cabin, sir.' Their eyes met. 'You will not be disturbed.' He opened the door for the surgeon and passed him without a glance. Like strangers, even though they shared the same wardroom.

Paul Lefroy, *Frobisher*'s surgeon, was round, even cherubic, more like a country parson than a man used to the grim sights of the orlop deck. He was completely bald but for a narrow garland of grey hair, and his skull was the colour of polished mahogany.

He waited until Bolitho was seated in his high-backed chair and then began the examination, his fingers probing around the injured eye like instruments rather than skin and bone.

Lefroy said, 'I had occasion to meet a young colleague who once served under you. You sponsored him, I believe, to the College of Surgeons in London.'

Bolitho stared at the light until his vision blurred. 'Philip Beauclerk. Yes, he was in *Indomitable* with me. A fine and promising surgeon.' But all he could remember was Beauclerk's eyes, the palest he had ever seen.

Lefroy wiped his hands on a cloth. 'We spoke of you, Sir Richard, as doctors will.' He beamed, the parson again. '*Must*, if we are to improve the lot of our people. He spoke, too, of the great man, Sir Piers Blachford.'

Another memory. Blachford and the rum-sodden Minchin, working as one while *Hyperion* gave up the fight and was starting to sink under them.

Bolitho said, quietly, 'He thinks nothing more can be done.'

Lefroy nodded slowly, his round figure tilted, untroubled by the angle of the deck.

'For someone in a position of retirement, free of the demands, to say nothing of the risks which beset every sailor, this damage might be contained for years.' He gazed around the cabin, the heavy guns straining at their breeching ropes while the ship heeled over. 'This is no such position, Sir Richard, and I think you know it well.'

Ozzard had appeared and murmured, 'Captain Tyacke is here, Sir Richard.' He shot a wary glance at the surgeon.

'Tell the captain I am ready.'

Lefroy was closing his battered bag. 'I am sorry, Sir Richard. You could attend another surgeon, much better qualified, were you not at sea.'

As he reached the door he paused and said, 'The drops you are using are excellent in their way, but. . . .' He bowed himself out, his baldness shining in the swinging lanterns.

His last word lingered like an echo in the air. As if someone had just slammed a great door. Like something final.

Tyacke strode in, his head bent to avoid the curving deckhead beams. He had seen the surgeon, but they had not spoken.

He did not ask Bolitho about it. He had seen enough of pain to read it now in the grey eyes watching him.

He recalled the words. *Now we are truly of one company*. He said, 'Now, concerning tomorrow, Sir Richard . . . .'

Bolitho leaned over the chart. *The lifeline*. The rest could wait.

Allday stood quite still, his razor reflecting the lantern light. Bolitho was leaning forward in the chair, his head on one side as if he had heard some new sound. But there was nothing, only a few muffled noises, and a sense of heavy stillness.

'The wind?'

Allday nodded. 'Aye, it's left us. Like the last time, an' the times afore that.'

He was talking to give himself time; he had no need to remind Bolitho of the moods and the madness of the weather. He knew them all, as he could feel the ship around him, her strength and her weakness. It was his life.

It was none of those things now. Bolitho had suddenly

gripped the arms of the chair and dragged himself upright, his mind wholly intent upon the ship, and the wind which had deserted them.

Allday glanced at the razor; he had been moving it downwards for the first stroke of the morning shave. He had barely a second to twist it away from Bolitho's face before its well-stropped edge laid open his cheek to the bone. Bolitho had not seen it.

Allday tried to relax the relentless grip of dread in his stomach. *He had not been able to see it.*

Bolitho was looking keenly into his face, his eyes clear in the light from the lantern.

'What is it, old friend? The pain?'

Allday waited for him to lie back again, unable to look at him.

'It comes an' goes, Sir Richard.'

He began to shave him with great care. *A close thing.*

There were voices now, loud and angry. Bolitho recognised Tyacke's, the other was Pennington, the second lieutenant. Then there was silence again, the ship holding her breath, creaking and clattering as she began to drift, her sails flat against the stays.

Tyacke hesitated by the door. 'I am sorry to disturb you, Sir Richard.'

Allday was mopping the shaved skin, relieved at the captain's interruption.

'The wind, James – is that it? We were warned we might expect it.'

Tyacke moved into the light. His shirt was torn, and streaked with tar.

He said, 'No, sir. We've lost *Black Swan.*' He was unable to contain his anger. 'I should have known! I ought to have picked the morning watch lookouts myself.'

Bolitho said, 'You command, James. You cannot carry every man's burden all of the time.'

Tyacke stared down at him. '*Black Swan* knows full well that she must be in company with the Flag at first light. A lookout with half an eye should have seen that she had gone from her station – at the first hint of dawn it should have been clear enough.' He waved curtly toward the stern windows, now grey-blue in the strengthening light. '*Gone!* And the fool only just reported it!'

Bolitho stood up, and felt the listless movement of the deck. Tyacke must have gone aloft himself to be certain, and vented his anger on Pennington when he had found the horizon empty, just as he was now blaming himself for another's carelessness.

He said, 'The wind will return, perhaps sooner than we think. Closer inshore, there could still be enough for the brig.'

He knew what Tyacke believed. That *Black Swan*'s eager commander had used the darkness to tack nearer to the land, to be the first to discover any shipping there and still return in time to resume his position for making and receiving signals. The dying wind had changed that dramatically. *Black Swan* was now without support, and *Frobisher* would be unable to see her, even if she required help.

The sentry's voice broke into their thoughts.

'First lieutenant, *sir*!'

Kellett stepped into the cabin, his face composed, probably prepared for this by the humiliated Pennington.

'Sir?'

Tyacke spoke instead to his admiral. 'I thought we should put down the boats and take the ship in tow, keep her head round, and cut the drift as much as possible.'

Bolitho said, 'I agree. God knows I've done it often enough myself.'

He saw Kellett relax slightly as Tyacke said, 'Detail the boats' crews yourself, Mr Kellett. Two-hour spells at the oars, more than enough when the sun finds them. Put the spare hands aloft to dampen the sails. I don't want to lose a cupful of wind.' As Kellett turned away, he added, 'It was not your fault. Sometimes we all expect too much.'

Kellett's mild eyes widened very slightly. 'I shall inform the second lieutenant, sir.'

Bolitho waved Ozzard aside and loosened his shirt. 'Not yet.'

He heard the trill of calls and the boatswain's harsh voice as he urged more men to the boat-hoisting tackles. Sam Gilpin was a boatswain of the old school, quick with an oath or one of his fists, but he rarely took a man aft for punishment if either of the options would suffice.

'Visibility?'

Tyacke dragged his mind back to the present. 'Heavy mist

inshore, sir. We are no more than ten miles out, but we're useless like this.' He glared around, as if the cabin were restricting him like a cage. 'I just hope young Sackville keeps his lust for glory on the leash!' Then he seemed to relent. 'That was unfair. I scarce know the fellow.'

Avery had arrived, stifling a huge yawn as he listened to what was being said, and to the urgent noises overhead.

He glanced quickly at Allday. 'Trouble?'

Allday shrugged. 'The wind's gone, so has *Black Swan*.' He wondered if he should tell him what had nearly happened with the razor, and decided against it.

Tyacke left the cabin and was heard calling out instructions to his lieutenants, and there was a responding creak of tackles as the first boats were hoisted up and over the gangways, ready to be lowered alongside. Avery imagined them all, all the faces he was coming to know, and the qualities behind them. Tregidgo the sailing master, the true professional, waiting with his mates by the unmoving helm, ready for the first hint of steerage way. Sam Gilpin the boatswain, whose voice was never silent for long: another old Jack, every finger a marlinspike, as he had heard Allday describe him. Kellett, always outwardly calm and unruffled; he would make a good captain if he ever got the chance. And all the midshipmen; *Frobisher* carried nine of them, with the usual contrast between the first-voyage squeakers, aged about twelve, to the more serious-minded ones who fretted on the threshold of that first, unimaginable step, to the rank of lieutenant. A step so vast, from cramped berth to wardroom, that it was almost impossible to imagine, except for those with influence or favour.

A ship's company, then, no better or worse than most; but this was a flagship, and the man whose flag flew from the main truck was a legend. That made the true difference.

He heard men calling from the upper yards and could see them, too, in his mind, hauling up bucket after bucket of sea water to pour over each limp sail. The salt would harden the canvas, so that when the wind found them again they would not lose even what Tyacke had called a cupful. He had seen the marine sentry grinning to himself at that, enjoying what he heard. He was not involved.

Ozzard had brought coffee, resigned, Avery thought, to his admiral's refusal to allow him to fetch his dress coat and hat.

Avery sipped the coffee. It was strong, and very good. One would never know Ozzard in a thousand years, but he could spirit food and drink out of thin air like a wizard.

He glanced at the discarded dress coat. Perhaps Bolitho needed, or wanted, to remain the ordinary man for a moment longer. He smiled privately. He could never be ordinary, no matter what he tried . . . .

Bolitho was waiting for Ozzard to refill his cup, unconsciously touching the locket against his skin, beneath the open shirt. Avery saw it, and was moved by what he saw. So far apart, and yet so close. It made him think of Susanna. It was hopeless, and yet he knew that if she merely crooked her finger, he would be her willing slave.

Bolitho said, 'I shall go on deck. A walk, George, before we begin to earn our keep?'

Ozzard almost ran for the admiral's coat, but let it fall again as Bolitho strode past him to the screen door.

He muttered quietly, 'What's the use?'

Allday looked over at the old sword on its rack. 'Use, matey? Only God knows that, an' he won't tell it to any poor Jack!'

He thought Ozzard unusually troubled. 'But how does he know, John? How *can* he know?'

Allday touched the sword. It was so unlike Ozzard to ask an opinion, let alone call him by name, that he was uneasy.

'I've never known him to be wrong.' He forced a grin. ''Cept in his choice of servants, that is!'

Ozzard snapped something and hurried away, pausing only to look back yet again at the discarded coat.

On the broad quarterdeck the air was almost unmoving; the seamen's bodies shone with sweat, and the salt water dripping from the limp sails pattered over them like tropical rain.

Bolitho walked back and forth, his feet avoiding the various ringbolts and gun tackles without conscious effort. How many times? How many places? Lieutenants touched their hats when they realised it was their admiral amongst them, and a nervous midshipman almost turned the half-hour glass a fraction too soon, until a scowl from a master's mate checked him.

Bolitho took a telescope from the signals midshipman, and, as he trained it along the ship and beyond the bows, he said casually, 'It will soon be time for your examination for lieutenant, Mr Singleton. I trust you are well acquainted with the signals procedure of our new allies?'

He did not see the youth's pleasure at being noticed and spoken to, and barely heard his stammered reply.

The boats were standing ahead of the ship, the tow lines rising at regular intervals to the pull of the oars. They were the launch and two cutters; any more would have caused unnecessary confusion. He saw a lieutenant in the leading boat, midshipmen in the others. Some might use a starter on their oarsmen to get better results, but he guessed that Tyacke's influence had made itself felt even in that.

And there was the shore. Africa, solid and hostile; no landsmen would recognise it on the chart.

'I can see the headland, Mr Tregidgo. A fair landfall, despite all else, eh?'

He heard the master's calm agreement. A far cry from being a Cousin Jack, but Cornwall was still clear in his voice. A fragment of home. He moved the glass slowly, careful to avoid the reflections from the sea. The haze or mist still shrouded the division between land and water; you could hide a fleet in it. *Frobisher* had probably been sighted, and her becalmed impotence noted with satisfaction. If, indeed, there was anybody to care.

He felt a nerve jump as a raucous squawk shattered the silence and expanded into a drawn-out crowing.

It was the ship's cockerel, penned in its coop. He heard Kellett saying something to Tyacke, and when he turned Bolitho saw the first lieutenant staring at the sea with obvious bewilderment. Tregidgo was actually grinning. He looked over at Bolitho and called, 'Old Jonas is never wrong, zur! Always crows when 'e 'ears a wind comin'!'

They all looked up as a voice shouted, 'Deck there! Gunfire to the south'rd!'

Bolitho strode to the nettings and stared at the empty sea. Like polished glass. No wind, then: Jonas had been mistaken.

Then he heard it. Sharp and irregular, with an occasional echo of a larger gun.

Avery was saying, 'I don't see how they can manoeuvre and fight without wind!'

Bolitho handed the telescope to the signals midshipman. He

recognised the sound of *Black Swan*'s small guns; the other was something much heavier, able to lie off and make every shot tell.

He said, 'Chebecks, George. Magnificent sailers – properly handled, they can outrun anything but a fast frigate.' He knew the others had fallen silent, and were pressing closer to hear his words. 'And when there is little wind they can use their sweeps to work around an enemy until they have discovered a blind spot.' A loud bang echoed across the water again. 'Like that.'

Kellett exclaimed, 'And here comes the wind, by God!'

It crossed the sea, ruffling it like silk, and then, as it found the ship, Bolitho felt the sails come alive again, heard the attendant clatter of blocks and rigging, and men calling to one another as the helm gave a shiver and then had to be restrained.

Tyacke said sharply, 'Recall the boats, Mr Kellett!' He saw Bolitho, and paused. 'Sir?'

'Recover the crews, James. We can tow the boats. It might give us time.'

He did not explain, but Avery saw in Tyacke's eyes that he understood, and was sharing each move with Bolitho, each thought, as if they were one.

Bolitho said, 'Take your glass, Mr Singleton, and go aloft.' He restrained the midshipman, gripping his shoulder. He felt the wind pressing his damp shirt against his skin. 'Tell me what you *see*, Mr Singleton, not what I might wish to hear.' He squeezed the young shoulder. 'You are my eyes today.'

Frobisher had reached her boats, and men were already swarming up the tumblehome to help warp them aft, to be secured astern.

Bolitho said, 'When you are ready, Captain Tyacke.' It was abrupt, and strangely formal. 'You may beat to quarters and clear for action. Have the gunner open the arms chests. I want each man ready!'

Tyacke touched his hat, equally formal. 'Aye, aye, sir!'

Bolitho felt the deck tilt very slightly, and heard the top-sails and topgallants bang noisily until they were filled like breastplates.

'Sou'east by east, sir! Full an' bye!'

The master looked at Bolitho, the question unspoken.

Bolitho said, 'Hold her as she is. As close as we dare. There may be no time to wear ship!'

The rest was lost in the staccato rattle of drums and the immediate rush of feet as seamen and marines stampeded to their stations, to clear the ship from bow to stern. To make her a floating battery, a fortress under sail.

'Ozzard's here, sir.'

Bolitho held out his arms and slipped into the heavy coat with its epaulettes and bright stars. How she had laughed when he had forgotten to tell her of the promotion. *My admiral of England* . . . .

He tugged on his hat, hoping it would shade the damaged eye.

'You may go below, Ozzard.'

Ozzard pouted stubbornly. 'Because of those pirates?' He sounded outraged that he should hide from such rabble.

Bolitho glanced up as the midshipman yelled, 'Six vessels on starboard bow, sir!' A slight hesitation, perhaps remembering his admiral's words. '*Black Swan* is all but dismasted!'

Tyacke swore softly. 'Stood no chance!' Thinking of his own *Larne*, how it might have been.

Bolitho snatched another glass. The mist had almost gone and the chebecks were clearly silhouetted against the dull land mass beyond. The same raked hulls he remembered, but more powerful now, with a square-rigged mainmast to give them additional power and speed; he could see the banks of oars churning at the water, the din and confusion quite silent in the lens. They were on a lee shore, and would need their long sweeps to regain sea room. One was still firing her heavy cannon, and Bolitho watched, his heart cold as more wreckage exploded from the helpless brig.

He said, 'Chain shot, Captain Tyacke.' He saw him nod, could sense his anguish as he urged his ship through the water.

'Get the royals on her, Mr Kellett! Put more hands aloft!'

Tyacke must have been right about *Black Swan*'s young commander. Using the darkness to break free for a moment from the flagship's apron strings, to see and act for himself. It was common enough. *I did it myself in* Sparrow, *a lifetime ago*. He lowered the glass as more smoke and sparks burst from the embattled brig. Sackville was paying for it now. But

211

here and there a gun still fired, and splashes fell amongst the chebecks, when before they had been unable to bear.

He felt the sudden fury rising inside him. Captain Martinez must have been well aware of these Algerine pirates and what they were doing. Like the two frigates they had seen from the citadel; they knew. But, for him, it was like being in the dark.

Tyacke said, 'I can open fire in half an hour, sir. Extreme range, but any longer and I think we'll lose them.'

'Very well, James. If we cannot take *Black Swan* in tow, we'll lift off her people in our boats.' He glanced aft, and saw them still towing astern.

Kellett shouted, 'Two of the chebecks are coming for us, sir,' incredulous that such frail-looking craft would dare to challenge a powerful two-decker.

There was a dull report, and then a loud slap as a ball punched a brown-rimmed hole in the foretopsail.

Bolitho said quietly, 'They can still bite, Mr Kellett.'

'Stand by to alter course to larboard!' Tyacke sounded very calm, totally absorbed. 'Alter course three points. That should do it.' He looked at Kellett. 'Pass the word to the starboard battery, and see that the lower gundeck understands what we are about!'

The helmsmen leaned back on their spokes and watched the driver flapping slightly, spilling wind while *Frobisher* answered the rudder.

'East-south-east, sir! Steady she goes!'

The two chebecks changed bearing as *Frobisher* edged around, every gun on the starboard side run out and ready. To most of *Frobisher*'s men, it would seem sheer madness to challenge a ship of seventy-four guns, and some of the crews were leaning through the open ports to jeer.

But the chebecks were moving faster now, and were using their square and lateen rigged sails to stand closer into the wind than any other vessel.

Tyacke had realised the danger; perhaps he had faced it before, when dealing with Arab slavers. If they could work around *Frobisher* and attack her from astern, any lucky shot could leave her rudderless.

He shouted, 'Full elevation, Mr Kellett! We can't wait any longer!'

His eyes found Bolitho across the crouching crews. He could have spoken it aloud. *We dare not.*

As if to give an edge to his words, another ball slammed into the lower hull. Through the telescope Bolitho saw several robed figures leaping up and down on the nearest chebeck's ramlike beakhead in what appeared to be a wild dance, beyond fear and beyond doubt. There was silence on the gundeck now, and only a handspike moving here and there to adjust the elevation or the training of each weapon.

'*As you bear!*' The pause seemed endless, each gun captain bent behind his port, trigger-line taut, his crew waiting to sponge and reload with the chain shot, hated almost as much by those who used it as by those who were its target.

The two chebecks were almost bows-on, and another flash of gunfire came from one of them, the ball smashing through the hammocks in the nettings and hurling two seamen to the deck, their blood like tar on the pale planking.

'*Fire!*'

Even the sound of the broadside was different, and as each gun threw itself inboard on its tackles it was possible to hear the chain shot, moaning and screaming like the fury of a hurricane. Bolitho imagined he could see its passage over the water, the sea's face torn into sharp fins as the whirling shot blasted above it.

The nearest chebeck seemed to stagger, as if it had struck a reef. The brightly-coloured sails were ripped away in the wind, spars, bulwarks, and men were smashed down in one bloody tangle. But a few figures still leapt about by the big cannon, and even when the chebeck began to heel over they were still there, waving their weapons and screaming defiance at their destroyer.

Tyacke lowered his glass. 'The others are coming about, sir! They intend to attack from the opposite side!' He gestured to Kellett. 'Larboard battery, run out. Those bastards are closely bunched. We'll give them a tune to dance to!'

But Bolitho was watching the first chebeck; somehow it had survived the broadside, and if anything had increased speed, even as her consort was torn apart.

Avery cleared his throat. 'Straight for us, sir! It's madness!'

Bolitho touched the old sword at his hip; he had not recalled Allday clipping it into place.

'They don't think so, George.'

'*Fire!*' The hull shook violently as the two larboard gundecks fired almost simultaneously. The range was down to half a mile. Not what British sailors had become used to, with an enemy hard alongside, and ships pounding one another into submission until one of the flags was cut down.

A single chebeck had survived the devastating broadside, and, like the first, showed no intention of retreating, or pausing to rescue the survivors who floundered amongst the flotsam and the drifting carnage.

'Marines, *stand to*!'

Tyacke turned toward Bolitho, his scarred face strangely calm. 'No time to reload, sir.' He drew his sword, and then raised his voice, so that men who were snatching up cutlasses and boarding axes faltered and stared at him. 'They intend to board us, lads! If one man, *just one man*, can get below, it will bring disaster!' He saw the uncertainty, and the doubt, especially on the more seasoned faces. 'This will be their last fight. Let it not be yours.' He looked at the dark blood where the two wounded seamen had been dragged away. 'So stand together!'

The marines were already crouching at the nettings, muskets trained, bayonets like ice in the sunlight. A seaman stood in the shrouds and took aim with his musket. Then he fell, his mouth wide in a final cry as he hit the water.

Frobisher's seamen abandoned their guns and clambered up to repel boarders.

Bolitho saw it all with an immense detachment, as if he were someone else, an onlooker, untouched by the sudden bang of muskets, and a deep baying chorus as the first chebeck surged alongside, sweeps splintering in the impact, men falling and yelling as the marines fired down amongst them at a few yards' range. They had no chance, but, as that onlooker, Bolitho felt no surprise when figures swarmed up and over the gangway, hacking with their curved swords, some still firing muskets and pistols while they clung to the chains and then the shrouds, driven onward by something even the stabbing bayonets could not repulse.

Avery drew his sword, and Allday moved closer to Bolitho, his cutlass resting on his shoulder, his eyes on the surging, swaying mass. But the squads of scarlet-coated marines were gaining the upper hand, their boots stamping in unison as, with bayonets parrying and pointing, they formed a barrier between the Algerines and the quarterdeck.

One marine slipped on the bloody deck and lost his balance. As though it were a scene in a nightmare, Bolitho saw a bearded giant whose robes were already soaked in blood swing his blade like a scythe, and heard the cries of outrage and horror as the marine's head rolled down amongst the litter of dead and wounded.

Lieutenant Pennington, a deep cut on his forehead, lunged at the giant but had his sword torn from his hand, and would have shared the marine's hideous death but for the diversion his admiral provided.

The giant, feet apart, raised his sword and held it in both hands, his eyes fixed on Bolitho, as if nothing and no one else existed. He must have been wounded several times; there was blood pouring unheeded down his thigh. His teeth were bared, in hatred or agony it was impossible to tell, but to Bolitho he appeared to be grinning, his teeth like fangs against his black beard.

Allday rasped, '*Leave it*, Sir Richard!' and bounded forward, but the great sword swung again. Sparks flew from the steel as the two blades clanged together, and Allday reeled across one of the guns.

Voices came from far away. '*Kill that bastard, Sergeant Bazely!*'

The crack of the musket was deafening, and Bolitho felt the sting of powder in his eyes as the marine fired, even as the sword rose again above his attacker's head.

When he looked again, the bearded giant had fallen among the others, a bayonet putting an end to his last, incredible strength. Weapons were being thrown down, but not many of the Algerines had survived, or perhaps they had been given no chance to surrender.

Tyacke was beside him, his hat gone, his sword still gripped in his hand. There was blood on its blade. He did not speak immediately, allowing the fury and the madness of the fight to release him.

'We lost a dozen men, Sir Richard, maybe a couple more. They're taking the wounded below . . . we'll know about them soon enough, I daresay.'

Bolitho stared up at the sails: unmoving again. Becalmed, with the remaining chebecks drifting alongside, crewed only by the dead.

Tyacke was still speaking. 'I've sent the boats for *Black Swan*'s people. We're safe enough here.' Then, with sudden venom, 'I'll be glad to see the last of this hellish place!'

Avery had joined them, and was gazing at the dead pirate as if he expected to see that inhuman strength rise up again. He said, 'It was you he came for, Sir Richard.'

'I doubt that, George.' He turned suddenly. 'Sergeant Bazely saved me just now. He must have been the only one left with a loaded musket!' He touched his sword, without knowing why. 'Where is he? I would like to thank him.'

Bazely exclaimed, 'I'm *here*, Sir Richard. With you.' He was grinning. 'Where a good Royal Marine belongs!'

Bolitho turned once more, and then covered his undamaged eye with his hand. There was no image, sharp or misty. There was nothing, only darkness.

15

The Next Horizon

Catherine Somervell gripped a vibrating stay and felt her cloak lift around her legs in the gusty wind. She had become used to ships and had always respected the sea, even before she had learned so much about its moods and hidden cruelties from the man she loved.

Grace and Bryan Ferguson had been openly despairing about her decision to take passage to Malta, and even Nancy, with the sea in her blood, had been concerned.

Catherine had travelled in all kinds of vessel, from humble merchantman to the ill-fated *Golden Plover*. None could compare with the East India Company's lordly and powerful *Saladin*. Even in the unreliable waters of the Bay of Biscay, *Saladin*, as large and imposing as any naval three-decker, had made the voyage more of an adventure than a discomfort.

She pulled the cloak tighter around her; it was the faded boatcloak of Richard's which she used for her cliff walks, doubly welcome now, like an old friend.

It was strange that she had hardly seen or spoken with Sillitoe since they had departed from Plymouth five days ago. There were a dozen other passengers, mostly merchants and their wives, privileged to be in this ship which was sailing to Naples to restore the severed links between Britain and the Neapolitan government after the escape of Naples from French rule, and the bloody recriminations which had followed it.

Strange, too, that Sillitoe should hold the same important role as her late husband, Viscount Somervell, although his appointment had been by the King when he had been in the early stages of madness. Whatever else the Prince Regent might appear to the public, he was genuinely determined to recoup the losses in trade brought about by the years of war with France.

She heard some sailors laughing together as they ran to deal with some rebellious cordage. Richard had told her a great deal about 'John Company' and its ships. Carrying trade to the ends of the earth, and when their flag was hoisted, it rarely came down. Well-manned and armed to full capacity, the company's ships were a match for any pirate or privateer, and had won several battles with enemy men-of-war. Richard had spoken of them with a kind of wistfulness, if not envy.

'Their men are well-paid and cared for, and carry a protection against impressment. They are true seamen, not held against their will. Perhaps when all this is over, Adam will be in a position to see those conditions in his navy. Think of that . . . .'

Sillitoe had touched only briefly upon his actual business in Naples, except to confirm that he was going to sign a new treaty and an agreement on trade. Nelson was still remembered there for his part in crushing the rebels and their French protectors, although Sillitoe had referred to the Neapolitans as 'fiddlers, poets, whores and scoundrels'. He had smiled at her surprise, and had added gently, 'Nelson's appraisal, not mine.'

She watched the gulls cutting back and forth across the ship's high stern and thought of the open boat, and their survival. *Tonight those gulls will sleep in Africa.* And the day after tomorrow, *Saladin* would anchor at Gibraltar. There might even be news of Richard and his ships.

One evening she and Sillitoe had supped alone, the other passengers apparently too sickened by Biscay. Even her new companion and maid, Melwyn, had crept quietly into her cot.

While they had sat listening to the sea against the hull and the muffled voices of men on deck, Sillitoe had said, 'I fear you cannot remain in Malta for long. When this ship returns from Naples, you must leave with her.' He had given that fleeting, wry smile again. 'With me. Nobody may question my arrangements; you have no such protection. In Malta's *society*, there would be talk of scandal. It could harm Sir Richard.' He had looked at her very directly. 'I can always offer that defence against envy and hypocrisy, things you know only too well. I can sometimes turn such hostility aside, and use it to advantage.'

Not once had he mentioned Oliphant and his attempt to rape her.

She had spoken to only a few of the other passengers, but had enjoyed her daily conversations with the captain, a bluff and very experienced officer who had once served in the navy as a lieutenant. He seemed much older than the captains she had met through Richard: boys who became men in the aftermath of battle.

And there was a master's mate, whom she had seen watching her when she had been walking on the poop. Not unlike Allday, a true man of the sea; like so many sailors he had been almost too shy to speak to her.

He had served with Richard in a frigate named *Tempest*, and it had been like sharing a fragment of his past. Richard had told her of the ship and her cruise in the Great South Sea, when he had almost died of fever, and Valentine Keen's first love, a Tahitian girl, had fallen to the same fate.

The man had fumbled with his belt and had said, 'We'm all that pleased to 'ave you aboard with us, m'lady. There's many o' th' lads who've served with Sir Richard Bolitho or knows all about him.' Then he had grinned, the shyness suddenly gone. 'We'll ne'er see *his* like again!'

She could almost hear Allday say, *An' that's no error.*

She could think of nothing but seeing him again; the reality of leaving so soon afterwards must not spoil it. She had agreed; they were Sillitoe's terms for this privileged passage. She had learned from one of the officers that *Saladin* would not have been calling at Malta but for Sillitoe's instruction. Powerful indeed. . . . Almost hesitantly, she thrust her arm outside the cloak and studied her wrist in the hard light. The marks were still there, like the memory of the cord tightening around her arms.

If he knew, or sensed in some way . . . .

We have no secrets. It was easy enough to say.

And she remembered Sillitoe's last words at their undisturbed supper, while the sea and the wind had boomed around them, but she had felt no fear.

He had said quietly, 'I am a willing party to this, and you must be sensible of my feelings for you. But I am curious to know what drives you . . . what carries you in the face of everything? Sir Richard is as safe as any flag officer can be. He has a good ship, to all accounts, and a reliable squadron. Not what he has been used to. So I have to ask myself, why?'

She had answered simply, without pausing to consider it. 'Because he needs me.'

Richard Bolitho stepped into *Frobisher*'s sick-bay and hesitated, unprepared for the brightness of its interior, the white-painted bulkhead and partitions, and the shelves of bottles and jars which rattled occasionally in time with the ship's motion. A world completely apart from the rest of the ship; Lefroy's domain. It was said that he even slept down here, rather than use one of the wardroom cabins, which, built as they were only of screens, could be torn down whenever the ship cleared for action. They were only temporary; here on the orlop deck, below the waterline, a place which had never seen the light of day since *Frobisher* had been built at Lorient, there was an air of permanence. On deck, in that other world, which he understood, Bolitho knew the hour was close to noon, the sky almost empty of cloud. In the sick-bay, time had no measure.

Lefroy was regarding him thoughtfully, more like a country parson than ever in the curious white smock he favoured when working among the wounded.

He said, 'Another has died, Sir Richard.' He sighed. 'Two amputations. A strong man, but. . . .' He shrugged, almost apologetically. 'Miracles are hard to come by.'

'Yes. Captain Tyacke told me. Fifteen killed in all. Too many.'

Lefroy heard the bitterness, and wondered at it. But he said, 'His name was Quintin.'

'I know. He was a Manxman. I spoke with him one night when it was his trick at the wheel.' He repeated, 'Too many.'

He glanced at the spiralling lanterns, and said, 'It's no better.'

Lefroy gestured to a chair. 'It was most unfortunate that the musket was discharged so close to your face. It could only aggravate the original injury.'

Bolitho sat and leaned back in the chair. 'I would be dead but for that Royal Marine's aim, my friend!'

Lefroy was wiping his hands, but thinking of the hours which had followed the fanatical attack on the flagship. He had only served under one admiral before, and could not have imagined him visiting the orlop as Bolitho had done, to talk with the wounded, or to take a hand in a strong clasp, and watch the life ebb from a man's face.

'I shall try this patch again.' The steely fingers adjusted a patch and placed it firmly over Bolitho's uninjured eye. The fingers again. Probing, stinging, another kind of ointment. He felt the heat of a lamp, so close that he could smell the wick. His eyelid was held, the eye wide open, while Lefroy said, 'Look right. Look left. Up. Down.'

He tried not to clench his fists, to contain the rising fear. What he had known from the beginning, when he had been unable to see the sergeant who had been right beside him. What he had been unable to accept.

Lefroy said, 'Anything?' He bit his lip as Bolitho shook his head.

'Nothing. Not a glimmer.'

Lefroy replaced the lantern. He had held it very close, so there could be no deception.

He untied the patch and turned away from the chair.

Bolitho looked around him. Everything the same as before; everything completely different.

He said quietly, 'As you said, miracles are hard to come by.'

Lefroy said, 'Yes,' and watched Bolitho stand again, the casual way he adjusted his coat, then touched his hip as if he expected to find his sword still there. A remarkable man, one who had been wounded several times in the service of his King and country, although he somehow doubted if the admiral would regard it in that light.

'I shall prepare something for it, Sir Richard. It should afford you no discomfort.'

Bolitho glanced at his reflection in a hanging mirror. How could it be? The same face, the same eyes, the same lock of hair which hid the deep scar there.

He thought of Catherine, that night in Antigua when he had found her again. When he had stumbled in a shaft of light. Now he would not stumble; there was nothing to deceive him.

'When we return to Malta, Sir Richard. . . .' He was caught

221

off guard as Bolitho answered, 'Tomorrow morning, early, if Mr Tregidgo can be believed.'

'I was going to suggest that you might visit a local doctor. I am no expert in this field.'

Bolitho touched his arm and reached for the door. 'See to the wounded. I shall be all right.'

On the quarterdeck once more, he stood for a few minutes staring at the dark blue water, the spray leaping over the beakhead with a movement like flying fish.

Tyacke had been waiting for him, but Bolitho knew he would never admit it.

'All well, sir?'

Bolitho smiled at him, warmed by his concern. A man who had suffered so much, and had never been allowed to forget it; who had almost broken when the woman he had loved had turned away. *And all I think about is what Catherine will see when she looks at me again.*

He said, 'I shall walk with you a while, James.' He paused. 'But for Sergeant Bazely, I would not be doing that!'

Avery had been looking at the signals log with Singleton, the midshipman in charge. Bolitho had been down on the orlop for only a short while, although it had felt like hours.

He heard Bolitho say, 'There may be some letters for us when we anchor – that would sweeten the pill, eh?'

He heard them laugh, saw some seamen look up to watch them pass.

Midshipman Singleton said, 'My ambition is to be like that, sir.'

Avery turned sharply, surprised by the seriousness and the sincerity of this youth who had seen men die screaming on this same deck.

He said, 'Keep to your studies, my lad. One day you might remember what you just told me. I hope you do.' He stared unseeingly at the open log. 'For all our sakes!'

Singleton was still gazing at the two pacing figures, remembering how the admiral had gone to speak to each of the survivors from the brig *Black Swan*. It had been impossible to save the brig, and she had been set alight to prevent her capture and repair by the Algerines.

He would remember that most of all. *Black Swan*'s young commander, wounded, but too stricken to accept attention while he had watched the dirty column of smoke against the blue sky. The end of his ship. He had heard the lieutenants saying it would finish his career too, at a court-martial table.

Bolitho had joined him by the nettings and had gripped his uninjured arm, held it until the other officer had turned towards him.

Singleton could still hear it. *The worst lies behind you now. Think only of the next horizon.*

He turned to Avery, but the tall lieutenant with the tawny eyes and the grey streaks in his hair was gone.

The first lieutenant called wearily, 'When you are through with your dreams, Mr Singleton, I would be *obliged* if you would bring me your log!'

Singleton stammered, 'Aye, *aye*, sir!'

Order and routine. But for him, things would never be quite the same again.

Daniel Yovell, Bolitho's round-shouldered secretary, dripped the red, official wax on to yet another envelope before sealing it. Then he shifted slightly in his chair, and peered through the salt-dappled stern windows, where the sun was touching the bright sails of some local craft as *Frobisher* made her final approach. He heard Allday moving restlessly in the sleeping cabin, still brooding over the short, savage fight on the upper deck when one twist of the Algerine's great blade had rendered him helpless to defend his admiral. His friend.

Yovell's frown softened slightly. People mocked him behind his back. *Old Yovell and his Bible.* But it had helped him in more ways in the past than people would ever know. Allday had no such release.

He was here now, looking at the pile of letters and despatches which had kept Bolitho, and Yovell's pen, busy for much of the time since the encounter with the chebecks.

Allday asked, 'What d'you think will happen?'

Yovell adjusted his small gold-rimmed spectacles. 'It depends. On what orders are waiting for us in Malta. On what the patrols may or may not have discovered about the two frigates at Algiers. I sometimes wonder if anyone ever takes heed of all this intelligence.' He made another attempt, for he was a kindly man. 'Try to forget what happened that day. You did your best. The pirate, from what I've heard, was a giant, and a savage, probably filled with some devil's potion as well as an unholy lust to kill.' He added gently, 'We get no younger, John. We sometimes forget that.'

Allday punched one fist into another. 'I should have stopped the bastard! Not left it to some bloody bullock!'

Yovell half-listened to the stamp of bare feet, and the sudden squeal of blocks as the ship began to change tack again.

He said, 'Sir Richard seems well enough. I think he always knew his eye would eventually fail him. It could have been worse. Much worse.' He folded his hands on Bolitho's desk. 'I prayed. I hope I was heard.'

Allday turned on him, but was moved to silence by the simple assurance.

He growled, 'Well, I think we should stop now. Haul down the flag an' let some other up-an'-comin' Nelson take the strain!'

Yovell smiled at that. 'Within a month you'd be burrowing round, looking for some job to keep you occupied. I would lay odds on it, and you know I am not a gambling man.'

Allday sat heavily on the bench seat, and glared at the nearest eighteen-pounder.

'I don't never want to become like most of the old Jacks you see. You knows 'em well enough, swingin' the lamp and sayin' how great an' fine it was to be raked by some bloody mounseer, an' to lose a spar like poor Bryan Ferguson.' He shook his shaggy head. 'Never! What we done, we done *together*. That's how I wants to remember it!'

The door opened and Avery entered the cabin. He, too, glanced at the pile of waiting letters and despatches, and shook his head.

'I don't know what drives him so!' He waved Allday back to his seat and remarked, 'There might be some fleet mail for us.' He peered through an open gunport. 'I just saw a sight, a big Indiaman, making all plain sail with the skill and swagger of a first-rate! Young Singleton told me she was *Saladin*, on passage to Naples. On the King's business for a change, by the sound of it.'

Allday looked at him. 'I knows her, sir. We was just talking about Bryan Ferguson, back home. Him an' me went down to see her once when she dropped her hook at Falmouth.'

Avery said something vague in acknowledgement. Like

Singleton, this seasoned, unflinching sailor could still surprise him. *Back home. . . .* Not many landsmen would ever understand what that meant to men like Allday, worn out by war and unready for peace. *And what of me?*

He could hear Ozzard rattling glasses in his pantry, preparing for the ship's first visitors after they had anchored. He smiled faintly. *Dropped her hook . . . .*

Yovell was saying, 'In a few weeks it will be Christmas again. And we don't even know if the war with the Yankees is over.'

Avery, still gazing out idly, saw another local sailing craft pass *Frobisher*'s quarter. Eyes everywhere. The news of their destruction of the Algerine pirates would have preceded them, too. He thought of *Black Swan*'s commander, Norton Sackville. Even in the crowded wardroom, he remained alone. Avery knew what such isolation was like, while he had been waiting for the unwarranted court martial, and had seen former friends cross the road to avoid contact with him.

Ozzard appeared and said stiffly, 'Sir Richard's not here, then? Must be still on deck for entering harbour.'

Allday stood up abruptly. 'I'll take his sword.' It was suddenly important, and he knew Avery was watching him with his steady cat's eyes.

Avery said, 'It'll be a while yet. Another hour, the master informs me.'

Allday took down the sword, nonetheless. Remembering all those other times, the excitement, the madness, the survival. *Always the pain.*

It was still damp on deck, and the air was surprisingly cool, reminding him of what Yovell had said. It was November now, but hard to compare with England's bare trees and angry, autumnal coastline.

The watch on deck were at their stations, and Allday noticed the extra lookouts aloft for the final approach. He thought of Captain Tyacke blaming himself for losing the *Black Swan*; you could never be too careful with so many mindless natives controlling all these hundreds of small vessels. *Not a true seaman amongst them.*

He found Bolitho with Tyacke by the quarterdeck rail, shading his eyes while he watched the land opening out to greet them. There was an anchored sloop-of-war close by, her

225

yards and rigging full of cheering seamen as their flagship passed slowly abeam.

Allday gave a satisfied grin. *As it should be.*

Bolitho saw him, and the sword. 'That was thoughtful, old friend. . . . I was looking at the harbour, preparing myself for what we might expect.'

Allday fastened the sword into place. The belt needed adjusting; Sir Richard was losing weight. He frowned. One of Unis's pork pies, now, that would be more like it.

Kellett called, 'Signal that fool to stand away!' He sounded sharper than usual, on edge.

A master's mate said, 'Guard boat, sir!'

Bolitho walked to the side and saw the smart pinnace with a midshipman and a captain of marines in the sternsheets coming about to lead them in; the marine stood to raise his hat in salute. He had always enjoyed the moment of entering harbour, no matter where it might be, but his heart refused to rise to it. He thought suddenly of Keen; he would be married by now, and a port admiral in his own right. He wondered who else would have been at the wedding. Bethune, perhaps even Thomas Herrick. He bit his lip. No, not Thomas. He had never healed the rift between himself and Keen.

She would be good for Val. Strong enough to stand up to his overbearing father, woman enough to help him forget.

'Guard boat is comin' alongside, sir!' The master's mate sounded shocked at such a breach of procedure.

Kellett shouted, 'They have a message for the admiral! Lively there, Mr Armytage! Your people are all like old women this morning!'

'Stand by for entering harbour! Hands aloft, Mr Gilpin!'

Bolitho raised his arm to the guard boat as the oars backed water, and swung the stem towards the sand-coloured fortifications once again.

Tyacke said, 'Carry on, Mr Kellett.'

Armytage arrived on the quarterdeck, still flushing from Kellett's rebuke and the grins from various seamen. It was his first commission as a lieutenant.

He saw Avery and hurried across, a small package, wrapped in oilcloth, in his hand.

Bolitho said, 'Here, Mr Armytage!'

He felt the others watching him, as if unable to move

while the ship and her tall shadow carried them forward, some invisible force in command.

'Thank you, Mr Armytage.' He unfolded the oilcloth carefully, his head turned very slightly to correct the imbalance of his vision. Then the paper; for a moment he held it in his hands. A carefully pressed rose, velvet-red, as he had seen them so many times. Again he read the card, the writing he knew so well. *I am here. We are together.*

Avery's voice broke in anxiously. 'Is something amiss, Sir Richard? Can I . . . .'

Bolitho could not look at him, remembering yesterday's verdict from Lefroy. He answered quietly, 'A miracle, George. They do happen after all.'

They stood side by side on a small balcony which looked down over a cobbled courtyard and an arched entrance from the street. There was a fountain in the centre of the courtyard, but, like the cobbles, uncared for, and full of weeds browned by the Maltese sun. There were servants, unobtrusive and unseen, their presence marked by fresh fruit and wine in the room behind them.

Even the island's sounds were distant and muffled, someone singing, or perhaps chanting in a strange, quavering voice, and the regular clang of a chapel bell.

She turned slightly inside his arm, which had never left her waist since they had stepped on to the balcony. She felt his fingers tighten, as if he still could not believe it, as if he was afraid to release her, and like a dream it would all be lost.

She said, 'I wanted to go to the jetty and watch you come ashore. To meet you and hold you. I wanted it so much. Instead . . . .'

They both glanced down as an old dog turned over, panting in the sunshine before dragging itself into the retreating shadows.

He tightened his hold around her waist, thinking of the haste with which he had cut short his immediate duties to come ashore, to this quiet street, to her.

She had told him about Sillitoe, how he had arranged this passage, how even this house belonged to one of his friends or associates, someone who owed him favours. He had felt no resentment or jealousy. It was as if he had known.

As he had slipped out of his heavy coat she had told him the rest of the story, or most of it. How Sillitoe had come with his men to her aid, and had saved her.

Then Bolitho had held her for the first time, pressing her face to his, stroking her hair, his words muffled until he had lifted her chin in his fingers and had said without emotion, 'I would have killed him. I *will* kill him.'

She had kissed him, and had whispered, 'Sillitoe is a law unto himself. He will deal with it.'

'He is in love with you, Kate.' She had flinched at the familiar use of the name. 'Who would not be?'

'I am in love with you.'

He thought of the piles of despatches which had been brought by the last courier from England. Once so important; he had barely scanned them, and had left Tyacke to sift through them.

She turned again in his arms and looked directly into his face.

'I would have done anything to be here with you. When the ship sailed into the harbour and your *Frobisher* was not at anchor, I thought I would die.' She moved against him. 'And then you came. My admiral of England.' She struggled with the words. 'Will you be able to stay? *Saladin* is returning in a matter of days. If only . . . .'

He kissed her face and her throat, and felt the pain draining away like sand. 'It is more than I dared to hope for.'

She led him into the room and closed the shutters.

'They know you are here?'

He nodded, and she said softly, 'Then they will know what we are doing.' He reached out for her, but she twisted away from him. 'Pour some wine. I must do things.' She smiled, and pushed some hair from her face. 'Oh, Richard, I love thee so!' Then, like the dream, she was gone.

Bolitho thought of Avery and Allday, who had accompanied him ashore. Each unwilling to abandon him in a strange port, and yet both so determined not to display their anxieties.

And she was here. It was not another dream, wherein she was torn away from him. He felt again the anger and shock as he recalled her careful description of the attack, and what

Oliphant had intended. It was as if Oliphant represented all those nightmare figures, the rivals and lovers which were always a part of his fears.

And she had shown a courage which he could only imagine; it was not even something he could compare with the shipwreck, or their first embattled meeting aboard the *Navarra*.

She called through the door, 'What of tomorrow?'

'I must meet the garrison commander, and receive some officials.'

'Afterwards?'

He felt the sudden excitement. 'I shall be meeting a very beautiful girl.'

She came into the room very quietly, her feet bare, her body clothed from neck to ankles in a fine, white gown.

She put her arms around his neck and held him tightly.

'A girl? If only I still were.' She gasped as he cupped her shoulders and ran his hands down her spine.

She said softly, 'And I missed your birthday. It was all done in such a hurry. Perhaps I shall buy something here in Malta . . . .'

She stood quite still, her arms at her sides as he found the gold cord and pulled it towards him. The gown was so thin that, in falling, it scarcely made a sound, and she watched him, her lips suddenly moist and parted in the filtered sunlight, as he held her against him before lifting her, and carrying her to the bed.

Her fingers were like claws in the sheets as he kissed her nakedness, her mouth and her throat, each breast, with a lingering pressure which made her cry out as if in pain as her nipples hardened in his lips. Once she had dreaded that this reunion would only bring back the disgust and the terror of that night. But it was as if she had no memory, and no control at all; she felt her body writhing as he came to her and she drew him down, touching and caressing, taking him into her, as if it was for the first time.

He kissed her, deeply, and tasted what might have been tears. But their need of one another drove all reserve, all memory, into the shadows. She arched her back so that he could lift her, to join them even more closely; they were one.

She turned her head from side to side, her hair spreading across the disordered sheets, her face damp as if from fever.

229

'I can't wait, Richard . . . I can't wait . . . it's been so long . . . .'

The rest was lost as they fell, entwined like broken statuary, and there was nothing, only the sound of their urgent breathing.

When, eventually, they stood again at the shuttered doors the shadows were deeper, and the old dog had disappeared. Together they drank the wine, neither noticing that the glasses were hot from the sun.

She put her arm around his shoulder, and did not look away when he turned his head to see her more fully.

'I know, dearest of men. I *know.*'

He felt her move against him, and the need of her again.

She tossed the mood aside. 'I am out of practice! Come, my love . . . I shall do better this time!'

Faint stars were in the sky when they finally fell asleep, in one another's arms.

There was a smell of jasmine in the room. The miracle was complete.

16

Lifeline

Captain Adam Bolitho walked slowly to the quarterdeck rail and, for only a few seconds, laid his hand upon it. Like the rest of the ship, it was cold and damp, and he felt a shiver run down his spine like some ghostly reminder. He was very aware of the crowded maindeck, the upturned faces, still anonymous and unknown to him, the swaying lines of scarlet-coated marines, the blue and white groups of officers and those of warrant rank. Soon to be a ship's company. *His* ship's company. People, individuals, the good and the bad, but on this bitter December day they were strangers. And Captain Adam Bolitho was quite alone.

On the lively passage back from Halifax to England, he had still imagined that he would be replaced at the last moment. That his one hope would be gone.

It was not a dream. It was not a reward. It was now, today. What his uncle had sometimes described as *the most coveted gift* was his by right. His Britannic Majesty's Ship *Unrivalled*, a fifth-rate of forty-six guns, was in almost every sense ready to join the fleet and perform whatever task might be ordered. So fresh from the builders' hands that in places below decks the paint was not yet dry, but up here, even to the inexperienced eye, she was a thing of beauty. She moved restlessly on the current, her holds and stores yet to be filled, like her magazines and shot-lockers, to give the graceful hull stability and purpose.

It was an important day for all of them. The fruitless, bitter war with the United States was all but over. *Unrivalled* was not only the first ship of her name on the Navy List, but also the first to be commissioned under the promise of peace.

Adam glanced at the taut shrouds and blacked-down stays, the new cordage touched with frost like entwined, frozen webs, and he saw the breath of one seaman hanging over him like smoke.

It was misty, too, and the houses and fortifications of Plymouth were still blurred, like a glass out of focus.

He felt the ship move again, and pictured the Tamar River which he had seen when he had first arrived. Beyond it was Cornwall, his home, his roots. He had heard that Catherine had gone to Malta to visit his uncle, and it had seemed pointless to challenge the rutted, treacherous roads merely to visit an empty house. Even more so to venture further, perhaps to Zennor.

He pushed the thought away, and drew the scroll from inside his damp coat. This was all that mattered, all that counted now. There was *nothing else*, and he must never forget that.

He looked steadily at the assembled company for the first time. The seamen were uniformly dressed in new clothing from the purser's slop chest, chequered shirts and white trousers. A new beginning.

Unlike any other ship in which he had served, Adam knew that *Unrivalled* carried not a single pressed man. The ship was undermanned, and some of her company he knew were felons from the assizes and local courts who had been given a choice: the King's service or deportation. Or worse. There were seasoned hands too, a tattoo or some skilled piece of tackle to mark them out from the rest. With ships and men being paid off with unseemly haste, why did some choose to remain in this harsh world of discipline and duty? Perhaps because, despite whatever they had sacrificed or endured, it was all they trusted.

Most of them would have heard other captains read themselves in at some time in their service, but as always it was a moment of significance for every one. The captain, any captain, was their lord and master for as long as the commission dictated.

Adam had known good captains, the best. He had also known the tyrants and the petty-minded, who could make any man's life a misery, or just as easily take his life from him.

He unrolled the scroll, and saw men leaning towards him

232

to hear more clearly. There were visitors as well, including two vice-admirals, and a small group of burly men in rougher clothing. They had been surprised to be invited, and proud, too; they had built this ship, had created her, and had given her life.

The commission was addressed to Adam Bolitho Esq, in large, round copperplate writing; it could have been Yovell's, he thought.

'Willing and requiring you forthwith to go on board and take upon you charge and command of captain in her accordingly.'

It was like listening to someone else, so that he was able both to speak and take note of individual faces: Vice-Admiral Valentine Keen, now the port admiral at Plymouth, and, with him, Vice-Admiral Sir Graham Bethune, who had come from the Admiralty in London for the occasion.

He recalled the moment when he had been pulled around the ship, and she had been warped to her first mooring. The figurehead had intrigued him: a beautiful woman, her nude body arched back beneath the beakhead, her hands clasped behind her head and beneath her long hair, her breasts out-thrust, her eyes looking straight ahead, challenging and defiant. It had been made by a well-known local carver named Ben Littlehales, and was said to be the best work he had ever done. Adam had heard some of the riggers saying that Littlehales always used living models, but none of them knew who she was, and the old carver would never tell. He had died on the day *Unrivalled* had first quit the slipway.

Adam saw Bethune and Keen exchange glances as he drew near to the end of the commission. Strange to realise that both of them, like himself, had been midshipmen under Sir Richard Bolitho's command.

If only he were here today . . . .

'. . . hereof, not you nor any of you may fail as you will answer to the contrary at your peril.' He pulled his hat from beneath his arm and raised it slowly, saw their eyes following it. So many strangers. Even the gunner's mate, Jago, who had accepted the invitation to become his coxswain, looked like a different man in his new jacket and trousers. Jago was probably more bemused than anyone at the turn of events.

He thought suddenly of the boy, John Whitmarsh, who had

died in that brief, bloody fight. He would have been here, should have been here. . . . and *Anemone*, the ship he had loved more than any other. Could this ship, and this new beginning, replace either of them?

He called, 'God Save the King!'

The cheering was loud, unexpectedly so, and he had to fight to contain his emotion.

He thought again of the figurehead; the old carver had chiselled an inscription at the foot of his creation. *Second to None*.

. . . . He would have to entertain his guests in the great cabin. It seemed so large and so bare, devoid of every comfort, and occupied at the moment only by some of the frigate's armament.

Valentine Keen stood back as the builders and senior carpenters crowded round *Unrivalled*'s first captain. Adam had done well today. Keen had sensed the thoughts possessing him, the memories, on this bleak morning.

So very like his uncle; changed in some inexplicable way from the flag captain he had left in Halifax. The confidence and resolve remained, but there was a new maturity in Adam. And it suited him.

And what of me? It was still all so new, and a little overwhelming at times. Keen had a full staff, two captains, six lieutenants and a veritable army of clerks and servants.

Gilia had surprised him with her grasp of this new life, her ability to win hearts, and to be equally firm when she thought it was necessary. With each passing day the old shipboard life seemed to fade further into the distance; perhaps eventually, he thought, he would be like Bethune, with only a painting or two of a ship or a battle to remind him of the life he had known, for which he had bitterly fought his father, and now had, voluntarily, given up.

Boscawen House, his new home, was an imposing place with fine views over the Sound; sometimes, when he was alone, he had tried to imagine Zenoria there. *The admiral's lady*. . . . He stared at the land. Like the image in his mind, it was misty, and eluded him.

Graham Bethune felt the damp, cold air on his face, and was glad he had come for this day. By using what influence he possessed, he had made certain that *Unrivalled* would go to no other captain. It was for Richard Bolitho; it was what he would want more than anything.

He recalled Catherine's pride and anger at the reception when Rhodes had presented Bolitho's wife. And later, when he himself had faced Sillitoe's fury and unrestrained contempt, he had known that this commission was for her sake also.

She was said to be in Malta with Bolitho; if anyone could manage it, she would. He thought of his wife's hostility, her shock and astonishment when he had turned on her and said coldly, 'Honour? What would you or your family know of that?' She had scarcely spoken to him since.

He sighed. But neither had she spoken out against 'that woman'.

He walked over to Adam Bolitho and thrust out his hand. 'I am so glad for you. It is a day one never forgets.' He saw the shadow in the dark eyes, and added kindly, 'There will always be thoughts.'

Adam bent his head. He had once said as much to John Whitmarsh.

'She's a fine ship, Sir Graham.'

Bethune said, 'I envy you. You cannot know how much.'

Adam joined the others and walked aft to his quarters, where a party of Royal Marines had been detailed to act as messmen. When they had all departed the ship would close in on him, and make her own demands.

He paused, the first laughter and the clink of glasses washing over him, unheeded. There was so much to do before they would be ready to put to sea, to teach, to learn, and to lead.

He pulled out the heavy watch and held it in the grey light. In his mind he could still see the shop in Halifax, the ticking, chiming clocks, the proprietor's interest when he had chosen this odd, old-fashioned watch with the mermaid engraved on its guard.

Aloud, he said, '*Unrivalled*. Second to none.' He thought of his uncle, and smiled. 'So be it!'

Paul Sillitoe sat at his broad desk and stared moodily through the windows, across the swirling curve of the river to the leafless trees on the opposite bank. Everything was dripping from an overnight rain; it seemed that it would never stop.

The new year of 1815 was only two days old; he should

be filled with ideas and proposals to put before the Prince Regent at their next meeting. Today, if His Royal Highness was sufficiently recovered from yet another celebration.

The unwanted and costly war with the United States was over, ended by the Treaty of Ghent, which had been signed on Christmas Eve. There would still be battles between ships or even armies until the news was officially confirmed and carried; he had known several such incidents, partly due to the difficulties of communication across sea and wilderness, but also, he suspected, because the officers in command were not prepared to ignore any prospect of action.

He knew that his valet was hovering behind him with his coat. He pushed some papers aside, angry at his inability to summon any enthusiasm for the day's work, let alone a sense of urgency.

His valet said, 'The carriage will be here at the half hour, m'lord.'

Sillitoe said curtly, 'Don't fuss, Guthrie. I shall be ready!'

He stared at the river again, remembering the night when he had burst into her house in Chelsea. It was rarely out of his thoughts, like a curse or a fever from which there was no escape.

He had been surprised at his own behaviour on board the Indiaman *Saladin*, that he had been able to see her and greet her as if they were total strangers. *Which we are.* Sometimes he had confined himself to his quarters in order not to meet her, in case she should think he had forced the encounter. But when they had met, and supped alone, there had been a new awareness, something he had never known.

He had not greeted her when she had rejoined the ship on the return from Naples, but had found her on deck, hours after *Saladin* had worked out of Grand Harbour and had suddenly been totally becalmed, the island still in sight, like copper in the sunset.

She had repeated, 'I am all right, I am all right,' and for a moment longer Sillitoe had believed she had heard him approaching, and had wanted to be left alone.

Then she had turned towards him, and he had realised that she had not known he was there.

'I am sorry. I shall take my leave.'

She had shaken her head. 'No. Please stay. It is hard

236

enough to leave him. To be tortured like this is cruel beyond measure!'

He had heard himself say, 'When I reach London, I will do what I can.' Even that had astonished him, to offer to seek on her behalf a favour which, if granted, would deprive him of any chance he might have believed he had.

He smiled grimly. Nevertheless, Vice-Admiral Sir Graham Bethune would be leaving for the Mediterranean in a matter of days, to take charge of a squadron of frigates which could be used against pirate or corsair. A sea-going appointment; there would be no accommodation for Lady Bethune.

He had seen the orders himself. They would release Sir Richard Bolitho from duty, and he could return to England. To Catherine.

He had also been kept informed of Captain Adam Bolitho's affairs. Why anyone should want to throw his life away on the sea was quite beyond him. Ships, to him, meant only trade, communication, and a means of travel. And even that . . . .

He glanced round angrily, but it was Marlow, his secretary, this time.

'Yes, what is it?'

'Some letters, my lord.' Marlow's cautious eyes took in the unread news sheets on the floor beside the desk, the coffee and the glass of madeira untouched. They were inauspicious signs, and, with Sillitoe, almost unknown.

Sillitoe shook his head dismissively.

'I'll attend to them later. Make my excuses, Marlow. I shall go now to the Prince Regent.'

'I have all the necessary papers, my lord.' He broke off. Sillitoe had not even heard him.

'After that, I shall be engaged.' Their eyes met. 'Understood?'

Marlow did understand. He was going to that house, so discreet, so private. Where a man of influence could lose himself completely in the arms of a woman, without fear of scandal or condemnation. He had become used to Sillitoe's difficult ways and scathing comments, but it troubled him to see him so disturbed, like some ordinary being.

To his knowledge, Sillitoe had not visited the brothel since the incident in Chelsea.

237

Sillitoe allowed his valet to help him into his coat, and stared around the room as if he had mislaid something.

Then he said, 'There is one letter, Marlow, for Lady Somervell in Falmouth. Please send it post-haste. She will want to know.'

He could already see it in his mind, the tears and the joy with which she would receive the news that her lover had been ordered home. He could deceive himself no longer. He heard the carriage on the cobbles and strode from the room.

Like a duel, when you have fired and your opponent is still standing. He had lost.

His Britannic Majesty's schooner *Tireless*, messenger, courier and bearer of news, good or bad, lived up to her name. Rarely in port for longer than required for storing and watering, she would be off again with all haste to her next rendezvous.

She was a smart, lively little vessel, a young man's command. On this February morning the lookout had reported sighting the flagship *Frobisher*, and, taking full advantage of a soldier's wind under her coat-tails, she had set more sail to run down on the slow-moving two-decker. Lieutenant Harry Penrose, the schooner's captain, was well aware of the significance of his despatches, and very concerned that he should make a perfect approach to the flag of one so famous; it was a name with which he had been acquainted even before he had entered the navy.

Penrose would have been astonished had he known that the admiral had been watching *Tireless* since first light with equal anxiety.

In *Frobisher*'s great cabin, the man in question listened to the bark of orders and the tramp of hardened, bare feet, as the flagship altered course slightly to meet the schooner and afford her some protection, although the sea was little more than a gentle swell. He clenched his fists. Weeks of it, of lack of news, of uncertainty, and of this sense of no purpose. There had been some activity when Barbary corsairs had attacked other small and defenceless vessels, but they had fled before any of Bolitho's thinly-stretched squadron could find and destroy them. And until more ships were released from the Channel Fleet and the Downs squadrons, it seemed unlikely that matters would improve.

238

Tireless might bring something. He tried not to hope for it. Perhaps a letter from Catherine. . . . So many times, he had recalled every detail of their reunion, the ache of parting after the big Indiaman *Saladin* had returned from Naples, in what must have been record time. He had thought of it again when Tyacke had come to report the sighting of *Tireless*, remembering with anguish how the Indiaman's pyramid of canvas, gold in the sunset, had remained becalmed outside the harbour as if to taunt him. He had watched the ship until darkness had hidden her. And he had known, even before her letter from England, that she had done the same. She had written to him about Adam, and the confirmation of his new command. Of the dazed reaction to the combined attack on Washington, and the burning of government buildings in retaliation for the American attack on York. As Tyacke had once said, *and for what?* He had watched Tyacke while he had trained a glass on the approaching schooner. Remembering his own first command, perhaps, or the powers of fate which had brought them so close together, as his friend and flag captain? And Avery. He would remember his own service in the schooner *Jolie*, which had ended in disaster and court martial. The tawny eyes gave little away; he might even have been thinking of the letter for which he waited. The letter that never came.

The strain of weeks at sea without activity was telling on *Frobisher*'s people. Ships and men being paid off: a sailor's dream rather than a safe reality, but it gave rise to flarings of temper and outbreaks of violence, even in a well-disciplined company. He could hear Gilpin the boatswain, bawling out to some of his working party. A grating was to be rigged immediately after the despatches had been passed across, and *Frobisher*'s own mail sent into *Tireless* in exchange. It was anyone's guess when those letters would reach their destinations.

He knew Tyacke hated the ritual of punishment, as much as he did himself. But he, more than most, knew the dangers of sailing alone when the ringing phrases of the Articles of War were not always enough. The Royal Marines of the afterguard, and the lash, were the only known alternative.

Yovell stood by the other door, his spectacles on his forehead.

'Everything has been signed and sealed, Sir Richard. I've had the satchel sent on deck.' Unruffled, unchanged, and yet the one man he might have expected to remain a misfit. Amused, gentle, devout: they were not qualities common in a man-of-war.

Allday was there, too. Pretending to examine the two swords on their rack, but obviously fretting more than ever about the possibility of a letter from that other, quiet world of the Helford River. Avery would read it to him as usual, if it arrived; theirs was an odd and a warm relationship, upon which neither of them ever remarked. Avery would be thinking of the fair Susanna. In vain . . . .

And Sillitoe, the one man he had never expected to become involved on his behalf. He could hear Catherine's voice in the darkness, remember her warm breath on his shoulder, while she had spoken of that night in Chelsea, distancing herself from it, more like an impartial witness than one who had been face to face with terror. He had wanted to feel doubt, suspicion, even hatred. But Sillitoe remained as before, remote, even in the desire he so obviously felt for Catherine.

And all the while I remain here in the Mediterranean, waiting. Probably with no less intolerance than the seaman who would be flogged at six bells of the forenoon watch.

Avery entered by the screen door and removed his hat.

'*Tireless* is shortening sail, Sir Richard.' He glanced briefly at Allday. 'She has signalled that her captain is coming aboard.' He added, 'Penrose, Lieutenant.' And then, more lightly, 'I would have thought he'd be here and gone, in case his admiral finds him some errand!'

Bolitho laughed. Avery had not forgotten.

'Very well. Bring him aft, and I'll speak with him myself.'

It took another hour for the ships to draw close enough for a boat to be put down and pulled over to the flagship, where young Lieutenant Harry Penrose was received with no less respect than if he were a post-captain.

Two seamen carried the satchels of mail and the despatches, and when Allday finally returned to the great cabin Bolitho knew that he had been lucky. Just a nod. That was all it took.

Lieutenant Penrose had a small bag of letters for Bolitho.

240

'From the courier-brig when I was last at the Rock, Sir Richard.' He became almost confidential. 'Her captain made me promise that I would deliver them personally.'

Bolitho took the letters; there seemed to be four of them. The link, the lifeline. He would make them last.

Penrose was saying, 'I fell in with the frigate *Halcyon*, Sir Richard. Captain Christie was making for Malta, but sent word to you in case I found you beforehand.'

He raised his eyes from the letters.

'What "word"?'

'The two frigates reported in Algiers have put to sea.' Penrose looked suddenly troubled, as if it were his fault.

Avery watched Bolitho as he slit open the first, crumpled letter, saw the way he turned his head as if to read it better, the damaged eye now obviously useless. By his appearance, one would never guess, and to share the knowledge was both moving and terrible.

He recalled the moment when Catherine had left Malta. He thought it had been Tyacke's idea; they had sent *Frobisher*'s barge for her, each oar pulled by a captain or one of the squadron's officers, with the admiral's own coxswain at the tiller.

As people saw them, and remembered them; as they spoke of them in the alehouses and the coaching inns from Falmouth to London. *The admiral and his lady*.

Bolitho looked up at him. 'I thought we might learn something of their intentions, but we were unlucky. They could be anywhere, under any flag. It would take a fleet to break into Algiers, not merely this squadron, and even then . . . .'

Avery said, 'Even then, nobody would thank you for beginning another conflict, though it would seem inevitable, whichever aspect presents itself.'

Penrose coughed politely. 'I must take my leave, Sir Richard. The wind favours me, and . . . .'

Bolitho held out his hand. 'My best wishes to your company, Mr Penrose. When next we meet, I shall expect to see epaulettes on your shoulder.'

The door closed as Avery led the schooner's captain away.

Yovell remarked, 'That was kindly said, Sir Richard. That young man will remember this day.'

He heard the trill of calls, and imagined the schooner's gig

241

pulling away from the flagship's side. *Tireless* would soon be gone. Meeting and departure. Their world.

Then the calls shrilled a different tune.

'All hands! All hands lay aft to witness punishment!' The immediate response of hurrying feet, the boots of the Royal Marines as they took up their stations across the poop.

Allday passed him without a word to close the cabin skylight, so that the sound of the punishment would be muffled.

It was a strange fact about Allday, Yovell thought. He loathed officers who abused their authority, but showed no sympathy for any man who raised his hand against it.

Bolitho said, 'I shall dictate orders for the squadron. Some will already know, but if the two frigates intend to reinforce the Barbary corsairs against allied commerce, it is essential that each captain recognises them as the enemy.'

He looked at her letters. She must have written every day. So that he could live her life with her, and share it, week by week, season by season. He clenched his fingers again as the drums beat out their staccato roll. Then the lash, a loud crack across the naked flesh, followed by the shout from M'Clune, the master-at-arms. '*One!*'

Then the drums again, and the sharp crack of the cat. One of the ship's hard men, Tyacke had said, who had threatened a petty officer.

'*Two!*'

Yovell looked at his interlaced fingers below the table. It only took one rotten apple, Allday had often proclaimed.

'*Three!*'

Yovell glanced up again, and then stared as Bolitho got abruptly to his feet, a canvas envelope still gripped in one hand.

He said, with great anxiety, 'What is it, Sir Richard?' conscious only of the expression on Bolitho's tanned face. Surprise, disbelief, but above all, a release which he had rarely seen before.

Bolitho seemed to hear him for the first time.

He answered quietly, and yet even the urgent drums could not quench it, 'From the Admiralty.' He turned, and looked for Allday. 'We are to pay off, old friend. *We're going home.*'

Allday let out his breath, very slowly.
'Well, that's it an' all about it!'
The waiting was over.

17

'Until Hell Freezes'

Yet another forenoon watch was ending, working parties preparing to gather up their tools and equipment, eyes alert for any over-zealous petty officer. The sailmaker and his crew had squatted cross-legged in any shade they could find, needles and palms moving busily like backstreet tailors. The carpenter and his men had continued their endless search for material in need of repair. At times like this, the upper deck was aptly known as the market-place.

Aft, below the poop, some of *Frobisher*'s midshipmen waited with their sextants to shoot the noon sun, some frowning with concentration, and very aware of their captain's tall figure by the quarterdeck rail.

In his mind, Tyacke was seeing the ship's slow progress, east by south, and some one hundred miles to the east of the Sardinian island. It was a sailor's vision, and that of a navigator, but to any layman the sea would appear an empty, glittering desert, as it had been for days. For weeks. They had met only one of their frigates, and had been in contact with another courier vessel; otherwise, they had seen nothing. He saw the first lieutenant making his way aft, pausing to speak with one of the bosun's mates. Like the other officers, Kellett was showing signs of strain. *Frobisher* had been shorthanded even before her fight with the chebecks, shorthanded long before she had commissioned at Portsmouth, and that, he thought, was due largely to her last captain's indifference.

The thought of Portsmouth brought another stab of anger. More men had been excused from duties because of sickness: poisoned meat, the surgeon had insisted.

Tyacke had an innate distrust of all victualling yards, and an immense dislike and suspicion of the common run of ships' pursers. Between them, yard and purser could dispense food already rotten in the casks without any captain's knowledge, until it was too late. A lot of money changed hands this way, and Tyacke had often heard it said that half of any naval port was owned by dishonest pursers and suppliers.

The casks in question had been put aboard at Portsmouth a year ago. How old they really were would remain a mystery; the date markings burned into every such barrel had been carefully defaced, and men were laid off as a result. Tyacke tightened his jaw. It would not end there.

He glanced at the poop, and imagined the admiral going through his despatches yet again. Was all this a waste of time? Who could say? But, as the captain, Tyacke had to consider the demands of his company, the growing shortages of fresh fruit and even of drinking water. An armed marine sentry by the water cask on deck was evidence of that.

He was staring at one of the midshipmen without realising it, and saw the sextant quiver in his hands. This, perhaps, was not what he had expected when he had donned the King's coat.

He turned away and gave his attention to the topsails, filled but only just; the weather was part of the general malaise. It was the usual north-westerly wind, but without life, sultry, more like the sirocco of this region at a later time of the year.

He considered the orders Bolitho had given him to study. When *Frobisher* eventually ended her mission and returned to Malta, Bolitho's successor would be there to relieve him; he had very probably already arrived. Vice-Admiral Sir Graham Bethune. Tyacke had sensed Bolitho's surprise at the choice; he knew the officer, and they had served together. The navy was a family . . . .

The thought uppermost in his mind returned; it had come, increasingly, to haunt him. *Frobisher* would be returning to England; Sir Richard would be allowed to lower his flag, to pass the burden to someone else. For a change.

He had heard Kellett and the others discussing it, when they thought he was out of earshot.

Going home. He had to come to terms with it; it was a concept totally unknown to him in all his years of service. *Going home.* He knew what it meant to Bolitho, even to

Allday. But to him, England had become something alien, a place only of more scrutiny, more revulsion, more pain. Until that last letter from the woman he had once intended to marry. Interesting, warm, mature, truthful. . . . He had tried to dismiss it, to laugh at himself, to accept that there was nothing for him.

In his heart, he knew that Bolitho had guessed some of it, but had said little. That was their strength.

It had all come to a head when Kellett had blurted it out, a day after they had parted with the schooner. The whole wardroom had been alive with speculation and concern for the future. What would happen to *Frobisher*? To them?

Tyacke had already asked himself that. Would she end up an empty hulk, in ordinary in some crowded dockyard, or allowed to sink still further to the status of a storeship or a floating prison? It had happened to other ships; Bolitho's *Hyperion* and even Nelson's *Victory* had been dragged from ignominy to serve again when the country was in danger of invasion and defeat. To find glory when others had been prepared to let them rot.

Kellett had asked him in his usual quiet fashion, 'When we return to the fleet, sir, may I ask, what shall *you* do?'

It had been then, without any hint or warning, that Tyacke had found his way, his purpose.

'I shall remain with the ship.'

Running away was not the answer. It never had been. He belonged.

And Marion would be there to help him. For all kinds of reasons, reasons he would have previously denied, or laughed at, they needed each other.

He thought of Bolitho and his Catherine. Love was the strongest bond.

He heard a step on the deck beside him, but it was not the first lieutenant; it was Avery, squinting at the sea and tugging at his shirt while he stared around from horizon to horizon.

Tyacke said, 'I have to see Sir Richard.' He hesitated over his choice of words. 'It is my duty to advise him.'

'I know.' Avery watched the vivid blue eyes, Tyacke coming to a decision. He said, 'Sir Richard knows this cannot continue much longer. As soon as we return to Malta, it will be out of his hands. But you know him well enough – he cannot let it rest. It seems there is some flaw in it, in the pattern, which refuses to fit.'

'I know. He spoke of the Spaniard, Captain Martinez, the one you met in Algiers.'

Avery nodded, and felt more sweat run down his spine. He often thought of that fine house in London, and of the lovely Susanna; even those, he would exchange at this moment for a bath in pure, clean water.

'There was a brief mention of him in the last despatches from Admiralty. Someone took the time and trouble to look into Sir Richard's report, a lowly clerk most likely!'

Tyacke watched some seamen loitering by an open hatch; they could smell the rum being issued. With little fresh water, and all the beer long gone, rum might be all the spark that was needed.

'A renegade, and an agent for the French when they were preparing to drag Spain into the war. Not that they needed much encouragement!' He heard Kellett clear his throat, and added impatiently, 'Is that all the information we have?'

Avery said, 'It troubles Sir Richard.'

Tyacke turned to Kellett. 'This afternoon, Mr Kellett – is that what you were about to ask?'

Kellett gave one of his rare smiles. 'Aye, sir.'

'Lower gundeck. Both batteries. See if you can knock a minute or two off their time.'

He turned back to Avery, his voice very calm. 'If Sir Richard requires it, I shall wait until hell freezes.' He paused. 'But it may take more than extra gun drills to keep the people mindful of their duties, if we delay much longer, eh?'

The cabin skylight was open, and Bolitho heard Avery laugh. Tyacke was a patient man, and he knew his trade better than any he had met.

He returned to the chart, and pictured *Frobisher* sailing sedately above her own reflection in this Tyrrhenian Sea. So wrong for a ship of her size and quality; this was a place more used to beak-prowed galleys with banked oars, and bearded warriors in plumed helmets. A place of the gods, of the myths of Greece and Rome.

He smiled at the notion, and opened his notes once again; he held his hand over his blind eye, out of habit, and was surprised that he could accept it. Catherine's letter had given him the strength; their lordships of Admiralty had done the rest.

It was strange about Bethune; he had seemed so suited to the ways and powers of London. Perhaps he had offended someone, which was easy enough at the Admiralty. Even Lord Rhodes' name seemed to have been dropped from despatches and orders. Was Sillitoe's hand in that, too?

He dragged his mind back to that meeting with Mehmet Pasha and his Spanish adviser, Martinez. They had known all about the two frigates moored there; nothing could move without the governor's permission, and his complicity. Martinez had been a successful and daring agent for the French revolutionary government. For Napoleon.

Tyacke needed to provide for his ship, and Bethune was probably waiting in Malta to assume command of the Mediterranean squadron.

I must go home. He did not realise he had spoken aloud to the empty cabin and its dancing, dazzling reflections.

There was no proof that Martinez was any more than he proclaimed. His roles had become less important and possibly more dangerous over the years, and in his own country he would never be trusted again. He thought of his brother, Hugh. A traitor was always remembered for his treachery.

If only he had more ships, especially frigates. This venture was a needle in a haystack; or was it merely vanity, a belief that no one else could see the hidden dangers?

He could smell the rum, and imagined the seamen and marines throughout the flagship, isolated now, and idle, no longer participating in the great events of other times and places.

As he leaned over the table he felt the locket, filmed with sweat, adhering to his skin. It would be spring when they reached England again. So much time lost, so much to rediscover.

He heard Tyacke's shoes outside the door, and, quite suddenly, made up his mind.

Tyacke entered and removed his hat; with his face in shadow, it was barely possible to see the full extent of the terrible scars.

'Join me in a glass, James.' Ozzard had appeared, as if by magic. 'I think I have pursued my instincts too far this time.'

They both watched the wine filling the glasses for a moment, then he said, 'We may run down upon *Huntress* before sunset. I would wish to speak with her captain.'

Tyacke nodded. 'It is possible, Sir Richard.'

Bolitho raised his glass. 'Either way, we shall return to Malta.' He smiled. 'In all truth, James, I wish you the happiness you deserve in your new life!'

Their glasses clinked, and the watchful Ozzard saw some wine splash across the admiral's white breeches. Like blood, he thought. But the admiral had not seen it.

Tyacke was on his feet again. 'I shall pass the word, Sir Richard. It may lessen the toils of gun drill!'

Ozzard went into his pantry and found Allday there, carving yet another model ship.

Ozzard could usually conceal his feelings, but on this occasion he was glad that his friend was so engrossed.

Now, even Captain Tyacke had somebody waiting for him.

He thought of the street in Wapping, and heard her dying screams. There was nothing left.

Lieutenant Harry Penrose gripped the companion ladder, and leaned back to stare at the sky while his schooner, *Tireless*, scythed through a ridge of broken water. It never failed to excite him, like riding something alive, which, of course, she was.

The rectangle of sky was duller than usual, with large patches of cloud moving like an untidy flock of sheep. Against it he could see the towering fin of the schooner's mainsail; that, too, seemed darker. Perhaps it would rain. They were not short of water, but just to hear rain running through the scuppers and wetting the sun-dried planking would make a welcome change.

He continued on his way, and heard the squeak of a fiddle from one of the tiny messdecks. She was a small ship, and a happy ship, a command for the young. Penrose was twenty-two years old and knew he was lucky to have *Tireless*, and would be sad to leave her when the time came; just as he knew he would not shirk his duty when it called him elsewhere. It was his life, all he had ever wanted, and had dreamed about as a child. His father and grandfather had been sea officers before him. He smiled. Like Bolitho. He had thought many times since of that unexpected meeting, when he had delivered despatches to the flagship. What had he anticipated? That the hero, the navy's own legend, might prove to be only another imposing figure in gold lace?

He had written to his mother about it, embroidering the story a little, but the truth was still fixed firmly in his mind. *The next time we meet, I shall expect to see epaulettes on your shoulders.* The sort of man you could talk to. The kind of leader you would follow to the cannon's mouth.

He felt the wind on his face, damp, clinging, but still enough to fill the schooner's sails.

Tireless's only other officer, Lieutenant Jack Tyler, waved vaguely toward the bows.

'Masthead just reported a sail to the sou'east, sir.'

Penrose glanced at the sea creaming back from the raked stem.

'I heard the hail. Who is the lookout?'

'Thomas.'

'Good enough for me, Jack.'

They worked watch and watch, with a master's mate standing in when it was convenient. You got to know the ability and strength of every man aboard, and any weakness too.

Tyler said, 'He thinks it's a frigate, but the light's so bad, we may have to wait until tomorrow.'

Penrose rubbed his chin. 'First light? Another day lost. She must be *Huntress*, our last rendezvous.' He thought of the solitary bag in his cabin and added wryly, 'Important, no doubt. Officers' tailoring bills, tearful letters for the mothers' boys, all vital stuff!'

They laughed, more like brothers than captain and first lieutenant.

They both looked up as the masthead pendant cracked out like a coachman's whip, and Penrose said, 'I think we might do it before dark, Jack. When she sights us she's bound to claw up as quickly as she can. They must be sick of being the last of the patrols, a guardship of nothing!'

He made up his mind. 'All hands, Jack! Let's get the tops'ls on her!' He could not contain his excitement. 'Let's show those *old men* how she can shift herself!'

Only one pipe was necessary; the fiddle fell silent, and the schooner's narrow deck was soon filled with bustling figures.

Tireless did not have a wheel like most vessels, but still mounted a long tiller-bar fixed directly to the rudder head. The helmsmen gripped it between them, glancing at the mainsail and masthead pendant, with only an occasional scrutiny of the compass. For a moment longer all was confusion, or so it might appear to the ignorant landsman, and then, heeling to the thrust of canvas and rudder, *Tireless* settled on her new course, spray bursting over her jib and spurting through the sealed gunports, where her sole armament of four four-pounders tugged at their breechings.

'Sou'east, steady she goes, sir!' Even the senior helmsman was grinning, his sunburned face wet with spray, as if it had indeed started to pour.

The lookout called again, 'Frigate, sir! Larboard bow! *Huntress* right 'nough!'

Penrose nodded. Thomas would know; he had eyes like a heron. And they had met with *Huntress* more than a few times on her endless patrols. Penrose thought of her captain. Older than most frigate men, with experience in other ships, and probably in merchantmen too, he was friendly enough, but one who stood no nonsense. Penrose had noticed that he never received anything but official letters with the despatches.

He lifted a telescope and waited for the image to settle in the lens, and at the same time accustomed his legs to the schooner's lively plunges. The habit and the motion had become part of himself.

Even in the dull light he could see the familiar outline, the shining black and buff hull, the chequered line of closed gunports. A fifth-rate, not new, but a fine command. He smiled to himself. For a younger man, of course.

He saw her ensign curling from the peak, so clean and white against the dull backdrop. Ant-like figures in her tops, some watching, hoping for a letter to bring back the precious memories, a face, a touch.

Tyler said, 'The bugger's not changing tack! Making us do all the work!'

Penrose grinned. The light was holding. They would pass the bag across and be away before dark, back to Malta. And after that? Not that it truly mattered . . . .

Tyler was speaking to the master's mate. 'We'll overreach

him at this pace, Ned.' He looked at Penrose. 'We shall have to come about, sir!'

'I know. Take in the mains'l!' He moved the glass again as a tiny patch of colour appeared at the frigate's yard.

'She's made her number, sir!'

Tyler was yelling to his men, and the air was alive with banging canvas and the squeal of blocks.

Penrose did not move. He could not.

He shouted, '*Belay that order!*' He did not recognise his own voice, hard and desperate.

He ran up the slippery planking and stared at the compass. 'Let her fall off, steer due south! She can take it!'

He seized the lieutenant's arm and saw him staring at him like a stranger.

'Why should he make his number to *us*, for God's sake?'

'Look, sir!' The seaman was almost incoherent. 'Christ Almighty!'

The telescope in Penrose's wet fingers felt like ice. He had just seen it. A moment later when they would have been wallowing round on to a new tack, they would have been close enough to hear it: the sound of trucks, even as the line of ports opened along the frigate's side to reveal the guns, and the men who had been crouching there, prepared to fire them.

The great sails filled again, and the taut rigging rattled and hummed in protest. But nothing carried away.

Penrose watched the other ship, his mind as cold as the glass in his hands; everything was clear. *Huntress* had been taken, and within minutes it would have been too late. Someone had tried to warn them, in the only way a seaman would know and recognise.

He felt a muscle jerk in his throat as smoke billowed from the frigate's side to blow instantly inboard again, so that the long tongues of fire looked solid, like furnace bars.

He heard voices crying out as iron crashed across the schooner's deck, and a length of the larboard bulwark was shivered to fragments. Men had fallen, how badly injured Penrose could not tell. But the masts were still standing, and the sails as hard as steel. Only a topsail had been punctured by a shot fired too soon, the wind tearing the canvas to ribbons like a giant ripping paper.

He levelled the glass again, shutting his mind to the pitiful cries, and to the fear which would follow if he allowed it.

The *Huntress* was changing tack; no wonder she had left it so late. Even in the spray and fading light, he could see the battering she had taken on her opposite side. They had not surrendered without a fight, although that was little enough, for what they had given in exchange.

He swung round and saw the master's mate tying the lieutenant's wrist with his neckerchief.

He strode to his friend, and steadied him. 'Hold on, Jack.' He did not blink as another ragged broadside exploded somewhere. As if it were happening in a dream, and to somebody else.

'We must find the flagship, Jack. The admiral must be told.'

Tyler tried to speak but the pain made him gasp.

Penrose persisted, '*Huntress* was the last patrol. The guardship.'

Tyler tried again, and managed to say one word. '*Elba.*'

It was enough.

Bolitho leaned back in his chair, his shirt clinging damply to the warm leather. Beyond the stern windows there was only darkness, whilst here in the cabin the shaded light from a solitary lantern threw shadows across the paintwork and the chequered deck covering, like strange dancers keeping time with *Frobisher*'s uneven movements.

How could a ship so large be so silent? There was only an occasional sound of feet overhead, or cordage being manhandled to trim a yard, or take the slack out of a sail.

He knew that he should sleep, just as he knew that he would be unable to do so. He covered his blind eye and looked at the unfinished letter which lay open on top of his chart.

Writing to Catherine always gave him a sense of conversing, of sharing the days and nights with her. *Frobisher* might be on passage for England before this particular letter was concluded.

He stood up and moved about the cabin, his hand brushing against one of the tethered guns. Even the metal felt warm, as if it had been fired only hours earlier.

They had not met with *Huntress*, and in his heart he knew

Tyacke had been humouring him with the belief that they would make a final contact before Bolitho handed over his command.

At first light they would come about and head for Malta. But until then . . . .

Allday was taking great care not to intrude upon his thoughts, but he was unable to conceal his relief that they were finally going home.

How would Allday settle down, what would he do? Proprietor of a small country inn, seeing the same faces every day, in a world where men discussed crops, livestock and the weather with equal authority. Not the sea. . . . But he would have Unis and little Kate. He would have to begin learning all over again. A different life. *Like me.*

He thought of going on deck, but knew that his presence would worry the watchkeepers. On the same tack and under reduced canvas, it would be hard enough for some of them to stay awake without their admiral pacing up and down. Tyacke would be in his cabin, planning, preparing for his ship's immediate future, and his own. Tyacke was probably the one person who had never expected hope to hold out its hand to him; the one man who so richly deserved it.

And what of Avery; would he remain in the navy or reconsider his uncle's offer? It was hard to imagine any one of his little crew in any life but this.

In fact Avery was on deck, clinging to the empty hammock nettings, and listening to the ship shuddering and groaning above and around him. Alan Tollemache, the third lieutenant, had the watch, but he had retreated to the poop after two attempts to open a conversation.

It was not that Avery disliked him, even though he tended to brag about himself and his family; it was simply that he wanted to be alone, to have only his thoughts and memories for company. It was difficult enough for any flag lieutenant to fit completely into wardroom life with its rules and traditions, and where every thought and idea was shared. It had to be that way; the lieutenants were a group apart, *us* and *them.* It was natural enough, but Avery had never been able to be anything but himself, and solitary.

He had been thinking deeply about the future, and what he might do when Bolitho's flag came down. Promotion, and perhaps a small command of his own? He could sense a hundred arguments before he could even consider it. He served Sir Richard; to be appointed aide to some other flag officer was out of the question. His powerful uncle, Baron Sillitoe of Chiswick, then? He admired Sillitoe for having offered him a future, one of substance and prosperity, partly because he sensed what it had cost him to bend so far. He smiled, and tasted the raw salt on his lips. The prospect would certainly attract the beautiful Susanna. But even poor luffs had pride, and pride pulled in both directions.

With a sigh, he walked aft, tossing a casual wave to the dark group of figures around the compass box, and pausing as the poop's black outline loomed over him to glance again at the sky. No moon, and only an occasional star. It was a fine night after all, even during the hated middle watch. He was about to feel his way to the companion ladder when something caused him to hesitate, and to turn, as if someone had called his name.

But there was nothing. It was an intrusion into thoughts which had been quiet, meditative, and for some reason he was troubled by it.

When he climbed into his swaying cot the disquiet remained with him, and sleep was denied him.

As in all men-of-war, shorthanded or not, *Frobisher*'s company were turned-to when there was barely enough light to mark sea from sky. It was always a time of bustle and purpose, and on this day there was not a man jack aboard who did not know that the ship, which was their home, their way of life, their reason for being, would soon be turning her jib boom towards the west, and eventually to England.

Kellett, the first lieutenant, was in charge of the morning watch, as the decks were washed down and the water casks filled with some of their last supply. The lazy breeze was heavy with greasy smells from the galley funnel.

Kellett saw the signals midshipman watching him, and said, 'Aloft with you, Mr Singleton, and see if you can be the first to sight the wretched *Huntress*! And cling to the thought while you climb: after this, *you* may be the one giving orders to some snotty midshipman, if your wits serve you well in your examination!'

The midshipman ran to the shrouds and began the long climb up the ratlines.

Someone whispered, 'Cap'n, sir.'

Tyacke strode to the compass and glanced at the topsails, then his eyes found Singleton clawing his way past the maintop.

'He'll see nothing, I daresay.'

Kellett was watching the working parties being dismissed, and thought of the tasks he had detailed for the day.

Tyacke was saying, 'If the wind holds steady, we should make a fair passage.'

Kellett listened with some curiosity. The captain rarely made idle observations, any more than he ever showed uncertainty in the presence of his officers. He had been in awe of Tyacke when he had suddenly accepted this command, and resentful also. Now he could not imagine *Frobisher* without him.

Tyacke was observing Singleton's progress, remembering how Bolitho had once confided in him, and told him how the fear of heights had disturbed him as a 'young gentleman'. He had heard Kellett's remarks to the youth concerning promotion, and, reluctantly, he had concluded that Singleton might make a good officer, provided he had a captain to drive him.

Oblivious to all of them, the midshipman had reached the crosstrees, where a tanned and scarred seaman was already on duty. Singleton had seen him fumbling with a packet when he had appeared beside him, and guessed that the man had been chewing tobacco, a punishable offence while on watch.

Singleton unslung his telescope, pleased that he was not out of breath. He would not report the offender, and he knew that the seaman, an old hand, would remember him for it. He trained the glass with great care, recalling the admiral's words to him. *My eyes*.

There was an horizon at last, very thin and hard, like polished silver.

It would be strange to leave this ship, he thought, to take that once unimaginable step from midshipman's berth to ward-room. To be able to speak openly with fellow lieutenants, who, up until now, had seemed bent on making every midshipman's life a perfect misery.

The old seaman was studying him, the seriousness on his young features. With one or two of the others, he would have remained silent, but the signals midshipman had always seemed fair enough.

He said calmly, 'There's a ship out yonder, Mr Singleton.'

Singleton lowered the heavy glass and stared at him. 'If I can't see it with this, then I. . . .' He grinned, and raised it again. 'Where away?'

'Larboard bow, very fine.'

Singleton tried again. Nothing. He knew about some of the older lookouts; it was a second sense, someone had told him.

He held his breath and waited for *Frobisher* to lift again. *And there it was.* How could he not have seen it?

He screwed his eye closer and saw the image strengthen. Catching the light from somewhere. A sail, touched with yellow gold, standing up from the hard horizon; like a feather, he thought.

He looked at his companion. 'I see her.' He smiled. 'My thanks.'

On the quarterdeck, every face was raised as Singleton's voice echoed down from the mainmast.

'Deck there! Sail, fine on the larboard bow!'

Tyacke exclaimed, 'Well, I'll be damned!'

Kellett said, 'Shall I inform the admiral, sir?'

Tyacke looked at him. 'When we know a bit more.' As Kellett hurried away, he added, 'He won't need telling.'

It was another hour before the masthead could recognise the newcomer. Tyacke watched Bolitho's face keenly as he told him.

'*Tireless*, James? Not *Huntress* after all?' He smiled, but the mood seemed to elude him. 'Well, she may have news for us, although from that direction I doubt it.'

When admiral and flag lieutenant joined the others on the quarterdeck, Tyacke noticed that Bolitho was dressed in a clean shirt and breeches. He looked rested and alert now, even though there had been a light burning in his cabin throughout the night watches.

Avery said, 'May *Tireless* not have seen *Huntress*, Sir Richard?'

Bolitho did not answer, trying to gauge the depth of his feelings. He could feel nothing but a sense of inevitability, of destiny. As if his reluctance to return to Malta had been justified. He saw Allday watching him; even Yovell was here on this bright morning.

Singleton yelled down, '*Tireless* has hoisted a signal, sir!'

Lieutenant Pennington murmured, 'We are all agog, sir.' Nobody laughed.

Singleton must have been very aware of the signal and its importance, even though he would not understand it. But his voice did not break or quiver.

'From *Tireless. Enemy in Sight!*'

Bolitho looked at Tyacke, ignoring or detached from the babble of disbelief and astonishment which separated them.

'So now we know, James. The trap is sprung. All else was delusion.'

He turned away, one hand on his shirt, and Tyacke thought he murmured, 'Don't leave me.'

Then he smiled, as if he had heard her voice.

18

Final Embrace

Bolitho pressed his face against the thick glass of the quarter-gallery, and watched the little schooner's distorted shape as she clawed her way across the wind.

When he turned he saw the stains of salt water on the deck covering, where *Tireless*'s captain had stood after a hasty pull to the flagship.

So young, so earnest, perhaps not able to grasp the magnitude of these events. He had almost pleaded, 'I can stay in company, Sir Richard. We're no match for close action, but surely we could do something?'

Bolitho had said, 'You have done enough. The signal, for instance.'

Penrose had forced a smile. 'I heard it said that you used the same ruse to deceive a more powerful enemy, so that he should believe you had sighted friendly ships.'

How could Penrose have known? It was beyond trickery now.

Bolitho had said, 'They will not run. They dare not. There is too much at stake.' He had taken his hand. 'Go to Malta with all haste. Tell the senior officer. I shall rely on it.'

Tyacke was standing by the table now, Avery by the fine wine cooler, his hand touching it as if to reassure himself. Beyond the screen there was utter silence except for the muffled sounds of sea and rigging. A ship holding her breath.

Tyacke said, 'Shall I remain on this course, Sir Richard?'

Bolitho walked to the table and lifted a corner of the chart. His unfinished letter still lay there; it had been hidden by the chart. Lieutenant Penrose could have picked it up, put it inside his spray-dappled coat before returning to his little command. And, sooner or later, she would have read it . . . .

He recalled what Tyacke had asked him; he had not questioned or even doubted him. So much trust. It was like a betrayal, and he was suddenly angry.

'Those *fools* in London, what do they know or even care, until all at once it is too late! All they can think about is grand receptions, peerages and self-congratulation! Men have died because of their arrogance and complacency! And will go on dying!'

Avery had stepped away from the cooler, his eyes very bright in the filtered sunshine. He had never seen Bolitho reveal his anger before, even though, many times, he had guessed it was there.

Bolitho said, '*Huntress* was taken, a vital link in the chain of an overstretched squadron! What did their lordships expect? Perhaps that the tyrant would remain passive, indifferent? This is not merely a man, but a colossus, one who has cowed and conquered every force that stood against him, from Egypt to the snows of Russia, from the Indian Ocean to the Spanish Main. What in hell's name did they expect?'

He calmed himself with an effort. 'There are hundreds, perhaps thousands of men who owed their power and influence to Napoleon. Without him to direct them, they are nothing.' He thought of Penrose again, and his signal. 'Oh, they will come, and we shall be ready for them.' He plucked his shirt from his body. 'But the trap is sprung. The *maybes* and the *if onlys* have no place here.'

He looked at Tyacke, his eyes very clear. 'You thought, perhaps, that nobody but a fool would challenge a ship of the line?'

Tyacke glanced at the chart, and saw the letter beneath it.

'*Frobisher* will dish them up, Sir Richard, you have my word on it!'

Yovell had appeared silently, and ventured, 'Then it will be war, Sir Richard?'

Bolitho said, 'We shall soon know.'

They all looked at the open skylight as the lookout's voice pealed, 'Deck there! Sail to the nor'east!'

Bolitho turned to Avery. 'Take a glass, George. I need your experience today.'

Avery snatched up his hat. 'Could it be *Huntress*, Sir Richard?'

Another voice reached down to the great cabin. It was Midshipman Singleton this time.

'Deck there! Another sail to the nor'east!'

Bolitho pushed the lock of hair from his forehead. 'I think not, George.' Then he smiled, and Avery was very conscious of the warmth in it. 'And fetch down Mr Singleton, or he'll have no lungs left!'

The door closed and Tyacke waited, blue eyes watching every movement, every changing mood, like reflections on the sea's face.

Bolitho nodded slowly. 'Yes, James, the two we saw in Algiers. Privateers, renegades, pirates, who can say? They will fight. They cannot afford to fail.'

Tyacke glanced around the cabin, imagining it stripped of all things personal, precious to this unbreakable man. A place of war.

'I would like to speak with the people, Sir Richard.'

Bolitho touched his arm as he walked to the opposite side. 'Good. It is their right.'

Tyacke understood. *What you would do in my place.* What so many would not.

Their eyes met, and Bolitho said quietly, 'Ten minutes, then? It will be enough, I think.'

Tyacke closed the door behind him, and Yovell, too, prepared to leave.

Bolitho said, 'Wait a moment, Daniel. Bring me a pen. Then you may put this letter in the strongbox.'

Yovell went to the desk where he kept his pens. Pipes shrilled, and he was surprised that he was unafraid.

'All hands! Clear the lower deck and lay aft!'

He looked toward the tall figure by the table, remembering. *It is their right.* Then he pulled open a drawer, his mind clear. He would fetch his Bible; it had never failed to comfort him. He placed a fresh pen on the table and saw Bolitho press the letter between his hands. His profile was composed, as if he was able to detach himself and his mind from the din of running feet, and the voices calling to one another. Voices offering hope and reassurance, and he was moved by them.

And then there was utter silence again; he thought of

261

the flag lieutenant up in the crosstrees with his telescope, probably looking down at the ship and the assembled seamen and marines, so rarely seen all together at one time.

Bolitho did not look up as Yovell padded quietly from the cabin. He read the first part of the letter very slowly, and hoped she would hear his voice when she read it. How could he be so sure that she would even receive it, or that they would be victorious today?

The pen hesitated above the letter, and then he smiled. There was nothing to add.

He wrote, *I love thee, Kate, my rose.* Then he kissed it, and sealed it with great care.

He was aware of the Royal Marine sentry outside the door, shuffling his feet and probably trying to hear what the captain was saying on deck.

The adjoining door opened and Allday entered, pausing only to close the skylight. His own way of holding the things he hated at bay. He said offhandedly, 'Young Mr Singleton says there are two frigates, Sir Richard.' He glanced at the eighteen-pounder gun near him. 'They'll not do much, no matter what they thinks, an' that's no error!'

Bolitho smiled at him, and hoped that there was no sadness in his heart.

But we know differently, my dear friend. We have done it ourselves. Can you not remember?

Instead he said, 'We've a fine day for it, old friend.' He saw Allday's eyes move to the swords on their rack. 'So let's be about it!'

Ozzard was here also, Bolitho's coat over his narrow shoulder. 'This one, Sir Richard?'

'Yes.'

It would be a hard fight, no matter what Allday thought about it. *Frobisher*'s company would need to see him. To know they were not alone, and that someone cared for them.

Then the drums began to rattle, urgent and insistent.

'*Hands to quarters! Clear for action!*'

He slipped his arms into the sleeves and took his hat from Ozzard. The one she had persuaded him to buy in that other, timeless shop in St James's.

My admiral of England.

He held out his arms and waited for Allday to fasten the

262

old sword into position. Ozzard would take the glittering presentation blade with him when he went down to the orlop, when the guns began their deadly symphony.

Allday opened the door for him and the marine sentry slammed his heels together, waiting to be released from this duty so that he could be with his comrades.

Allday closed the door from habit, even though the ship would soon be cleared from bow to stern, screens and cabins torn down, personal possessions stowed away until they were recovered by their owners, or sold to their mates if fate turned against them.

He found time to notice that Bolitho did not look back.

Captain James Tyacke stood by the quarterdeck rail, his arms folded while he surveyed the ship, *his* ship, in this moment of instinct and experience when nothing could be overlooked. He could feel the first lieutenant watching him, perhaps seeking approval, or preparing for some sharp criticism. But he was a good officer, and he had done well. The chain slings had been rigged to the yards, and nets spread to protect men on the maindeck from falling debris. There were boarding nets also. They could not estimate the strength or the determination of the enemy. If fanatics from a chebeck could hack their way aboard, this was no time to take chances.

He looked along each line of guns, the eighteen-pounders which made up half of *Frobisher*'s artillery. Until action was joined, each remained a separate unit, the gun captains sorting over the rows of black balls in the shot garlands. A good gun captain could select a perfectly moulded shot just by turning it in his hands.

A glance aloft, to the small scarlet clusters in each fighting top: marine marksmen and others who could aim and fire the deadly swivel guns. Known by the Royals as daisy cutters, they could scythe anything more than an inch high to the ground, or to the deck. Most sailors hated the swivels; they were unpredictable, and could be equally dangerous to friend and foe alike.

The decks had been well sanded. It was said to prevent men from slipping in the heat of action, although everyone knew the real reason for it.

'Well done, Mr Kellett.' Tyacke took a telescope from the rack and raised it to his eye. Without looking, he knew that Kellett was smiling his deceptively gentle smile, satisfied.

He felt his jaw tighten as the first pyramid of sails appeared to rise out of the shark-blue water like a phantom. He moved the glass again. The second frigate had luffed, and was drawing away from her consort. Almost to himself, he said, 'They hope to divide our fire.'

He lowered the glass slightly and glanced up at *Frobisher*'s spread of canvas, topsails and forecourse, flying and outer jib, with the big driver angled across the poop, the White Ensign streaming out from the peak. He knew that Tregidgo, the sailing master, was watching him. He ignored him. They all had their vital roles to play, but he was the captain. He must decide.

The wind was as before, from the north-west, not strong, but steady. Enough to change tack when required. She would handle even better when the order was given to slip the boats from their tow-lines astern; the main deck looked strangely clean and bare without them. Always a bad moment for sailors, when they saw their means of survival cast adrift. But the risk of flying splinters was far greater.

The sky was clearing, so different from the dawn. Long banks of pale clouds, but the sun already stronger and higher. He grimaced. A perfect setting.

He turned to face Kellett. 'I want to make this quite clear. When we get to grips with those fellows, I want every available man at his station. Provided he can walk, I need him *today*, and I'll not stand for carrying passengers! The lower gundeck is the key to any fight with faster vessels. Inform Mr Gage and Mr Armytage that I expect them to maintain rapid fire no matter what may be happening up here. Is that understood?'

Kellett nodded. He had heard about Tyacke's experience at the Nile, when he had been on the lower gundeck with the big thirty-two pounders. Guns which, if properly laid and trained, could pierce nearly three feet of solid oak. Or so it was claimed.

Kellett had only served on a lower gundeck once, as a very junior lieutenant. The noise and the inferno of fire and smoke had been enough to drive some men to panic. It was a place and a time where only discipline and rigid training could overcome fear and madness. How it must have been for Tyacke . . . .

He remarked, 'They wear no colours, sir.' It was something to say, to ease the tension.

Tyacke raised his glass again. 'They soon will. And by God they'll lose them, too!'

He concentrated on the leading frigate. There was a fine display of gilded carving around her beakhead. He smiled, unconsciously. She was Spanish, or had been once. He wondered what had happened to *Huntress*; perhaps they had put her down after the failure to lure *Tireless* beneath her broadside. He thought of his own depleted company. He must keep the enemy at a distance, cripple at least one of them.

How easy it was to regard strange ships as enemies; he had been doing it for most of his life. He thought suddenly of Bolitho. He was in the chart room, probably keeping out of the way, when every fibre in his body was tugging at him to take command, as a captain again. But there was neither fleet nor squadron this time, and some of the waiting seamen would be thinking as much. Their fate lay in the hands of three captains, and the man whose flag whipped out from the mainmast truck.

Tyacke heard Midshipman Singleton instructing his signals party by the halliards. The boy seemed different in some way, not yet mature, but indefinably different.

Tyacke moved to the compass box and gazed at the group there, the backbone of any company committed to action. The master and his mates, three midshipmen to carry messages, four helmsmen at the tall double wheel, and beyond them, the rest of the afterguard, the marines and nine-pounder crews. Protected by nothing more than tightly-packed hammocks in the nettings, they would be the first target for any sharpshooter.

He said, 'Converging tack, Mr Tregidgo.' He saw him nod; Tregidgo was not one to waste words. 'We will engage from either side.' He looked at their faces, stiff, empty. It was too late for anything else. *I have decided.*

He walked to the rail and gripped it. Warm, but nothing more. He smiled tightly. That would soon change. He looked along his command yet again, sobered by the thought that she might not be his for much longer. At the Nile, his own captain had fallen, and so many others on that bloody day. Could Kellett fight the ship if that happened? He shook himself angrily. It was not that. He had faced and accepted death many times. It was the navy's way, perhaps the only way. To make men confront and accept what was, in truth, unacceptable.

It was Marion. The new belief, the hope that a hand had reached out for him. Something he had sometimes dreamed about, but too often dreaded. He thought of Portsmouth, gazing at the nearest gun's crew. When all this had begun, when she had come to find him. With such quiet warmth, and such pride.

He thought of Bolitho's unfinished letter, hidden by the chart in the great cabin. Marion could never have realised what strength he had found in her.

He heard Allday's voice from the poop, and turned in readiness. He saw Bolitho, apparently quite calm, and Allday walking with him. As a friend, an equal. He smiled. No wonder it was so hard for people to understand, let alone share.

He touched his hat. 'I would like to alter course, Sir Richard. Those two beauties will try to harry us, to use haste to avoid being dismasted.' He waited while Bolitho took the big signals telescope from Midshipman Singleton, saw the way he held his head at an angle to obtain the best image. It was not possible to believe that he was blind in one eye.

'They'm running up their colours, sir!'

Tyacke levelled his glass on the leading frigate. Had he really clung to a last doubt, a hope? He could see the Tricolour standing out to the wind. More than a gesture; it meant that this was war again, even if the rest of the world was ignorant of it. Napoleon had escaped from what had been, at best, a token captivity. He recalled Bolitho's rare anger, his despair for the men he had led, who, in his eyes, had been betrayed by complacency. Tyacke glanced at him now, and saw the bitterness on his features as he returned the glass to Singleton.

Then he looked directly at his flag captain. 'So it is war once more, James.' There was a cold edge to his voice. 'So much for the Bourbon Restoration.' He looked around at the silent gun crews and the waiting seamen, and the marines, faces shadowed beneath their leather hats. Very quietly, he said, 'Too much blood, too many good men.'

Then he smiled, his teeth very white in his tanned face, and only those close enough could see the pain and the anger which lay there.

'So cast the boats adrift, Captain Tyacke, and let us give these scum a lesson, teach them that now, as before, *we are here*, and ready!'

Somebody gave a wild cheer, and it was carried along the deck to the forecastle and the men crouching at the carronades, although they could not have heard a single word.

It was infectious. A madness, and yet so much more.

Tyacke touched his hat with equal formality. 'I am yours to command, Sir Richard.'

Allday watched the cluster of boats drift haphazardly away from the counter. There was no cheering now, nor would there be until the flag came down. Theirs or ours, the rules never changed.

He touched his chest as the pain moved through him like a warning. Then he grinned. One more time. And they were still together.

Bolitho stood beside Tyacke and watched the oncoming ships. The range was closing, and, at a guess, stood at about three miles. An hour and a half had passed since *Frobisher* had cleared for action; it felt like an eternity.

The two frigates were almost in line ahead, their sails overlapping, as if they were joined. It was the usual illusion; they were perhaps a mile apart, and pointing directly towards *Frobisher*'s larboard bow. The wind had not varied by a degree; it was still north-westerly, light but steady enough. The frigates were close-hauled on the starboard tack, probably as near to the wind as they could manage.

'Shall I run out, Sir Richard?'

Bolitho glanced at him, at his burned profile, and the steady blue eye.

'I think they intend to tackle us separately. They'd never risk a fight broadside-to-broadside, not against our armament. If I were in command, I would change tack at the last possible moment. The leader could then lie athwart our hawse and be able to rake us as he passes, and we'd not be able to bring a single gun to bear.'

Tyacke nodded slowly, seeing it. 'If we try to follow him round, which we can do with the wind in our favour, the other one will go for our stern, and pour a broadside through us while we are engaged. I think we should run out now, and try to cripple one of them with our heavy battery.' He looked at Bolitho. 'What do *you* suggest? You're a frigate captain, and always will be. I'd welcome your experience!'

Bolitho smiled. 'That was bravely said. It is just a feeling.' He could not keep the excitement out of his voice. 'Those two captains are desperate, to engage us, to cripple us, above all to provoke close action. The wind is in our favour, but they can match our strength with their agility. I think that the *unexpected* will win the day. We can come about into the wind, be taken aback in all probability, but we can give each a broadside before either captain can stand away. What say you, James?'

Tyacke was staring at the two oncoming frigates, as if they were being drawn towards *Frobisher* by an invisible force, like a line on a chart.

'I'll pass the word.'

He looked down as Bolitho touched his sleeve. 'When we turn, run out the upper guns, James. Keep the lower gundeck sealed. It will give them something to ponder over.'

Tyacke smiled. 'It might just work, by God! Trick for trick!'

Bolitho saw Avery watching him, brushing threads of cordage from his breeches after his hasty descent to the deck.

'I'll send *him*, if I may, James. Captains and admirals should sometimes keep their distance.'

He saw Tyacke's smile open into a grin. Because of the unlikely plan of action, or because he had not been too proud to ask for advice? But he was already calling to Kellett and the other lieutenants to outline what he required of them.

Avery listened to Bolitho without comment, his expression thoughtful, curious.

Bolitho repeated, 'No double-shotting, no grape. I want every shot to find its target. Tell the lieutenant on the lower gundeck to keep firing, no matter what!' His grey eyes moved towards the waiting gun crews. 'Otherwise it will be bloody work up here.'

Avery looked at the other ships. Was it only his imagination, or were they much closer?

'And Napoleon, Sir Richard? Where will he be, at this moment?'

Bolitho heard the crash of a solitary gun, but could see no

telltale fall of shot. A signal, one ship to the other? A misfire, perhaps?

He answered, 'He could be anywhere.' He added quietly, 'He may have gone to his home in Corsica, but a few miles from Elba. Can you imagine a more reckless place to imprison such a man? But my guess is France, where his real strength lies, where people will rise up and follow him yet again.'

'You admire him, don't you, Sir Richard?'

'*Admire*? That is too strong a word. He is the enemy.' Then he gripped his arm, the mood changing again. 'But if I were a Frenchman, I would be there to welcome him.'

He watched Avery move away, and said, 'Take young Singleton, for the experience.' He shaded his eye to look at the masthead. 'I shall need no signals today.'

Avery hesitated, and saw some of the seamen running to the braces and halliards, Tyacke consulting the sailing master and his mates by the compass. In a moment the ship would alter course to larboard, into the wind, into the enemy. He looked at the distant pyramids of sails. Half an hour, at the most. He beckoned to the midshipman and together they hurried to the companion ladder.

After the brightness of the upper deck, the lower hull seemed like a musty vault.

When they reached the lower gundeck, Avery had to stand for several seconds to accustom his eyes to the gloom, and the sudden sense of danger. A little, feeble light filtered through the tiny observation ports on either bow, and from lanterns protected behind thick glass. The guns were manned and loaded, and he could see the eyes of some of the seamen glinting as they turned to watch him. Was that why Bolitho had told him to take Singleton with him? Because he was known to these men, young or not, and because as flag lieutenant he himself would be, and would remain, a stranger?

Objects were taking shape on either side, the great black humps of the breeches, the powerful thirty-two pounders, fourteen on either side. Tiny pin-pricks of light, like malevolent eyes, flickered in each match tub, slow matches in readiness if the more modern flintlock should fail or misfire.

He was joined by the two lieutenants in charge, 'Holly' Gage and Walter Armytage. He met them often enough in the wardroom, but it went no further than that.

He could feel the intensity of their concentration as he explained what was intended.

Gage said doubtfully, 'Might work.'

His friend laughed, and some of his men leaned over to listen. 'I shall tell our people we need a miracle today!'

Avery touched his arm. 'If the order comes, you'll know they're trying to board us.' He gestured toward the guns. 'Seal the ports and clear the deck. We'll need every man jack to repel an attack in strength!'

As they moved to the ladder again, he saw the side of the hull, dull red in the feeble light. If the enemy's iron burst into this crowded deck, at least the paint would conceal the blood.

Singleton said, '*Will* it work, sir?' He sounded very serious, but not afraid.

Avery thought of all those other times, and replied, 'If anyone can do it, *he* can.'

The light seemed blinding on the upper deck. Avery saw Tyacke turn towards the admiral, one arm half-raised as he said, 'Now, sir?'

Bolitho nodded, and gripped his sword against his hip.

'Stand by on the quarterdeck!'

'*Ready ho!*'

Tyacke barely raised his voice. 'Put the helm down!'

As the wheel was hauled over and the ship began to turn to larboard, men were already running like demons to let go the headsail sheets, spilling out the wind so as not to hamper the ship's head from swinging.

Instead of the peace and the menace of their approach, everything was noise and orderly confusion, the sails banging and flapping wildly as the ship continued to turn.

Bolitho walked to the opposite side and watched the enemy. Perhaps they had been expecting *Frobisher* to stand downwind to give battle to the leader, exposing her stern to the other frigate. Now it appeared as if they and not *Frobisher* were turning, separating, one on either bow.

He glanced aloft, at the writhing sails pressed against masts and yards. The ship was aback, unable to pay off on either tack, but the frigates were in a worse plight, sailing so close to the wind that they had no choice but to alter course. *Frobisher* was almost hove-to, and might even have lost steerage way, but it made no difference now.

He shouted, 'At 'em, lads!'

The port lids were hauled up, and to the shrill of a whistle the main deck eighteen-pounders trundled their black muzzles out into the sunlight.

'As you bear! *Fire!*' That was Lieutenant Pennington, his face scarred from the fight with the Algerines. The leading frigate seemed to turn away, her foremast and rigging reeling over in the carefully-aimed broadside, gun by gun, each shot controlled by Pennington and another lieutenant. Up forward, the breathless crews were already sponging out and ramming home new charges, oblivious to the banging canvas and the yells of topmen high above them.

'As you bear!' Tyacke's sword blinked in the sun as he brought it down. '*Fire!*'

The second frigate had recovered and was already setting more sails, to continue with her original attack or to escape further setbacks, Bolitho could not tell. She was standing across the starboard bow, changing tack, close enough to her damaged consort to be able to see the destruction and the upended guns.

Bolitho looked at Avery. '*Now!*'

Avery, with Singleton at his heels, ran for the companion ladder, tugging a whistle from his shirt as he stumbled and almost fell down the last steps.

Smoky daylight scythed through the gundeck as the port lids opened as one, and the crews threw themselves on the tackles to haul their massive charges towards the enemy. Each 'Long Nine', as these guns were nicknamed, weighed three tons, and the naked backs of the seamen were soon shining with sweat.

Lieutenant Gage was pressed up to his small spy-hole, then he turned, his face wild. 'On the uproll, lads!'

Avery heard Singleton shout, 'Cover your ears, sir!' Then the world seemed to explode, smoke billowing through the deck, where men were already serving their guns and others waited with handspikes and rammers to compete with their messmates. The same men who served these guns slept and ate beside them; the guns were the first things they saw upon waking every day, and, too often, in dying, the last.

Each gun captain held up his fist, and Armytage yelled, 'Ready, sir!'

271

'*Fire!*'

Again the guns crashed inboard on their tackles, but suddenly another whistle shrilled, and the same crews were struggling to secure them and close the ports to prevent the enemy boarders from attacking them in their midst. In their home.

Armytage was shouting, 'Arm yourselves!' As he ran past Avery, he called, 'We're going to foul the first bugger, George! We've done for the other one!' He was grinning, mad with excitement, but all Avery could think was that it was the first time he had called him by name.

On deck, Bolitho watched the second frigate with something like disbelief. An enemy, driven by hatred and revenge, but a thing of beauty, two broadsides from those thirty-two-pounders had reduced her to a mastless wreck. He turned and stared at the mainmast of the frigate which had taken their first, carefully aimed broadside, when *Frobisher* had caught the enemy completely by surprise. A collision was inevitable; *Frobisher* had not regained the wind, and the other ship was out of command. Seamen and marines were already running to the point of impact, bayonets and cutlasses shining through the seemingly immovable pall of pale smoke.

There were cheers, too, as more men came pouring from the lower gundeck, either already armed or snatching up weapons from the chests prepared earlier by the gunner.

Bolitho saw Captain Wise of the Royal Marines striding, not deigning to run after his men as they crouched by the hammock nettings and searched for targets.

Shots cracked and whined overhead or smacked through the heavy canvas, and here and there a man fell, or was dragged away by his companions. But their blood was up; no boarder would survive this day.

He saw Avery and Singleton hurrying toward the quarterdeck; the midshipman was almost knocked over by a charging, wild-eyed marine.

Tyacke waved his sword. 'Board 'em, lads! Cut that bloody flag down!'

Bolitho strained his eyes through the smoke, and saw men already on the frigate's forecastle. There was resistance, but the harsh blast of a swivel gun scattered the defiant ones like torn rags.

Singleton's voice cracked for the first time. 'They've struck, sir! They're done for!' He was almost weeping with excitement.

Bolitho turned to Allday. So it was war again. But even war would not keep him from her.

A seaman running with a boarding pike slipped on blood and would have fallen, but for Bolitho's grip on his arm.

He lifted his eyes in disbelief, and managed to stammer, '*Thankee*, Sir Richard! I be all right now!'

Allday was about to say something, he did not know what, when he felt the pain again, so intense that he could barely move. But it was not the old wound this time. He saw Bolitho turn and stare at him, as if he would speak, but seemed unable to find the words.

He heard Avery shout, '*Hold him!*' Then he saw Bolitho fall. It was like being given new life, new strength; he leaped forward and caught him around the shoulders, holding him, lowering him carefully, everything else without meaning or purpose.

Men were cheering, some firing their muskets. It meant nothing.

From the starboard gangway Tyacke saw him fall, but knew he must not leave his men while they boarded the enemy, following his orders. Midshipman Singleton, who had become a man this day, also saw him fall, and was on his knees beside him with Allday and Avery.

Bolitho turned his face away from the sunlight which lanced down between the shrouds and the limp sails. His eye was stinging in the smoke, and he wanted to rub it. But when he attempted to move, there was no response, no sensation, only numbness.

Shadows moved across the sun, and he could hear faint cheers, as if they came from another time, another victory.

They were all here, then. *Waiting*. A sudden anxiety ran through him.

Where was Herrick? Herrick should be here . . . .

Someone reached around him and dabbed his face with a wet cloth. He recognised the sleeve; it was Lefroy, the bald surgeon.

He heard Allday's painful breathing, and needed to tell him, to reassure him. Everything would be the same.

But when he tried to reach out for him, he realised for the first time that his hand was tightly gripped between Allday's. Then he saw him, watching him, his hair shaggy against the smoke and the sun.

Allday murmured, 'Mr Herrick's not here, Cap'n. But don't you fret now.'

It was wrong that he should be so distressed. One who had done so much. He tried again, and said, 'Easy, old friend, be easy now.' He felt Allday nod. 'No grief, we always knew . . . .'

Lefroy stood slowly, and said, 'He's gone, I'm afraid.'

Tyacke was here now, his sword still in his hand. He stood in silence, unable to accept it, and yet knowing that all the others were looking to him. To the captain.

Then something made him reach down and grip the sobbing midshipman's shoulder. Like that time at the Nile.

He said, 'Haul down his flag, Mr Singleton.' And then, gazing unseeingly at Allday's bowed head, 'Help him, will you? There's none better for the task.'

He saw Kellett and the others watching, the fight forgotten, the victory now pointless, empty.

He turned, as Avery stood and said quietly, 'Goodbye, dearest of men.'

As if she had spoken through him.

It was over.

Epilogue

The carriage wheeled into the stable yard and came to a halt
with practised ease, and a stable boy ran to take the horses'
heads. To pacify them, perhaps, after so short a journey from
the harbour.

Adam Bolitho opened the door without hesitation. This was
the only way he knew, to go through with it.

He climbed down and stood on the worn cobbles and stared
at the old grey house with a certain defiance.

Young Matthew had remained on the carriage, his face grim
and downcast, almost a stranger, like the stable boy.

It had been Bryan Ferguson's idea to send the carriage, as
soon as he had received word that the frigate *Unrivalled* had
anchored in Carrick Roads.

Adam glanced around now, at the carpets of daffodils and
bluebells amongst the trees, seeing none of it.

This was the place where he had come for help, for sanctuary,
when his mother had died. Then, from midshipman to post-
captain, a life full of excitement, elation and pain; and he owed
it all to one man, his uncle. And now he, too, was dead. It was still
stark and unreal, and yet, in some strange way, he had sensed it.

When *Unrivalled* had entered Plymouth after her first weeks
under his command, he had known it then. The port admiral,
Vice-Admiral Valentine Keen, had put off in his barge to meet
him personally. To tell him. *We Happy Few.*

Napoleon had escaped from Elba, and a few days later had
landed near Cannes, to be greeted not with hostility or fear
but like a conquering hero, especially by his marshals and Old
Guard, who had never lost their faith in him.

He had walked the streets of Plymouth, grappling with it, fighting it. His uncle had fallen on the very day that Napoleon had stepped ashore.

Even through his grief, he had sensed the mood in that seaport which had seen so much. Anger, frustration, a sense of betrayal. He understood their bitterness; there was hardly a village in England which had not lost someone in a war against the old enemy. And in seaports like Plymouth and in garrison towns, there were too many cripples in evidence to allow them to forget.

In Falmouth, it had been much worse. Falmouth was no city but lived off the sea, and the ships of every size and flag which came and went on the tides. *Bad news rides a fast horse*, Ferguson had said. Enemies were nothing new to these people; like the sea, the dangers were always there. But this was different, close, personal. Falmouth had lost her most beloved son. The flag above the church of King Charles the Martyr was at half-mast, and idlers had dropped their eyes when he had climbed from his gig, as if they were unable to face him. During the short journey from the town square, past familiar fields where he had seen men and women working together in the warm spring sunlight, some had looked up as the coach with its familiar crest rattled past, as if they still believed, dared to hope, then, as quickly, they had looked away.

The pleasure of his new command seemed unimportant; there was no one with whom to share it now. Even the names and faces of his ship's company were blurred, a part of something else, irrelevant.

He himself had remained composed, withdrawn; he had seen too many men die in battle to be unprepared, or to reveal the distress which was now tearing him apart.

He saw Ferguson climb down from the carriage, using his solitary arm as if he had never known anything different. He was a good man, a reliable one, and a friend. Ferguson understood him well enough to ensure that he was spared the agony of being greeted by the people who worked here and on the estate, especially his wife Grace, who would have been unable to contain her tears.

How quiet it seemed, the windows in shadow, watching.

Ferguson said, 'We got the news two days back. A cutter

276

came into port. I told Lady Catherine myself. She left for London immediately.'

Adam turned and looked back at the stables, at the big mare Tamara, tossing her head up and down.

Ferguson saw his glance, and said, 'Lady Catherine will come back. She'd not leave Tamara.' He hesitated, his hand twisting at his belt. 'John Allday. D'you happen to know . . . .'

'Safe.' Bethune had sent a full report to Keen, probably quite a different kind from that which he would write for the Admiralty. But until the others came home, they would not know the full story.

Keen had tried to explain to him, and Adam had guessed much of it. *Frobisher* had returned to Malta to land her dead and wounded, although there had been few of either. Bethune, Tyacke, Avery; someone close to Sir Richard must have suggested a sea burial. To avoid the splendid ritual which had attended Nelson's death, the ostentatious displays of grief and mourning from people who had hated England's hero in life. To spare Catherine the agony of seeing the same mockery made of her lover's sacrifice.

They had buried him at sea. Adam had seen it as vividly as if he had been there. Wrapped in his flag, an admiral of England, at a place marked on a chart of which few would know. Surely no better resting-place, by his old ship *Hyperion*, and so many of her company whom he had never forgotten.

He found that he was on the stone steps, and knew Ferguson had stopped by the tall, double doors to allow him the time and the solitude for this reunion.

It was all exactly as he remembered it, the grave portraits, the great hearth where he had lain with Zenoria, some fresh flowers on a table, the door to the library partly open, as if somebody might appear there; he could even imagine the smell of jasmine.

He clenched his fists as he saw the sword, lying on a table in a patch of sunshine. Bethune must have sent it with his courier, perhaps not knowing what he should do with it. And Keen had sent a cutter to Falmouth with his own letter of condolence to Catherine. It was strange that he had not mentioned it in Plymouth.

He picked up the old sword very slowly, and saw the sheet of paper which had been folded beneath it.

It was Catherine's writing. What it must have cost her to sit here in anguish, and yet be able to think of him.

> *Dearest Adam,*
> *The sword outwore its scabbard. Wear it with pride,*
> *as he always wanted. God bless you.*

Ferguson stepped quietly into the room and watched, holding his breath, as Adam Bolitho unfastened his own sword and clipped the old blade in its place.

In this room, and in this light, it was not Adam but Richard standing there, all those years ago, and he was deeply moved by it.

When he looked again, Adam was smiling, and holding out both hands to him.

It needed no words.

The last Bolitho had come home.

ALSO AVAILABLE IN ARROW

Man of War

Alexander Kent

Antigua, 1817, and every harbour and estuary is filled with ghostly ships, the famous and the legendary now redundant in the aftermath of war. In this uneasy peace, Adam Bolitho is fortunate to be offered the seventy-four gun *Athena*, and as flag captain to Vice-Admiral Sir Graham Bethune once more follows his destiny to the Caribbean.

But in these haunted waters where Richard Bolitho and his 'band of brothers' once fought a familiar enemy, the quarry is now a renegade foe who flies no colours and offers no quarter, and whose traffic in human life is sanctioned by flawed treaties and men of influence. And here, when *Athena*'s guns speak, a day of terrible retribution will dawn for the innocent and the damned.

'One of our foremost writers of naval fiction'
Sunday Times

arrow books